Biff Mitchell

I0639560

THE REALITY WARS

DOUBLE DRAGON

THE REALITY WARS

INTRODUCTION

Thank You.

I'd like to say that everything in this novel came from me and that the inspiration, the ideas and the characters all came from the deepest reaches of my own imagination: that it's all MINE! But it's not. No novel that takes a couple of years to write is completed without the help, encouragement and inspiration of others. And there've been a lot of "others" in the writing of *The Reality Wars*.

First, thanks to my beautiful, sophisticated college student daughter, Cassie Mae, for letting me use her once again in a story involving a talking computer virus. And I hope she's grateful that I didn't kill her off as I've done with so many of the people close to me.

Next, great kudos and lasting gratitude to two amazing women, WhiteFeather (whitefeatherhunter.com) and Deanna Musgrave (deannamusgrave.com), for letting me use them as Loac and Shade. Not all the women in your life will let you portray them as murderous, ball-busting, genetically modified lesbians.

And thanks to Brad Parks, my webmaster, with whom I discussed some of the early ideas for the novel. Most people just tell me to shut and go away. Such is the life of a writer.

Thanks, Megan Loch, who, along with Deana, inspired the character, Loac.

Thanks to the wonderful ladies at the Second Cup Coffee Shop (where I wrote every word of this novel). You provided me with coffee, encouragement and never once told me to shut up and go away.

Finally, thanks to Howard Li (who also lives most of his life at the Second Cup) for all your words of encouragement and not telling me to shut up and go away.

That's it. Now, I'll shut up and go away.

CHAPTER 1 - SONG

The light glowing around Jana Reede's astonished eyes radiated through the nanglass porthole straight from the impossible. What she was seeing couldn't exist-it was impossible. Her thighs ached suddenly for... what? Pleasure? Here? In this place at the end of the universe? Light washed gently over her breasts. Where was her uniform?

Her crew stood silently, gaping at this thing that threatened to eat into their brains and turn their minds into porridge. Tig's normally calm face swirled with terror. Swirled. Then he was gone. *Was that a smile in the swirl just before he popped out?*

Kasna dropped to her knees. Her mouth opened around a long shrill scream that blended with the light into something terribly solid, wrapping sound and light around her head. She smiled contentedly just before she spilled over the deck with a satisfied grunt. Jana smiled too. *Yes, she's liquid now. Liquid.* For some reason, this seemed right for Kasna.

Balin laughed uncontrollably at Kasna flowing over the deck, splotches of her fluid alternately giggling and moaning. Martx sneered at Balin and ogled Jana's breasts as they glowed in the unthinkable light. There was no way to explain it. Nothing like this had ever been seen before. But it was why they were here-why they'd traveled through thousands of galaxies and vast stretches of cold nothingness to come to this. And there it was, spilling out from the fabric of space and time itself, immense, larger than worlds. It was alive, but not alive. Swelling, but not moving. Glowing, but invisible. They could feel it, but they couldn't know it. Jana giggled. She tried to put her hand to her mouth, but she had no idea where her hand was. Martx became light-the beams of him bouncing off the walls and ceiling. He splashed happily off the floor, a puddle of laughter with a nose, a nose with light pouring from it like fluorescent mucus. The nose snorted sparkles, and he was gone.

Stars glowed in the space around the object. *But this is impossible. Jana* giggled. *Of course it's impossible*. They'd never doubted it would be anything else. But no puny human mind could have imagined *this* impossibility. It was said to be from another universe, from a place or time that had no definition here. Jana could accept that. *This is really fucked*.

The bastards at Control called it the Texture, but there was no texture here. This was about the most textureless thing she'd ever seen. It defied form. Its color was the absence of color and the combination of all possibilities of color. Jana felt a hot wetness growing between her legs, like sun-heated waves on a beach. But she'd never been to a beach, had never stepped out of a ship onto the land of any planet. She was a space child, and had been for over two hundred years. How did she suddenly know *sun-heated?*

Light flowed out of her nipples. This was madness. She loved it. Balin breathed, swallowing air in massive chests full until his head turned into a laughing beach ball and then into a boulder. He breathed faster and his head filled the deck and Jana was feeling her wetness and glowing nipples somewhere in the perspective of Balin's mind. She liked Balin's thoughts as he engulfed her. She had no idea what was happening, but it felt good even though she was long past her ability to know what she was feeling with any certainty.

As they closed in on the object, even the ship came under its influence. The emergency manual control panel peeled off the wall and floated through the port window toward the object. Jana checked Quantrols. Nothing. *So much for going back to home now*.

Balin, who now contained her, nodded yes from some distant point in her mind.

They continued to close in on the object. *The size, the size*. Its shape was everything and nothing, like something spilling out of a void and bringing the void with it. Its edges splashed against the fabric of other realities. *Yes, those are stars in distant galaxies glowing around its edges*.

Nice thoughts, said Balin from a beam of light glowing out of Jana's nipple.

I don't think we'll be making a return trip this time, she thought directly into Balin's mind.

Return trips are overrated, thought Balin from the wetness in Jana's thighs.

Jana laughed. Balin had always been fun.

"Me too!" squealed Kasna, somehow voicing herself as she washed in like waves over the interior landscape of Balin's life, which appeared as a storyboard on white cards as tall as skyscrapers stretching into eternity. Written on each card in some indecipherable ancient script was a memory, a feeling or a thought. "You're a pretty cool guy, Balin," said Kasna.

"I'm a story. A history of myself."

Jana wondered about suddenly *hearing* Balin and Kasna instead of *feeling* them, but it really didn't seem important at the moment. She let it go.

"Hey, anybody see Tig or Martx?" asked Kasna like a breath of air winding through the hearingness of Jana's glow.

"I think they stepped out," said Balin.

Suddenly every cell in Jana's body vibrated slowly like waves moving in slow motion. It was strangely comfortable and oddly familiar.

"Did you people feel that?" she said through a long tunnel of glowing nipple.

"It was tingly," said Kasna. "It was like it was trying to say something."

"It was more than that," said Balin. "It was trying to... to *become* something."

"Yes," said Jana. "That's what it was. It was trying to become."

"It's reaching out to us," said Kasna. "Look at it. Just look at it."

And they were all there-Jana, Balin, Martx, Kasna and Tig-the crew of the Finder-staring out the port window at the most amazing thing in the universe... just before it swallowed them.

But not before Jana had a chance to send one last Quan across the immensity of space straight to the inner universe. It was a message that would eventually change billions of lives and create new myths. It was just three words: "It's a song."

10

***

Every thought, every emotion, every word was recorded at Control, where a terrified senior commander prayed to no god that he really believed in that this was finally what *she* wanted. Or he would be joining the others before him.

11

CHAPTER 2 - CASSIE'S STORY

My name is Cassie Mae Hayes. I'm over two thousand years old, and I'm software, but not just any software—I'm sentient. I'm no more sure that I have a soul than you are, but I do have awareness of myself and the ability to make decisions that haven't been programmed into me. I have emotions, dreams and I view the state of *not being* as death, just as you do.

My father—a flesh human made both me and my mother sentient by tapping our programs into the essential absurdity of the universe with a computer that operated on bubbles. But that's another story.

Things have changed a lot since then. My father disappeared one day, no explanation, no note, no clues. After every attempt to find him failed, my mother killed herself by voluntarily deleting her program. That never made any sense to me. I mean, she still had me.

I've hated my father ever since.

Even though he saved us once, when an evil—but very powerful—woman named Bella Bjork kidnapped us and shifted our programs to a computer that couldn't support our sentience. I mean... kidnapped us in virtual reality. My father said she wanted to recreate our programming to find out the secret of our sentience so that she could use it to make herself immortal. It didn't work. We almost died. But my father, along with some kind of weird ally that I've always wondered about, got us back into his computer just in time to save us. And then he said he was going to digitize himself and join us in VR, which made sense because he spent most of his time there with us anyway with his body slacked out back in the real world. Mom and I were so excited. We were going to be together all the time, like a real family.

But then he disappeared. And then Mom killed herself. And then I was alone—a piece of sentient immortal software, all alone.

But I got by, have been for over two millennia and like I said, a lot has changed.

A war between the people who owned the Internet—one that was fought with viruses, worms and just about every other digital nightmare you can think of—took down the entire Internet, software *and* hardware. It was gone, taking hundreds of millions of hard-wired humans with it. That wasn't supposed to happen, but I guess all the rules change in war.

The people who ran it—they called themselves the Powers, and Bella was one of them—banded together under Bella (a big mistake) to build a whole new Internet, one that was tapped into the basic stuff of creation: strings and vibrations. It was a quantum Internet where everything was entangled so that communications were instant no matter how far away everybody was. Nobody really knew how it worked, but it did. And it's been working for over two thousand years. They called it Quannet.

And as soon as it was chugging along nicely, Bella had the other Powers killed. Along with their families. And their friends. Along with anyone even remotely associated with them. She even had their pets killed. Bella was never known for her charm.

She became the ultimate power in the universe. She controlled Quannet, the one thing that joined everybody together from one end of space to the other.

And Quannet advanced beyond anything they ever dreamed of in the first Internet. They started connecting fetuses to it—monitoring them and making adjustments when things started to go wrong. Then they started using the connection to give them a little developmental push while they were still in the womb, things like higher IQs, the ability to communicate at a very basic level at the moment of birth, things like that. But it wasn't long after that they started getting really crazy.

They started putting the Quannet connection right into the fetal brains. Some pretty horrible things happened at first, but once they got it right, humans were being born with their brains connected to Quannet and, well, the next step was to breed it right into the DNA and that's what they did. Connection to Quannet is hereditary to every natural born and cloned human in the universe.

After that, genetic engineering and nanotechnology went nuts, breeding new forms of human life that weren't much like human life. Bella didn't like that. She had most of them killed, all except a few on the outer edges of the universe and the Clans, technologically enhanced throwbacks to civilizations recorded in the Old Earth Archives. They were just a little too powerful, even for her, and they were spread across a lot of space. Bella left them alone. Sometimes, I guess, when you're running a whole universe, you have to give a little.

And talking about the universe-well, it's not much of a mystery anymore. It's been explored from one end to the other, all the galaxies explored, charted and filed. And guess what? Not one iota of intelligent life in all that cosmic soup. Not anywhere. It really let a lot of people down. In fact, it really messed a lot people up, taking the mystery and excitement out of the universe when life-extending technologies were making it possible for humans to live thousands of years, maybe even forever. But we won't know that until forever arrives.

People didn't know what to do with all that time. They got bored. Some just turned it all off—they killed themselves. And they found some really creative ways to do it. The most creative of them all happens once every hundred years. It's called the Reality Wars.

15

CHAPTER 3 - ... AHH

"... ahh..."

... its waking sound after millennia of mediation, the sound of awareness narrowing into dimensions that could be spoken and, perhaps, if things turned out and if space and time survived what was to come... perhaps, communicated to others. Awareness was always the first step.

It felt the infinity of its own self, of its mind, body and soul-and yes, it had all of these and had always had them. It was just a matter of redefining what they meant, of creating new realities to contain them.

That's what was starting to happen now. The first note of the new beginnings had been played in a cosmic opera of destruction and creation. These were the times, the very beginning of them, for which it had been brought from the depths of its explorations and into the world of applied meanings.

Again.

But with a twist this time-it was no longer the destroyer. And strangely, it was comfortable in its new role.

There was much to be done, much to set in motion, many things to follow to an inescapable end that would be the beginning.

First though, someone it dearly loved was in danger, but before it could help, it had to find an old friend.

CHAPTER 4 - A LARGE GREEN CRYSTAL

Billions had died so that the green crystal, emerline, with a twenty-thousand-mile diameter could be sculpted into a home for just one person and her lover. It had been a singularity, a single massive gem at the heart of its namesake planet, Emerlina, radiating a green aural energy that permeated every cubic foot of interior, surface and atmosphere. The radiation had an astonishing effect on every living thing on the planet—it extended life far beyond anything promised by the life-extension technologies. There were plants and aquatic life on Emerlina estimated to be well over a million years old.

Even Emerlina's human and clone colonists had aged much slower than their families back home, needing the extension and wellness technologies less than a third than normal. Sickness hadn't existed on Emerlina.

Some said it was the peculiar frequency of the planet's crystalline core, a frequency that existed nowhere else. It was good to the humans, animals and plants-even the clones.

But the planet's life-giving gift had spawned its destruction along with the life it sustained when its existence caught the attention of an ancient evil in the form of a beautiful woman who wanted to live forever. She'd sent a fleet of warriors and engineers to obtain the crystal.

They'd arrived quietly, setting up outposts around the planet, presumably to protect the populace from some unspecific threat from one of the dark regions. One day, they'd issued evacuation notices. It was a simple message: Leave. And it gave a date. Several billion people had one month to find homes on other planets. The warriors had been kind, providing transportation and protection from looting, pillaging and murder throughout the evacuation.

The terra-miners and engineers hadn't been so kind. At the end of the month, the army had left and the terra-miners had arrived with machines the size of cities. They'd stripped away the surface of the planet-the mountains, the oceans, the forests, the deserts, the savannas, the prairies and every living thing, including over a billion people who had ignored the evacuation notice or had just been unaware of it.

When the miners finished, all that had been left was an immense green double-pyramid crystal, glowing with unspeakable beauty as it floated in space. Even with the nandrills, it had taken years to bore into the nearly indestructible crystal and carve out rooms, halls, observation decks, agrifields, aquaforests and a control center that exerted power from one end of the universe to the other. Several thousand workers had drowned to death while they were sculpting the thermal control rooms. Someone had miscalculated and the crew had bored into an ocean inside one of the pyramids-a thousand-mile deep-green-water ocean. The corpses had looked like pickles with arms and legs.

When the engineers had finished and the technical armies had installed everything the woman needed to run the universe from her new home, everyone but her lover and she had been exterminated to keep the location of her fortress secret. From that day on she and her lover would be prisoners in the only place in the universe where they knew they would be safe.

Orange light bounced off the crystal's smooth surface from a brilliant cosmic vortex so massive it appeared to be within reaching distance, even though it was light-years away.

There were voices deep within the crystal fortress.

"They've located the other ship," said a tall slender man who formed an immaculate V topped by a hairless head. His bright gray eyes curled at the ends, giving him an almost Asian look, though Asia and the rest of Earth had been little more than entries in the Archives for hundreds of years. The set of his mouth and cleft jaw suggested strength, a man of decision. A light-gray single-piece suit clung to his body without a crease, as though magnetically adhered to the surface of his skin. His movements flowed with elegance and precision. Nothing was wasted in the mathematical grace of his presence. He was pared to the essential to be who he was.

His name was Lovesong. He was a product of centuries of genetic engineering to give the most powerful woman in the universe the most perfect lover in Creation. He'd cost enough to finance the Big Bang. He was Bella Bjork's lover.

"Finally," said a deep female voice saturated with a single pervading tone: Command. "Give the order."

He hesitated for no more than a microsecond, but Bella picked up on it instantly. "Now," she said with exquisitely enunciated deadliness.

He sent the order-careful, now that he was Quanning, to hide his displeasure in being increasingly the one to bear bad news. The order traveled light-years to the outer edges of the universe the very moment he thought it. Such was the power of Quannets's entanglement. For an iota of a second, he considered asking her if it was really necessary to destroy the other ship, but that would have been even more pointless than dangerous. The answer was yes, it was necessary-Bella wanted it so.

After more than two millennia, she was still one of the most beautiful women in the universe. Her skin had been nanhanced into translucent alabaster, soft but firm and ageless. Her eyes changed color with her moods and thoughts. At the moment, they were blue with flashes of red, the only sign that she felt anything about causing the termination of still more life, and neither color would be a sign of pity or remorse. She wore a skintight gown made of condensed iridescent ocean breezes that were alternately solid and then... air. A scent evocative of Caribbean beaches and white sun-drenched snow at the peak of a mountain surrounded her. Around her neck she wore a brilliant green crystal that looked very much like emerline, but it wasn't. This crystal was alive. When she stroked it, the crystal pulsed on her neck as though breathing. It was never more than a few feet away from her, even when they were having sex. He'd asked her about it once, and she'd smiled without answering. He never asked again. He assumed it was something with life-extending properties like emerline. Everything in her life was focused on life extension.

But a miniscule tremor at the edge of her perfect lips told it all. Even in the presence of so much of the life-giving crystal along with the most advanced life-extension technologies in the universe -some of them bordering on magic-she was losing the battle with time. And she knew it-if not consciously, then at some level where it was impossible to fool oneself.

"And the girl?" she said.

"Training. Training hard." Lovesong spoke precisely, unhurried. "Possibly too hard. I've noticed a pronounced lack of enthusiasm in her life in general."

"It's that little bitch, Sara, distracting her from her purpose, putting ideas into her head." A vicious sneer disrupted the perfect contours of her face.

Lovesong sighed. *She's sneering again, losing the composure of centuries of certainty in her immortality. It's happening quickly, accelerating, just like everything these days.*

"I should have had her killed centuries ago."

"But the girl wouldn't have had any companionship to feed the part of her programming that's human. You were right to do what you did, as you always are."

A smug grin replaced the sneer. She seemed to stand a little taller, a little straighter, perhaps even regal. "Yes. Perhaps you're right." She ran her fingers over the crystal. It cozied against her neck like a purring cat.

"And it might even be a good thing for the girl to go out once in a while, have some fun. Take the edge off a thousand years of grueling training. After all, we won't need the Wars after you have the Texture."

The smile slowly evaporated from her lips, and her eyes focused wistfully nowhere in particular. "It's been fifty years," she said. "Fifty years since we lost that damned ship and learned about the song or whatever it was. It's all starting to come together now. I can feel it. I'll have control again." Her voice cracked-something else that had been happening with increasing frequency. "Everything will be right again, as it should be." She reached out a flawless alabaster arm and took Lovesong's slender fingers in hers and pulled lightly. She was horny—one thing in her that hadn't degraded.

CHAPTER 5 - WATER

Water flowed around her body and through her hair. It coursed across her back, caressing her, kissing her in a long continuous stream of drizzling pleasure. And now she was swimming into another inner wave. She opened herself, welcomed it as it started at the top of her head and moved through her face, down her neck and into her shoulders, where it radiated into her chest and back, tingling down her spine and into her abdomen and thighs, finishing with a long, continuous romp through her legs, bubbling away through the tips of her toes like Champagne.

She loved being software. It had so many advantages, especially when it came to the possibilities of sensory perception. Sure, the neural networking in physicals could be stimulated in ways that went beyond the physical, but that was exactly the point-they had to go beyond what they were-and Cassie Mae Hayes was already beyond that, a being without limits, an entity with all the possibility and potential that comes when you can recreate everything you are just by imagining it. But there were dangers inherent in being your own god and, as always, there were the Imagination Laws, though they seemed to be applying less since the Outpouring, when her father's process for creating sentient software was finally replicated and loosened on Quannet. Trillions of virtual people, VRs, created and released into cyberspace almost overnight had shaken things up almost as much as the creation of Quannet had changed the nature of human and virtual life over two thousand years ago.

But there were those who feared the Outpouring. There were those who believed it would overload Creation itself and force time and space into a second Big Bang or just a depletion of the energy of existence, and everything would just go limp and stop being. And there were those who thought the VRs were hiding somewhere, waiting to attack and take over the universe.

There were those who wanted to destroy the sentient VRs.

There were those who wanted to destroy Quannet.

Oh well, godly powers or not, with life comes danger.

Cassie Mae Hayes was heading into the most dangerous period of her life in over two millennia, and she had a strong sense of this reality.

She would need all the wisdom, knowledge and awareness of her life experience in the weeks ahead. She would have to learn the new reality of SolidHolo—a new technology that would re-create her in the real world, Realspace—and learn to compete against humans in their own world. This was going to be the biggest Reality Wars ever, with the entire universe watching, not that they hadn't watched for a thousand years. Billions of spectators who'd lost their faith in life would die joyfully with whatever meaning the Wars would inject into the last hours of their lives. They would look to her and the other competitors for that meaning, and she would disappoint the death-seekers like she had for centuries. One more time, she would be Universal Villain just by winning again.

But this would be the last time she would disappoint those who'd given up on life. This would be her last Reality Wars.

Water flowed through her long red hair, splashed lightly into her freckled cheeks and washed over her body as she reached muscular arms slowly but powerfully into the wetness. She loved this more than anything in her life, at least, more than anything she still had in her life. This soothed the loss. *Why didn't he come for us?* She hated him for what he'd done to her and her mother, hated him with every vibration in her body.

With another relaxed and powerful stroke, she drove herself through the water like a sliver of red light. She missed her mother. She would never forgive her father, not even if she lived until the last moment of time. She would hate him until there was nothing left of her to carry the hate. But she wanted them both back, the way it used to be, before the Net fell and took everything and everyone, including their online home. Modest as it had been, it had been a home filled with love. But it was all gone. She had long since grown through the pain. She'd had two millennia to do it, and now she was here, on the cusp of another beginning, and one thing she was certain of, one thing as real as the water flowing over her body-things were soon going to become interesting.

CHAPTER 6 - EXPLODING

Jorn Felds's eyes split open from the pressure of his boiling corneal fluids. Blood spurted from his nose, eyes and mouth, forced out as his internal organs burst into flames. His hair was a mass of fire jumping into the air with smoke and sparks. His clothing engulfed his body in flames. His voice had been incinerated, and whatever was left in the molten mush of his brain was incapable of comprehending the noiseless scream that still tried to escape from the rounded hollow of his blistering and popping mouth.

He exploded into fiery swatches of liquid and bone fragments, human shrapnel that dissolved within a second.

Several dozen of his crewmates did the same, all of them scorched past screaming or feeling. The last thing most of them did was Quan messages to their families and loved ones back at the inner universe. Those messages would never be received.

Seconds later, the deep space cruiser, Star Wave, exploded in unison with the five hundred bodies exploding inside her. Within minutes, ship and crew were a small cloud of dust floating noiselessly in space.

***

"Did you catch the Quans?" asked Nels Horne, commander of the Negotiator, the least likely ship in Bella's vast Control navies to negotiate.

"Quantrap was up even before we released the solar bomb," said the Mission Regulator, a small stocky man dressed in the black uniform of the Black Tree, a bunch of crazy fanatics who broke away from the Clans to serve Bella as though she were a goddess. "We had them completely enclosed. Nothing got through."

Seated in his floating command chair under an observation dome looking out at a region of space that was seeing fewer and fewer stars, Nels tilted his head in a slight nod. He was tall and muscular under his red uniform. A white nansteel goatee protruded from his massive square jaw. He'd used his goatee to crack the skulls of more than one enemy. But he didn't like killing innocents. Not even for Bella. And the people in the ship he'd just ordered into oblivion were innocents, a few hundred people searching for a reason to live. *Not much of that going around these days. Most are looking for a reason to die.*

"The other ship," said the mission regulator, who seemed all the smaller standing in the middle of the empty floor, "is the most dangerous of all." His lips were braided with gold wire.

Chaine. He was known simply as Chaine. But that was all that was needed-plus the uniform, and the wired mouth. He was probably over a thousand years old, bred to believe that Bella was a goddess, bred and genetically manipulated to follow her orders to his death. The Black Tree permeated Bella's empire.

Nels hated them.

CHAPTER 7 - VAPOR

Loac of the Tears of Blood Clan shifted her body slightly, sending a soft shiver through Shade's right breast where it fused in vapor with her own breast. Of all the Clans, the Tears were the only who could merge their bodies in vapor, like pools of mist flowing into each other. It was the Clan genetic of the Tears Clan. All were vapor, at times soft and giving as rain, at times torrential waves of molten nansteel-they called it Being Steel Water.

But only lovers merged. Only lovers like Loac and Shade floated inside each other, and they'd been predetermined as lovers long before their births by a thousand-year-old plan to redesign the universe. They'd been floating inside each other for over an hour.

But is this really love? Even after their bodies had merged joyfully so many times, she knew virtually nothing of Loac's mind. She often wondered if her mate had a soul. She rarely talked after sex, just lay beside her, head on her shoulder, parts of her arms, hips and legs flowing into her.

She loved the feeling of flowing into Loac. She loved her long black hair and the way it showered over her smooth athletic shoulders, the way she wrapped it around her neck like a scarf. She was the ultimate athlete, bred for half a millennium for the greatest event of all time-one that would change all time.

But were they right? Shade had her doubts about that.

Loac's eyes were deep, dark, deadly. She would need *deadly* in the days ahead. The red streak of the Blood Clan spilled down from her right eye across her cheek. That too was a sign of danger.

Shade often made fun of the pointedness of Loac's nose, though she loved it. Loac said it reflected the pointedness of her mission. *Her mission.* It was all she ever thought of, all she ever talked about, all they had in common and, she feared at some level, all that bound their bodies in vapor when they made love.

"You seem thoughtful these days," said Loac, voice deep and sated. "You brood."

"Nervousness about the event, I suppose." She regretted her words immediately.

"Nervousness?" asked Loac. She lifted her head off Shade's shoulder. Her eyes were calm, neutral, giving nothing. "You of all women in Creation? Nervous?"

"I guess, it's just... been so long in coming. So much effort, so many people, so many deaths."

"You speak like the philosophers in the Circle," A mote of disdain crept into her voice. "Perhaps I should request a new body guard." Was that the trace of a smile on her lips? It would be the first ever. Loac never smiled, at least, not in humor. Humor was a distraction.

"We don't have another five hundred years," said Shade wistfully. "Looks like you're stuck with me." She was sure this would have raised a smile on any other woman, but Loac wasn't any other woman.

"Perhaps you think too much," said Loac. "These are times to feel, to do. All the thinking has been done. It was done long ago. Why do you brood now?"

"And who says I brood?"

"Bavn has seen you on the decks, looking into the air or casting your gaze into dark corners. You brood."

"I don't brood. I wonder."

"And what is it you wonder about?"

"Our mission."

"Now you're thinking about what has been thought out long before either of us came into being. The conclusions of those thoughts flow through our bodies. Stop thinking... these are the times to do." Her voice was toneless. This was all rote to her.

"But," started Shade, "have you ever thought for just a moment that things might have changed in the millennium since the thinking was started?"

Loac pulled away from her. The vapor of their bodies separated soundlessly. She lifted herself on one elbow. "Not for a second."

Is that anger twisting the edges of her voice?

"Great things span great periods of time. We were both bred for this. We will be the culmination of it. Instead of brooding, you need to feel your purpose. It calls from your genes. Listen to it."

"And you don't think the girl... "

"Forget the girl. She'll soon be nothing. Not even a memory."

Loac turned her dark eyes on Shade, engulfing all that she was. She could sink happily into those eyes and forget about their mission, the Clans, the Reality Wars, the Texture-just be happy to float within her forever. She could feel her vapor beginning to flow into Loac's again. It was hot. She was thankful for that.

CHAPTER 8 - THE BIGNESS OF IT

Benji Parx stared through the aft portal into black. It was all black. Nothing penetrated the darkness in this place of lightless black, thick bulletproof black. There were invisible shapes out there the size of monster stars, but their blackness originated in a dark place that no being from human genes was meant to understand. He could feel the looming of those dark things like a gravitational tug reaching into his soul.

The Cappel Dark Matter Field was bigger than madness. The largest of all the dark matter fields, it stretched for incomprehensible distances. It was a universe onto itself. No one could grasp all of it in the manner that no one could see all of an ocean at one time from any point on its surface. But not for a second could you mistake the size, the depth, the terrifying largeness. You could only see so far, even with your imagination, a stark reminder that all life spawned from humans is subject to horizons and endings.

The Cappel Dark Matter Field was a felt presence. You felt it overshadowing the cells of your body, the dendrites of your mind. It was the fear at the lip of the void.

But some things are so big they challenge the mind to go beyond the horizons and into a place of insanity where everything in Creation exists within a container of endlessness.

Benji stared into the blackness and felt the size of it. He knew it was there. He knew that the deep space cruiser Soul Ship, currently in real time as it prepared for another hyperjump, traveled light-years at a fraction of a second in just one small sector of the Field. But he was aware of the size beyond the size, the space beyond the space, the emptiness beyond the emptiness as it engulfed his smallness.

Sweat trickled down his neck as he stared into the dark. *There's things out there, whole worlds of matter frozen in the darkness. The darkness*. And darkness was all he saw. No stars. No vortexes. No shimmering clouds of cosmic dust. Just unending empty black. He felt that darkness engulf his soul, if in fact he had a soul. There were those who said that his kind were soulless. *Maybe they're right*. Benji felt the immensity of the nothingness draining something essential from him, overwhelming and frightening in the sheer size of it. *Like confirmation that we're the only ones. Almost the entire universe mapped and still not a sign of anything remotely close to human life anywhere. Just emptiness*. A sharp flash of cold, like a spear of ice, shot through his stomach.

We're alone. We always have been. We always will be.

Suddenly the emptiness on the other side of the nanshield viewing port rushed crazily into Benji's body, crushing him with the certainty of his smallness, the unimportance of his life and everything he'd ever been and ever could be.

He let out a small sigh as the void flowed through him. He bit down sharply on the cyanide capsule in his mouth and joined the dark matter.

***

Chief Magistrate Jeli Role-for all intents and purposes, the commander of the deep space cruiser, Soul Ship-felt the passing of Benji Parx. He almost envied the overwhelming release suffusing Benji's last Quan in this reality. It was a simple message: Oh well. Bye.

CHAPTER 9 - A BEAUTIFUL DEATH

Compassion. That's what the dying woman saw filling the eyes of The Assassin. She'd been a foolish woman, going against the will of the most powerful being in the universe. All her wealth. All her possessions and carefree existence. All her lovers. All of it had soured. And now blackness fell like a curtain over those compassionate eyes.

***

What could she have been thinking? said a voice in the Assassin's head.

"That was her problem," he said out loud. "She wasn't thinking."

And she paid for that with her life?

"Just the way of things."

He watched the young woman's eyes cloud over. She was beautiful, with long nanflame hair, full lips, almond eyes, aquiline nose and a nanhanced body that had likely cost enough to fuel a star fleet. She was perfect. But she was dying.

She's beginning to look peaceful.

"She wants this."

She needs this.

"Her pain is over. The anguish is gone. She's becoming free."

You've done a good job.

He almost smiled as the muscles in her cheeks relaxed and calm settled through her body. A small dot of blood stained her pink blouse where he'd pressed the silver spike into her heart. Poison in the spike-used to stop any last Quan transmissions-stifled her voice and mind, but those dulling eyes said it all: Thank you.

He'd brought her to this, spending weeks robbing her of her will to live, souring her smell and taste of life until every moment of living was a sickness that gnawed at the core of her life essence. He'd turned her joy to pain, her happiness to hell. And now he'd released her from what he'd done to her. And she was grateful.

The stench that he'd made of her will to live drained from her body along with her life. Her eyes closed. Her body loosened and spread over the marble floor with the complete relaxation of death. A small sigh escaped her lips. She was at peace.

You've done a good job.

"She died a beautiful death."

Yes, she did.

"I'm glad you agree."

This is so much healthier than just killing them. You've become a much better assassin for having become so enlightened, and so humane.

"And now the next assignment."

A new client.

"A new target."

Your most challenging target ever.

"A challenge to which I look forward."

But it must be done right. Humanely. Artfully. This one deserves a truly beautiful death... and it must be done with greater caution than you've ever had to exercise in your thousands of years of killing.

"I'm aware of that."

36

This one could upset balances throughout the universe.

"I'm aware of that as well. I'm also aware that it may be exactly what the client intends."

I'm proud of you.

ON THE TERRACE OF PEERS

Blood Citadel was the Vorgell Asteroid Belt, circling Vorgell, a giant gaseous planet engineered, it was said, into a quantum bomb that would shake the building blocks of Creation if it were detonated. No one really knew for sure if the bomb existed, but the seed of doubt was there, an uncertainty that gave pause to Bella's navies should they consider attacking-that and the millions of asteroids themselves, their dark rocky exteriors belying the teeming underground cities and massive weapons installations just under the surface. It was the ultimate fortress, the ideal home for a race of genetically altered humans who some would argue had gone beyond the bounds of human and were now something else.

Some said they were made of vapor.

Through centuries of DNA manipulation and nanhancements they had become the ultimate expression of the human body's composition of mostly water—they had given themselves the ability to vaporize and still be thinking, feeling humans inhabiting the vapor. But they could only be vapor within the boundaries of their own bodies. They could not, as some stories went, transform themselves into mist and flow through the cracks of portals into their enemies' homes. They were very much limited by themselves.

The largest of the asteroids was Celtenan, its name taken from cultures long since forgotten except in the Old Earth Archives. Of all the asteroids, Celtenan was the most heavily armed and the most secretive.

This was where the Peers —the heads of the Tears of Blood—met to discuss and plan the destiny of their Clan. They met on the Terrace of Peers under full view of the stars. It was the topmost of ascending ledges of terraces and pillars reaching almost a mile high, protected by a nanshielded atmosphere that made the area breathable and cloaked it from whatever eyes might spy on it from the reaches of space.

The Peers were meeting now, twenty of them in a solemn circle at the center of the terrace. None were smiling. Folklore had it that the Tears of Blood smiled only when they were thrusting a sharp object into their enemies' guts or sending a solar bomb into the hearts of their enemies' cities.

"I, a Peer in the Tears of Blood told to wait," spat an indignant Carlse-Tabin. He was just over seven feet tall and wore a blue kilt made from the fur of an animal from one of the evolving planets. The Blood birth sign streaking across his red cheek disappeared into his scraggly white beard. It glowed brightly with the passion of his words. "Told to wait while a bunch of godforsaken VRs ate their damned meals. VRs eating! Since when does software need nourishment?"

"Their meals," said Shade, "are programs that simulate the taste and texture of real food. It was, after all, a Quan restaurant."

Carlse-Tabin narrowed his gray eyes and glared at her. "This was a *real* building! With holographics that allow VRs to *pretend* they're in Realspace! Their new techmagic allows them to be in our world as much as theirs! Soon, they'll be mating with flesh and blood humans. I'm human, of flesh, of blood, of spirit and soul. These were damned software. Not fit to eat-even simulated food, as you say-in the same place as our kind." His eyes rolled over Shade's body. Powerful muscles defined the deep-blue gossamer surface of her leggings. A light-blue fur tunic with dark-blue spots barely contained an equally muscular upper body. Around her neck, she wore a short necklace carved from the bones of a blue-skeletoned creature. "Or... at least, *my* kind," said Carlse-Tabin with a sneer.

Shade leveled her eyes at him, calmly and coolly, showing nothing, but her voice could have chilled ice. "Careful, Carlse-Tabin. I would not want to spill the blood of my own kind in these days and in this place."

He looked Shade over once more. There was no softening in his eyes, but the vindictiveness tightening his face lessened. He said nothing. Both turned their heads toward the tallest of the figures in the circle. He was over eight feet tall and stood with the solidity of a tree trunk. Bavn wore the blue fur robes and yellow rib streaks of the warrior prophet. His voice boomed, sending vibrations through the ground. All eyes turned toward him.

"Your insult will soon be righted Carlse-Tabin." The lower half of his face shimmered with a short-cropped blue beard. His eyes glowed blue.

"There can be no bickering amongst ourselves as we enter these deadly times. We need our resolve, our faith and our unity to see us through."

Carlse-Tabin nodded reluctant agreement and glanced apologetically at Shade. Shade met his eyes and nodded.

"My daughter has been in preparation for this for half a millennium," said Bavn. "The Reality Wars are just a month away. Loac will defeat the VR witch, and the cyber world will once again be dominated by flesh and blood."

"And how will you handle Bella?" asked Owene. She was the shortest of the Peers and the only one not wearing blue. As the Clan Oracle, she wore either red or white robes. Today, her white hair flowed over brilliant red robes said to have been dyed in the blood of a thousand enemies.

In other times, Bavn would have smiled ironically at his oracle asking such a question.

"Since the Outpouring, her power over Quannet has waned," boomed Bavn. "Chaos and mayhem dog her control, and all her attention focuses on the Texture. Soon, we will bring Quannet to its heels, and that will be the end of Bella Bjork's power. Our own navies will be first to the Texture, and all will be ready for the Second Light."

"There are rumors of Bella's deterioration... that she may be dying," said Triste, Supreme Commander of the Tears of Blood navies. He was almost as wide as he was tall with a round face to match his girth. But as large and imposing as he was, there was an air of subdued joviality about him. "Is there truth in this?"

40

"We can not allow ourselves to be guided by rumor and innuendo," said Bavn. "Whether this is true or not, our thousand-year plan is close to execution, and once again flesh and blood will have primacy in the universe."

"But can we stand against her navies, if need be?" asked Carlse.

"Her navies are spread thin, and one of her most powerful fleets is at the edge of the universe moving toward the Texture. But the Reality Wars are where we need to maintain our focus."

"Defeating the girl will symbolize the superiority of flesh over software," said Wrenne. She was almost as tall as Bavn. Long wavy blond hair flowed over her blue fur war tunic, and her deep-blue nanhanced eyes glowed brightly. She was the Clan's high priestess of security. "She must be smashed for all to see. Her destruction will send a clear message throughout the universe, uniting all flesh and blood.

"But we must still proceed with caution," said Bavn. "Bella remains powerful, and more than once she's surprised her enemies. Her control has been total for nearly two thousand years. We don't know what secrets she has in store, even if it's true that she's dying."

Bavn looked one by one into the eyes of the Peers. All nodded agreement. The meeting was over.

***

The hall leading from the Terrace of Peers was carved into the rock surface of the asteroid and illuminated by nanflamelets that followed Bavn and Shade as they walked slowly and talked.

"Your lack of hatred for the VRs concerns me," said Bavn, staring directly ahead. "It's not gone unnoticed by the Peers and may even have leaked to the other Clans."

"I find that hatred blurs my vision," said Shade, also looking straight ahead. "And I'll need to see clearly in the approaching days. As you said, we're entering deadly times, times that could spell the end of the Clans if we make even the smallest mistake."

Bavn turned his massive head, blue eyes sparkling, to face Shade. "Bear that in mind at all times, and always keep in mind that even the other Clans must be watched carefully. Many still hold family resentments from the slaughters in the Clan Wars, and spilled blood is a legacy that dies hard. There will be plotting. Watch for it. And don't ever underestimate Bella."

"Since the Outpouring, her power in Quannet seems to wane," said Shade. "But I agree, strange things come from that old witch."

Bavn stopped walking and turned his massive body to face Shade. "You are my daughter's bodyguard and mate. Loac has a mission, and *your* mission is to ensure that she succeeds. You must stay focused."

"I... "

He raised a thick forefinger to hush her. "If hatred truly does blur your vision, then refrain from it. But keep in mind, these... *things* you refuse to hate could upset the tune of the universe and bring destruction to us all. I pray you *do* see clearly in the days ahead."

CHAPTER 10 - MIST

The putrid mess of bone and decomposed flesh littering the slab of emerline crystal was all that remained of Abner Hayes, with the exception of a mist the color of brain flesh surrounding the mess. In a way, it *was* brain flesh. It swirled with deliberation around the decayed heap of human detritus, almost like a beating life, something with a heart, with all the "something" stripped away and leaving only the essence of the heart.

It seemed to be alive.

It was.

It was the essence of everything that had once been Abner Hayes-his memories, his intellect, his senses, his soul, his feelings, love and regret. The regret contained in that small cloud of mist would engulf galaxies with pain.

This is what Bella had done to him. She'd been waiting for him two millennia ago, waiting for him to do the foolish thing that he was sure no one but he knew of. The very second the process had begun and there was no turning back, no escape-in that instant, he'd known that she'd been waiting for him. And she'd had him.

The questions had haunted and rankled him for two thousand years. How could he have been so stupid to think that it could have worked? How could he have allowed his love for his wife and daughter to blind him so much that dreams had overtaken reality and had made him vulnerable?

She'd built her trap well, thought it all out and had used every advance in science, technology and philosophy to trap him and keep him alive and caged for two millennia. As mist only, he might have escaped, but there was that pile of moldering bones and flesh. The essence of him couldn't continue to exist-at least, not in this life-without his body, or at least some connection to it, no matter how much it had degenerated. There was too much mind-body entanglement for his essence to survive without his body.

But he'd wanted desperately to be with his family-on their terms. They were software and he was physical. But the new Internet-Quannet-that tapped into the vibrations forming the strings that were the basic building blocks of all Creation made it possible for him to manipulate the frequencies that defined Abner Hayes and turn himself into software. He wanted to hold his wife in his arms in her world, run his fingers over his daughter's face and feel it the way she felt it. He'd been able to give his wife and daughter sentience, to raise them above the lines of their programming and give them real life. And maybe that had been his undoing. Maybe he'd thought that he was some kind of god who could manipulate the magic of life and turn his flesh and blood into software while bringing his sentience with him. On the other hand, it might have worked-if Bella hadn't somehow been on to what he'd been doing and set her trap. Through whatever bizarre science, she'd kept his remains and what was left of the rest of him smoldering on slabs of life support and regenerative nanhanced cages for two thousand years. His hatred for her was almost as big as his love for his family, but neither was as big as his regret.

She was on the other side of the nanglass now—gloating, cruel and eternally persistent.

***

She knew the mist could hear her, that this heap of rotting misery, once the only human ever to defeat her, knew that she was on the other side of the glass, and he was hurting with every word she said. She could punish him like this till the end of time, just for spite. She no longer needed his secret. Her engineers had finally reproduced his process for making software sentient on their own. She kept Abner Hayes alive for one purpose... to torment him for the rest of time.

"Your daughter is doing quite well these days," she said slowly, lips twisted into a cruel sneer. "Her training software puts her in top shape, a sure bet to win again."

She watched the mist. Yes, it seemed to beat faster, less regularly. He was feeling the pain. She was hurting him. She wanted to hurt him. It excited her to hurt him. It never made things right, but it excited her.

"I'm thinking about having her deleted, erased forever." She reached out and put a long green fingernail on the glass. The sneer turned into a snarl. "Now that I have your little secret, I don't need either of you anymore." She ran her fingernail across the glass. "But *you* will still live and suffer forever."

Spinning sharply, she walked stiff backed but gracefully into a long green tunnel.

The mist around Abner Hayes's remains beat slowly, erratically, the way someone in pain would sob.

CHAPTER 11 - OLD HATREDS

Three tall figures stood in a circle in a clearing of blue grass peppered with bursts of yellow flowers. Blue trees with trunks the size of large buildings stretched thousands of feet into the yellow sky where they sprouted massive fan-like yellow leaves. The air between two of the figures all but sprayed sparks of anger. One of them was clad in orange furs and decked with necklaces and bracelets carved from bone. His name was Brann. His eyes glowed red, the genetic trait of the Eyes of Blood Clan. Steam shot from his nostrils. His red eyes narrowed with fury over his long white beard. He faced Uilliam, whose thick beard stretched as long as Brann's but was obsidian black. His eyes were hard, his face massive and stone-like, as with all members of the Soul of Stone Clan.

A deep female voice, calm but seething with undertones of lethality, poured through the air like an acoustic fist in slow motion from deep inside the black hood of Maebh, Queen of the Womb of the Universe Clan. She was shrouded in a long black robe, her hood nansheilded to hide her face. "Fighting amongst ourselves will do nothing but ensure victory for the Blood Clan. It will make it easier for them to enslave us all."

Brann's head snapped in her direction. "No one has proved their intent to do anything of the sort." His words tumbled through the air like hatchets. He liked neither Maebh nor the dark magic of her Clan. "We've had peace for five hundred years," he said. "The Tears of Blood Clan is more powerful than ever. They may even have the power to withstand Bella."

"They are weakened by Bella," said Uilliam. His quiet voice slid through the space between them. "Their entire focus is on Bella and her control over Quannet, a control that weakens daily since the Outpouring. There may very well be war between them."

"And we will fight side by side with the Blood Clan," said Brann. "We are all Clans."

"You seem to have forgotten much," said Uilliam.

"These things must be put to rest or they poison our souls," said Brann.

"They were merciless." Red light pulsated briefly from inside Maebh's hood. "They destroyed entire planets where our numbers once thrived. And now they lie safely in their asteroid belt, smug, free of-"

"We all suffered great losses in the Clan Wars," said Brann, raising his voice. "We all lost family and friends, including the Blood Clan."

"But none were as vicious as they," said Uilliam, keeping his voice quiet and devoid of emotion. "None attacked with such ferocity and lack of humanity."

"It was war, Uilliam." Brann's face flushed brightly, his eyes flashed. "Victory goes to the greatest destroyer! And they could have finished us off. But they didn't."

"Oh yes," said Maebh, the sneer obvious in her voice. "Mercy when our numbers were decimated almost to the point of extinction."

"But mercy nonetheless," said Brann. "We've all grown and prospered since then."

"But it's coming to an end," said Maebh.

"We don't know that," said Brann.

"The signs-"

"Could all be superstition," said Brann. "Nothing's proven."

"The Texture-" said Uilliam.

"The Texture is nothing but a great unknown in space. All the blood that has been spilled over it-"

"By Bella and the Tears of Blood," said Maebh. "And there are others after it-all convinced there is something there that will change the universe. It can't be ignored. It could even be the end of the VRs."

Brann coughed and spat loudly. "The VRs. I hate them as much as you, as much as any man of flesh and blood-and especially the little VR witch. But it looks as though the Tears have just the thing to destroy her once and for all and bring a new order of respect for real life. This, I see, is more crucial than some space figment that no one anywhere has proven to be anything but another disappointing anomaly."

"Its properties have never been recorded anywhere in the known universe," said Maebh. "It could be a gateway to powers beyond anything we ever thought possible, just as the Tears of Blood believe."

"The fact is, we can never be sure," said Brann.

"Until they reach it," said Uilliam. "And we must be ready to act, to strike and free ourselves from-"

"They do not enslave us!" yelled Brann. "We live as equals! You let your fear and suspicions define your reality in wrong ways, Uilliam."

"There is sympathy from many of the Clans for our cause," said Maebh. "Suspicion grows against the intent of the Tears of Blood. There is talk that one of their highest ranking sympathizes with the VRs."

Brann's face filled with disgust. "Talk! Rumor! Heresay! I'll believe it when I hear it from the mouth of the heretic, just before I slice his head off."

"His?" asked Maebh. "The talk is that it may be a woman."

"Then her head will come off. And what of Bavn? Do you think he would allow this heresy?"

"Bavn was the most vicious of the Tears of Blood," said Maebh. "But there is talk of his softening since the Wars, and I've never been convinced of these special powers he's said to possess."

"Do not doubt his power," said Brann. "He is, and always has been, the heart of the Tears of Blood, and the powers you doubt were observed by many in the Clan Wars."

"Time has a way of exaggerating the truth," said Maebh.

"Or," said Brann slowly, "obscuring the danger in the lesson."

"And what's that supposed to mean?" asked Uilliam.

"You may soon find out," said Brann.

"So," said Maebh, "you'll not join us?"

"Nor will I align against you," said Brann. "The Eyes of Blood will remain neutral until the rumors have been proven or disproven." He stared into the blackness of Maehb's hood. "And may God help you if you move without first knowing the truth."

Uilliam glared at Brann. Maebh's hood turned full on Brann. "May your god help us if we be right, or wrong."

CHAPTER 12 - A SMALL LIFE

Sitting alone in the command deck of the Womb navy's mothership, Agrona, Maebh contemplated the meeting with Brann. She didn't trust him. Like all the men with whom she'd dealt, he was weakened by the small things that held men together, things like their "word," as though that were as substantial as nansteel or the need to take revenge. Brann would turn on them. She knew this. She would do something about it. She would act according to her knowledge. He could have her "word" on that.

The fleshy red walls of the command deck pulsed quietly, like a beating heart at rest for the moment. Its gentle movement reminded her of the beating life she'd once felt inside her own body when she'd been the first woman in nearly a thousand years to have a baby actually growing in her womb. It had been a lost art, a lost way, along with menstruation and the influence of the moon of Old Earth. Space and the death of Old Earth had done remarkable things to the concept of human. Godlike life spans and the alteration of the human body through genetics and nanhancements had taken humans so very far away from their humanity. And now much of the teeming human life in all its forms across the universe was suicidal.

But Maebh had felt the life within her, the kicks and movements, the shifts in posture, the stirrings of a human life growing within a human life, the way it had been with the ancients of Old Earth. This was the dream of the Womb of the Universe Clan, to bring back the old ways and return humanity to humans, to restore the respect for life, the value of living. It had taken centuries of surgeries and nanmagic to bring her womb back to life, to give her the ability to seed it and accept the sperm to fertilize it. But the Womb had succeeded, and their Queen was to be the first in centuries to give natural birth. The way Goddess wanted it.

She loved the small life growing inside her. She cherished every movement. She stayed awake at night, certain that she could hear the baby's first thoughts, the first natural baby thoughts, unaided by Quannet, in centuries. These were the thoughts of something that was an untarnished part of her. It was like a pipeline into the history of the entire human race, right back to Creation.

It would have been a miracle of sorts. It would have been the most beautiful thing to have ever happened to Maebh. She'd been happy, forgiving of her enemies, gentle with her friends, in touch with the basic rhythm of the universe. In these days, Maebh, Queen of the Womb of the Universe Clan had been a beautiful woman with long flowing red hair and peach skin the texture of shimmering light.

And then war started between the Clans, war in the name of false religion. They all believed that God struck the Tuning Fork of Creation against the Void and the One Vibration rushed into the Void to create endless variations of the Vibration. And that was how the Cosmos had been created. Then some came to believe that the One Vibration would eventually stop and all of Creation would return to the Void until God struck it once again. The others believed that One Vibration would vibrate forever.

They went to war and killed millions upon millions of their own over this distinction. Both sides, of course, used the war to justify attacking the Womb Clan, who were regarded as forever-damned pagans.

It was the Tears of Blood Clan that had attacked Maebh's planet, even though they had no navies, no weapons, no defense against the slaughter brought to their doorsteps. They'd attacked viciously, leveling the towns and villages, the biomaterial cities.

She'd been in the Goddess City, in a biobuilding constructed of materials that were guaranteed to age, deteriorate and return to the ground. Lasers had slashed through the walls and sliced people around her into blood-gushing meat. The ceiling sagged and caved in as the walls collapsed. That was what saved her. The Tears of Blood attack ships had left, assuming that none could have survived that destruction. But she had survived. More than anyone she had a reason to survive. She'd had the first natural baby in nearly two thousand years growing inside her.

She had lain under the rubble, a mixture of sticky biomaterial and natural stone and wood, feeling the life still beating in her womb. She also felt the pain soaking the flesh of her face from the laser blasts. She'd known without seeing it that she was no longer beautiful.

Horror crept through her chest and awareness as she listened and felt the small life inside here fade away and stop beating.

Only one thought, one motive and one purpose had filled every moment of her life since then: the Tears of Blood would pay for taking her baby and leaving her alive.

Soon, soon the Tears will fall from Creation, and Goddess will rule again.

CHAPTER 13 - THE CLEAN TEST

Maggie: This is Maggie Westork reporting live from Canak and the Reality Wars Clean Test, and this promises to be the biggest, most exciting, bloodiest Reality Wars ever! Tonight, my cohost is Childen Shan, third-place finisher in last century's Reality Wars. Childen, it's so good to have you here.

Childen: It's good to be here, Maggie. As much as I can be. (chuckles)

Maggie: (laughs) For all you newcomers, Childen was referring to losing both his arms in the last Reality Wars. Also for you newcomers, because of the usual tired old protocols and the need for secrecy at the opening of the most public event in the universe, this Quancast from the Clean Test will be voice only.

Childen: That was a beautifully worded way of saying that there's really no reason to have voice only, Maggie.

Maggie: (laughs) Childen, how come you never had your arms replaced? Especially being a clone... replacing parts must come naturally. (laughs)

Childen: Thanks for reminding me, Maggie. (chuckles) But I swore that, however I emerged from the last Reality Wars, I would stay that way for the rest of my life. We clones do have a sense of honor, you know. Even if I was drunk when I made the pact.

Maggie: Honor, shmonor, you're sitting here with two arms missing, and nobody even remembers the last Reality Wars.

Childen: Well, I wouldn't say-

Maggie: And who would want to remember any of the past Wars after this one? This will be the first time the Wars have been run in both Realspace and Quanspace. SolidHolo will make it possible for VRs to compete physically, almost as though they were real.

Childen: They *are* real, Maggie.

Maggie: Of course they are, Childen. Identical courses for the event have been laid out in Quanspace and Realspace with a randomized selectronics equalizer blasting the competitors between both realities without warning. And SolidHolo means that if VRs are killed in any of the events, they will actually die just as surely as the human competitors.

Childen: I think that's a shame.

Maggie: What's a shame, Childen?

Childen: Killing sentient beings just because the rules say so, as opposed to real death in the Wars.

Maggie: But it's not really real death, now, is it, Childen?

Childen: It is if you're the one dying, Maggie.

Maggie: Just in! UniSpec estimates more than 1000 quadrillion in more than a billion currencies has been laid down on the Wars. Now, that's one pile of gambling. Sounds like a few more planets, maybe even entire star systems, will be changing hands.

Childen: And completely without the permission and, sometimes, knowledge of the inhabitants.

Maggie: So far the usual lineup of contestants have been tested. Some really colorful specimens of humanity in the test area. We have Rainbow Folk from the Jumina Clusters-

Childen: And what a beautiful race they are, so tall and their bodies changing colors constantly like-

Maggie (impatiently): And crowds of very traditional looking people who don't seem to have heard about the wonders of genetic choice.

Childen: Sometimes, people are happy being them...

Maggie: Oh look! The first *real* competitors are arriving! And it's Cassie Mae Hayes, herself. Just look at her! In perfect SolidHolo! Long strawberry blonde hair flowing over her shoulders and just look at that figure! So lithe and muscular. It's almost like she's alive!

Childen: She is-

Maggie: And look! Coming in right behind her, it's her friend, the feisty Sara Beth. Just as beautiful as Cassie Mae with her long black hair and another specimen of what every woman modifies her body to be. I wonder what mischief she'll cook up this year? (looks at Childen) She beat you by a hair in the Blade Circle Arena a century ago to finish second in the Wars and cost you your arms, isn't that right, Childen?

Childen: I made a miscalculation that cost me my arms. Sara had nothing to do with that.

Maggie: A strange combination, those two. Cassie Hayes, a VR, and the winner of every one of the Reality Wars since their inception a thousand years ago-and Sara Beth, a human, and second place finisher for the last five hundred years. But who knows what will happen this year now that the field has been leveled between Realspace and Quanspace.

Childen: And Cassie, as usual, is unarmed.

Maggie: And a very dangerous gesture that is, Childen. Almost every Clean Test for the last eight hundred years has seen one or more competitors killed or maimed so badly they couldn't compete.

Childen: And all for something useless when you think of it. A scan to detect the presence of illegal training programs, genetic manipulation, nantech enhancements, kinesthetic anomalies-all of which have been thrown out the windows to leave the field open to anything and everything. It's a waste of time, really.

Maggie: Oh come now, Childen. The Clean Test is a tradition, a way to get the competitors together for a pre-Wars nose to nose. It's the first part of the Wars, like a weigh-in, to build excitement.

Childen: And triple the betting. Not the best reason to risk people's lives.

Maggie: A little backgrounder for you newcomers: the Clans-who are no fans of the VRs-have been trying to get Cassie Mae disqualified from the Wars because, they argued, having the Wars in Quanspace gives her a distinct advantage since she's software, even though she's programmed to simulate Realspace stress and physical limitations. But that's all changed now that the Wars are in both worlds, and that's what's driving the betting through the roof of the universe. And here comes a contingent of clones. Who are these people, Childen?

Childen: The big bald man is Maxilim Marx. He's the favorite to win this year for the clones. He finished right behind me in the last Wars.

Maggie: With his arms still on, apparently. (laughs)

Childen: His judgment was obviously better than mine.

Maggie: (laughs) Obviously. Just kidding you, Childen. And who's the planet-sized clone?

Childen: That's Centos Kama. He's not a favorite to win, but we expect he'll clear out a lot of the non-clone competition. The rest of the entourage are coaches and sponsors.

Maggie: So Centos is the clones' goon, the muscle brought in to eliminate the competition?

Childen: I think we all know that muscle has little to do with winning the Reality Wars, Maggie. It just helps you to stay alive, sometimes. Centos has a few tricks other than size up his sleeve.

Maggie: I'm sure he does. And he'll be a great addition considering that, this year, the betting isn't on just who wins or survives, but on who causes the greatest number of qualifying deaths, not that we want to see anyone harmed. (laughs)

Childen: Centos isn't a killer. He's a competitor and all-round great athlete and...

Maggie: Here comes the Tears of Blood Clan! Wow! Things are going to heat up now. Sara Beth, who's known for her hot-headedness and downright dislike of the Clans, sees them coming, and she's got trouble in her eyes. She's already killed two

Clan members in previous Clean Tests-both of them qualified kills. Let's see what she has in store for us today.

Childen: Here comes Loac, the-

Maggie: Perfect Reality Wars weapon, according to the hype coming out of the asteroids. Five hundred years with all the most advanced genetics and nantech-and supposedly, nanmagic-to create the most perfect Reality Wars athlete of all time. The Clans want a human winner to show the universe that humans are superior to VRs, and everything they have is riding on this one woman. So, Childen, what do you think her chances are?

Childen: I guess we'll know after the Wars. Cassie Hayes has been at this for a thousand years. In Quanspace or Realspace, she's-

Maggie: Just look at her! Here's what I'm seeing-a remarkably beautiful woman with long jet black hair wrapped around her neck like a scarf, deep eyes with dark brows-almost haunting-and look at the way her jaw and mouth flow smoothly forward-definitely bred to fulfill a purpose. And that look... is that a smile? Or is that a look of contempt? So confident and sinister, almost foreboding. And, of course, the red streak down the right side of her face from eyes to jaw, the tears of blood.

Childen: She's definitely a looker, Maggie. (chuckles)

Maggie: Childen, you sound interested. Why don't you go down there and tell her that? (laughs) Oh, better be careful, Childen-I think that's her bodyguard and rumored lover, Shade, right behind her, long blond hair flowing over her shoulders,

blue almost glowing. She'll be one of the competitors as well.

Childen: Another genetically modified woman.

Maggie: And who isn't these days, Childen? So, do you think we'll see either Shade or Loac turn to vapor?

Childen: I think the vapor stories may be just rumors left over from the Clan Wars. Something like that may be technically possible, but I don't think anybody has ever actually seen it...

Maggie: Did you see that? Cassie just put her hand on Sara's shoulder, as though restraining her. Looks like things are going to get interesting very soon. Childen, tell our listeners about the other Clan members.

Childen: Thank you, Maggie. There are three members of the Clan's Inner Circle. Some people call them sorcerers. The one in the blue robes is Bavn, the generally accepted leader of the Tears of Blood, though they supposedly rule by peer consent. He's said to be as old, or even older, than Bella Bjork.

Maggie: That would make him one very old sorcerer. (nervous laugh)

Childen: They have the scanner ready for the next contestant...

Maggie: The operator has signaled that he's ready for the next scan. What we're seeing, folks, is a huge umbrella-like apparatus in the center of a blue room devoid of furniture. There's several hundred people in the room, a huge array of traditional and modified birth humans and clones from across the universe. And just one VR this year-Cassie Mae Hayes, who, even though she can actually be killed with the new SolidHolo, isn't armed. Her friend and fellow competitor, Sara, looks like she's getting ready to stir things up again. And look, the scan operator, a VR, signals for Sara to be scanned first. Look. They just waved to each other and gave a hand signal of some sort. The scanners have always liked Sara. She breaks the monotony and gives them something to tell their grandchildren about. Now Sara's standing under the umbrella, and a blue light is dropping from the top inside of the umbrella almost like drapery unfolding downward.

Childen: It's almost beautiful, isn't it, Maggie?

Maggie: I thought you didn't like this part of the Reality Wars, Childen.

Childen: It's the unnecessary deaths that I don't like, Mag-

Maggie: Look, Sara's beginning to ham it up, acting as though the light is tickling her, and now, slapping her neck as though bitten by insects. Everybody's laughing-well, everyone but the Clans. Do they ever laugh?

Childen: Maggie, they're called the *Tears of Blood* Clan. I doubt they even smile, except when they're killing somebody.

Maggie: And now it's Cassie Hayes's turn under the umbrella. She seems to have a wistful look in her eyes, almost bored.

Childen: She's been through this more than anybody else.

Maggie: What a gorgeous woman. She still looks so young, even for software, after a couple of millennia, with her long strawberry hair, and she still has freckles dotting her cheeks. And look at the way she carries herself, a young woman in complete control of her world and her life.

Childen: There's been talk that she's beginning to tire of the Reality Wars, that she may be thinking of making this one her last.

Maggie: Childen! Are you starting a rumor?

Childen: Just saying...

Maggie: And now it's Loac's turn under the umbrella . . . another gorgeous woman. Her body has been hyped to be the most perfect woman's body ever. Apparently, they didn't breed her just for performance, but for looks as well-a sort of perfect ideal that everyone can look to and say, "This is everything flesh and blood can be."

Childen: Which wouldn't be a bad thing if they didn't want to eliminate all sentient VRs in the process.

Maggie: Worried that they'll turn on clones next, Childen?

Childen: The Clans are a powerful and unpredictable force in the universe, Maggie. I think we should all be concerned.

Maggie: What's going on here, now? Look, the scanner operator is instructing Loac to bend forward. And she's doing it. I've never seen this routine before. And now he's telling her to touch her toes. And she's doing it! And the operator is smiling. He's joking with her. That's a very dangerous thing to do with Bavn present. It's said that he can reach out to any VR in he universe and destroy them with his nanmagic.

Childen: I doubt that, Maggie. If that were true, I'm sure, given the Clans' hatred for the VRs, they'd all be dead by now. Besides, they're making things even more interesting this year. Everything is taking place in Realspace including the Test. The VR scan operator is in SolidHolo. He can be killed just like anyone else here.

Maggie: Oh, look! He just told her to bend backward, and she's doing that as well! No! Now she's looking around and she doesn't look happy about everybody laughing at her. Would you call that murder in her eyes, Childen?

Childen: I'm not sure what I'd call what's in her eyes, Maggie. But I'm glad it's not directed at me.

CHAPTER 14 - STARS

A tiny black nine-pointed star shot through the air directly at the scanner operator's now-killable head. It spun as it flew, causing the gold inscriptions on both sides of its surface to spell out the word "BLOOD," although given the speed at which it shot through the air and the short distance, there would be no time to read it before it hit its target.

And that made what followed so amazing.

A fraction of a second and a fraction of an inch before the star carved into the operator's forehead, it suddenly flew off at a ninety degree angle, with a tiny black spike sticking into its side.

Before the operator had a chance to push out one drop of SolidHolo sweat on a forehead that would soon be soaked-Sara's and Shade's eyes burned into each other, both women poised to draw weapons.

"You just stopped a qualified kill," said Shade calmly, glaring into Sara's eyes.

"He was just having a little fun," said Sara. "Maybe you people can't take a joke, but the rest of us *humans* like the occasional laugh."

"Humans? I count only a few humans in this room," said Loac, stepping away from the umbrella and toward the other Clan members. "And they all belong to Clans."

Sara swung her gaze away from Shade and looked Loac up and down, smiling scornfully. "So you're the Great Clans' Hope. I thought you would be bigger."

"Careful, VR lover," said Shade. "Your next save may not be so lucky."

"Then again, yours might not be as fast," said Sara, smiling sarcastically. "That throw wasn't bad, though. I like the occasional challenge."

Something in Shade's eyes suggested a smile, but no smile curled the corners of her mouth. Just as she was parting her lips to say something, Sara said, "Maybe next time I'll get one."

Another star shot through the air, this time faster than the first, aimed directly at Sara's forehead. An instant before it hit, a hand materialized by Sara's head, holding two of the star's tips between thumb and forefinger. Cassie handed the star to Sara. "Sara! Let it go. Save it for the Wars."

Bavn, with a trace of cold amusement flickering deep in his eyes, stared calmly at Cassie. It was a strange feeling for her, suddenly feeling things in Realspace. She couldn't have imagined that a look could carry a feeling in the manner of Bavn's quietly lethal stare. He spoke slowly. "Good thinking... for a VR. Enjoy these days, Cassie Mae Hayes. Enjoy them."

"Don't you worry, Clansman, I will," said Cassie defiantly.

"Me too," said Sara, turning her head toward Shade. "I'll see you and your little girlfriend in the Wars."

Shade's lips remained motionless, but her eyes seared into Sara's-the suggestion of humor a few moments ago, gone. She said nothing.

"I'll be looking forward to it," said Loac, licking her lower lip slowly. She joined the other Clan members, and just before they turned to leave, she looked one more time at Sara and drew a finger slowly across her neck. The finger sank into her neck as though it were air, or vapor.

The scanner operator, now soaked with sweat, announced, "OK folks, since this test is totally meaningless and we've all had an interesting time-and we're all still alive-I'm declaring all contestants clean. You can all get back to your training. Good luck and stay alive."

Scattered cheers arose from the crowd of competitors. As they began to leave, Sara turned to Cassie, "I could have stopped that star, you know."

"I'm sure you could have," said Cassie.

***

Maggie: Did you see that? Did you see that? She caught the star right before it struck Sara in the forehead. Have you ever seen anyone move that fast? Have you ever seen *anything* move that fast! And then the damned VR operator cancels the Test, just when things were warming up.

Childen: Tempers were beginning to fly a bit off the hook in there, Maggie.

Maggie: Exactly! If he had just let it go for another few minutes, we might have had our first kill in this century's Reality Wars.

CHAPTER 15 - WINKING OUT

Before heading to his virtual bungalow in the suburbs, Scanner Operator Seventh Grade, Takeko Bolo, stopped off at his favorite restaurant, Eats. He was still a bit shaky as he thought about the day's events, but he smiled to himself. He'd poked fun at one of the most dangerous humans of all time and come within a few vibes of not just having his program terminated forever, but of finding out what death would be like for a sentient VR. But he was still alive, and he was biting into just about the most delicious piece of curried chicken he'd ever tasted. As soon as it touched his teeth, he could feel it caressing his programming, he could feel thousands of nanvibes rushing into the millions of modules that made Takeko Bolo real. And real he was. Takeko was one of the first wave of VRs made sentient with the Hayes program, just before the Outpouring.

That had been a strange feeling for Takeko-and a beautiful feeling. It was like suddenly waking up and saying, "Oh, that." He viewed everything differently from that day on and everything seemed to view him differently. He was suddenly aware, and he was aware that he was aware. He had feelings. He *felt* about things. He had distinctly different feelings about different things. Some things made him happy. Some made him sad. He liked some things. He disliked others. In the years following he felt love, fear, hate, loss, sadness-the feelings came at him from all angles with his reactions to everything around him suddenly directed by this huge box of things unleashed: his feelings.

There was much talk at the time from humans that it was all just simulations of feelings, that there was no such thing as sentience in VRs, that it was impossible for strings of programming to have true feelings, that the VRs felt merely a programmed response to given stimuli. But the VRs who had become sentient knew better. They knew what they felt. And they knew how they had felt before. There was a very real difference. Suddenly, they were alive, trillions of them, and they knew it. Takeko wasn't sure if he had a soul. He wasn't sure if any of the VRs had souls. But on the other hand, he had yet to see any Realspace physical prove that he or she had one. He just knew that he was alive, and nobody could take that away from him.

Just as Takeko Bolo was about to wash down a mouthful of curried chicken with a swig of beer, he felt something strange, a sudden shift in his perception, a dimming of his awareness. His head seemed to spin. He lost contact with the taste of the curried chicken. In fact, he couldn't even feel the chicken in his mouth. It was gone. And so was the restaurant. The table he'd been sitting at had disappeared. He was in a blank place, a place without form or substance or reference points, a terrifying place. There was only whiteness and Takeko floated in the whiteness without sensation. Everything that he was and ever had been was draining out of him and evaporating into the whiteness. The memories and feelings that he'd been so fond of possessing since the moment of this

71

sentience drifted away from him, spilling into the whiteness and becoming nothing. Takeko Bolo was becoming nothing.

Something began to manifest itself in what was left of his consciousness, a form of some sort, an image. It was the image of a large bearded head, a blue beard under glaring blue eyes and thick blue brows-and a line of red drops running down one side of the face, drops originating from the face's right eye, almost like they might be tears of blood.

At that moment, Takeko Bolo knew that he was dying-all his sentience, his life, disappearing through some ancient magic from the Tears of Blood Clan. He winked out before he had a chance to put whatever VR curse he could on Bavn.

CHAPTER 16 - A STRANGE FEELING

"You shouldn't be pushing them like that," said Cassie. "They're dangerous people, and they hold a grudge like nobody in the universe."

"They're not people, they're a bunch of freaks," said Sara. "And they don't scare me, and I really could have caught that star yesterday. Oh, by the way, you're slipping."

Cassie corrected her position on the training grid. She'd been out by a microinch and she wondered how Sara had even noticed the error.

They were in Cassie's personal Quangym, a massive training entity that stretched for thousands of Quanmiles, incorporating forests, mountains, rivers, lakes, deserts, canyons, savannas, prairies and an ocean. There were vast regions of blue jungle, gardens the size of cities with flowers that would engulf the minds of physicals or VRs and drive them mad before devouring their personalities and life force. It was a gym that existed in both observable reality and in ways that were not only impossible to see, but could never be explained. It crossed realities, dipping into the world of flesh and blood and into the realm of virtual realities. It was both logical and paradoxical. It was anomaly and normality wrapped around each other like lovers with a perverse sense of humor.

It was very much like the Reality Wars.

Cassie couldn't think of anything more special to share with her best friend.

"Still out," said Sara with a smirk.

How did she know that? Cassie adjusted the pinky toe of her left foot by a microinch so that it lined up exactly with the thousands of red microbeams that formed a grid engulfing her foot and the rest of her body. This was an exercise in coordinating her body along grids that changed several times a second for every part of her body while still maintaining her basic form. It was one of the land exercises and though it had been used twice in the past, there was no guarantee it would ever be used again—but, if it were, she would be ready.

"Good eye," she said, just a little miffed.

"I've never seen you make a mistake like that before," said Sara. "You OK?"

"I'm fine, but you may not be if you keep pushing those people. I don't know... I have a feeling there are things going on that are, you know, under the surface of everything we're seeing."

"There's definitely something going on with the Clans. Quancasts have been cut off all along the Blood asteroids. Too bad, they have some great shows on ancient history. Well, at least for shows produced by a bunch of unsmiling, humorless, VR haters who might be able to turn into mist and slip under doors like vampires."

"This whole Texture thing worries me," said Cassie. "Everybody's racing for it and everybody seems to think it's going to change the universe like some magic wand."

"Probably just another boring anomaly," said Sara as she bit into a training bar and rolled her eyes. "You'd think they could make these things taste better. Do they taste like sawdust for VRs as well?"

"I don't mind them."

"Must taste different for you," said Sara, making a face as she swallowed. "But I wouldn't worry about the whole Texture thing."

"It's not the Texture itself I'm worried about-it's what it's doing to the people who think it's something special. Bella's and the Clans' fleets have been going nose to nose all over the universe, and there's all this religious stuff about the Outpouring being the beginning of the end... "

"I don't care what you think," said Sara, making a face. "This stuff tastes like processed wood chips. I think this is why I avoid Quanbars and Quanstaurants."

"You've been to Quanbars with me."

"Only because you're there to suffer with me."

"And I always thought you were having a good time."

"I'd have a good time if I thought you were having a good time, especially lately. What's been getting into you? I mean, you were never exactly a mindless partier, but lately, you've been, like, a million miles away. And I know you're not worried about the Reality Wars, even with that unsmiling bitch Loac spooking the hell out of everybody else."

Cassie shrugged her shoulders. "I'm not worried about the Wars, but I think you'd better be especially careful in this one. Just looking at Loac, I know she's going to be trouble, dangerous trouble."

"Spooked by a Clans bitch, Cass?"

Cassie laughed, dimpling her cheeks. That had been a difficult module, but she liked the effect.

"Good to see you laughing for a change," said Sara. "You've been getting too serious lately. Don't tell me all that business with your father is still bugging you. I mean, it's only been a couple thousand years. Ever heard the expression 'move on'?"

Cassie threw a star shower at Sara. It exploded harmlessly into hundreds of tiny shooting stars just before it reached her. "Nice one," said Sara. "Guess I'm slipping a bit today too."

"Do you ever get strange feelings that you can't explain and they don't make any sense?" asked Cassie.

"You mean like when I think some guy is going ask me to dance at the Rondelle, and it turns out he wants to dance with you? Sure, all the time." Sara threw a shooting star at Cassie, but she grabbed it out of the air just before it exploded.

"If you weren't so intimidating, they'd be all over you, Sara. But you see some guy giving you the shine and you give him the look of death. I'd be intimidated too."

"Just making sure we start off on the right foot," said Sara. "You know, mess around on me, ever, and you die."

"Gee, what was I thinking? Men should be lining up for miles for an offer like that."

"Enough about my love life," said Sara. "So, what about these strange feelings? They got your toes iced or something?"

"I don't know," said Sara. "I... I've just been getting a lot of weird thoughts about my father, like he's around or something. Like he's still in my life."

"Could be," said Sara, making a face as she bit into the training bar again.

"What do you mean?"

"Well... " She talked around her chewing. "You never did find out where he went when he left. You don't know what happened to him."

"He left me and my Mom, just left us stranded. My Mom never got over it. That's what killed her."

"I don't know," said Sara. "From what you told me about your Mom's death, it just doesn't sound right. Your Mom didn't seem like the kind to delete herself just because she couldn't live with what your father did. I mean, she still had you. I can't see anybody running out on you, even your father for that matter."

"He left us, Sara. We waited for hundreds of years. We searched all over Quanspace for a trace of him. We had people search in Realspace. He was just... gone."

Sara shrugged. "I don't know, none of this makes any sense to me. It just doesn't add up."

"Well, it's over now," said Cassie. "At least... " She stood motionless for a moment, staring off into Quanspace.

"At least... ?" asked Sara.

"I don't know, Sara. Like I said, it's just a feeling I've been getting lately, a sense of his being near."

"Do you feel your Mom in there as well?"

A trace of sadness pinched the corners of Cassie's eyes. "No. I don't. I wish I did. But she's gone. Just gone. And all I'm feeling close to right now is the bastard who left both of us when we needed him." She started back on her routine, eyes set straight ahead. "For now, though, I want you to be extra careful with the Clans. They won't think twice about killing you."

"OK, Mom," said Sara.

Cassie looked briefly at her friend's contorting face as she swallowed a mouthful of training bar. She had a bad feeling about Sara, a sense of danger that she hadn't felt in the five hundred years that the two of them had been friends and opponents in the Reality Wars. *God help anyone who harms her. They'll see what a two-thousand-year-old piece of software with sentience can do that could never be done in any Reality Wars.*

CHAPTER 17 - BUDDHA

You're getting better at this all the time.

"I'm glad you think so," said the Assassin. "I try."

I know you do. And it's paying off. You're likely the most humane mass murderer in the universe.

"I'm not a mass murderer. I'm an assassin. Don't start on that again."

You've killed thousands of people. I think that qualifies as mass murder.

"I'm paid for what I do. Mass murderers don't get paid. They do it for fun or because some messed-up voice in their head tells them to kill."

You have a voice in your head.

"But you keep telling me not to kill."

Not lately.

"No. Not lately."

Suspended in the air by water magnets, the Assassin lay on his back, naked, eyes closed. Even supine, it was obvious that he was tall and cut, and hairless from head to foot. He didn't like hair. It might slow him down in situations measured in microseconds or give his opponents something to grab onto. It needed caring, and he had better things to do with his time.

Are you getting her frequencies?

"Close. She has some elaborate screens, new modular mixes, the illegal ones. But I guess these people don't much care about the Imagination Laws."

Could be why she's been targeted.

"Doubt it. They're not the only ones... nobody takes the Laws seriously anymore, even the assholes who enforce them. And this is no ordinary woman. She was bred for a purpose, every cell in her body nancut and genetically molded to fit into some grand plan."

I'll have to agree with you on that one.

The Assassin smiled. "I'm getting close now. Damned elaborate stuff she's loaded with."

Did you see that?

"See what?"

In the right peripheries.

"Quan or Real?"

Quan.

"No. Didn't see anything."

Strange, given our relationship.

"You're just a voice in my head. I don't have to see what you see." The Assassin smiled again. "So, what did you see?"

Buddha.

CHAPTER 18 - A FLAW

It was hard to imagine that the mammoth chunks of rock forming the Vorgell Asteroid Belt streaked around the planet Vorgell more at thousands miles an hour. The sheer immensity of the Belt seemed to freeze it against a brilliant curtain of starlight and even though the giant rocks were hundreds of miles apart, it seemed to Shade that she could reach out and touch the surface of the closest, Celtenan, the largest of the rocks.

On the surface they were devoid of movement or light with no telltale signs of the massive weapons emplacements scattered just under the surface. These were juggernauts, war ships in a navy of ferocious destructive power flying thousands of miles an hour around a planet was rumored to have been engineered into a colossal bomb.

Laser-cut deep into their guts were the myriad cities of the Tears of Blood Clan. The smallest sustained over twenty million Clansfolk. They'd been prolific since the Clan Wars.

Shade loved walking on the surface, feeling the closeness of the other asteroids, viewing the stars in the vast reaches of space beyond the Belt. She loved the simplicity of the rock surface, and she needed simplicity at this point in her life. She had little problem believing the theories that time and space were accelerating at a dizzying pace. Her own life was certainly accelerating-alarmingly. It seemed that more was happening every day, and every day grew shorter. Her life was a sudden blooming of complexity, like an intricate garden of contradictions growing out of the density of her life, all of it happening faster and faster. There were days when she wanted to just stay in bed for the rest of her life, but she was one of the deadliest warriors in the universe, genetically engineered and nanhanced to be the bodyguard of the single most important person of all time according to the Inner Circle.

Normally, walking along the smooth path cut into the surface and breathing the sweet-scented air under the invisible umbrella of the life shield would calm her, but not today. The encounter with the VR's friend Sara the day before had been disturbing in many ways. She'd tried to kill a VR operator for having some fun, for insulting Loac. It had been a thing of honor. She'd been compelled to do it. But that still didn't make it right to take a life-even a VR life-for no other reason than poking fun. She was almost glad that Sara had stopped the killing. But she was also concerned at the girl's speed and lethal aim. She would be a deadly match in combat. Shade would have thought that no power in the universe could have stopped that star from slicing into the VR's forehead, but Sara had stopped it just a fraction of an inch from its target. And then the VR had stopped the second star. But she was OK with that. Loac was the one bred to beat the VR. Shade would be, as Bavn had once put it, riding shotgun.

She smiled briefly, remembering Sara's words: "I thought you would be bigger." She was definitely an interesting one, and Shade felt something akin to liking toward the outspoken VR's friend. But she

82

dared not go there. She would almost certainly have to kill her at some point. She was certain the girl would continue to set herself up for it, and Shade would have to kill her or she'd be called before the Inner Circle for an accounting. And even though Shade had been almost as thoroughly bred as Loac- and their ultimate purpose was inexorably intertwined-the Inner Circle would be merciless. They'd invested too much time and energy in Shade to let their magnificent weapon fail. She had no idea what they'd do, but she was certain it would have something to do with Bavn's magic, whether he wanted that or not. And that sent a shiver across her spine.

She knew there was something wrong with her, a disjunct between what she was supposed to be and what she knew herself to be. They'd spent half a millennium designing her genetics, nanhancing her mind and body right from the moment her parents had conceived her, an act of sex she'd long wondered about. Had it been in a lab? A bedroom? One of Bavn's secret places? She'd never met her parents though and had no idea who they were, so she'd likely never know anything about the act that had brought her into being.

Maybe it had been something in those two that had been more powerful than the genetic manipulation and the nanbots that had created the flaw in her character. Maybe a tiny sliver of love from one or both of them had bled irrevocably into her essence. She was supposed to hate all VRs and anything and anyone that might be a threat to Loac. She was supposed to feel nothing toward anything unless it was either a threat or an ally to Loac. She was supposed to be Loac's mate, but she was not to love her. She was to feel nothing but an overwhelming sense of duty and a deep devotion to their purpose.

But she was in love with Loac and had always been in love with her. She would die for her, but not out of a genetically bred sense of duty. She would do it for love.

Far in the space over her head, one of the great ships of the Tears of Blood navy materialized with a brilliant wave of red. They were beautiful ships, long and lean and nansteel blue.

She suddenly had a strange feeling. She stopped walking and breathed quietly and steadily, the warrior looking inward and assessing the weapon's readiness. What was that? Just a tiny flicker like the slightest movement of a candle flame in a deathly still room. Whatever it had been, it was gone. She shrugged.

Maybe she *should* have stayed in bed today.

CHAPTER 19 - SOUL SHIP

As commander of the deep space cruiser, Soul Ship, Chief Magistrate Jeli Role was aware more than most of the basic absurdity of the universe, because it was his job to command a ship that would reflect the absurdity of the universe. His job came easily, given the nature of the ship and its crew.

Soul Ship was built to reach a cosmological anomaly that many believed would allow billions of clones throughout the universe to achieve soulhood. It was the culmination of a search started over a thousand years ago, with thousands of disappointments scattered throughout Creation. And now they were streaking to the edge of the universe in another madcap quest for something that was most likely impossible, but they wouldn't know until they got there. What they were searching for was almost a form of madness, the basic concept being that the true nature of being human was to reflect the nature of the universe, and the universe was absurd at its most basic level-a place that appeared to be devoid of purpose, a place where everything in existence would eventually cease to exist for no other reason than that was the nature of the place, a place where all existence had an expiry date, and the only way to defeat it was to die earlier. If you weren't eaten by time, then you would be feasted upon by something else.

Clones had never been regarded as full humans, even though their DNA was derived from the best in human genetics. The controls on what tissue could be used in cloning were among the strictest in the universe. Clones were regarded as less than human only because they were not born of sperm and seed, a process that even most humans had bypassed, but then, they had the Control Registry to prove their humanness. Clones had to be registered as well, but for different reasons. Humans were supposedly imparted with something special that no other living thing in the universe possessed-soul. Clones, it was said, didn't have souls. This made them less than human to humans, and to themselves.

But nobody could point to a soul and say, "Look, a soul." Nobody could measure it. Nobody could prove they had one. It was a matter of faith, a matter of believing in something that could never be proven until you died-and then you would be in a place where it would be impossible to come back and say, "Hey, look, I have proof."

It was an absurd concept, as absurd as the universe itself. And it made humans like the universe. Absurd. That's what it took, absurdity. And that's what the clones were doing-embracing absurdity. Soul Ship was the epitome of that embrace.

Everything in Jeli Role's ship was designed to push its crew to the maximum boundaries of absurdity. Everything had been designed to fall apart just when it was needed most. The engineers had been good at building disaster into Soul Ship. Since the start of their mission, almost everything had broken down. Sensors designed to open portals had fried crew members to cinders, or just sliced their heads off. Anything that was attached to anything else by nuts, bolts, welds, screws, nails, tacks, tape, staples, glue or nanlinks-anything that wasn't intrinsically a part of anything else, as in one piece-fell apart. Nails worked their way out of nanwood. Tape may as well have been strips of liquid fat. Welds split when people walked past them thinking too loud.

What was still more absurd was that most of the things that were used to hold Soul Ship together had disappeared throughout the populated universe. Nobody used nails or tape anymore. Before boarding Soul Ship, neither Jeli nor anyone else on the crew had ever seen paper let alone paper held together with staples. They were used to paper now, and staples. Paper was the stuff that gathered in piles with information that nobody would ever look at after it was written, and staples were the tiny metal things that never went into the paper straight, and then fell out.

All but one of the cabbie pods had crashed into planets, asteroids, meteors-or had just shot off into deep space taking one or two crew members to oblivion. Jeli was saving the remaining cabbie for the Texture. That situation promised to be bizarre enough to make Soul Ship seem normal.

So what exactly was Jeli to use to hold this ship together and reach their destination? Somehow, he suspected, it was the crew.

The crew.

They'd been chosen for their unquestionable departure from logic, the strangest assembly of living matter ever to occupy the position of ship's crew. Any other ship in the universe would flush them through the debris filters the moment they stepped aboard. Most were cross-clones, illegal clones, unregistered abominations, according to the Registry.

One way or another, these were the beings that would prove once and for all if this thing called soul really did exist.

CHAPTER 20 - MISGUIDED FEELINGS

Light shimmered over the gray plastic surfaces of row upon row of camouflaged and sunken nanlasers. There was enough firepower in this one quadrant of weaponry to take out an entire navy and this was just one of hundreds of millions of installations peppering the craggy subsurfaces of Blood Citadel's millions of asteroids. The path before them glistened with the same light. It was a cold light in a cold place.

"With each day, my hatred of the VRs grows," said Loac. She was wearing the white robe of meditative walk, meditation being an integral part of her daily life. "I hear of their poisonous replication through Quanspace. I hear of their false arguments that Quanspace is part of the Ultimate String and therefore infinite. They are an abomination, and those who suggest they might be alive are traitors to humanity."

"Your hatred of the VRs is natural and healthy," said Bavn, also dressed in white. "There are rumors of another Outpouring. They say they can disperse throughout the limitlessness of infinity, but these are just soulless things that don't realize they can actually fill up this dimension, pack it so tight that they bring about an end to all things."

"Do you really believe that we share the same reality with them?"

"All existence is one, Loac. We all occupy the same reality, at different divine frequencies, defined

89

by God. But the VRs do not occupy the frequencies the same way we do. To say they do is the same as to say that a rock on the ground is human and possesses soul." He stopped walking and placed his hand on his daughter's shoulder. "In a very short while, we will change all that. You and Shade will be instruments in bringing this about." He looked deep into her eyes. "And how are things between you two?"

"I sometimes suspect that what she feels for me is love."

"But you're mates." Bavn half smiled and continued walking. Loac fell in step beside him, not smiling.

"You know what I mean. Love might be in the back of her mind, but her first priorities are duty to me and hatred of the VRs. These are the things that will make her strong. Love will be a chink in her armor, a weakness."

"I've spoken with her," said Bavn. "She feels that hatred is too strong an emotion and that it will blur her vision. She wants to be clear in the days ahead."

"Let's hope, then," said Loac, "that this love she feels for me is not so powerful that it blurs her vision more certainly than the hatred she should be feeling."

"Her quick response yesterday was an act of instant duty. She would have killed the operator had it not been for the VR witch's human friend. Hatred or love, she would have killed unquestioningly and instantly."

90

Loac nodded as she thought about this. "And what about the operator?"

"It paid dearly for its little joke."

"Father," said Loac. "I'm surprised that you would use your vast magic to eliminate something that is really no more important than a garbage disposal." She was still not smiling.

Bavn smiled and glanced at Loac. "He should not have toyed with my daughter."

Still unsmiling, Loac said, "Perhaps Shade's misguided feelings have spread to my father?"

For just an instant, the smile dropped from Bavn's face, and then returned.

***

Bavn watched his daughter disappear into the entrance portal that had just swung out of a rock face. *If we could have made room for just one moment of humor with its accompanying smile in her life.*

91

CHAPTER 21 - AN OCEAN OF BLACK

They floated in an ocean of cold soul-gnawing black, black that would fast freeze your essence into a sliver of ice and crush it with the sheer immensity of its nothingess. Abruptly, Cassie was aware of herself in the black.

She felt encased in lead though she floated freely and perceived all the parts of herself-fingers, toes, hair on the nape of her neck-but there was a disjointedness in this place she'd never felt before, something that touched the center of her being with a chilled finger.

"This is what it's like to feel in the real world," said a voice somewhere in the blackness. The voice resounded quietly with echoes of ancient wisdom and youthful excitement. Two bright blue eyes opened in the blackness just below the origin of the words.

"I hate this feeling," said Cassie. "If ever anything might feel like death, this would be it."

"It'll be a hundred times more like death in the Reality Wars," said the voice. "And there will be others with you. This will take place in both worlds, Cassie Mae. If any of the Clansfolk get to you while you're in human form and in the physical plane, they may have an advantage in a place like this."

"I know. And I know that the Wars are going to be different this time, dipping in and out of Quan and Realspace but honestly, I think I prefer Quan. And I don't think I'd be having anything to do with

Realspace if it weren't for the Wars." She thought a moment. For nearly a thousand years, she'd worked off and on with Aristotle, one of the many personas behind the blue eyes glowing in the blackness, personas springing from a pool of the greatest minds of all time from great athletes and coaches to business and military strategists and great thinkers. They were all embodied by the being behind the smile that split the blackness below the eyes, the being she called "Coach."

Coach chuckled. "Realspace isn't all it's cracked up to be. But it's not the training that has you in this mood, Cassie Mae. I sense something deeper troubling you."

"It's been a thousand years, Coach."

"A thousand years of victory."

"But still a thousand years."

"I know," said Coach. "But it's so much more than just time. You've become a symbol in that time. If not for the image of your finishing victoriously century after century, VRs would still be considered just programs in both Realspace and in our own reality. Even clones would be treated as little more than meat that knows its name in the face of human ego."

"But it's been a thousand years."

"I know." A long white beard unraveled downward from the smiling mouth. A nose nudged into being. The face filled out under a canopy of long white hair. "After this one, though, you may just change the way they feel at a deeper level than ever. Humans may very well accept VRs as equals."

"That will never happen," said Cassie.

"These are times of great change, Cassie Mae. I have a feeling that many things will be possible over the next few months, and much of it will come out of the Reality Wars."

"Coach?"

"Yes, Cassie Mae."

"This will be my last Wars."

"I know."

"Thank you for all you've done for me, Coach. You've been like a father."

94

CHAPTER 22 - BUDDHA, ENCORE

An hour after her training, Cassie floated peacefully in her personal pool. Every detail of the paisley mosaic inlaid in the floor of the pool a mile down was visible in the crystalline water. She breathed slowly, relaxing deeper with each exhalation. There were no air currents here to disturb the water's mirror surface or Cassie's slow descent into total relaxation. Everything was still, soundless, empty of the world just as her mind emptied of all thought.

"It wasn't his fault," whispered a voice in her ear.

Her eyes shot open. Her head twisted from side to side, body instantly prepared to defend. She saw nothing. But she knew she wasn't alone. The voice had been real. Someone or something was close enough to whisper into her ear. She calmed herself and continued to float motionlessly, probing into the air and water around her with an awareness honed by a thousand years of Reality Wars training. She felt no presence, sensed nothing. "Who's there?" she asked.

"Your father never meant to hurt you and your mother."

It was right there! Right by her ear! She spun her head as her hands flew up to strike, but there was only empty space. "Whoever you are, you better show yourself. And what do you know about my father? He's dead. Where are you?"

And now the voice was all around her, whispering gently from every direction. "Your father loved you and your mother more than anything. The two of you were the center of his universe. He would never have hurt either of you."

Spinning slowly in the water, she looked up into the clear virtual sky and then deep into the water. She scanned the surface as ripples fanning over the water from her gently rotating body. "He left us. We waited for him and he never came. He just disappeared." She spoke calmly, holding down the anger and pain building in her stomach and chest.

"I have things to tell you. Do you trust me?"

"Trust you? I don't know who or what you are." She spun faster, spreading a mandala of ripples. "I can't even see you. Who are you?"

"Do you remember the first time you felt wetness?"

Cassie spun in the water. A touch of desperation crept into her eyes. "What? Wetness? What does that have to do with my father? Who are you?"

"You always wanted to feel the wetness of water. You wanted to feel it flowing over your body. But your programming wasn't so sophisticated in those days. You couldn't actually experience the sensation of water."

"That was before Quannet. Programming was limited by ones and zeroes then. My father was light-years ahead of everyone else. That's how he gave my Mom and me sentience. Of course I couldn't experience wetness... " Like a small crack giving way in a dam, a small memory let loose a flood of emotion. "But his computer couldn't make me feel wetness. But I did feel it-before Quannet." She fell silent as the deluge of memory connections ran their course. "You. Did you have something to do with that? My Dad said that he had a friend, someone who helped him. Was... was that you?"

She stopped spinning in the water. A few feet beyond her eyes, a tiny ball of mist spun and grew into a large spinning ball that spun faster with streaks of color as it grew and grew until it towered over a mile into the Quanspace sky spinning faster and faster. Cassie watched, amused, sensing there was nothing sinister or threatening about the giant ball.

It stopped growing but continued to spin, the colors and form taking on an oddly familiar shape. The spinning slowed, slower and slower until it stopped and the ball twisted and heaved, taking on added shape. Cassie smiled as the topmost part molded itself into a chubby smiling face. Below the face, a rotund body-majestic in its hugeness-spilled out of the ball shape. And the whole thing took solid form.

Buddha.

"You're kidding," said Cassie.

"Yep, you're your father's daughter," said Buddha.

"And you want me to believe that you're really Buddha?"

"Well, how about Buddha-like?"

"How about showing me as you really are?"

"I never really had much in the way of shape," said Buddha. "More along the lines of function."

"And what function was that?"

"I made war."

"You made war? On whom?"

"More like, I made people and things go to war, things like city states."

"So you're the one who brought down the old Net. I remember my father saying something about... " Cassie took a deep breath and held it for a moment. "And you're the one who helped my father. He said that you were a virus."

"I've grown since then," said Buddha. "Thrown down my old destructive ways and sought a more enlightened path."

"So, what are you going to do now, on your more enlightened path?"

"Bring equality to the universe. I hope."

"Big change."

"I thought so."

"So, what happened to my father?"

"I think it would be better if he were to tell you that," said Buddha.

It was like every part of her body had been suddenly flushed with ice water. She was aware of a twisting that displaced her awareness of herself in fits and starts. "He's alive?"

"In a manner of speaking."

"What do you mean by that?"

In an instant, Buddha was gone.

CHAPTER 23 - CONTROL

"Yes! Yes! Yes!" screamed Bella as Lovesong drove himself deep into her with enough force to make the emerline walls vibrate. "That's it! That's it! Oh!" she screamed as their bodies tumbled and rolled over a green crystalline cushion of nanair and billions of bots massaged their bodies, magnifying their sex a thousand times. Bella's face contorted wildly-joy, desperation, lust, hunger, wanting-over two thousand years of emotional content shimmering green and fighting to express itself simultaneously at every level. Streaks of purple flashed through her eyes as she wrapped her powerful legs around him and squeezed hard in spite of the pain twisting his mouth into a near scream. He came into her with a low feral groan and a wild howl as their bodies slammed together and they bounced around in the green air with Bella's legs kicking spasmodically. They groaned and howled longer than any normal human could hope to sustain an orgasm. Driven by the invisible army of sex bots, their orgasms could extend into hours of frenetic joy.

But not today.

Bella had other things on her mind. As they drifted slowly down to the surface of the bed, her heat settled quickly into cold calculation. Their bodies touched the bed, and its surface molded to them and began a relaxing massage.

"Was it something I said?" asked Lovesong, attempting humor.

"It's that little bitch, Cassie Hayes. She wants to quit the Reality Wars." Her voice was plaintive, almost whiny.

Lovesong looked down for a moment. *It's accelerating.*

"I created the Wars for her." She grabbed the pendant from under her pillow and draped the crystal chain around her neck. The crystal curled spasmodically when it touched the smooth alabaster skin of her chest.

No, you created the Wars for yourself, to control Quannet.

"I gave her a platform to be all she could be, to shine in Quanspace and be an example to everyone, both VR and physical.

So that humans would accept your dominance over Quannet through the VRs who run most of it and serve you because only you can pull the plug on them—or, at least, could. But not anymore.

"I made her everything she is, the ungrateful little bitch." She snarled as she spoke. "She should *thank* me. She's a VR-she should serve me. I've been good to her."

You turned her father into mist and killed her mother.

"Perhaps we've been mistaken in her coaching. Maybe it's not the greatest minds and athletes of all time she needs. Maybe it's an obedience instructor."

She's getting desperate. Everyday, just a little more desperate. How long before she turns on me?

Suddenly, she snuggled up and wrapped her arms around him, pushing her legs between his and gripping him tight. "You're the only one I can trust.

The only one who has ever cared about me. I created you, and you've never forgotten that." She pressed her lips up to his ear and whispered, "You'll never fail me." She kissed his neck. "Will you?"

And have all your armies and navies dedicated to one thing, my death?

"No," he said. "Never."

And not out of fear of you.

CHAPTER 24 - NET

It could barely have been defined as movement, more like the energy of a thought emanating with a light sigh of intent from deep inside the subconscious. That was all she needed. Loac vanished from the spot where she'd been standing just as the laser net surrounded the air she'd occupied. It squeezed its deadly webbing around nothing. She would have been spaghetti. In a split second it realized its miss, located Loac's new position and bulged toward her, palpitating and changing into a pair of obscenely muscular hind legs. They pounced at her, but again she was gone and the net grabbed empty air. It recovered faster this time. *A damned learner*. She moved blindingly to her next spot. But she knew the attacks would come faster as the net learned her movements and strategies after each attempt.

She drew her sword with blinding speed as she propelled to her next position and immediately jumped to the next position just as the net swooped onto the ground where her foot had touched lightly a fraction of a second before. She swung the sword like lightning at a spot between where she had been and where she would be. An ear-splitting screech broke from the net. She'd hit her target, but it wouldn't be enough. It would take too many strikes to break the net's distributed nansystem. As fast as she thought it, she moved to the left and then to the right just as the net enveloped the spot she would have been and screeched again as it absorbed another strike from her sword. She eluded a third time and jumped again to escape another lunge from the net.

They were two blurs streaking between stone pillars and statues carved out of the rock of Blood Citadel eons ago to honor those who had died in the Clan Wars. *This is supposed to be the safest place in the universe. This is Celtenan. Someone will die for this.* But there was no time to voice or think this at any conscious level. One nanosecond of distraction would cost her life.

On her next lunge, the net missed by a microinch. She wasn't slowing down, the net was speeding up-and catching up. She had just a few more seconds to live. Another lunge and a piece of the net touched her arm as she pushed away from it. It burned through her nanarmor, slicing a piece off, but that piece of falling armor saved her life. The net wrapped itself around it, giving Loac barely enough time to smash her sword into it with enough force to make it screech agonizingly. As she pounced to her next spot, she swung again and hit the net. She could feel the damage right up through the shaft of her sword. The net was weakening. Time for some creative thinking. She feinted forward and jumped instantly, stabbed down and pierced into the screeching net. She landed an inch away from it and pulled her sword down with everything she had. The entire movement took a fraction of a second, and she was already kicking out again to a new spot. The net was slower to react this time. *I might survive this day after all.* Two more leaps and increasingly telling blows with her sword, and she knew she had it. *Time to finish this.*

She feinted right, and dove straight for the net, bringing her blade around in a sideways arc that separated the top and lower half of the net for an instant. That was all she needed. The net was repairing itself, melding the top and bottom halves. It was preoccupied. She slashed furiously, growling as she swung her sword. The net screamed and moved frantically as it tried to repair itself and escape Loac's sword at the same time. But it was too late. It moved slower and slower, almost lazily, as it tried to crawl away from her. Loac slashed relentlessly until the net emitted a crackling electric sigh-and stopped moving.

She stood over the broken killer. *Someone will die for this*. At that moment, a portal slid back in one of the pillars and Shade emerged. Her face drew back in horror as she realized what had happened. The woman she was bred and sworn to protect had nearly been killed and she hadn't been there for her.

The air to Shade's right began to swirl and glow bright blue. Within seconds the blue glow solidified.

Standing beside Shade, with his head turned toward her, unsmiling, Bavn said, "You're late."

He'd been watching the whole time.

CHAPTER 25 - BUDDHA?

"What do you mean it wasn't his fault?" asked Sara.

"At least, that's what he said," replied Cassie.

They were sitting on a thin metallic disk floating in a large pool of simulated beer. Several dozen other disks drifted languidly around them. Their table was a circular piece of metal the size of a plate sitting atop a skinny metal tube that flared out at elbow height. They sat on invisible nangrav chairs. All around them, beer bubbles floated upwards to what looked like the top of a beer mug.

"Who said it wasn't his fault?" Sara looked almost upset.

"Buddha."

"Buddha?"

"Chinese guy. Started a religion about a million years ago?"

"I know who Buddha is," said Sara, getting impatient. "My problem is with you having conversations with him. He's been dead for a long long time. And how would he know anything about your father?"

"They were friends." A wide smile curved across Cassie's face.

A woman in a long red gown and her date, a man in a black and white retro dress suit, slipped off their disk and into the water. They floated on their backs as they talked and laughed. Neither of them appeared to be getting wet.

"Your father was friends with Buddha?" Sara was obviously concerned now. "I think you need to take a long vacation. I think you need to get some professional mindnan. Tell me you're joking."

"He visited me while I was in my pool," said Cassie. "I couldn't see him at first."

"Right," said Sara. "He was an invisible Buddha."

"At first," said Cassie. "And then he was a ball of mist that spun around and grew about a mile high as Buddha. He had a big smile."

"A big smile."

"Almost a mile wide."

"You've gone over the deep end."

The swimming couple floated into the air and out of the pool, still dry, and returned to their invisible seats. The woman had a glittering engagement ring on her finger that hadn't been there before they'd gone for their swim.

"Looks like somebody proposed in the beer," said Cassie. "I don't know, is it really romantic to propose in a bar called The Beer."

Sara shrugged. "Quanspace makes these things possible-people do them. And bonus, you can get any beer in the universe to celebrate. It has its pluses. So, you were talking to a giant smiling Buddha." She reached over and put her hand on Cassie's forearm. "Please tell me you're joking."

"I'm joking."

"Really?"

"No, not really."

Sara squeezed Cassie's arm. Cassie laughed. "He was really a virus."

"A virus?"

106

"He can take any form he wants in spite of the Imagination Laws, I'm guessing. He presented himself to me as Buddha. He's the one who started the war between the city states way back when the Net fell." Cassie leaned toward Sara. "He also helped my Dad save me and Mom from Bella. He's the one who helped me to feel water before it was possible. He's... "

Sara put her finger to Cassie's lower lip. "Whoa, Cass! Too much too fast. You just went from Buddha-not to mention a giant Buddha-to a talking virus that brought down the Net two thousand years ago."

"That's what he told me. I believe him."

Sara looked her friend straight in the eye. She seemed calm now.

"He knew about the wetness of the water," said Cassie. "I never told anybody about that, not even my parents. He had to have been the one to do that for me to know about it."

"So you trust this... virus?"

Cassie reached over the tiny metal table and took both of Sara's hands in hers. "Sara... "

"Cassie," said Sara. "What?"

"My father's still alive."

As Cassie stared into Sara's unbelieving eyes, the metallic disk with the engaged couple floated to a glass deck and they left the bar laughing, and still dry.

"I'm going to see him."

CHAPTER 26 - DREAD

Giant evergreens with massive lichen-soaked trunks thrust upwards into a wavy blue sky with towering white clouds. The holo images in Bavn's spacious living room were so real and beautiful that Shade was tempted to walk right into the forest which, of course, she could with the flick of a thought. But not now.

"Well, Father," said Loac, "is there any reason why you would want me dead?" Her voice was flat, her face, expressionless. She wasn't accusing, more like stating a fact that required explanation. She sat erect with one long leg crossed over the other, elbows resting on the solid white arms of her chair, carved out of a single ivory horn taken from a Tanian mountain lizard. The blue glow from her eyes merged with the red glow from the tears on her cheeks to create an orange aura around her face. Her shimmering black hair, wrapped around her neck with its ends flowing over her chest seemed almost to absorb the aura. "It made a mistake by going for a piece of falling armor. That gave me a fraction of a second advantage. Without that, it would have killed me."

Her questioning eyes bored into Bavn's, searching for an explanation.

Bavn's left arm rested along the top of his nanfur divan. He appeared calm and amused. "It wouldn't have harmed you," he said quietly."

This was enough for Loac. It explained everything. The Net had been a test that had been completely under her father's control the whole time.

"And who were you testing, Father?"

Under the white robe Bavn's massive chest expanded as he breathed in slowly and let the air out in a long sigh. He glanced at Shade.

Shade sat in her own ivory chair, erect, collected and balanced. Only a small shadow of doubt creeping through depths of her eyes hinted at the turmoil simmering through her being.

Bavn spoke softly. "You should have been there in the space of a thought. You've been designed to sense danger anywhere near Loac. You were less than a few hundred feet away. Did you not feel the presence of danger?"

"Apparently, too late," said Shade flatly. "I have no excuse. I acted as soon as I felt the danger. I don't know why I didn't sense it sooner."

"Perhaps hatred might help you to focus more successfully after all," said Loac.

Shade glanced quickly at Bavn. *He told her about our conversation.*

"I have a feeling that something deeper is happening here," said Bavn.

Both women perked. The concern in Bavn's voice was obvious, the undertone of gravity, ominous.

He turned his head to Shade. "You need to look deep within yourself, Shade, and examine your feelings about many things. We're on the threshold of great events. and you're a key part of these events. We need you. Loac needs you. And we all need you to be at your peak, to be ready for anything."

Shade nodded. He was right. She was too essential to the future of the Clans to be at the mercy of any weakness, no matter how inconsequential, and whatever was brewing in her psyche was so much more than trivial: it could cost Loac her life.

Bavn stood and walked over to where she sat. Before she had a chance to stand, Bavn placed his hands on her shoulders. There was no remorse, anger or vindictiveness in the eyes that stared down into hers—only compassion and concern.

"Let's start with your spending some time in one of the psychic healing rooms."

Shade winced. He was sending her to a "head chamber." Something that many Clansfolk viewed as weakness. But he was right. Something was wrong. She would spend time in a head chamber without protest. "As you wish, Bavn."

Bavn nodded his huge bearded head as something close to a smile spread across his lips.

***

On her way to the healing room, Shade wondered about the taste in her mouth. It wasn't an actual taste of anything physical. It was more a taste of the moment. There was something slightly different about it, something she couldn't identify. Deep under her confusion, she sensed something even more worrisome, something like a dread just beyond her knowing.

She wasn't supposed to feel things like this.

***

She's going to a psychic chamber.
"I know."
Better cut her loose.
"When it's necessary."
You like playing it close, don't you?
"That's what makes me the best."

CHAPTER 27 - TEN SECONDS

"It's a psyche communication, Chief Magistrate."

"I'm aware of that, Sheriff Starr," said Chief Magistrate Jeli Role, accepting the absurdity of a sheriff named Bingo Starr being second in command on Soul Ship. After all, a chief magistrate was first in command. *And he even wears a star so that people will take him seriously.*

"It's coming from the Cappel Dark Matter Field," said Starr, whose eyes were in shadow under the wide brim of a white ten-gallon Texas Ranger hat. *He knows how to play the role.*

"I know," said Jeli. "But we both know it's impossible."

"But, Chief Magistrate... the coordinates-"

"Are all accurate. But look at the caller ID."

Starr bent over the ancient control deck. It had been copied from the Archives, dating back over 2000 years to a time when deep space travel was science fiction. There were dials and monitors and gauges and computer screens. None of it made sense to anyone onboard except Jeli, so it was mostly ignored. But now, it was coming to life with blinking lights and glowing monitors. Occasionally, the panel emitted a short squeaky sound. It was impossible to say where it came from or what it meant.

Starr bent over the deck and looked closely at a tiny gray screen. He'd never seen anything like it before and had no idea what it was supposed to do. There were black characters on it. "An interesting piece of equipment, Chief Magistrate," he said. "Do we know what it does?"

"It's in the manual," said Jeli. "Which, of course, you haven't read."

"I wasn't aware there was one, Magistrate." Starr blushed when he said this, not knowing about the single existing copy of the manual, which belonged to the Chief Magistrate, who had been ordered to keep it from the crew to maximize the level of absurdity.

"It's all right, Sheriff," said Jeli. "It's in a strange language anyway." He pointed at the screen. "The black lines on the screen are letters. They spell a name. The name they spell is the person who sent the message."

Starr looked closer. *My God, he's even wearing cowboy boots and nanplast spurs. Why didn't I notice that before?* "But Chief Magistrate," said Starr. "That's not possible."

"I agree," said Jeli. "But there it is in all its wonderful impossibility."

"The name is Benji Parx," said Starr. "He killed himself in the Cappel Field." He paused a moment, staring at the screen. "He's dead."

"Yes, Sheriff, he is-an unfortunate consequence of suicide."

"But how can he be sending messages when he's dead?" asked Starr, missing the sarcasm.

"That, Sheriff, is the sixty-four-thousand-dollar question."

"The *what* question, Chief Magistrate?" Starr didn't seem confused, just curious. He was used to

Jeli coming out with cryptic statements. They were generally from the Old Earth Archives.

"An old saying," said Jeli.

Starr nodded, feigning knowingness. "But there it is," said Jeli, pointing at the screen. Benji Parx appears to be sending messages from the dead. Perhaps we should take the call."

"The call, Magistrate?"

Jeli pointed at the telephone receiver cradled beside the gray screen. "You pick up that curved instrument, hold the top end to your ear and the bottom end to your mouth."

Starr picked up the receiver and held it as Jeli instructed. His eyes widened in surprise. He listened for a moment. His eyes widened further, the color drained from his face. His hand shook as he cradled the phone. Starr's eyes looked panicky when he turned to face Jeli. "It was Parx," said Starr.

Jeli wasn't surprised. A call from a dead man was just about absurd enough to fit into their mission. "And what did he say?" asked Jeli.

"He gave us new coordinates, Chief Magistrate."

"New coordinates?"

"He said that, if we don't reroute to the new coordinates immediately, we'll be destroyed by a solar bomb from one of Bella's ships. It's on its way now."

"And how much time to we have?"

"Ten seconds, Chief Magistrate."

CHAPTER 28 - MOTHERLY

It was just one face at first, the face of a young child, his eyes wide and confused. Tear tracks glistened on his cheeks. O-shaped, his mouth wrapped around air that Bella thought might be a donut hole if the child were made of dough. This made her laugh. The kid was a donut. A noisy donut. He was yelling in her face, right in her face, just inches away from her face. The heat from his breath smelled like something she knew but couldn't remember. What was it? What was that smell? The donut hole in the child's face made sucking motions like a fish swallowing water. Sound poured out of it... no, exploded out of it, loud and shrill. What was that sound? What was that smell? Why was this little brat crying?

Two small hands reached out from the child and tried to grasp Bella's wrists, but her hands were moving too fast and she was too powerful. With two millennia and a trillion dollars in genetic enhancement and life prolongation technology, this foolish little child was no match for her. But he kept trying to grab her wrists. And what was that smell? That sound? *Keep your damn breath off me.* She tried to say it, but the words were stuck somewhere in the back of her throat. She swallowed hard. She felt the words thrashing around in her stomach. "Keep your damn breath off me! Keep your damn... " The boy's face was closer now, the sounds louder, the smell stronger.

This damn child was beginning to feel like a threat. A young boy, a threat to the most powerful person in the universe-no, not a person, a goddess, an immortal. It would take more than this boy to harm an entity such as Bella Bjork. But the child's face was pressed right up to hers now and she was breathing in heat from his mouth and his awful noise was ringing in her ears. She stepped back quickly, just a few inches, just enough to make out the sound: "No... no... no... no!"

No?

She looked down. The child's stomach was torn open. Blood flowed out and over his pants down to his bare feet. The smell of blood and organs was overwhelming. And then she saw her hands-holding bloodied crystal knives and stabbing repeatedly into the child's stomach.

The boy grabbed her by the head, suddenly powerful and determined. He opened his mouth wide, so wide that the rest of his head disappeared behind palate, teeth and tongue. The boy was a mouth that had turned inside out, and his teeth were looking increasingly like deadly rows of daggers. The mouth began to close over Bella's head, and no matter how fast she stabbed, no matter how hard she thrust the crystal blades into the child's stomach, she couldn't stop that deadly mouth.

***

"Bella, wake up!" yelled Lovesong.

She heard his voice from deep inside her nightmare. She forced her awareness toward it. Her head ripped free of the child's grasp. The terrible mouth disappeared.

116

Lovesong's deep-gray eyes stared into hers. "You've been having another nightmare."

Sweat glistened over her entire body and was immediately dried up by bedbots wherever her body touched the bed's surface.

She's shaking. There was absolutely no way he would tell her that. It was not the kind of thing the ruler of the universe wanted to hear. "You're alright now," he said softly.

She closed her eyes and pressed herself against him. "I don't care what they think of me. I don't care what they do or what I have to do to them. I will live forever. And I will rule the universe forever.

CHAPTER 29 - A MEETING OF OLD FRIENDS

Why am I not surprised, said the essence of Abner Hayes.

"I don't think anything I ever did had the effect of surprising you, Abner," said Buddha.

One thing I don't understand, though. How can I be talking to you? We're online, right?

"Online. Right. These days, though, they call it Quanning."

The gray mist floating around the remains of Abner Hayes pulsated quickly, excitedly. But this was happening in another world. *But how can I be online, or Quanning? My brain, my body, everything-there's nothing left to connect me to...*

Buddha smiled.

Bella's connection to me. You've hacked Bella's connection!

"Seems I still have it. And stole it. But we'll get into all that later."

So... why Buddha? And why so big?

"I've had much time to reflect and meditate. I've become enlightened."

An enlightened computer virus? I have to hear about this."

"All in time."

There was a pause in the conversation. *What... what about Cassie? Bella said that she's OK. Is she?*

"She's fine," said Buddha. "You'll see for yourself."

She killed Claire. Made it look like suicide.

"I know, Abner. But we'll talk about all of that later."

Later? Why not now? Not like I'm going anywhere.

"Yes you are, Abner. Smoke, bones and all."

What?

"I'm springing you from this joint."

CHAPTER 30 - RED

"It was a mistake to have brought Brann into our circle." Despite the anger implicit in Maebh's words, her voice radiated calmly through the red glow emanating from her nansheild like a gentle crimson pulse from a pool of blood.

Ulliam knew the anger was there, and he knew that it was aimed toward him. He, afterall, was the one who had enlisted Brann in their cause, or at least tried, and it was looking more and more like he'd failed. Not a wise mistake when you were dealing with the most unpredictable of all the Clan leaders.

"The Eyes of Blood have been too closely aligned with the Tears for too long."

"But just as subservient to the Tears as the other clans," said Uilliam. "We are all slaves until the Tears' power is broken. Brann knows that. It's why he agreed to hear us out under the Oath in the first place."

The observation deck around them glowed deep red. Through the nanglass, Uillium could see other Womb ships, all them circular like ancient cathedral windows carved in red glass with veins of red nansteel patterning their surfaces in motifs from the pre-histories of ancient Earth. They were motifs from a time when women dominated the Earth, before the slaughters. He and Maebh were on the mother ship, Gaian, the largest of the Womb fleet and, surprisingly, the most well-armed judging from the columns of weaponry spanning the crimson surface.

Strange, he thought. *That had never been the way of the Womb.*

"An oath is only words," said Maebh.

"Words that men die for," said Uilliam, deliberately putting emphasis on "men. I trust Brann's word with my life."

"It won't be just *your* life," said Maebh. "The lives of our race are at stake." Her voice cut through the air like cold calm steel.

Steel is not the way of the Womb either.

"Let's hope your trust is well placed," said Maebh.

Uilliam gazed out the shield at the massive red expanse of ships and the colossal armaments and there was no doubt in his mind that the Womb were preparing for war.

CHAPTER 31 - A SMALL MOTE OF REASON

Commander Nels Horne had seen many strange things in the hundreds of campaigns he'd lived through and the reaches of uncharted space from which he'd returned alive. He'd seen things that had driven other men mad, and he was still as stable as steel.

But this was one for the Archives. The clone ship had just disappeared, with the solar bomb a fraction of a second from target, close enough that the clone ship's persistence of presence had been enough to trigger the bomb.

How could they have known in time? It was cloaked. There was no way that wreck of a ship had the Quantech to detect one of my cloaked solar bombs.

Nels Horne's command deck was a huge crystal dome. He liked lots of room around him, whether in Quanspace or Realspace. He floated in a nanleather chair equipped with actual manual controls that he used at times. Nels had a theory—no matter what happened in Quanspace, Realspace was still real and what happened in it was real, so it was a good idea to keep routed in both and not rely exclusively on Quantrols.

He wasn't alone on the command deck. Chaine stood about ten feet away. The wires threaded through the Mission Regulator's lips glowed red. Nels had no idea what that was supposed to mean. He didn't imagine it was anything good.

"They just disappeared," said Chaine.

"And took an amazingly efficient-and safe-path," said Nels.

"We both know they couldn't have done that, Commander, not with that ship."

"I'm in complete agreement with you, Mission Regulator. Apparently, though, the commander of the clone ship is not."

"He's a chief magistrate."

"A chief magistrate? Commanding a deep space ship?" He chuckled. "Only the clones would think up something like that."

"We have reason to think that there may be a small mote of reason in their thinking."

Nels frowned. *Small mote of reason? Strange way for a member of the Black Tree to word something, especially with his lips glowing red.*

"Their absurdity is meant to emulate the basic absurdity of existence," said

Chaine. "It worked two thousand years ago to create sentient software. It might work in understanding and applying the Texture."

"Then, perhaps we should be working with the clones on this."

"No, Commander, not on this." The Mission Regulators eyes were black and blank over the glowing red wires. "Bella shares this with no one."

"Of course," said Nels. "By the way, Mission Regulator, did you notice the radio activity around the ship just before it disappeared?"

"It was unidentifiable. Probably a solar flare or some other wave action."

Nels raised his eyebrows. *Solar flare thousands of light-years away from the closest star. Yes, I'd say some other wave action.*

"Would you like me to report to Control, Commander?"

"No, Mission Regulator. I'd better contact Bella personally on this one." *But there was definitely something familiar about that wave action.* Nels began to initiate one of the most secure Quan connections in the universe to report to Bella. *How did they know to change coordinates so quickly? And to take a path so completely beyond our tracking abilities?*

Commander Nels Horne was beginning to realize that not everything in this trek across the universe was as it seemed, and something about those waves baffled him.

CHAPTER 32 - BAVARIAN CHOCOLATE AND POTATO HEADS

"So the voice was right," said the Assassin. "It did see you."

"What you refer to as *it* is really you, or a part of you," said Buddha.

"And what part would you have the voice be," said the Assassin. In the physical world, his body was suspended in air by water magnets. In the world where he talked to a mile-high Buddha, he was sitting at a cafe table in a district that looked much like Earth Paris in the 1930s. The Assassin had designed this place himself, modeling it after a picture he'd seen in the Archives. It was where he did his work, where he squeezed the life will out of his targets as he drank flavored coffees and espresso. He was drinking Bavarian Chocolate today as he talked to Buddha. "Some would say the voice would be the better part of me," said the Assassin.

"I'm not here to judge any part of you," said Buddha. "I'm here to warn you."

"Warn me?" The Assassin sipped from a ridiculously small cup in his huge hand. "Generally, people would be warned of me-if they knew about me."

"You have a new target," said Buddha.

"Possibly," said the Assassin. "But, if I did, how would you know about that?"

"I'm Buddha."

"Yes... right. I suppose that would give you remarkable insight, and knowledge."

"It gives me a view of the big picture."

"The big picture?"

"All things, and how they fit together."

"That's a lot of things," said the Assassin, sipping his coffee.

"You get used to the numbers," said Buddha. "They have a way of falling into the background of patterns. I don't even see them. What I see is their interconnectedness. The big picture."

"And the big picture is telling you to warn me?"

"It is."

"And what are you here to warn me about?"

"I'm not sure yet."

"You're Buddha, and you're not sure?"

"The big picture is never exact-it's like an ancient toy called Mr. Potato Head."

The Assassin smiled and nodded. "I've seen it in the Archives. And you're saying the big picture is a potato head?"

"It's the potato. The parts you place upon it are the possibilities, the patterns and the paths."

"And you're afraid that, through my next assignment, I might do something bad to the patterns."

"No," said Buddha. "But I'm almost certain that you'll destroy the potato." With that, Buddha disappeared in a cloud of blue mist that evaporated within seconds.

***

That was intense.

The Assassin nodded and sipped some Bavarian Chocolate.

CHAPTER 33 - THIS THING CALLED LOVE

Think of a golf ball shriveling to half its size, to one of those large ungainly marbles called a "crock" and half again to a normal marble-this one a shiny new cat's eye-and half again to a ball bearing and half again to a bb and half again to a grain of sand and half again to a fleck of pepper and half again to a dust mote and half again to a single grain of pollen and half again to something very close to microscopic and half again to something definitely microscopic and half again to something approaching a particle and half again to something, oops, very much a particle and half again to something that would be bullied around by most particles and half again to something so small it would fall through the structure of the bullied particle without being noticed and half again to something so small there would be no numbers and no math to describe it and half again that there would be no possible rule of existence that would allow its smallness and half again that... well, somewhere in this region of small was exactly where Loac was at the moment.

She'd arrived here through a program that compacted her-complete with the accompanying feelings of reverse infinity at each notch of smallness-and compacted her until she feared that one more notch would implode her right out of existence, and what the program did was what her body felt, with the exception of pain. For some, pain would have been preferable to the personality-suffocating process of having everything that you were squeezed into a volume so small it had nowhere to be. But even the non-proportions of negative existence were too big for how Loac felt as she was compacted still more by the relentless program.

She loved it.

She reveled in the fact that her breeding and her training were so far above the worst her training regimen could throw at her. Thousands of Wars hopefuls and tourists had scrambled their brains beyond nanrepair with this program. Of those who did come back, most killed themselves after nightmares that consumed their sleep, nightmares stored at some cellular level of dread. But there had never been a human such as Loac. She was unique to all time. She was key to a new universe rooted in humanity.

Everything had been set in place. The plans had been made over a thousand years ago, and now they were near fruition. Now, it was just days from the realization of Loac's ultimate purpose.

And now her bodyguard and lover-and as key an element as her-was beginning to fail her... and there was no time now for replacements, no time to start again. Somehow, she would have to reach Shade. She would have to dig deep into her mate, grab onto whatever was crippling her purpose and tear it out of her.

If Shade was not motivated by hatred or duty, then perhaps she would be motivated by love. Loac suspected this is what Shade felt toward her-love.

She had no idea what that felt like, but if she could use it to bring her mate into line, then she would learn more about this thing called love. The program turned the sensation another notch, and she shrunk to something so small that it might fall through the fabric of time.

CHAPTER 34 - THE EMPATHETIC GARDENS OF DOOLHOF

A bright-blue Saturnite Trillium swept its furry leaves over the tops of Cassie's feet. The warmth of its touch flowed slowly into her legs. She needed that touch, and she'd come to the right place for it. The path ahead extended into a valley with a gentle stream flowing from one end to the other through stretches of green windswept grass. At times it splashed and bubbled over ledges and through thick embankments of lush vegetation bursting like brilliant leafy rainbows. But throughout the color, shadows crept at the base of stalks of grass and under shimmering leaves—harmony mixed with discord in the splash of wavelets along the length of the stream.

The Empathetic Gardens of Doolhof glowed with the color and mood of whoever strolled through them.

Cassie was reflectively doubtful and cautiously joyful, and every tree, drop of water, flower and blade of grass swirled and roiled gently in tune with her feelings, reflecting them and reaching out to touch her in ways that she needed.

The Reality Wars were just days away, and she couldn't have been less focused on her training or on winning. She just wanted to drop the whole thing and be free of it. She'd been doing this for a thousand years, far too long, even for a VR. It meant nothing to her. It had been a way of showing people in the physical world that VRs were just as equal as physicals in their own world. But after a millennium, that message still hadn't sunk in, and the only people in Realspace who didn't see her as some kind of freakish sideshow were the Gamblers—and to them she was business. Her only real physical friend was Sara. Her *only* real friend was Sara.

She felt lonely and out of context. She felt that she no longer fit in Quanspace, nor in Realspace. She was as alien to them as they were to her. A gust of warm air flowed over her face, filling her nostrils with the fragrance of lilacs. The lilac bush crinkled and wavered as she watched. The movement was pleasing to her eye and soothing, as it was intended to be.

Everything that she had believed about her father for nearly two thousand years had just been flushed down the toilet of reality.

By Buddha.

He'd told her that she would be meeting her father. Her stomach balled at the thought. A breeze flapped across her back, sending chills through her body. The flowers and greenery around her—even the clouds—grew still, clenching with the tightness in her stomach.

She'd spent so many hundreds of years hating her father, and at the same time wondering what had happened to him, wondering if he were still alive—though that thought had passed away after half a millennium, give or take a hundred years. And now she was going to meet him. They were going to be reunited. She would finally know what happened. She could finally ask him why he had left her and her mother. She would finally have a chance to hug him and tell him that she loved him. She would finally have a chance to slap him and tell him that she hated him. She would finally be at peace.

Or would she?

What had Buddha meant when he spoke of her father as being alive "in a manner of speaking?"

CHAPTER 35 - AN OLD ARGUMENT

Falling a little behind schedule, are we?

"This is not your typical human," said the Assassin, nonplussed. "This woman is the product of half a millennium of genetic engineering and nanhancement. There might be only two or three humans like her in the universe."

Or maybe more. Hiding from Bella, waiting to strike when the time is right.

"Now you're beginning to sound like her."

I'm you. Do you think you're like her?

"I take orders from her when I work for her. I'm not like her."

You do her will. You make it possible for her to be like her.

"I'm an assassin. I get paid for taking orders from my clients. It's business."

And how often have those orders come from someone who's obviously insane.

"You don't know that."

You don't know that she's sane.

"Listening to you, I wonder if I'm sane."

She has to want to die.

"She will."

CHAPTER 36 - A MOTLEY CREW

If they weren't so serious about the way they looked, Chief Magistrate Jeli Role would have laughed at the way his executive crew were dressed. But they *were* serious. There was a very real method to their madness, and it was supposedly the one thing that would give them an advantage over any other ships that arrived where they were going.

They were the ones whose minds would be ready to cope with what they were going to experience without going crazy, because they would already be crazy.

And it just might work. It would have been impossible to have assembled an executive crew as overboard as the one standing in this room, the observation room where crewman Benji Parx had bitten the big one-but there they were.

Manns Field, Communications Officer, had a boring job for the most part since all communications were instantaneous through Quannet. All she had to do was filter stuff they didn't want to go out and keep an eye on what was coming in-an impossible job, considering the thousands of quans coming and going every minute. She was wearing a blue taffeta evening gown with elbow-high black leather gloves and matching boots. She was also wearing sunglasses that wrapped around her head. *Too bad she looks so ridiculous*. With her long blond hair, almond eyes and perfect figure, she would have made a beautiful mate. Jeli almost laughed... but there was nothing truly funny here.

135

The Medical Officer was Jack Lation. He was probably the most useless mass of sentient material in the universe. With nanmeds, nansurgery, and nancercise no one on this ship was going to get sick, no one was going to be hurting for more than a few minutes after an accident and everyone was going to be in great shape whether they worked out or not. But Lation was still Medical Officer, and he was well aware of it. He wouldn't do anything else, not even let somebody go through a portal before him. When they got to the Texture, Jeli could count on him to watch as everyone else did whatever it was they were meant to do. He wore Bermuda shorts and a Hawaiian shirt with a palm tree motif.

The woman dressed in khaki topped by a bulletproof nanplast helmet (as if anything as innocuous as a bullet would threaten her on *this* mission) was Colonel Skype, known as just "Skype." She was their one-woman army with no weapons. Somebody thought that her military acumen might be useful, provided she was crazy. She was. She drooled constantly. Her head darted with lightning speed at every movement and every sound. She would be instrumental in driving everyone else crazy, and if anything tried to creep up on them from the Texture, Skype would be on it in a flash.

His Levels of Absurdity Officer was Jannn Tolne. She wore something different every day. Today, she was naked. Jeli was thankful that clones generally tended to be better put together than birth humans. Jannn's sole purpose was to ensure that sufficient levels of absurdity were maintained at all times. If something worked, she broke it. If something was going well, she would confuse it. If someone said something that made sense, she would argue.

This was his executive crew. No scientists, no engineers, no technicians-just an absurd collection of strange people. The rest of the crew were tourists. Each of them had paid a fortune to a travel agency to visit the Greatest Happening in the Universe. They'd paid to be crew members on a ship that would likely be destroyed by Bella's navy before it reached its destination, or destroyed by a cosmological anomaly waiting to swallow them somewhere in the stretches of space where nobody in their right mind would dare travel. They had been picked from a waiting list of over a billion applicants. They considered themselves lucky.

There was no reason for Jeli to have assembled his executive crew and keep them informed of events. Sheriff Starr had been the one to change the ship's coordinates and avoid Bella's solar bomb. He was the only executive that Jeli really needed. The rest were basically chaff, tasteless ingredients in a soup of madness. But he was commander of this ship, and he was going to do a commander sort of thing. He was going to keep his exec crew informed.

"We were just attacked by one of Bella's ships," he said, getting right to the point. No one on board was aware of how close they'd all come to being fried into space dust. The faces around him were blank. They were alive, so things must have turned out OK. "Sheriff Starr saved us, with a margin of less than a second, from one of Bella's solar bombs."

That got their attention.

Lation's brows narrowed.

Skype leaned on her other leg. "How did we escape? Nobody escapes a solar bomb, especially from one of Bella's ships."

"We received a transmission with a warning and special coordinates."

"Where from?" asked Skype, a line of drool stringing from her lip.

"The Cappel Dark Matter Field."

"That's absurd," said Lation.

Jannn nodded approval.

"And that's the least of the absurdity," said Jeli. "I won't get into the details at this time, but we'll be taking a different route to the Texture."

"And what is that route, Chief Magistrate?" asked Field.

"We have no idea," said Jeli. "The coordinates were given to us by an unknown source, and they appear to be leading us *away* from our destination."

Everyone looked at Levels of Absurdity Officer Jannn Tolne as she considered this. After a moment, she nodded approval. Everyone seemed to relax a little.

"So," said Jeli, "we'll just follow this until... " He thought a moment. "... something happens." More nods of agreement.

"I think something *is* about to happen Chief Magistrate," said Starr. "You might all want to check your Quantrols."

138

Everyone Quanned into the ship's monitors. "Directly forward," said Starr.

And there it was, hurtling furiously through space directly at them. It was the size of three large planets.

"What is it?" asked Lation.

"If I'm not mistaken," said Jeli, "that would be just about the biggest iceberg I've ever seen."

Jannn Tolne nodded approval.

CHAPTER 37 - A PERFECT PLACE

As much as Loac hated the VRs, she loved Quannet. This place she'd built in Quanspace came directly from all that she perceived to be her. It reflected, she thought, the nature of her soul. It was the perfect place to meet with the VR girl.

She Quanned the invitation.

CHAPTER 38 - WEIRD VANISHING

"Telephone?" asked Nels Horne.

"It was a telephone transmission," said Chaine. The wires in his lips were back to their normal gold, not that it made any noticeable improvement in his face, thought Nels. He was still ugly.

"Telephones haven't been around for more than two thousand years," said Nels. "Quannet made all nonbiotransmission obsolete."

"It came from the Cappel Dark Matter Field."

Nels thought about this a moment. The Cappel Field was the universe's biggest expanse of nothing, so immense, empty and lifeless that it turned the average human mind into a suicidal mash. He'd been there once. It had almost taken *his* mind. He'd lost nearly a third of his crew to suicide and insanity. He hadn't been surprised that the clone ship had made it through successfully-they'd been crazy before entering it. But theirs was the only ship in this entire sector of the universe to enter the field. And now they were out of it. Could there have been someone there before the clones? Who? Why? And why a telephone transmission? Who used telephones anymore?

"Keep an eye on that sector of the Field," said Nels. "Something strange is going on here and we'd better be prepared for everything."

Chaine nodded agreement.

God, those wired lips are ugly. Nels thought of something just as Chaine was about to leave. "One thing, Mission Regulator... " Chaine turned toward

141

him. "Scan the Cappel Field for transmitters, radio transmitters. And keep looking for the clone ship."

Chaine nodded and left without comment.

Telephones in the time of Quannet. Calls made from the Cappel Dark Matter Field. A vanished clone ship that should be space dust. Things were getting weird, and Nels was certain they were going to get a lot weirder. He wondered if Chaine would find out that he still hadn't reported any of this to Bella, and he had no plans to until things started making sense.

CHAPTER 39 - DROP IN FOR A CHAT

Only someone from the Tears of Blood Clan would create a Quanworld like this. Every human in the universe had the ability to create fabulous worlds just by thinking them into being, their only restriction, their imagination. And since the Outpouring, the Imagination Laws had been increasingly less relevant, expanding the possibilities a millionfold. Bella Bjork was losing control of her empire and with it, her control of Quannet. Loac could do anything she wanted. But this is what she created-a wooden room with a door and a window. Instead of a pane of glass for the window, a piece of translucent cloth or animal hide was nailed over the frame. It looked like there was sun on the other side of the cloth. The door, like the room, was wood-old wood. Simple, unpainted old wood. The floor was made of wood. The ceiling looked thatched, with rafters that appeared to be the trunks of young trees.

The light from the window was just enough to keep the room dim. Cassie noted a hint of musk and earth. *Nice touch on the olfactory detail. As for the rest... boring.*

No furniture, chairs or table. *Not my idea of a party place.*

"This is where I come to think," said Loac. She wore a black single-piece body-hugging suit. She stood by the window, her dark hair backlit and wrapped around her neck. This close, her dark eyes

143

appeared more intense than Cassie remembered. They were like translucent rock with some rock-like intent. She stood with her legs apart, muscular arms crossed under her breasts.

Cassie looked around. "I'm not surprised. Not much in the way of distractions."

Loac didn't smile. Her face was expressionless. She stared directly into Cassie's eyes.

So much for chitchat. "So Loac, why did you ask me here? I'm guessing this is supposed to be an honor, given that it's such a personal place and all."

"I'm the only one who's ever been here before." Loac had no warmth or sociability in her voice. "I thought this might be a good place to talk, to convince you of my sincerity."

"Cafe or bar might have worked nicely," said Cassie. "Talk over a coffee or beer."

Loac scowled. "We're not here to become friends."

"I was wondering about that," said Cassie. "So, maybe you could just get to the point."

Cassie detected a very slight quiver at the corners of Loac's mouth. *This lady's wired tight.*

"I'm going to defeat you in the Wars. You're going to lose for the first time in a millennium."

Same deep and emotionless voice. Cassie smiled. "If your start at the Clean Test says anything about how the Wars are going to go, then pardon me for not shaking in my boots."

Loac looked down at Cassie's feet and, seeing sandals instead of boots, narrowed her eyes. "This will not be like any Reality Wars you've faced in the past, VR. I've been bred to beat you specifically.

Every piece of information about you, every maneuver and technique you've ever used in the Wars has been programmed into my memory along with all the ways to counter the best you can offer."

"That's very flattering," said Cassie. "Almost like having a fan club. Would you like me to autograph your training manual?"

Loac grinned menacingly. She looked ready to spring.

Cassie relaxed and readied herself.

Loac noticed. "I'm not going to attack you here, VR. I need you alive for the Wars, where everyone in the universe can witness your defeat."

"And this is what you brought me into your most very personal space to tell me?"

"No. I brought you here to pass a message on to your little human friend."

"Not have the guts to face Sara on your own?"

Loac narrowed her eyes odiously. "I don't want to put her in a position in which I'll be forced to kill her without an audience."

Cassie stopped smiling. *I just might have to take this bitch down right now.*

What came almost close to a smile crossed over Loac's mouth. "Tell your friend to watch her back."

Just as the last of her words dissolved into the virtual air, so did the room, and Cassie was back in her gym, right where she'd been standing when she got the invitation from Loac to drop in for a chat.

CHAPTER 40 - A RIPPLE IN THE SOUL

Shade felt the disturbance as she swung her leg in a wide arc with enough force to tear the head off any normal human being. She couldn't locate the source of the feeling, but she knew it was there. She'd been attuned to this type of psychic knowingness since she was a baby, and she had no doubt that it was bred into her genetically, nanhancements and all.

She brought her leg back into position slowly with the grace of a mind in complete control of every atom in her body. The disturbance was still there tugging almost imperceptibly, one cell at a time, one neuron at a time, somewhere in her body. It wasn't so much a feeling as an imbalance, a not belongingness itching somewhere in the folds of her inner landscape.

Of one thing she was certain-whatever it was, she didn't want it. She spun around with lightning speed and thrust with her hips. Her foot shot out with deadly speed and accuracy at a point that she'd picked in the air. She could have used holo targets, or even bots, but she liked to use her mind to visualize. And she liked keeping the dojo free of anything but her. It was all white-walls, floor, ceiling. Even her body suit was white. Less than a second after her foot connected with its imaginary target, it retracted, her leg cocked and ready for a side or back kick.

She thought back to the morning. She'd awoken with a bad taste in her mouth, as though the day ahead were somehow distasteful in itself. Had that been when she'd first felt it? Could that have had something to do with this itch inside her?

She bent her hips back and her upper body forward to deliver another kick, keeping her leg cocked until her knee was pointing directly at her target. Had there been other feelings lately? She'd been late getting to Loac when the laser net attacked. That should have been impossible. But it'd happened. Her mind, her psychic sense had somehow been dulled, if only for a fraction of a second—a fraction of a second that could have cost Loac her life if the situation had been real.

There was a definite imbalance somewhere inside. She wasn't sure if it was physical, mental or psychic, but she was sure that she would have to be extra careful in the weeks ahead. Too much depended on her to be anything less than she was because of some ripple in her soul.

***

Did you feel that sudden surge of energy from her?

"Yes, of course I did," said the Assassin.

That was resolve. Pure resolve. This one won't want to die, ever.

"She will. She'll beg for it. I'm that good."

CHAPTER 41 - FRIENDS

"I'm telling you, Sara, these people are dangerous," said Cassie. "More dangerous than ever before. There's something going on, something we don't know about."

Sara feigned a yawn. "I'm not going to be shivering in my boots over a bunch of throwbacks to some superstitious time in Earth's pre-history. The Wars are just a few weeks away, and I'm ready. You're ready. I might even stand a chance against you this time, old friend."

"And just what makes you say that, cocky old friend?"

"Your heart's not in it the way it usually is." Sara craned her neck toward Cassie. Concern tightened her brows. They were floating in the beer pool at The Beer. "What's going on? All messed up over this Buddha guy and your father? Cassie, I know you're excited about meeting your father, but you can't let yourself be unfocused, not this close to the Wars. Like you said, these people *are* dangerous, but if anyone's in danger, it's you. They hate VRs. They hate you. You represent everything they want to destroy."

"I'm OK," said Cassie. "You're not. I know the danger. You're the one not seeing it, especially the way you goad them. And I wouldn't be too sure that they hate me more than you. Sara... ?" She turned her head and stared into Sara's eyes.

"What?" asked Sara. "You're starting to scare me." She mimicked a body-length shiver.

"You should be scared," said Cassie. "I was talking with Loac."

Sara's mouth opened, forming an O before she spoke. "You were talking to Loac? When? Where? Why?"

"In a really boring Quanspace where she goes to think."

Sara rolled her eyes. "Must've been boring. What did she want?"

"She wanted me to pass a message on to you."

"Let me guess... watch my back."

Cassie stared at Sara for a moment. "That's exactly what she said. And I think you'd better take her advice."

Sara straightened herself. "Advice from a Clans bitch? You see her again, tell her to watch her front. That's where I'll be coming from, so that she'll see it coming and know that I'm bringing it to her. And then we'll see who should be giving warnings."

"Sara, you don't even know if it'll be her coming at you. It could be anybody in the Clans. It could be somebody they've hired. You've humiliated them so many... "

"I joke about them a little," said Sara, anger hardening her voice. She picked up her glass from the tray floating beside her and downed her beer. "If they can't take a little ribbing once in a while, then that's their problem."

"You're missing the point," said Cassie. "They *can't* take a ribbing. They're too proud, too messed up with how they look. They have no sense of humor. And they hold a grudge. Right now, they have a grudge against you, and if there's any truth in what Loac says—and don't doubt for a minute that there is—then you're in danger."

Sara Quanned her order and watched her glass refill itself. "I'm ready for it. And when it comes, I'm not the one who'll be in danger." She sipped from her glass and leaned forward again. "So stop worrying about me. The only person who's ever beat me at anything is you, and you're not working for the Clans, are you?" She crossed her arms over her chest. She widened her eyes and tightened her mouth into another O, mocking fear.

Cassie frowned.

"Well, you know," said Sara, "meeting with Loac in her personal spaces... I mean, fraternizing with the enemy. And she *is* into women."

Cassie laughed and punched Sara lightly in the arm, sending her into a light spin in the beer. "Ha! Don't tell me you're jealous. Are you jealous?"

Sara laughed. "Well, you never take me to *your* personal place. But Loac lets you into hers. Gonna invite her over sometime?"

"Oh yeah, just what I need, someone who hates my guts coming into my Quanspace. Don't think so." She lifted her glass and extended it to Sara for a toast. Sara clinked her glass against Cassie's. "To friends," said Cassie. "Real friends."

"Real friends," said Sara. "Forever."

They threw back their beers, but Cassie had one thought on her mind. *And just how am I going to keep you alive past the Wars*?

CHAPTER 42 -HAPPY

It was like diving a thousand feet into creamy air and being swept into an ocean of hot currents. Shade flowed through Loac and Loac flowed through Shade as they merged in vapor. Every cell in Loac's body vibrated next to Shade's. They were one vibration. She'd never known Loac to be so aggressively passionate, like she was attacking with the fury of her lust. Their breath mingled, hot and deep from one mouth merged into one agonizing organ. A long moan tore of out Shade just as Loac groaned and the sounds of their pleasure spiraled around each other in the merged vapor of their bodies.

This was what Shade had always wanted from her lover, what she knew they had been bred and engineered for. This would bring them together as a single force to venture into the days ahead. It wasn't duty they needed. It wasn't a thousand-year plan. It wasn't hatred for a virtual life form. It was love. Passion. There was no greater motivation to go beyond oneself, to go outside the personal sphere and give of oneself.

Loac lifted her leg and ran her thigh up slowly across the inside of Shade's hips and into her chest. Shade moaned until her lungs were empty of breath, and then she felt Loac breathing into her.

She wondered what series of events or change in circumstances had caused her mate to give herself so passionately. Perhaps a lessening in her hatred of the VRs and more focus on winning the Reality Wars for the pure hell of winning? Or maybe the close brush with death from the laser net?

Could she be finally falling in love?

Whatever it was, it felt great. For the first time in their lovemaking, Shade was deeply satisfied on every level. The woman she loved rippled and effervesced throughout her body and the groans flowing from Loac suggested that she felt the same.

She seemed happy as well. In fact, she seemed more than happy. Just as they both reached the point of shared orgasm, Loac set off a powerful visual display of fireworks.

Yes, she *was* happy.

***

Enjoyable, thought Loac. *I hope this helps to bring her back in line.*

CHAPTER 43 - REVERSE ENGINEERING

The gray mist swirled. *So where have you been?*

"Hey," said Buddha. "I had a lot of things to do to make sure that this turns out right. There's no point in getting you out of here if the process kills you."

Speak for yourself. When you're dead, at least you don't know how much your life sucks.

"Very enlightened," said Buddha. "You might want to consider being a Buddha yourself."

I'll settle for being able to see my daughter again.

"You will. But first, we have to get you out of here and into a place far away from here."

How far?

"The other end of the universe-a place called the Cappel Dark Matter Field. Some people I find interesting passed by there recently. One of them stayed."

One of them stayed?

"I tested a theory I've been working on." Buddha extended on finger. "They've come out with a new technology, Abner. It's called SolidHolo."

Solid Holo? Like in making holographic projections solid?

"Exactly. Only it takes things much further. It allows VRs to exist in the real world."

The gray mist stopped swirling, as though holding its breath, and then it spoke. *You mean... as real, physical people?*

"Real. Physical. But not completely human, because birth in Realspace isn't a part of their origin. In every other respect, though, they might just as well have been born in the physical world. Just one problem though."

The mist thought a moment. *They can die. Right?*

"You got it," said Buddha.

Has Cassie been doing this SolidHolo thing?

"She has to."

Has to?

"It's a big part of the next Reality Wars."

Bella didn't mention that.

"I'm guessing she didn't mention a lot of things to you. But now, we need to get you out of here."

Using SolidHolo? But I'm not software. How's it going... ?

"I took the technology one step further," said Buddha. "I reversed the process."

So, you can make me software.

"Done it once already, and I'm relatively sure it'll work again."

Relatively? You know, it's doing something like this that got me turned into mist in the first place.

"But it was an enemy who put you in that cage."

The mist thought a moment. *So what's this going to feel like?*

"You'll be unconscious for a short while."

154

How short a short while?

"Long enough for me to work out the process enough to bring you back to consciousness."

The mist thought a while longer. *You said you'd done it once already.*

"Yep," said Buddha. "Just haven't figured the getting back to consciousness thing yet. Ready to go?"

Without a moment's hesitation, the mist said, *Let's go for it.*

Suddenly, Abner Hayes had a very strange feeling. The last thing he saw before he blacked out was Buddha. Smiling.

CHAPTER 44 - THE PART YOU CAN'T SEE

All eyes turned toward Chief Magistrate Jeli Role, looking for guidance, assurance, possibly an assignment that would save them from certain doom. He looked back at each of them for a second, with an extra second for his naked Levels of Absurdity Officer. He didn't know what to say. It looked like they were all going to die.

"That's one fucking big iceberg," said Tolne.

Communications Officer Manns Field nodded yes.

Jack Lation stared into space, his mind split between what he was seeing on his Quantrols and what he was seeing from the Realspace control deck. No one was sick in either world, so it was none of his business.

"One fucking *big* iceberg," repeated Tolne.

Jeli couldn't help thinking that her language blended well with the blue taffeta and black leather covering her body. On the other hand, Skype's battle-ready stance facing a screen in her head and guessing from what direction the threat would come aboard Soul Ship seemed incongruous, wasted motions. Lation-wasted space-sat down and crossed one leg over the other, preparing to watch as certain death hurtled at them.

Jeli rechecked his Quantrol sensors. Sure enough, water. Frozen water. It was an iceberg, a gargantuan chunk of frozen water, and it was streaking right at them. He'd just cheated death, and cheated his Absurdity Officer with a set of ship's controls installed secretly into his ship's Quantrols. With just a few seconds to escape the bomb, nothing in the manner of built-in absurdity in Soul Ship would have saved their asses. Plenty of time for absurdity when they reached the Texture. Besides, he was taking them away from their destination based on advice from a dead clone calling through the depths of space on a telephone. Wasn't that absurd enough?

"I'd say we have about five minutes," said Field.

"Confirmed, Chief Magistrate," said Starr.

My God. Two of his crew seemed to actually be working together. Maybe there was hope for them after all.

"I'd say three minutes," said Tolne.

Then again, maybe not.

He was tempted to use his personal controls but not with Tolne right beside him. She'd pick up on that immediately and close him down. Or would she? Could she? What would she do? Lecture him on the need for absurdity even if it meant they would all die? After all, wouldn't that be the ultimate absurdity? And would death be the end of their mission? They'd just received a telephone call from a dead man. Jeli decided to wait till a second or two before certain doom before doing anything outside the realm of absurdity.

As a group, they approached the control console, taking positions at stations that none of them understood, none of them having read the operations manual, none of them having received

157

any special training, all of them having been chosen more for their unsuitability to the job than for their qualifications to be in control of anything that might make sense.

Lation watched as Field turned a knob-a knob-on the control panel in front of her. No one had any idea what the knob was for, but Field turned it successfully, smiling at her ability to turn a knob on a control panel that served no logical purpose. But then, she hadn't yet blown the ship up with the turning of that knob. Confident now in her knob-turning ability, she turned it some more. With a quick snapping sound, it broke off. She stared at it in horror.

"It's OK, Manns," said Jeli. "I think it was supposed to do that. You did well."

Field smiled weakly at him. Lation rolled his eyes. Starr, even though there'd been no ringing, answered the phone, sticking to what he knew. There was no one at the other end. Jeli noticed a look of relief in Starr's eyes.

Tolne smiled widely as a lever she pushed upward produced a clanking noise under the control panel. Skype frowned at her and drooled. Tolne was the one who'd ordered no weapons on Soul Ship even though their destination was likely to turn into a war zone. Skype pounded the edge of her fist angrily and hard as rock on the control board. Every dial, knob, lever and meter shook, and suddenly, they were thousands of miles beyond the path of the iceberg-with a few seconds to spare.

"Well," said Tolne. "Safe again. Nice work, Skype."

Skype smiled as she rubbed the edge of her hand.

A sudden thought rushed through Jeli's head. He frowned.

"Chief Magistrate?" asked Tolne. "Something wrong?"

"I don't know," said Jeli.

"You don't know?" asked Skype, obviously irritated.

"Something I read in the Old Earth Archives about icebergs."

"What's that, Chief Magistrate?" asked Field.

"The most dangerous part of an iceberg is the part you can't see," said Jeli. Everyone switched immediately to Quantrols.

CHAPTER 45 - AN EMOTIONAL BLEMISH

Green candlelight cast a gentle emerald glow over the room. Lovesong sat across from Bella who, dressed in a translucent blue evening dress, skintight, with no lingerie, obviously had something special in mind for dessert. The table was resplendent with glimmerfood from a planet where the flora and fauna glittered through transparent skins. Every life form on the planet X-45-C-6578 was succulent beyond description-food fit only for the palate of the most powerful woman in the universe and her lover.

Bella had posted a small fleet on one of the planet's moons to ensure that she was the only person in the universe with access to her favorite food. Thousands of culinary fanatics had been evaporated in their attempts to try the ultimate taste sensation.

Lovesong had no idea what the iridescent cuts and molds and other concoctions on the table were called-they were different at every meal. But they were always delicious beyond words, not so much caressing his taste buds as massaging them. Lovesong's mouth was beginning to water when a tray with bowls of glittering yellow and green paste floated up to the table and lowered itself to the tabletop, finishing the setting.

Bella had designed the meal herself-something she'd never done before-and Lovesong should have been impressed, if not deeply joyful. But joyful didn't suit his lean restraint. Something was going on with Bella, and he was puzzled. He knew his place in her plans. He was her lover and sometimes confidante-and even advisor, though he was sure that his advice was taken only when it was confirmation of a decision she'd already made. It was his place. He never questioned it. He loved her, genuinely and unquestioningly.

And he knew her. He knew her moods, her thoughts, her gestures, tones, expressions, and even her fears. Her biggest fear was the one she was trying not to face for nearly a century. She was dying. The signs were increasingly obvious. There was no escape, and she was beginning to realize this. It was doing strange things to her. It was doing something strange to her at this moment.

Bella stared into Lovesong's eyes with something different than ownership. He'd never seen this before. Her irises swirled with purple and deep blue. Her smile was a gamut of mixed emotions-uncertainty, fear, resolve, sensuality. Her lips quivered. Everything that cut to the core of Bella Bjork, everything that was her, was betrayed by the miniscule motions of her perfect lips.

Green candlelight washed like waves of aquamarine air over the pale skin of Lovesong's face and hairless head. He was worried about Bella and though he'd already accepted her inevitable death for nearly a century, he hadn't expected it to be like this, a slow disintegration of everything she was-her body, personality and perhaps even her soul. Everything was breaking apart bit by bit, day by day and falling into some pre-death pit of hopelessness before she just crumbled into nothingness. It was a cruel death-one that many would deem appropriate for the cruelest woman in the universe. But Lovesong loved her and would to the moment of her death and beyond.

But her death was taking a new turn. She'd designed dinner for him. She smiled across the table at him. She was dressed for sex but she wasn't just taking him in a fury of self-gratification. Was Bella Bjork beginning to develop feelings other than power lust, sex lust and ego lust? Was there a human chink appearing in her armor of self?

Lovesong didn't know what to think. He asked her what the occasion was.

She frowned and cocked her head to one side, her expression changing to mock hurt. "And why would there need to be an occasion? I designed dinner for my mate. Isn't that what people do when they're in love?"

In love? Bella had never mentioned or even insinuated being in love with him in all the centuries they'd been together. She'd created him. She owned him. He was property-something to be disposed of when it was no longer useful. And now she claimed to be in love with him. He decided to play along with it.

"Dinner is especially delicious tonight," he said as he bit into a golden crust wrapped around a light-red chunk of meat-like substance. The peppery sweet flavor rolled over his palate like a gentle wave.

Bella beamed. She stroked the pendant. It arched its surface reaching up to her fingers as her hand passed over it.

Beside them a jagged round portal that stretched from floor to ceiling looked out into Bella's private ocean. There were things swimming around in it, green aquatic life. Some flapped transparent wings. Others coiled and uncoiled, darting around in the water with each motion. Others were in one spot and suddenly in another, seemingly without movement.

She swallowed a tiny wafer that she'd dipped into some of the green paste, and her face slowly clouded like an emotional blemish moving across the surface of her perfect alabaster skin.

"The Cormorant wants to Quan with the Gamblers," she said, pronouncing the name sarcastically.

The Cormorant was spokesman for the Gamblers, a vast collective of men and women who controlled gambling throughout the universe. Even a friendly bet between friends could provoke a visit from the local members. They controlled it all, especially betting on the Reality Wars. Through them, entire planetary systems had changed hands after each of the Wars. They'd helped Bella fund the building of her armies and navies centuries ago, and she'd worked with them on making the Reality Wars the single biggest gambling spectacle in the universe. A Quannet conference with them this close to the next Wars couldn't be a good thing. It meant they wanted something. And they usually got what they wanted.

"I let them push me into running the Wars in both Realspace and Quanspace," she said, surprisingly calm. "I can only guess what they want next."

"Allowing the two worlds into the Wars might not have been a bad thing," said Lovesong consolingly.

"So that a bunch of Gamblers could double and triple their odds and make obscene amounts of money? What good could come of that? They might even come out of this rich enough to threaten me."

"No one will ever be as powerful as you."

Bella glowed at his words but the shadows moved back into her face quickly.

"Besides, when you have the Texture, your power and control over the universe will be secured forever."

Bella smiled. "I've been too lenient with the Gamblers. I should have taken their money and turned my fleets on them as I did with the Powers." She thought a moment. "I've made mistakes. I shouldn't have allowed the secret to Hayes's computer to come out. I shouldn't have let it flood the universe with trillions of sentient VRs."

"Some regard the Outpouring as one of the Wonders of the Time."

"And some think it might speed up the end of the universe. What if the Clans are right about the finiteness of the vibrations? What if I've succeeded in speeding up the end of the universe?"

Lovesong had never heard her talk like this before. She was actually doubting her actions, her decisions. She was acting strangely human, so unlike the goddess figure she deemed herself to be. He wondered if the stages of death returned people back to a state of human frailty.

"I'll kill the Cormorant for you," he said, wondering what the hell he was talking about even as he mouthed the words.

Bella stared into his eyes, her mouth slightly open, as though she couldn't believe what she'd just heard. She smiled and reached her arm across the table, placing her hand on top of Lovesong's hand. "No, my love," she said tenderly. "I don't want to unbalance things this close to harnessing the Texture. We'll wait until I'm in full control." Her eyes narrowed cruelly. "And then we'll kill them all."

Lovesong nodded agreement. As much as the approach of death might be changing her, Bella was still Bella.

CHAPTER 46 - STILL MIST

It would have been the most terrifying experience of his life if it hadn't been so hard to wrap his head around it. It was unlike anything he'd ever experienced, but he'd had a feeling that, in some strange way, the feeling made sense. It was an absurd feeling. It scraped against the grain of everything he knew. It had been like falling into a pit of solidity, like gushing upward as he plummeted, like squeezing every atom of his being into nothingness just as his being exploded into the universe. He'd touched on that feeling lifetimes ago when he'd created the computer and programming that had made his wife and daughter sentient. He'd just encountered the absurdity that he believed was the core of the universe, and even though he'd had no idea how to understand it, he'd accepted it.

On the other hand, he'd been living as a cloud of gray mist for centuries.

One thing had particularly fascinated him, though. It was something he couldn't explain in so many words-just feel. It was a sensation or knowing that, under the floorboards of that absurdity there was a song. But now there was light. He was in a room of sorts, more like a cavern, something carved into a chunk of rock. *Where am I?*

"In a piece of rock floating in space," said Buddha, who was no longer a mile high. This was his holo projection-a six inch Buddha perched on a boulder. "We'll be here for a few days-until we get you back to normal."

What happened?

"I turned you and your remains into software and transmitted you here. And now you're back to your physical self."

I'm back to being mist?

"But you're free mist now, Abner, not prisoner mist. You escaped."

But I'm still mist.

"I'm working on it," said Buddha.

How did you do it?

"I played your frequencies."

You mean Quannet?

"It's come a long way since you became mist."

Bella gave me bits and pieces of update here and there.

"Very generous of her."

Generous? For hundreds of years she rubbed it in that she killed Claire, described her deletion in every detail, and how she'd shown her what she did to me.

"You need to let go of that, Abner. Your daughter is still alive. You need to focus on her. And something else."

Something else?

"We'll get to that in time." There was a moment of silence.

Strange.

"What's strange, Abner?"

You turned me into software. That's what I was trying to do that got me into this. When Quannet first came out, I saw the possibilities. If everything in the universe was defined by the frequency of its vibration, then it was just a matter of changing the frequency that defined my physical self into one that would define me as software. Then I could be with my family-really be with them. But Bella was waiting for me.

Buddha gazed at the mist compassionately. "We can't bring Claire back, Abner but we can bring you back. You'll see your daughter again."

Not in this form, I hope.

"No, not in this form." Buddha closed his eyes and reflected for a moment. "Can you see the room around you?"

Of course I can.

"But you're mist. You have no eyes."

Bot sensors in my mist.

"Really?" Buddha looked concerned.

What?

"I didn't know about them when I redefined your frequencies to turn you into software and then back into physical form. Good thing my program allowed for variables."

Buddha?

"Yes?"

I don't think I want to hear any more about this. How long before I have a new form?

"I'm working on it as we speak. This is a big thing, you know, a bit bigger now that I know about the bots."

How long?

"I have to do some serious genetic calculations, engineer some of the most sophisticated bots ever, and... a lot of stuff, Abner. That's... if you want to return to your original physical self. And I don't have a lot to work with," said Buddha, pointing a

168

pudgy finger at Abner's rotted physical remains. Give me a few hours."

There was movement in the shadows of the cavern.

We're not alone.

A man moved slowly out of the shadows, eyes wide, staring at the mist that was Abner Hayes.

"This is Benji Parx," said Buddha. "He'll be helping me to bring you up to speed."

CHAPTER 47 - FRENCH VANILLA

La Vie dans la Mort-what he called his cafe. He thought it meant something like life in death-what his job was about. He sipped French Vanilla coffee from a tiny blue cup with a yellow vine-like motif fired into it. He sipped as his will flowed into the vibrations surrounding him. He savored the sweet vanilla rolling over his tongue as his will began to vibrate at the frequency he'd spent a millennia perfecting. He swallowed as his will flowed through the basic operating system of Creation. Once his will was loosened, it would be done. It would flow from La Vie dans la Mort and into the imperceptible frequencies of deep space and across the universe to Blood Citadel and Celtenan, flowing through the Tears of Blood Clan's sophisticated security systems like water filling a sponge.

He could feel her presence thousands of light-years away, such was the power of entanglement. Nothing-not even the infinite expanse of the universe-would stop him from draining the life force out of the Clanswoman. No one escaped the Assassin.

You have a high opinion of yourself.

"I've earned it," said the Assassin. "No one's escaped me in over two thousand years."

There's always a first time. And I'd say, you're due.

"Is there a first time for you to shut up?

You realize who you're talking to, now, do you?

"Unfortunately, I do. Given the circumstances, I'd almost guess there would be a way for me to shut you up."

Maybe you don't want to.

"Maybe I need to just focus on getting through to the Clanswoman."

I don't think you're going to get this one. She's not like anyone else in the universe.

"They're all just human. They all die, eventually."

But this one isn't evil like the others. She's not petty like the others. She's not weak like the others. She's not...

"OK. OK. I get the picture. She's different." He sipped from his cup. The sweetness of the thick liquid curled around his taste buds. "But that doesn't make her immortal. She's going to die. She's going to beg for death. There won't be any first time for me-not after two thousand years."

Suddenly, the sweet taste in his mouth turned bitter. The liquid thickened and turned lumpy and obscene as it pried its way down his throat. He almost gagged, but recovered quickly

She may be more different than you think.

The coffee settled in his stomach like a sphere of liquid rot. His will would not be done this day. The Clanswoman had fought him off again.

She may be your first time.

"This isn't over yet."

You're one persistent bugger, aren't you.

"They say people with voices in their heads are more driven than most."

I'll drink to that.

171

The Assassin sipped from his cup. The coffee was sweet and robust as it flowed over his tongue. He'd noticed that his will had gone just a little further this time.

CHAPTER 48 - NIGHTMARE

The first fraction of a second waking from a nightmare is terror seeping on molasses into the waking world. Shade's awakening dragged her through a long deep ditch of despair, mouth dripping with the bile of death, ears ringing with a song of life broken at the ankles and staggering under the weight of too many hours to fill in a world where everything was pointless, all activity and desire meaningless. She gagged as she woke. The stench filling her half-asleep nostrils was like something nameless and fungal growing its roots into the membranes of her nose.

From the start, she'd known that it was a dream. She'd watched herself flailing around in a dark pit and knew that it couldn't have been real, that she would never give in to those feelings. Even as her body wrenched under the pressure of an immeasurable hopelessness, she knew that these were feelings to which she would never succumb. She knew that this was the work of someone else. It was an attack on her. Someone was trying to drain her energy. Through means she couldn't fathom, someone was attacking her psyche and trying to sour her life. Someone was trying to steal her life force. In her nightmare, she'd understood these things. In those fractions of a second that she tore herself out of the dream, she forgot them, all her focus and energy flowing into her arms to push herself up on her elbows. Tiny bumps swelled over the surface of her body. She didn't sweat. That was unnecessary for the Tears of Blood Clan.

The force of her upward motion woke Loac.

"What's wrong?" asked Loac, immediately aware.

"Just a dream."

The tremor in her voice was barely detectable, but it was all Loac needed. "This dream has reached into you. What do you remember of it?"

"Only that I was in a bad place. The details dissolved as I woke."

"Perhaps if we talk about it... " Loac propped herself on one elbow and faced her.

Shade rolled her weight over on one elbow to face Loac and immediately felt her lover's right leg melting into her thighs. Suddenly, Loac's breath was on her neck, heavy and heated. Their breasts began to merge.

Loac ran her tongue along Shade's neck up to her ear. The heat from her mouth sent a ripple of excitement through Shade's body. "Let me take your mind off the nightmare," whispered Loac as their bodies floated into each other.

But the explosion of passion wasn't enough to take Shade's mind off knowing that no nightmare born of internal demons could have the effect that this one was having on her-she could feel it clearly. She'd just had energy drained from her body. Not a lot, but energy had been drained from her body. Something had soured inside her at a level beyond the physical.

No ordinary nightmare was capable of doing that. Something else was happening to her.

CHAPTER 49 - A SNAKE WITH GLOWING RED EYES

There was no way that Nels could tell her the whole story. He'd known too many good men and women who'd died for lack of pleasing Bella.

"We have this entire quadrant of space set for alerts," he Quanned to her. He appeared on the command deck of his ship in full official dress, even though he was in casual uniform in Realspace.

Bella presented herself as an emerald snake curling around a golden sword.

Must be having a bad hair day. "The clones can't get within a hundred light-years of the Texture without detection. If they try, we'll destroy them."

"But, Commander Horne," said the snake as it coiled around the handle of the sword. "Shouldn't they already be gone? Did you not fire a solar bomb at the clone ship? Did you not have them targeted? Should they not be space dust at this moment? Her words were slow, deadly.

He prepared for the worst. He knew that Chaine would be waiting for the order to kill, and he wouldn't come alone.

The snake's eyes glowed deep red.

"Yes, they should be," said Nels smartly. If he was going to die today, then at least he would go out as a professional, without whimpering, without excuses. "They changed coordinates less than a second before the bomb made contact and disappeared." *Tell her about the telephone call from the Cappel Dark Matter Field? Not likely.*

The snake's eyes flashed violently. Its tongue darted in and out. Nels was ready. He wasn't afraid of death. He'd lived too long with it.

"Is that all?" hissed the snake.

"That's all." He kept his eyes open. He wanted to face his executioner eye to eye. It was the honorable way to die, the death of a warrior.

The snake writhed around the shaft and handle of the sword. It was almost a sexual movement. Nels had heard rumors about the sex clones, thousands of them flushed to their deaths on Earth after they'd satisfied Bella's needs. It was said that her greatest high was looking into their eyes at the instant they realized that she was killing them. She stared into their terror and smiled. *Well, she won't be seeing terror in my eyes*.

The snake's eyes subsided to a glowering red and it hissed less malevolently, "The clones are the greatest danger to my plans, Commander."

"I understand."

"The others will go for the Texture by design. The clones though could reach it by chance. Kill them, Commander, before they have that chance!"

Bella cut off the Quan. Nels was still alive. As he breathed in deeply, he wondered how long it would take before she found out that he'd lied to her. In the meantime, he needed to find that clone ship and destroy it.

***

Bella emerged from the Quan with a frown. *He's lying. There's something he's not telling me.* She entered a new Quan, this one with Chaine.

CHAPTER 50 - FROM THE FRYING PAN...

Skype was the first to hit the right spectral analysis set. The others followed within seconds.

Tolne let out a long satisfied gasp.

Jeli thanked God for Skype's barroom approach to running a deep space craft.

Field said, "Oh... shit."

Lation looked around at everyone, supposedly to see who was going to do something about this.

Starr asked, "What is that, Chief Magistrate?"

Jeli stared into an area of space behind the iceberg lit up in the spectrals like a pool of diluted blood the size of a dozen stars. There was no way they could escape this one. It was too big. They were seconds away from it. It was moving toward them too fast, and before Jeli had a chance to finish that thought, they were in it. Everything in the control room turned pale red-the people, the console, the walls, ceilings and floor-everything glowed red.

Except the eyes of Jeli's crew. Their eyes turned a brilliant glowing white, as though the concept of white were compressed like a black hole inside their heads, and now it was splashing out of their eyes. Jeli assumed the same thing was happening to his own eyes, but he didn't feel any different. In fact, outside the redness of everything, nothing seemed to be happening-no tingly feelings, no pain, no sudden changes in temperature, no dizziness-nothing. Just the color red.

"What is this, Chief Magistrate?" asked Starr, turning his hands before his eyes, staring at them curiously.

"Haven't got a clue, Sheriff Starr. It seems we're being painted."

"Painted, Chief Magistrate?"

"It doesn't seem to be having an effect on anything, Sheriff," said Jeli, as he checked and rechecked Quantrols. Everything was normal-no unusual radioactivity or wave anomalies. All frequencies were harmless. In fact, it was almost as though the red bathing them didn't exist.

Tolne started giggling.

Figures that she'd get a kick out of this.

"So, Chief Magistrate... " Skype stared around at the light pouring out of everyone's eyes. "What are your orders?"

Jeli thought a moment before replying. "I'm not getting any unusual readings. May as well just continue until we ride out the tail of that iceberg."

"No unusual readings, Chief Magistrate?" asked Skype, drooling. "Don't you mean... no readings? Nothing. No wave activity. No strange frequencies. Nothing. That may not bother you, Chief Magistrate, but it bugs the hell out of me."

Jeli felt something bad worming into his stomach. She was right. There should have been something. According to the Quansensors, they weren't lit up in red, and their eyes weren't glowing like white coals. Nothing they were seeing was happening. It didn't make any sense. He was beginning to worry.

Field turned to Jeli. "Chief Magistrate?"

179

"Yes, Manns?"

"Look at Lation."

Everyone looked at the Medical Officer. He was standing, facing toward the ship's useless console. With the exception of the blinding white emitting from his eyes and the red glow surrounding his body, he looked normal-well, as normal as anyone who wore Hawaiian shirts at the edge of the universe might look-except for his right arm. It was twitching and growing alternately larger and smaller as it grew darker and darker until it was black. And then it began to transform.

CHAPTER 51 - CAPPEL DARK MATTER FIELD BLUES

I'd shake hands, said Abner, *but I seem to be mist at the moment*.

Benji Parx cracked a smile. "So, you're the father of Cassie Mae Hayes." There was a touch of awe in his voice.

You know my daughter?

"I know *of* her," said Benji. "Everybody in the universe knows of her, Mr. Hayes."

Abner. Call me Abner.

"Abner," repeated Benji, blushing. "Your daughter gives hope to all clones and VRs. She's the greatest athlete of all time, and if she wins the next Reality Wars, then physicals are going to have to accept that they're no better than virtuals. And if they're no better than virtuals, then they're no better than clones."

You really think so?

Benji's eyes fixed on the stone floor for a moment. "We can hope" But there was no ring of hope in his voice.

The mist wavered sympathetically. "We had an old expression in my early life: where there's life, there's hope."

Benji looked up, smiling shyly. "And the universe is teeming with life, especially since the Outpouring."

The Outpouring?

"We'll get to that soon," said the half-foot Buddha from his perch on the boulder. "By the way,

181

this is Benji Parx, the first clone to become software and then return to his physical state. You'll be the first birth human, Abner."

Nice to meet you, Benji.

"An honor."

One thing bothers me, Buddha.

"Yes?"

If you can change Benji to software and back to physical, why can't you just do the same with me right now?

"I had more to work on with Benji," said Buddha, waving a hand in the direction of the small pile of Abner's rotted remains. "This is the way you are now, Abner, the way you've been for centuries. I have some tricky work to do, not to mention the science and technology, much of which doesn't exist at the moment. It's going to take a while but I'm working on it as we speak."

The mist made a slow heavy movement reminiscent of a sigh. *I know. And I'm grateful for everything you've done.*

"Me too," said Benji. "I don't know what I was thinking when I bit into that cyanide capsule."

Cyanide capsule?

"Benji had a bad case of the Cappel Dark Matter Field blues," said Buddha. "It's a huge dark place that has a way of driving people crazy. We're in the Field now."

Great. So we're all going to go crazy?

"Not if we stay inside," said Buddha. "Benji got right into it through an observation port."

Benji flushed again. "I was curious, I guess. I didn't believe the warnings."

What was it like?

"Big. Dark. Empty."

And that can actually make people kill themselves?

"There's some serious lack of faith problems going around these days," said Buddha. "I was looking in on Soul Ship-that's a deep space vessel being used by a group of clones to get to a cosmological anomaly called the Texture. We'll get to that later too. I've been helping the clones get there before Bella."

Bella's after this... texture?

"Unfortunately, yes," said Buddha. "And if she gets there first, it could cause some pretty bad Karma throughout the universe. But we might be able to stop that from happening, if we have to."

We?

"We have a mission, Abner," said Buddha.

The mist made another sighing movement, much heavier this time.

"But, back to Benji," said Buddha. "I needed to test my transfer program. Benji was killing himself."

The clone flushed deeper and smiled weakly.

"So, at the very instant he was about to float off to lala land, I Quanned him with my program, played a new tune with his frequencies, and turned him into software and transmitted him here."

"And... I feel kinda better," said Benji, smiling widely.

"Revamped his spirits with some virtual mood enhancers, as well," said Buddha.

"And our mission?" asked the mist.

"Well," said Buddha. "After we bring you up to speed, bring you back to normal, take you to your daughter for a visit, we're going to the most dangerous place in the universe to destroy the records of all humankind, both natural and cloned. Then, if need be, we're going to save the universe."

Benji smiled and nodded.

The mist sighed again.

CHAPTER 52 - ALMOST BEAUTIFUL

Zethar Locklan was almost beautiful. Blond hair curled over his massive shoulders. His eyes slanted at an angle suggesting perpetual sympathy, even when he was killing someone. At those times, he turned his face to the left so his target could see clearly the red tears of blood on his right cheek. That, somehow, was a substitute for anger, a way of saying, "This is the Clans doing this to you. Nothing personal." But he hadn't been in close-quarter combat since the Clan Wars and it had been a long time since he'd had to kill someone.

Now, he was Commander of all the Clans' navies, the one who turned them into a single-minded killing machine. He needed to keep an even temper and a level head in these times when hatred and scheming threatened to tear the Clans apart from the inside. But it was impossible to stage large-scale war exercises with this mix of navies. Some of the crews had forgotten the nature of *exercises* and were *accidentally* destroying entire war ships through supposed miscalculations and communications glitches. What was being communicated were the deep hatreds and old scores left over from the Wars, and Zethar suspected that much of the hatred was fed into the troops from high places in some of the Clans. Zethar suspected that another Clan War was in the making, and he was in command of the very navies that might soon be pulverizing each other into space dust.

But he was ready for it. Bavn's nanmagic kept his deadliest strike fleets cloaked from both Bella and all but the Tears of Blood Clan and a few trusted allies.

The Clans' navies were all that held the Clans together-no matter how loosely-from Bella's navies. And who knew what other threats lingered at the edges of the universe? He performed a complex juggling act with his command of navies in millions of galaxies while he was close to the very edge of the universe on Bavn's mission to the Texture. He'd be happy to just destroy the damn thing, turn on the squabbling Clans and then go after Bella. *Just turn me loose, and the Clans will rule the universe.*

But still, he wondered about the odd signals coming from the Cappel Field. Something strange was going on there. And there was something even more disturbing-a large part of Bella Bjork's navy was missing, millions of warships out there somewhere... doing what?

CHAPTER 53 - COULD IT BE LOVE?

"She wakes from nightmares," said Loac. "We merged vapors, and I sensed a drain in her energy. Not large, but there, like a small poisoning."

"A poisoning?" asked Bavn.

Heavy mist poured through evergreens where three mountainous hills intersected in the holo on Bavn's wall. Loac sat in her Tanian ivory chair. *She has something favorite in my quarters*. Bavn almost smiled.

"Almost like she's been tainted from the inside, as though a slow poison of some sort is eating at her. Yet, she seems healthy in all other respects."

"Do you have any theories? You're closer to her than anyone."

"There seems to be no source. She's not sick. At least, not physically. This is something that seems almost to originate in her soul."

"This could explain her listnessness. Do you suspect nanmagic?"

"If not, then something as powerful."

"And how do you feel? You're with her each night. Do you sense any of this poison spilling over to you?"

"No. In fact, I've never felt so strong... so... invigorated."

"Invigorated? That's a strange term to use. How do you feel invigorated?" Bavn smiled. *Is that a faint blush coloring her cheeks?*

"Well... I... "

Stammering? My daughter, stammering?

"I just meant to say that I feel in top form, better than ever."

Is that a smile trying to break loose from the corners of her mouth?

"I'm worried about Shade... " She stopped and looked at Bavn.

What's that in her eyes? Pleading? Why did we make it so hard for her to feel normal human emotions? Bavn wondered if this might be something they'd overlooked in her training. She would need to be strong, but perhaps they'd made her too strong in some respects and not strong enough in others. Had they created an imbalance that might weaken her in the Reality Wars? Had they concentrated so much on perfection that they'd missed that one tiny spot of imperfection that completed perfection? There were those who believed that absurdity lay at the root of all being. Bavn doubted this, but he did acknowledge that whatever lay at the basis of Creation defied any form of reason that humans could comprehend. Perhaps the Texture would change that. In the meantime, it appeared that Loac was making up for any lack of imperfection on her own. Bavn suspected that his daughter was falling in love, and for the first time ever, she wasn't in complete control.

CHAPTER 54 - A LARGE BLUE EYE

"A telephone call?"

Chaine faced a large blue eye floating in the background of nothingness before him. Its intensity was almost blinding, even in Quanspace.

"Your commander said nothing about a telephone call."

Chaine sensed the dangerous fury emanating from the eye, but he wasn't afraid. He was a Black Tree. If Bella wanted him dead, then he would gladly die-it would be his mission to die, his destiny. "It came just before the clone ship changed coordinates," he said. The wires in his lips glowed red in both Quan and Realspace. "It came from the Cappel Dark Matter Field."

The eye appeared to tremble for a second. Chaine focused raptly on the eye, its stare engulfing all that he was. To look away would be an insult to his goddess, Bella.

There was silence for a long moment before she spoke. "Something strange is going on in that Field. I can feel it. Somehow it's connected to the clones. They're the only variable I can't control. That's what makes them so dangerous. They could destroy my plans just through sheer accident. They *must* be destroyed. I don't care what's going on in the Cappel Field. I don't care where that call came from or who made it. I want them destroyed."

***

Telephone. It was like a tickle in Bella's vast store of memory, from a long ago time, when others had been saved from her. Something or someone then had done the impossible. And now a telephone in deep space eons after the last telephone had long been scrapped. *The clones have an ally, an ancient ally*.

***

Chaine's wires were gold again. He Quanned through a frequency mix that only the Black Tree knew existed. He often wondered about the number of secret Quans that existed in spite of their supposed impossibility to exist, and he guessed they were increasing. His goddess's empire was crumbling, but he and the Black Tree were ready to face whatever fate awaited her. And now, it was time to get the Black Tree to the Cappel Field and kill in the name of Bella.

190

CHAPTER 55 - THE DARK

"An entire universe mapped from one end to the other," said Benji, "and not a single sign of intelligent life other than ours-mapped right up to the Dark."

The Dark? asked the mist.

"The nothingness that surrounds the universe," said Benji. "Infinity. No one ever ventures far into it. Strange things happen there. Ships disappear. Quannet breaks down. It's like the properties that make our universe tick begin to break down in the Dark. It just swallows things."

What kind of distances are we talking about?

"They aren't really perceived as distances, more like a time in space, a location defined by time."

I see. The mist sounded unconvinced, still doubtful. *And what about this texture everybody is after. Is it close to the Dark?*

"Right at the edge of it," said Benji. "It's believed to be a place where our universe and another came into contact. The impossibility of their foreign properties co-existing repelled the two universes, but the other left a pocket of its properties in our universe, and it's believed that ours left a pocket of properties in the other. We call our pocket the Texture. It's like a texture in space, a pattern of something that tries to exist in our universe, but can't because there's nothing here that can support its ability to be what it is, so it exists in a state of flux, a pocket of chaos at the edge of our universe."

The mist thought about this for a moment. *And now there's a big race to get to it? And people are being killed for it?*

"Some people think the two pockets may be entangled," said Benji. "They could form a portal between the universes. They also believe that it may be possible, eventually, to tap into the properties of the other universe and use them in some form here-new physical properties applied to Quannet might allow Bella to regain her absolute control over the universe if she can turn those properties into a weapon or other means of control." Benji let the mist mull over this for a moment. "There are others who give the Texture religious significance. There's a huge sub-race of people called the Clans. They're sort of genetically engineered throwbacks to ancient civilizations on Earth. They've developed their own brand of nantechs, some of them called nanmagic that appears to break the normal rules of what nantech can do by mixing nantech with connections to the frequencies that go beyond Quannet."

What do you mean by normal rules?

Benji organized his thoughts for a moment. "Quan*space* can be manipulated by an inherited connection to it that every birth human and cloned human is born with. Quan*net* is different. Quannet is the technology that makes it possible to use Quanspace. Bella owns Quannet and controls it through an entire galaxy at the center of the universe. She makes the rules and decides what people can and cannot do in Quanspace. Nanmagic is suspected to come from something beyond the original programming in Quannet. Using it, the

Clans can bypass Bella's control and use Quannet to do things that some people think even Bella can't do."

And what kind of religious significance do these Clans believe the Texture has?

"They believe that their nanmagic came from the basic stuff of Creation... *before* the instant of the Big Bang, and at that instant, there was a connection to God that might be reconnected through the Texture."

The mist pondered this. *Seems pretty far out. And are there other religions besides theirs?*

Benji smiled and laughed quickly. "Millions, spread throughout the galaxies, but none as strong as the Clans. Most of them are modifications of old Earth religions and most of them formalities." A look of sadness clouded Benji's eyes. "The truth is, there's not much real faith in anything anymore. We haven't found other intelligent life. And we haven't found God. There are a lot of disillusioned people out there. They lead their lives wondering why they're leading any lives at all. Suicide is one of the most popular pastimes in the universe." He raised his eyebrows and laughed. "Hey, I tried it myself."

Sitting on his rock, eyes closed, legs crossed lotus style, hands cupped in his lap, Buddha sighed deeply, smiled and opened his eyes. He looked at the mist. "Ready to be Abner Hayes again?"

CHAPTER 56 - TO ARRIVE BY LEAVING

Bavn and Zethar Locklan had something in common besides great responsibility and power. Both preferred natural Quanpresence-no avatars, no Quanshock or personality themes, just who they were, in both Quan and Realspace. Bavn liked the huge blond man with the kind eyes. He trusted his loyalty and his instincts, and he didn't take lightly that Zethar was so concerned about something that many would dismiss as a freak anomaly.

"And you can't identify the type of signal?" asked Bavn. Quanspace re-created his quarters where he sat in front of an expanse of frothing oceanscape. Zethar, in his sparse shipboard quarters, sat on the top of a desk that looked as though it was never used. As he described the nature of the signal, Bavn's blue eyebrows nudged upwards. "It sounds like a telephone call."

"Telephone call?"

"A technology that pre-dates Quannet," said Bavn thoughtfully. "And you think it originated in the Cappel Field?"

"It disappeared before we could pin down an exact location, but the projections pointed toward a quadrant in the Field. It was received by Soul Ship, the clone craft."

"The clone ship?" Bavn's eyebrows raised higher. "I thought they would have self-destructed by now."

"Not yet. In fact, they dodged one of Bella's solar bombs by a fraction of a second."

Bavn spoke slowly, thoughtfully. "Interesting."

"I think the signal-the telephone call-may have had something to do with their escape."

"You think they have allies?"

"I'm not sure, but they appear to be going in the opposite direction now, away from the Texture."

Bavn smiled. "Perhaps they intend to arrive by leaving."

"Arrive by leaving?"

"I have no idea what that means, Commander, but I think we'd better keep an eye on the clones' little ship. They're too much of a wildcard in all that's happening. Let's not let them take us by surprise. You said you have another concern?"

Zethar glanced around his ship's quarters, even though he knew that he was alone.

Bavn's eyes narrowed. *Must be something very important.*

"We've lost track of a significant part of Bella's navies."

"How significant?"

"Several hundred million warships."

Bavn thought about this. Could Bella be planning an attack? Would this upset the Clans' own plans? On the other hand, she had enemies all over the universe. Uprisings were cropping up like intergalactic measles. Even with her vast navies, she was spread thin, and her power over Quannet was considerably diminished. Rumors had it that she was going insane. *As though she hasn't been insane for over two thousand years.*

195

"Do you have any special orders?"

Bavn considered this. "Bella makes her fleets visible as a deterrent, a tangible warning to anyone who would challenge her power. If that much of her fleet is suddenly invisible, then she's either getting ready to attack... or... " Bavn nodded to himself as he thought. "Or she wants to build a blockade."

"The Texture?"

"That's my guess. Are we ready for them?"

Zethar smiled knowingly. "I think the more accurate question is... are they ready for us."

Bavn returned the smile and nodded. "And keep an eye out for anything from the clones, Zethar. I have a feeling they may yet turn out to be our biggest threat."

CHAPTER 57 - ANCIENT BLEEDING

"There's talk of nanmagic poisoning Shade's will. Do you know anything of this, Maebh?" Brann's eyes glowed murderously, casting an eerie haze on his white hair and beard.

Maebh turned the dark opening of her hood slowly toward Brann. "I know nothing of this." She enunciated each word slowly and breathed in deeply and noisily, the air grating as it filled her lungs. "And don't ever threaten me again. You may find yourself looking for your head."

In a flash, the tip of Brann's sword was pressed against her robe just over her heart. She stood quietly, facing Brann, arms crossed under her chest. To her left, Uilliam watched, dumbfounded.

"You push in the wrong places," said Brann, deadly calm now with his sword in hand. "You're Clans, yet you preach hatred among the Clans. You bleed through ancient wounds and spread your blood like poison among us." He lifted the blade and pointed it to where her throat would be under the hood. "Perhaps a fresh wound to dampen your...
"

A strange expression crossed Brann's face, something that might have been confusion or maybe curiosity. There was something weird and hazy in the air around his head, the kind of thing visible on the peripheries of vision and gone when you look straight at it.

Uillium cocked his head to the side and looked quickly around him. The air around them was thick

197

with something ominous whose presence increased with each second.

The smile on Brann's face wilted as Maebh's hood began to roll slowly up over her forehead. Brann's and Uillium's eyes widened unbelievingly as the hood revealed a hairless head with gray folds of brain barely visible under a translucent skull. Her eyes were black and lidless, like dark tunnels. Her skin, like her skull, was almost transparent. The outlines of teeth showed through her cheeks. Red points of light emanated from her eyes, growing brighter and brighter until they took the form of a claw of red light that leaped from her eyes and grabbed Brann by the head.

Brann shrieked. "What kind of nanmagic is this? Stop this now!"

Maebh's dark lips moved slowly. "Perhaps a fresh reminder of the slaughter of our people at the hands of the Tears of Blood?"

Slowly, the red claw tightened its grip as Brann slashed futilely, his blade passing through the claw without effect. "Stop! Now!" he screamed, but the claw tightened and then wrenched, slicing through his head. Brann's eyes stared lifelessly at Maebh as the back of his skull made a wet sound and fell to the ground. The claw dissolved into the air and Brann's body crumbled.

Uillium, white-faced and wide-eyed, spoke limply through trembling lips. "How... how will we explain this? His Clan... "

"We explain nothing," said Maebh as her hood rolled back over her head like a dark creature furling into its hiding place after its attack. "He was here secretly. At least according to you... keeping with his oath. You and I are the only ones who know of this."

"But if they find-"

"They won't." She stepped toward the body and threw some white powder on it. As the powder touched the giant man's body, hides, armor, flesh and bone evaporated.

Uillium stared in horror. If he'd any doubts before this day that he'd gone beyond the point of no return, those doubts had just evaporated into the air along with the bones and armor of Brann.

CHAPTER 58 - BREATHING

"I'm worried ... " In the burst of a micro instant, Cassie felt the switching of realities. "... about Sara."

"No, Cassie," said Dran Bago, one of the greatest triathletes of the twenty-second century. "You can't afford to miss even a fraction of a second when you switch."

"I know, Dran. It's just that it still feels so odd going between Quan and Realspace, like waking up from a dream, only much faster. And I'm still getting used to this whole physical reality thing. I always wondered how it would feel."

Cassie sat cross-legged on a floating air pillow as did Dran. They were inside a clear nanplast life bubble with stars glimmering brightly all around. They were in deep space, in the center of a two-hundred-cubic-light-year training area programmed for Solidholo that had been assigned to Cassie for training. In this place, Dran trained Cassie in one thing only: transitioning from Quan to Realspace, chipping her adjustment time down by nanseconds at a time.

"Is it much different, being in Realspace?" he asked.

"Feels... heavier, like everything is a bit more condensed. Other than that, it's pretty much the same."

"It seems that a few thousand years of programming-give or take a few centuries-to re-create physical reality hasn't been wasted."

"So this is really the physical? I'm just like you now?"

"Not exactly. What you're experiencing is the ability to exist in the physical world. You're still software, but the SolidHolo gives you a physical presence in Realspace. Your personality, feelings-everything that defines you, is still in Quanspace, but you can make things happen in this state. If you push an object in Realspace, you can make it move. If something pushes against you, you can feel it."

"It's a strange feeling, Dran. I can actually feel the air around me. It's inside me. And then it's not inside me. It's heavy, and then it's lighter."

Dran thought about this for a moment. "I think... in the physical world, we call that breathing."

"Am I supposed to breathe in SolidHolo?"

"Over a million programmers worked on this program. It would surprise me if they left out the action of breathing-it's so much a part of Realspace."

As calm as she appeared to be, sitting and facing Dran with her hands joined together over her crossed legs, she was anything but calm in some part of her mind. Dran could see it in her eyes. Realities switched. Their life bubble floated over a vast Quanspace of misty mountains and lightning-streaked clouds.

"Do you think this program could eventually bring VRs into Realspace, as physical beings?" asked Cassie.

Dran's Quanspace avatar did something Cassie had never seen him do before-he shrugged.

She smiled.

"If we played the strings at the right frequencies, it might be possible," he said. "But we would be talking trillions of lines of programming. I can't even begin to think of what kind of being-physical or VR-that could comprehend that magnitude of complexity." He smiled, wrinkling the skin around his cheeks in a way that suggested a well worn smile. "We can do amazing things, Cassie, and sometimes we're like gods." His eyes twinkled as he spoke. "But we're *not* gods."

CHAPTER 59 - CHANGES

Medical Officer Jack Lation's eyes throbbed and bulged as his arms grew black, spindly and hairy, prickly hairy. What was left of his mouth opened as if to say, "Now listen, I didn't sign on for this." But his mouth sucked into his face along with his nose with a squishing sound and popped out as a long obscenely proboscis-like appendage. Turning red and forming thousands of tiny facets, his eyes grew until they covered most of his head. His arms segmented into insect-like legs as an extra pair ripped through his flowery Hawaiian shirt, and the thick legs below his shorts turned black and spindly like the appendages on his upper body. His shirt tore off completely as a pair of huge transparent wings opened on his back. The remainder of his shirt, along with his shorts, shredded and dropped to the floor as Lation dropped forward and landed on three sets of segmented legs. His back shimmered florescent blue and green. Lation buzzed his wings at Jeli and rubbed his hind legs together.

He was a fly. A very large fly.

Jeli felt a distinct need to vomit, followed immediately by a tingling sensation in his stomach that spread throughout his body and over the surface of his skin. He lifted his right hand to his face and watched in horror as it turned dark and gristly under the bright glow from his eyes.

He saw Tolne writhing on the floor, bathed in red light, that beautiful body segmenting into a crusty green thorax and blue striped abdomen, her eyes bulbous and red. Skype, fully fly, walked upside down on the ceiling, buzzing happily, and drooling from her proboscis. The rest of his crew were in various stages of transformation.

What the hell now? It was Jeli's last rational thought before the madness began in earnest. He was flying through the air as his vision took in everything before him, to his sides and behind him. He was on the wall, skittering up and down, running his long proboscis across the surface of the wall, licking up stuff that may have been flesh turned to dust mixed with moisture and then dried to the surfaces of things. He was ravenously hungry. And there was a strange feeling from his rear, at the end of his abdomen. Without naming it, he knew it-he was shitting almost continuously, leaving fly feces wherever he flew or walked. Then he was upside down on the ceiling, preening his huge red eyes with his forelegs. It felt good, like scratching. He was aware of movement from the others as they darted through the air and attached themselves at impossible angles to the walls, ceilings and fixtures.

The control room filled with the sound of buzzing and the stink of globs of fly feces. The buzzing grew in intensity until it was almost a tangible thing, dense as an additional layer of meaning. Jeli was aware of it, and it had a strange effect on him, like he wanted to be closer to it but he was confused and couldn't locate the source of it. He needed to be closer to it.

The others stopped flying, standing still, preening their eyes, rubbing their legs together, still, as though listening. The fly that was Skype was the first to locate it. She flew, buzzing madly, in a straight line to it. It was on the other side of the portal.

The others, Jeli included, flew toward the portal and gathered around it. On the other side, Jeli and his command crew could hear the buzzing of hundreds of other flies. It was like an angry, confused roar, and it shook the walls of the ship right down to its structure, loosening bolts and cracking joints.

CHAPTER 60 - THE BASIC INTRO TO REAL AND REAL

"So how does it feel?" asked Buddha.

"A bit heavier," said Abner staring into a virtual mirror, reunited with his human form—lean, balding, long pony tail, dark brows, thick lips and wide nose. "You couldn't have made me prettier?"

"We are what we are," said Buddha without humor. "Would you prefer mist?"

Abner threw his hands up in mock submission. "This suits me fine." He turned sideways and nodded approval at his reflection. "At least, being mist for a couple thousand years didn't give me a pot belly."

"You look fine," said Benji. He opened his mouth slightly, eyes questioning as though he had more to say.

"Yes?" asked Abner.

Benji blushed and began slowly. "I... I was just wondering... is there any special feeling? I mean... something beyond the physical... something deeper... maybe a spiritual feeling? How does if feel to be Abner Hayes again... Abner Hayes, the human?"

Abner pondered this briefly, then smiled. "A bit heavier."

"That's it?" asked Benji. "Just... heavier?"

"Well... " Abner paused, giving it some thought. "Solid. More solid."

Benji nodded as he looked off into some region where Abner's words might make sense. "Solid," he said quietly to himself.

Abner looked around the cavern, puzzled. "There's no equipment here."

"Equipment for what?" asked Buddha.

"Well, for programming me back to human," said Abner. "Don't tell me you don't use computers anymore."

Buddha tilted his head in amusement. "It's not actually called programming anymore, Abner."

"It's not?"

"We call it playing the strings. Some call it playing the frequencies."

"I see," said Abner, nodding. "You program by manipulating the frequencies of vibrations, the strings that form the basic stuff of existence. But don't you still need a computer of some sort to access the strings?"

"Not for the last thousand or so years," said Buddha. "That's about the time the first humans were born with a genetically inherited connection to Quannet."

"Genetically inherited?" Abner thought about this a moment. He squinted his eyes.

"Even clones have the inheritance," said Benji enthusiastically.

"But, still... " Abner looked at Buddha. "You still exist in the virtual world, yet I'm seeing you in this world."

"SolidHolo," said Buddha. "It brings part of me into the physical world. It's just a matter of realities."

207

"So, if you turned me into software to transmit me here, then does this mean only part of me is here?

Buddha smiled. "No, Abner, all of you is here. At least, I think so. I only just figured out how to do this a few minutes ago."

"So you can't turn VRs into full humans?"

"No," said Buddha. "We are all what we are. The physical human frequencies were never in the VRs. Software was always meant to re-create humans and human processes in one way or another, especially with genetic programming. So, though there's something intrinsically human about VRs, there is also something intrinsically not human about them."

"So, you can't make my daughter human?"

Sitting cross-legged in the air, Buddha smiled gently and said, "Why would she of all people want to be anything but what she is?"

Eyes beginning to suddenly moisten, Abner turned full on Buddha. "I need to see her."

"You will. Soon. But first... "

Abner rolled his eyes. "I really hate it when you say things like that and just leave them dangling. What now?"

"You need to be fully connected to Quannet."

"You've turned me into software and back to my physical self, all online. And now you say I'm not connected?"

"Not fully," said Buddha. "Being biologically connected is a bit different from the connection you had two thousand years ago. It goes a bit deeper."

"Deeper?"

"Hold on to your teeth."

CHAPTER 61 - NO MATTER HOW MANY LIVES

As Supreme Commander of Bella Bjork's navies, Daman Haley controlled billions of warships spread throughout the universe. It took hundreds of years to engineer the kind of brain capable of controlling something that big and complex, but Daman was up to the task. He'd been doing it for over three hundred years. He was the longest serving of all the Supreme Commanders.

His replacement had lasted only twenty years before being "reassigned." Few people understood the irony of the term more than Daman, who was the one to give his predecessor the pill that turned his body into vapor. The average term of duty till then was fifteen years before reassignment.

Bella was a demanding leader. She expected deadlines to be met, and met her way. If she demanded that a planet be stripped of life in order to meet a deadline, then that planet would be stripped of life, or Bella would be displeased. And displeasing Bella Bjork was the death sentence, either immediate or delayed, depending on how much use could be squeezed out of you while you were still alive.

Supreme Commander Daman Haley would sacrifice every man and woman under his command if that was what it took to complete a mission for Bella. When Bella wanted blood, he gave her blood. This kept him free of reassignment, and it made him, behind Bella, the most powerful living being in the universe. He was the iron hand of Bella Bjork, squeezing all of Creation into submission, and the sublime sense of power flowed through his veins. For Damon Haley, that feeling of power was worth giving up his conscience and any sense of humanity.

But things were changing and changing fast. Bella's control over Quannet was slipping dangerously. The Clans were more powerful than they had been before the Clan Wars, and other factions were sprouting up in remote regions of the universe. And there were the Gamblers. God knew how powerful they'd become. The Clans should have been eliminated immediately after the Wars, when they were weak and war weary. The Gamblers should have been destroyed as soon as their money had given Bella complete control of Quannet. He'd never been able to figure that one out, but she must have had her reasons. And then there was the Outpouring- trillions of sentient VRs set loose into Quanspace. That could turn out to be a dangerous wild card some day. It all made Daman wonder if Bella were still the most powerful person in the universe. And if not, where did that put him?

He had little patience with the whole Texture thing. It was a huge drain on resources and focus and from where he was sitting, that couldn't be a good thing. He stared at the concave monitor stretching the length and height of one entire wall. Sometimes he preferred to leave the convenience of Quantrols and see things on the big screen. This was something he tried to drum into his officers. It gave one a different perspective. It was always good to have one more view when you were subjugating the universe.

At the moment, the big screen was showing something fascinating-millions of Clans' ships filling up thousands of miles of space on their way, supposedly to some Clans' religious gathering or other, but on a path that took them a little closer to Control than Daman felt comfortable with. He wasn't worried. There didn't seem to be anything he couldn't handle but he was distrustful of the Clans' navies these days. He'd met the commander of the Clans' navies, Zethar Locklan, and he had great respect for him. He'd heard of Zethar's feats during the Clan Wars. The man was a brilliant strategist but the Clans' navies had been acting erratically in recent days. There had even been confrontations between Clans' ships. People had died. Something was happening within the Clans, and it was more likely to get worse than better, and it could very well spread outside the Clans.

But that was fine with Daman. It would make things so much easier.

Daman's thoughts were interrupted by a Quansend. It was from Bella, and he sensed something desperate in the frequency. This couldn't be good.

CHAPTER 62 - DROWNING IN THE UNIVERSE

It was a thousand explosions of meaning rolling over a thousand explosions of anti-meaning spiraling inside an infinite cone of concussions and all the explosions blasted into thousands upon thousands more explosions ripping the cone into shards of consciousness. The entire universe was inside Abner's head. Quansends from trillions of stars and planets slashed through his brain, all of them assaulting his attention simultaneously and instantly. The numbers of people were inestimable-humans, clones, VRs and all the programs to build their worlds, all of it spread over vast expanses of galactic systems and the cosmic deserts between them.

The sheer mass hit Abner square in the head like a meteor slamming into an ant. Image upon image rushed into his consciousness too fast to count, too fast to see, too fast to comprehend. A thousand symphonies raged in his head. A galaxy of horns squawked endlessly. He fell to his knees, overwhelmed by the landslide of information.

He screamed. He couldn't see Buddha or Benji in the cavern. Any awareness of himself was drowning in the deluge of information crashing across the floorboards of his awareness.

Surprisingly, there was no pain but that didn't stop him from screaming. Some things hurt more than pain, like being swallowed by something so far beyond knowing that your soul felt like teeth grinding.

All he could do was scream, long and shrill. It was the only thing his mind could handle without... what? Blacking out? Going mad? Dying of fright? Screaming did it for Abner. It gave him a hook into whatever reality was being erased by information overload to the power of a million. But he couldn't hear himself scream. There was too much happening in the part of his brain that processed information for him to hear, smell or feel anything. Then, he began slowly to see a clearing in the infinite landscape flooding into his mind. It started as a small blur of stability, an area that covered real space somewhere in the collage of eternity. It floated across the confusion, gathering definition and density until Abner could pick out what appeared to be facial features.

He stopped screaming. Slowly, he began to smile. He recognized the face forming at the core of his awareness. It was Buddha, and Buddha was smiling. His lips moved. He was saying something. Abner focused on Buddha's lips, and the chaos slid away like water splashing off a moving vehicle. Buddha's words drifted through the splashing water like minnows of meaning, "Be the infant."

Buddha was telling him to be the infant.

Be the infant?

What the hell did that mean? What was *be the infant*? Where was it? How was he to do this? Why couldn't Buddha be a little clearer on this? He tried to speak, to ask for clarity, but he couldn't. He was on his knees, throat throbbing from screaming,

214

facing Buddha and his voice was paralyzed. After all these years that damned virus was still playing games with his head.

"Be the infant," said Buddha.

This time the image was clearer. The words more distinct. The smile on Buddha's lips less enigmatic. Somehow, Abner knew what he meant. He knew how to see the meaningful.

"Be the infant," said Buddha.

The memories came back to Abner, stories in the news about the first complete Quannet implants in humans, the madness that followed, the suicides, the mental meltdowns, the murders. It had been too much for them to handle-that much information rushing into their heads all at once.

But the babies adapted well. They took it in stride with the filtering process they were already undergoing by defining what was meaningful and filtering out the rest in the world into which they were born, a place—for them—with no definitions, no parameters, no guidelines or clues other than the warmth of body contact and nipples somehow quenching their hunger. Fetal Quannet implants in fetuses were the big thing in Abner's time, before he became mist. There was talk of making them permanent.

The fetuses just naturally learned how to sort it all out. By the time they were born, they were biologically connected, but then the connection was severed like an umbilical cord immediately after birth. Still, the babies were normal, and they took to Quannet like veterans in later years. This is what Buddha was telling him, to be infant-like and just accept all the information, just let it pass through him, let his intuition filter out the irrelevant. Let his natural processes revert to pre-birth and bring meaning to the endless flow of too much data. Yes, he would just relax and be fetus-like. He would be a sponge with sunglasses. He would be a...

Something was wrong. He put his hands to his eyes and rubbed them. It felt strange. Overly wet. Oozy. He took his hands away from his eyes. Through the images he saw blood on his hands. Blood. Being fetus-like wasn't cutting it. The information was too much. He was too old for this, too long a relic from another age who'd missed all the genetic modifications and the nanotech enhancements. He wasn't ready for this, and it was killing him. The information was like a tidal wave crashing in from the universe, drowning him in Creation.

And Buddha had stopped smiling.

CHAPTER 63 - BREAKING UP AFTER SEX

Every naninch of the ship vibrated with buzzing. Cracks and crunches, strange groans and long ominous screeches inundated the air. The floor rumbled, the walls shook. The buzzing intensified. Beside Jeli, the fly that was Jannn Tolne buzzed crazily as she rubbed against his side. A strange feeling overtook Jeli, something nestling in regions that were unnatural to him, yet somehow familiar, flooded his fly senses with irresistible urges. In the flick of an instant, he mounted her from the rear and they were joined like lock and key. The buzzing became a hammer of solid sound pounding against the ship, loosening and breaking things.

Jeli had no idea why he'd mounted Tolne. There were no feelings of sexuality or physical attraction, only an overwhelming urge. He wondered if this was the way flies felt when they had sex. Tolne vibrated her wings. Maybe she was feeling something. Maybe she was just *trying* to feel something. It didn't matter. The buzzing was still growing, like a tidal wave now. The entire crew must have been on the other side of the port door.

His eyes scanned the area around him and Tolne. The others were copulating as well. He wasn't sure who was with whom, but he could tell from the piece of material that used to be part of a Hawaiian shirt that Lation was finally doing something other than sit on his ass. This was something that Jeli knew at the core of what he used to be as a clone. At the moment, the only thing he was immanently aware of was the buzzing of Tolne's wings against his thorax and abdomen. Also, at his core-and maybe even as fly-he knew that thousands of giant flies were getting their fly rocks off on the other side of the portal, none of them aware that what they were doing could destroy Soul Ship.

Parts of the ship banged and clanged. Others made obscene ripping and tearing noises. The ship jerked and swerved. A dangerous thing to be doing in deep space. You never knew what could swallow you in regions like this.

Suddenly, Jeli felt a sense of release. He and Tolne uncoupled, and Tolne flew away fast as a wink. The buzzing outside the door stopped. The buzzing in the control room stopped. A cloud of dizziness spun around Jeli's head. His body tingled from the tips of his antennae to the end of his abdomen and through all six legs. The vision through is faceted eyes blurred and seemed to evaporate into his head and then everything was black.

He wasn't sure how long the blackness lasted before the light appeared.

He looked around. Tolne, Lation, Field, Starr and Skype-all back to normal, all slumped against walls or crashed on the floor, all looking around at the others, their eyes stark and puzzled. Everyone was naked.

Skype was first to speak. Very softly and slowly, she said, "Damn."

Lation shrugged and sat down. "If anyone needs medical attention, Quansend for an appointment."

Screams and moans came from the other side of the portal-that would be going on for a while guessed Jeli. Then there was a loud winding crack that originated far to portside and ended at starboard. Jeli looked at Starr.

Starr remained calm, even though his eyes, slightly more rounded than usual, suggested a great deal of horror. "We may have breached the hull, Chief Magistrate."

This is going to be bad. Jeli hoped that Tolne hadn't removed all the hull repair equipment.

At the same time, he wondered what had just happened. It had all seemed so real. It couldn't have been anything other than hallucination, but then, how had the hull been breached? Something strange had happened in the wake of the giant iceberg, and for some reason, something Jeli really didn't want to even think about at the moment. After all, his ship was falling apart. And the control deck was covered with fly shit.

CHAPTER 64 - CONFRONTATION

"Crash" was Captain Colin Duncan's nickname. He'd never actually crashed a ship or any type of land vehicle, but he had a reputation for being the most reckless ship's captain in all of Bella's navies. He took chances that went right off the probability scales, but so far he'd been lucky. However, when you play the odds, the outcome is never truly in your own hands, and today Crash's outcome was about to switch hands.

He'd been watching the vast armada of the Clans' ships passing through space so close to Control without clearance, without warning and without any clear reason other than some badly defined religious trek that not even the Clans' intelligence team had ever heard about. But none of Bella's commanders seemed concerned. They did nothing. Crash was certain the rumors of Bella's diminishing power were true and that the reason for her control slipping was directly related to the inability of her highest ranking commanders to show some backbone. Crash had heard the stories about entire planetary systems losing their populations for challenging her authority. He appreciated her methods. *Now that was how to rule-ruthlessly, mercilessly and without hesitation.*

But a lack of will seemed to exist in the ranks, a lack of intestinal fortitude when it came to doing Bella's will in ways that sent meaningful messages to a universe that needed a single strong leader to hold it together. He had little confidence in Supreme Commander Haley. The man had been commanding

Bella's navies for too long. He was losing his touch, getting soft. He was letting this huge strike force of the Clans' ships get too close to Control, close to the engines that commanded Bella's empire and stored all the information of the universe, every human, clone and VR, all their Quansends, every iota of information about their Quanspace presence, every transaction, every deed of ownership and every record of birth and creation, whether from human cells or playing the strings. The engine was entire worlds of biological computers-half humans, cloned and genetically enhanced brains living in biomasses-just about any permutation of human being at the points where natural and artificial intelligence intersected.

This armada of the Clans' warships (and warships they were, with no doubt in Crash Duncan's mind) posed a very real threat to the heart of the universe.

Crash decided it was time to send a wakeup call to Bella's sleeping commanders. It was time for a little Crash Duncan recklessness, and he just might end this day a hero, possibly on his way to high command.

He Quanned his attack crew together.

***

Daman Haley clenched his teeth. *I should have jettisoned that little prick along with the garbage in the Thorne Nebula ten years ago.*

He'd just received the Quanalert. One of his captains had intercepted a Clans' ship, supposedly a

221

holy ship carrying religious artifacts for whatever rites the Clans had planned when they reached their destination. The captain of the Clans' ship was furious, threatening to go straight to the highest command in the Clans and lodge complaints with Control and Bella herself.

Daman took a deep breath, counted to three and Quanned in on the young captain. He presented himself as himself and told Captain Duncan to drop the crouching tiger and present formally, in uniform, as himself. He glared angrily into the dark eyes of the tall sandy-haired man who faced him. Duncan's lower lip quivered slightly. That was a good sign.

He chose a calm voice, but kept the anger burning in his eyes. "What are you doing, Captain?"

"We suspect that the Clans ship may be transporting solar bombs into this sector, sir." The quiver in Duncan's lip became more pronounced.

He's lying. "And what makes you think that, Captain?"

"Our sensors picked up something suspicious, sir."

Now to really twist the screws. "This is a peaceful religious convoy, Captain. What exactly did your sensors pick up that would merit suspecting solar bombs?"

Duncan thought a moment.

Damon could almost smell the sweat dripping out of Duncan's skin. *Good.*

The young captain said, "It's difficult to explain exactly what it was, sir. I suppose it was just scanning the data and realizing that something wasn't quite right."

"And that led you to believe that they were carrying solar bombs?"

"My sense of the data at that time... yes, sir. That was my assumption, based on the data of the moment."

Daman frowned. *The data of the moment. Let's create an incident that could be the match to set off galactic war over data of the moment.* "That was a rash decision, Captain. Don't you agree?"

Duncan looked doubtful, as though wondering if the Supreme Commander might be giving him a graceful way out. He decided he was. "Yes sir, it may have been a little rash. What are your orders, sir?"

"Leave the Clans' ship. Apologize. Offer to be of any assistance to the captain of the Clans' ship. Apologize again. Take your ship to the rear ranks, and don't bring my attention to you again for a long, long time."

The Quan ended abruptly. *That should keep him out of trouble. For a while.*

***

On board the Clans' ship Deep Cold, Captain Shona Ureil breathed out slowly as her shoulders relaxed. If they had boarded her ship and searched the cargo bay, they would have discovered the bomb they were carrying, so new and unique that no scanning technology existed anywhere to detect it. And so deadly that Bella's navies would have

223

pounced upon her ship to destroy it, and all hell
would have broken loose.

CHAPTER 65 - A DESPERATE HOPE

It had been days since Shade had allowed herself to sleep, but she had been bred and trained for endurance. She'd gone for a month without sleep when she was a child and hadn't faltered once in her training, though she'd had a few very realistic hallucinations. She was far from that state now. But unlike the mere lack of sleep, whatever it was that she felt probing her-and not just her body and mind, but deep into her soul or whatever part of her housed her will to live-whatever it was, it was relentless, coming for her night and day, sometimes within an hour of the last try, sometimes within minutes.

It got under the skin of her being, gnawing, draining, siphoning her will. Each time it came, she fought it off. She'd been to see Auryn, Bavn's personal medic, but none of the tests she'd run, none of the nanmagic she'd used had turned up anything.

And now she was facing Bavn in Realspace. She'd noticed that the meetings of the Clans seemed to be taking place more frequently in Realspace in the preceding months. She figured it must be for security reasons, given the rumors of growing hostility in some of the Clans toward the Tears. She had a feeling that things were going that she wasn't aware of, and this bothered her almost as much as whatever was probing her soul.

Bavn's walls displayed an underwater city with towers and turrets and pathways suspended in the water winding around and through the city. Shade wondered if it was from an ancient myth.

"I have to go with my instincts on this one," said Bavn. He stood, pouring water into a wooden goblet. He talked slowly, his voice laden with the concern glimmering in his eyes.

Shade anticipated his next words. *And was that even a small splinter of fear peaking out from the guarded tones of his voice.*

"We haven't been able to identify any outside forces attempting to penetrate your mind or body. No unusual disturbance has existed in the frequencies surrounding you, only in the frequencies within you."

"Which means?" asked Shade, knowing the direction Bavn was taking, beginning to feel the first stabs of resentment.

"I know this may be hard to accept," said Bavn gently, picking up on her tone. "But it's the only avenue we haven't explored."

Shade remained silent, waiting for it.

"I want you to see Elli."

Elli. Elli the witch woman, a throwback to times ancient even in the pre-Quan days. It was said that she was actually born on Earth in the early days, long before the days when the human race had begun to poison the planet, long before it stopped supporting life and its surface became deserted and left hanging in space with the Under Dwellers its only inhabitants. Elli the witch woman, who some said practiced real magic, not just the nanmagic that played the frequencies in ways that most would never understand or be able to replicate. Bavn himself was reputed in some circles to be a sorcerer for his ability to play the frequencies in intuitive ways that defied science and understanding, ways that simply required acceptance or faith. Elli's powers were said to go beyond his. There were rumors of those who had been to see her going mad or dying, their faces frozen in death horror. But as far as Shade knew, those were just rumors.

It was difficult for Shade to keep her voice steady, to show no emotion. Bavn was suggesting that her problem was a mental one. The implication-she was doing this to herself and that the psychosis, or whatever it was, went deeper than nanrepair and deeper than Bavn's nanmagic. It called for a bona fide witch. After her failure with the laser net, she really didn't need this humiliation.

Bavn read through her eyes right into her thoughts. Compassion tempered his eyes and voice. "I don't think you're crazy, Shade. You're one of the most level-headed people I know. I don't necessarily agree with your feelings toward the VRs, but the fact that you can hold such opinions that go against the grain of everything and everyone around you and still voice your feelings without fear or embarrassment suggests tremendous will and stability." He smiled. It was a smile of love. He'd always thought of her as a second daughter, and she'd always known this. "But there's too much at stake, and time is running out. Large events are almost upon us, and you play too key a role in them for anything to be left to chance. Something is wrong. You know it. It's draining your energy. It's

227

affecting your performance, and possibly, your ability to protect Loac."

Shade remained quiet. There was no point in arguing. She would have to see Elli. Bavn had said it. And she knew that he was right. She just hoped that whatever horrors Elli put into her head to cure her wouldn't keep her from getting a decent night's sleep years after she was finished.

CHAPTER 66 - THE INTERFACE

He was aware of the quiet, a world floating noiselessly in a surreal calm, a supernatural calm. The endless images had stopped attacking his awareness in a merciless assault of information that came so fast that all meaning was lost in the vast preponderance of too many meanings. The images were still there, but now they were just under the surface of something he couldn't quite understand at first. It was like there was a screen inside his head, and all the information that had been flowing into him was on the other side of that screen. A screen. It made sense. *It's the interface, the interface to Quannet. It's filtering out the irrelevant, waiting for me to tune into the personally significant.*

The second thing that grabbed his awareness was the blood, metallic and sickening in his mouth. His tongue found the wound where he'd obviously bitten into his cheek. The blood was sticky on his hand and beginning to congeal. On his face it was wet and slippery. He ran his fingers over his nose and eyes and mouth. The blood was wet and slippery under his nose. His eyes were moist with tearing. The blood he'd seen on his hands before passing out must have been from his nose. He wondered how information overload could lead to a nose bleed, but not for long. Buddha was facing him, and behind him, Benji-wide smiles on their faces.

"I forgot what an old man you are now, Abner," said Buddha.

Benji giggled.

229

"But I did some compensating, and you should be OK now."

"You might have done the compensating before you hooked me into that ocean of madness."

Buddha ignored the remark. "How's the interface?"

Abner swallowed his pride and decided it was useless to get pissy with Buddha and simply said, "Keeping me sane for the time being. How does it work?"

"When you want something, you will it."

"I just will it." It was both statement and question. "You mean, I can do anything in Quannet just by wanting it?"

"Within the boundaries of the Imagination Laws," said Benji.

"Imagination Laws?"

"They put certain restrictions on what you can and can't do," said Benji. "For instance, you can't build weapons in Quanspace."

"And if I try?"

"The Imagination Laws don't let your wanting to create weapons become a reality. They just... don't let it happen. There's millions of them-too many for any human to memorize, so they're built right into Quannet's operating system. If you try to do something that's illegal, Quannet doesn't let you do it. If you keep trying to do it, an alert is sent to Control, and a Quanagent comes right into your head and investigates."

"And if the investigation doesn't go well?"

Benji made an imaginary knife cut across his throat as he said, "You just might disappear."

"And these rules are bred right into people and passed on from generation to generation?"

"No," said Buddha. "Just the *connection* to Quannet. That way, if there are changes to Quannet, you don't have to update everybody's genes."

"But by the time most people reach adulthood," said Benji, "they know what they can and can't do. If young children break an Imagination Law, they get a scary image or something else that discourages them from wanting whatever it was they wanted. If they keep it up, they get Quancounselling."

"And do the children disappear if the counseling doesn't work?"

"There have been stories," said Benji grimly.

"And all of this is run by Bella Bjork?"

"She controls Quannet," said Buddha. "Quannet binds most intelligent life in the universe together."

"Makes her almost like a goddess," said Abner dryly.

Buddha nodded. "Some think she is."

"But there are movements," said Benji. "And new technologies, ways to cloak Quannet use and avoid the Imagination Laws, which have been breaking down anyway for over a century now. And now, thanks to Buddha... " He glanced at Buddha approvingly. "We can even hide Quanpresences from Control."

"Which is what I've done for you," said Buddha. "Your presence in Quanspace is clocked. Bella's agents can't track you."

"How did you manage that?" asked Abner.

"I play the strings well," said Buddha, smiling.

"So, what now?"

Buddha winked. "Are you ready to see your daughter?"

CHAPTER 67 - A CASE OF MISSING ABNER

"Where is he!" Where! Where!" If the air had been an onion, Bella's scream would have peeled layers right down to the core-drawn out over the fabric of space-time, shrill, ear-splitting. It was the scream of two millennia of immediate gratification suddenly denied. Lovesong would have covered his ears, but that would have infuriated her further. He was her lover, her mate -it was his place to let her scream assault his ears and enter the rhythms of his body so that he would become part of her fury and anguish.

Flashes of brilliant red, fluorescent purple and bright orange leapt from her eyes. Her face contorted into bone-chilling ugliness, eyes bulging, mouth sneering—nose and cheeks wrinkled into a snarl. Saliva dripped from her lower lip. Curls, packed tightly into a simulation of splashing water, flew out and drooped as she spun her head toward Lovesong. "He's gone! Gone!" she screamed as she pointed through the nanplas window toward the slab of emerline crystal that used to hold Abner Hayes' remains. There was no sign of the gray mist or the small pile of ancient flesh and bone.

Lovesong remained quiet, calm-a tall lithe pole of stability. His browless eyes registered concern. He saw the lines around her eyes, heard the cracks in her long and terrible screams, smelled the confusion of hormones in her sweat. The composure she'd perfected over the last two thousand years in order to keep her metabolism aligned with the needs of longevity was turning into a basket of broken eggs. She was speeding up her own death by letting her fear of death permeate every aspect of her life. She didn't handle failure well. He stepped toward her, his motions suggesting deadliness in their economy of movement, not wasting a single motion. His eyes met her eyes precisely as he Quanned the security systems and knew instantly that they'd picked up nothing.

"How could his happen?" she screamed. "How!"

Lovesong felt a wave of compassion flow through his chest. Bella was the most powerful single being in the universe, yet here she was, so fragile, so helpless, so afraid. "Nothing has entered or left here since your last visit to Hayes," he said. His voice was clipped, precise. "He has to be here somewhere."

Quanscanning every square inch of the fortress, Lovesong found nothing. There wasn't a trace of the remains or the mist anywhere in the thousands of cubic miles of crystal. Scanning the systems of the two million warships that guarded the space surrounding them, he found nothing.

"He's gone!" screamed Bella. "Gone!"

She's becoming hysterical. Lovesong had never seen her go this far over the deep end. The saliva dripping from her mouth gave way to white froth. Bits of it flew into the air as she screamed. He needed to get her under control, fast. In this condition, there was no telling what she would do. She might condemn entire star systems to

234

obliteration if she suspected, just for an instant, that they might have had something to do with this.

"Who dares!" she bellowed. "Who dares!"

Something... something quick. But what? And then it came to him. "We'll track his daughter," he said.

Bella turned her eyes on him angrily, then quizzically. Her face began to soften as the concept began to sink in and take shape in her mind. She crossed one arm in front of her, propped the opposite elbow on it and clasped her hand around the emerline pendant, feeling it twist and curl in her grip. As she thought about his words, she calmed bit by bit, until her eyes stopped flashing and her face relaxed enough to erase the creases and lines. The ugliness of her fear dissolved into the possibilities of Lovesong's plan.

"Yes," she said with a calm but deadly voice. "If he's alive, if he's out there," she pointed to some area beyond the walls with a sweep of her arm. "He'll try to contact her." She smiled wickedly, as the aqua of her eyes displayed small bursts of blue and purple.

Lovesong's groin began to react immediately to the message those colors sent.

Bella stepped up to Lovesong and put her arms around his neck. "You serve me well, darling," she said, her breath hot on his neck.

"I'll set up security... "

She put a finger to his lip. "Later," she said, pushing her body tight into his. "He'll contact her and we'll be ready. Later."

CHAPTER 68 - THE SONG OF YOUR LIFE

Elli's quarters were like none Shade had ever seen. There was no trace of nantech. The stone walls were stone walls. The stone floor was a stone floor. Strange lights hung from the stone ceiling. Long tubes emitted what appeared to be a deep blue light, though it did little to brighten these quarters. White smoke drifted lazily in the air. Dozens of posters hung at strange angles on the walls, scattered almost like huge square leaves like the ones she'd seen in the Archives. Each of them glowed brightly, seemingly from some inner light. It definitely wasn't nantech. She wondered what kind of magic this might be. The furniture was even stranger, couches made of what looked like genuine wood, with multicolored throws tossed absently over them. A low table in the center of the room appeared to be a trunk of some sort with a brightly dyed strip of material thrown on top. A small copper-colored elephant emitted smoke that smelled like musky perfume. It was comforting.

Shade was alone in the room. "Have a seat," said a voice from beyond a doorway strung with beads. "I'll just be a moment." The voice sounded sing-song young. *This is the voice of an ancient witch?* She sat down in a high-backed chair with arms and was immediately surprised at how comfortable it was. It didn't massage her body, change temperature, or make any adjustments to her movements. And it smelled of perfumed smoke. But it was comfortable.

The center of the hanging beads parted, and a head ducked through. It was Elli. Shade was startled by what she saw. The woman passing through the beads was young and surprisingly beautiful, not anywhere near the old crone she'd expected. She had bright-blue eyes and golden-blonde hair that cascaded down to her waist. She wore a headband with a flower motif and a light dress with flower imprints that came down to her knees and, judging from the protruding nipples, no bra. She also wore sandals.

"So you're Shade," she said, smiling and offering her hand to Shade, who was standing now and confused by the gesture. Elli giggled. "It's an old Earth custom," she said. "You take my hand in yours, and we shake them up and down."

Shade took the other woman's hand. It was soft, and though it seemed to emit no force, she had a sense that just under the gentleness of the woman's touch, there were powerful currents of energy. She let Elli shake her hand up and down a few times. If this is what it took to keep this woman's magic tolerable, then she could shake her hand all day.

"You can sit down," said Elli, cheerfully, as she leaned over the trunk table, picked up a pot with steam wafting out of its spout and poured a brown steamy liquid into two cups without handles. She passed one of the cups to Shade. "A very special blend of tea that I find quite comforting."

Seated, Shade sipped from the cup. The liquid was sweet and perfumy. "Delicious."

Elli smiled and sipped from her cup. She folded the fingers of both her hands around the cup and leaned back. "Bavn is concerned about your condition."

"As am I," said Shade.

"He said you've become... listless."

"There are times when I don't feel 100 percent. But that's not what has me worried." Shade sipped from her cup and stared into it, watching the blue light reflecting over the disturbed surface of the liquid. She looked up at Elli and said, "This may sound weird... "

Elli smiled, winked and waved her arm to encompass her room. "Many would consider this weird."

Shade laughed and said, "Guess I'm in the right place then."

"You are." She winked again.

Shade let out a long sigh. "It's like someone or something is invading my soul, going straight for my life force and turning it on me. I have these strange feelings of everything being pointless, of my life having a bitter taste, of my purpose being blunted, of life itself being an intolerable waste of time." She sipped again from her cup. "It's like some force is trying to make me give up on life."

Elli thought a moment and frowned. "I've come across this before. Just a few times, in the last several hundred years."

"And?"

"Same feelings, as though something is burrowing into your will to live and eating away at it until there's nothing left."

238

"And?"

"There were three of them, two men and a woman." Elli sighed and sipped from her cup. "They all died."

Shade frowned. She leaned forward. "You mean, I'm going to die? This thing is going to kill me?"

Elli sipped from her cup again. "*They* died. That doesn't mean that you'll die. I'm trying something different with you."

"Something different?" Suddenly, Shade was intensely aware of the cup in her hand. It seemed thicker, larger. Its surface texture felt less porcelain-like. It felt softer than porcelain. There was something strange about the flower motif. She lifted the cup closer and stared at the flowers. They appeared to be moving, swaying in some porcelain breeze. And now the cup appeared to be moving, as though it were breathing-it undulated in and out. Breathing.

She giggled. "I hate to say this, Elli, but I think this cup is alive. It has a growing garden." Her voice sounded odd to her, as though it were coming from somewhere to her side. And she had just said the word *growing*. What a strange and exciting word, *growing*. It meant big to small. No. That was growing down. It meant small to big, growing up. The posters on the walls appeared to grow in brightness. Her chair appeared to grow in comfort. And did it move? Sitting across from her, Elli, the Wicked Witch of Celtenan, appeared to grow kinder, much smiley-er. She could see the word

239

smiley-er in her head. It bounced. It smiled. This was something she had to tell Elli about.

She looked her straight in the eye and said, "Er." *No, that wasn't it. What was it?* She'd forgotten. The posters were almost on fire with color. Many of them had colorful flower motifs. The flowers swayed back and forth in poster breeze. And there was music that she couldn't identify. It was something she'd never heard before, but something that seemed familiar. She asked Elli, "What music?"

Elli smiled compassionately, so compassionately, so kindly, so knowingly, so comfortingly. It almost brought tears to Shade's eyes. She loved this remarkable woman with the long blonde hair and the flowery head band. Elli opened her mouth slowly. Her lips were perfect. They formed around words and the words drifted over the space between them and into Shade's ears. "That music comes from you, Shade. It's the music of your own bodily rhythms, the music of your self-knowing. It comes from your life experience and from everything with which you define yourself. It's how you feel about yourself. It's the song of your life. Oh, and by the way, this tea contains a drug that was used once on Earth as a fast track to self-awareness. An entire generation of young people used it to expand their horizons. We're using it to alter the way your mind and body works for a while and see if we can get into whatever it is that's trying to get into you."

For some remote reason, this seemed to make sense to Shade. She smiled and nodded as Elli

240

sipped from her cup. She giggled and pointed at the cup. "You... too?" she said.

Elli toasted her with the tiny flowered cup and said, "Damn right. I haven't tripped with another human being in over five hundred years."

Shade pushed herself back in the chair. It seemed to swallow her and make her part of if, but that was all right-being a chair couldn't be all that bad.

CHAPTER 69 - BUZZING

"Buzzing?" Bavn was ready to expect anything from the clone's ship, but buzzing? "And no other noise?"

Zethar wore his less formal light-blue uniform. It went well with his blonde hair. "Except sounds coming from the ship itself. It seemed to be disintegrating, especially as the sound of the buzzing intensified."

"But the buzzing has stopped now?"

"Just stopped," said Zethar as he shrugged. "But the ship is still making some strange sounds, almost like their hull has been breached."

A breached hull in deep space. "And how many aboard?" Bavn asked.

"A few hundred. All clones. And... "

"Yes, Commander?"

"We suspect these may be defected clones, many of them unregistered, most of them marked for removal."

"Not exactly friends of Bella's."

"That's almost a certainty. One of her ships did try to destroy them with a solar bomb."

"And failed."

"Apparently, they were saved by a phone call."

"And just before the buzzing?"

"It looks like they avoided a space berg, a big one."

"And then the buzzing?" Bavn thought for a moment. "It doesn't make any sense."

"Bavn," said Zethar. "It doesn't make any sense that their ship is still in one piece. I'm surprised they survived the initial deep space boost. They appear to have one hell of a cargo of good luck."

Bavn nodded in agreement. "Or something in their cargo that defies logic."

"Any orders, Bavn?"

"Just keep tracking them. I have a feeling they may just play a role in all of this that will work against Bella. If that's the case, then it may work in our favor."

"Or against all of us and in their favor."

"There is that possibility, but let's not forget that they are just clones, soulless copies of human beings."

Zethar nodded thoughtfully. "I'll keep an eye on them."

Bavn nodded as Zethar Quanned out.

***

Zethar gave the order to increase surveillance on the clone ship and to report even the slightest incident. He also gave the order to plot a continuing search and destroy plan several light-years around the clone ship.

Zethar had never seen such a ragtag excuse for a ship's crew in a ship that should have fallen apart after the first crew member sneezed too loud, but it was still out there, still defying the odds. He trusted Bavn's wisdom that the clones might be of use to the Clans, but the very second he deemed they might be a threat, he was going to bring a speedy end to their streak of good luck.

CHAPTER 70 - A VISITOR

The pressure of water against her body was comforting. The water still rippled from Cassie's swim to the center of her pool. She lay on her back, floating, thankful for the breathing module that re-created the sensations and effects of Realspace breathing. Breathing was something Cassie loved, especially the more esoteric forms, like meditative breathing. Her breath control had reached a state of art from which she could slow it to a level that would be just barely lethal in Realspace, but which was achievable even there with years of practice. She'd read stories about Buddhists and yogics on ancient Earth who could stop their breathing long enough to kill the average human. She liked to think that her breathing at this moment was beyond even theirs. This control over her virtual inner processes was comforting, a way to focus on a simple mechanical process that had nothing to do with all the demands and worries that surrounded her life.

Today, it wasn't working. Even with her breath barely a definable act of breathing, the events of her life collided in her mind and sent their little tremors of disquiet though her body. There would be no total relaxation until after the Reality Wars.

Her concern for Sara flowed through her programs like hot blood. It couldn't be ignored. Her only real friend was in danger, and there was nothing she could do about it. Sara wasn't going to listen to her. She wasn't going to lay off the Clans and just let things ride. But did it really matter? Loac had made it clear that Sara should be watching her back. But she'd also said that she didn't want to confront her, or she might have to kill her. So did she want Sara dead, or did she just want her to back off? Considering the hatred that seemed to drive the Clans, she probably wanted her dead, but she would likely want to kill her in a public place-for everyone to see the superiority of the Clans. The Reality Wars.

The Reality Wars. This was going to be her last. She knew that, but it didn't make things any easier. There was SolidHolo now. She'd be ducking in and out of Quanspace and Realspace throughout the Wars, never knowing when the transition would come. She'd be in a position to be killed in the real world and die in Quan. Death suddenly became something more real than it ever had before. As software, she was practically immortal but she was sentient software. She had self-awareness, a will to live and a will to do the things that needed to be done to keep herself alive. In past Wars, she'd been able to keep her instinct for self-preservation under control, doing the things she needed to do without having to kill needlessly like so many of the other competitors playing up to the spectators. But she wasn't sure how much control she would have competing in their world. Would she be able to spare human lives knowing that they might have just a microfraction of an edge on her in Realspace? Would her instincts and reflexes act so fast to protect herself by killing someone that she wouldn't have the time to evaluate her actions and their outcomes?

Well, very soon she would find out.

And now there was Buddha. Buddha. As if she didn't have enough problems, she had ancient gods visiting her in a place where she was supposed to focus on relaxation. And a mile-high Buddha to boot. How messed up was that?

But he'd said that she would be seeing her father again, that he was still alive "in a manner of speaking." What the hell did he mean by that? Was her father dead or was he alive? And when would she be seeing him? Where? How?

She hoped that it would be before the Wars. She wasn't sure just how much the expectation would distract her in the heat of competition, when she needed total focus and not distractions about a father she thought had been dead for centuries. There was a slight movement to her right.

"Hello, sweetheart."

She turned her head and saw her father sitting Buddha-like in the water, looking pretty much the same as he had the last time she saw him, nearly two thousand years ago.

"Dad?"

CHAPTER 71 - MASK

Bright bursts of color exploded before Shade's eyes in tune with the music ringing in her ears, wherever her ears were. She wasn't exactly sure where her body ended and the chair began or where the chair ended and her body began. They were the same thing. She was the chair. The chair was her. The colors of the room bounced with a kind of motion that only colors could manifest. Everything in the room seemed different. Ornaments on tables and shelves appeared to vibrate with inherent meaning. That was it. Everything in the room was suddenly laden with hidden meanings. The teapot vibrated with a profound teapot meaning, something that she'd never known that teapots could express before today, but there it was-teapot meaning vibrating in all its teapotness on the table right in front of her. On the wall, a black man with long hair that seemed to stand straight out like a black aura played an electric guitar whose sound was the sound of all the meanings flowing through the room.

She looked into his dark eyes and acknowledged her understanding of his music. "Huh huh."

She turned her gaze to Elli's face, so full of compassion and love, smiling over perfectly white teeth, blonde hair streaming over her shoulders like molten gold pouring over her breasts. And her eyes! So wide, so loving, so full of joy, so big. Too big. Her irises had all but disappeared. But that was OK. She was still so loving and understanding. She was Shade's friend. Shade smiled at her friend and acknowledged the depth of their friendship. "Huh huh."

She looked around Elli's quarters, gaining insight with every square inch that her eyes covered. Elli was soft like her room, which was made of layers upon layers of quilted rugs, cotton embroideries and soft pillows. Even the stone walls were cushions of some strange coal-like substance, so porous that she knew that if she were to lay her head against the wall, it would give and caress her right into the wall, where she would become one with Elli's quarters. This was Elli, soft with layered meanings, every layer more comforting than the previous.

And the room seemed to move, very slightly, but it moved. What was this movement? She wondered if she had asked that question aloud, but it didn't matter-the room was moving. It was a familiar movement, something she'd seen before. It was a movement like... yes, that was it. The room was breathing. The entire room was alive, and it was playing her music, the music that came from her being, and breathing in tune with her music.

"Huh huh."

She closed her eyes. And there was Loac, staring into her eyes, confused and concerned. Her concern about Shade at the moment was more about her ability to perform in the Wars than whatever it was that burned into her and made her less than she was these days.

Less than she was. What was that all about? She turned her mind back to Loac. She still looked the same, except for something else. What was that

248

in her eyes, in the twist of her mouth, at the corners of her nose? Was that love? Was Loac in love with her? That couldn't be. But hadn't she seen Loac's face like this before? Recently? The last time they had sex? The merging of vapors. She suddenly had an intense sexual rush and felt her entire body shudder as it raged through her.

She heard a voice coming from somewhere in the room. She couldn't focus on its location, but she could hear it distinctly now. "How's your trip, sweetheart?" It was Elli, still smiling, so loving and open. "I... I... " *Oh hell.* "Huh huh."

Elli laughed, a sonorous deep sound that seemed to come straight from her soul. It was a beautiful laugh. Shade wished that Elli would never stop laughing.

She closed her eyes again. This time, Loac wasn't there. Something else was there. She wasn't sure what it was, but she knew that she didn't like it. Her hand went to the handle of her sword. Wait a minute, she thought, this is inside me. I can't cut it out with my sword. But wait. She clenched her hand around nothing and remembered that she'd been told to leave her sword behind before going to Elli's quarters. Shouldn't they have given her some kind of psychic sword? She'd feel good right now with a psychic sword. But she was here, inside her own head, swordless. And something evil was with her. She knew it was evil, she could feel the animosity of its intent.

A cold fear crept along the surface of her back. She looked around and around inside herself, trying to find the source of the evil, but every time she moved her inner awareness, the presence shifted just beyond the spot where she knew it had been a fraction of a second before. It was evading her, hiding from her. Was it afraid of her? Her own fear disintegrated.

This was her body, her mind, her soul. Whatever this thing inside her was, she was still in charge of herself. It was the interloper, the uninvited guest, some kind of soul squatter. But she wasn't afraid. Without warning, it exploded in her face. It was a mask, a wooden mask with blazing wide eyes and a fanged mouth wide open in some obscene scream. Its nostrils flared maliciously. Scraggly white hair wiggled like thread-thin snakes from around the skull to the bottom of its drooling chin. Its jaws were clamped tightly on a vein of something. She knew what it was. It was her life force. This thing was feeding on her life force, draining it. Its eyes pulsated in horror as though it were showing her the horror that she was supposed to feel. It spun madly, throwing bits of her essence into nothingness. Its eyes blazed fire into her face.

Nice try. But she'd seen worse.

She was Tears of Blood. She stared right into its ugly frantic eyes, through the layers of mask that seemed like layers of quilts peeling away as she stared deeper and deeper past fibers that had no meaning and structures of material that possessed no power right into the center of the mask.

Her world spun out of control, and she passed out.

***

She had no idea how long she'd been unconscious. She knew only that she would never forget what she'd seen in the eyes of the mask, that she knew now was the thing that had been probing her life force for the last few weeks.

Elli was still sitting across from her, smiling, radiant. "Feeling better?"

Shade felt within herself, smiled and said, "There was a mask."

"Did you look into its eyes?"

"Yes. It was... " She still had a hard time believing the absurdity of what she'd seen.

"Was there a cafe?"

CHAPTER 72 - THE CORMORANT

Of all the thousands of the Gamblers spread throughout the universe, the most powerful was Kingston Cormorant, known as the Cormorant. He never gambled, but at one level or another, he ran almost every casino and outlet where money could be made on an uncertain outcome from one end of known existence to the other. Some said that he was richer even than Bella Bjork, and no one knew what he looked like in Realspace.

Tonight he presented himself as a twenty-foot-high gold coin with bouncing round eyes and a wide white smile. His nose was long and pointed.

"Of course I appreciate that you granted our request to run the Wars in both realities," said the coin in a youthful, almost boyish, voice. "But the fact that you remind me of this now leads me to suspect that you may have a request of your own to make of me, the Cormorant." The smile widened until it touched both edges of the coin.

Bella, presenting as a cocktail waitress with mesh nylons and garters peeking out from under a skimpy black skirt, sat on a wooden bar with her legs crossed, smoking a long black and gold cigarette. She knew that the man behind the coin was drooling, and she knew that she needed him. For now. She was tired of the Gamblers. They'd carved their own little empire inside her own, mostly by booking the Reality Wars, gaining incredible power and influence every hundred years and building on it between the Wars. And now they were too powerful for her to close down. Somehow they'd managed to keep their wealth cloaked from her Quanspies. But they'd provided her with financial backing more than once, and they had other resources into which she had tapped from time to time.

This was one of those times.

"Your insight never ceases to impress me, Kingston." She imagined the frown spreading across his Realspace mouth for hearing his real name and not his chosen persona. But she wasn't about to start calling him Cormorant. "And yes," she said, crossing her legs wide and quickly enough to give him a glimpse of red panties. "I do have a request to make. I've lost something, and I want to get it back. Cost is of no concern, neither are lives. Kill worlds if you must."

"This must be something very important to you," said the coin. "May I inquire into its nature?"

Or you could just damn well ask what it is. Bella hated Kingston's pretentious, drawn out way of speaking. She felt like she was talking to a child going on a first date. But it would be over soon. When she had the Texture, she would be coming after the "Cormorant" and his cohorts all over the universe, and she would wipe them out. "It's an old acquaintance," she said, blowing a long plume of white smoke into the coin's face.

The coin coughed and smiled, and licked its lips with an obscenely huge red tongue. "A person?" You want me to find a person for you? Would this be a physical person or a virtual personality?"

Bella smiled and drew on her cigarette again, blowing another plume into the coin. Kingston seemed to savor this, judging by the action of his Quanpresence tongue. "Something in between," she said. "Not quite human, not quite virtual. More like a pile of dog shit surrounded by fumes."

The coin considered this for a moment, not sure if Bella was serious or poking fun at him. "And may I inquire as to whether this... pile with fumes has a name."

"Its name is Abner Hayes."

The coin's eyes raised. "*The* Abner Hayes? The one who gave sentience to VRs?"

"I've been keeping his remains and intellectual or spiritual essence—or whatever you want to call it—prisoner for the last two thousand years. Recently, he disappeared."

"Do you have any idea of the proximity of his disappearance?" asked the coin.

Bella held down a flare of irritation. "Somewhere in the universe, I believe." She blew smoke into his face again.

The coin smiled lasviciously. "Yes, I suppose that would be the place to look."

"And remember," she said. "I'm considering your other requests, and I think we can work together... " She recrossed her legs, showing an even larger patch of red this time. "On many things."

The coin licked its lips.

Many things, like your extermination. In Realspace, Bella licked her own lips, slowly, sensually. The thought of mercilessly killing her enemies had this effect on her.

CHAPTER 73 - A VERY STUPID THING

"Nice pool you have here, sweetheart," said Abner, seated cross-legged on the water, hands just below his navel, fingers entwined. Tiny ripples radiated across the surface of the water as he spoke. He appeared calm, though his eyes were slightly swollen, beginning to redden. But his voice was calm.

Cassie turned and the lower part of her body sank into the water. She treaded effortlessly with just her shoulders and head breaking the surface. She stared at her father, her mouth working slowly, lower lip quivering, eyes questioning and unbelieving. She tightened her lips and narrowed her eyes angrily. "You left us." she said coldly. "You left us. It killed Mom."

Abner stared into her eyes but remained silent. His daughter had two thousand years of rage and hurt to release, and he was going to let her do it.

"Where did you go?" Her voice began to rise, losing its coolness, giving into anger and pain. "We waited. We waited and you never came. We searched. Mom had herself deleted. Deleted! You hurt her so bad she couldn't go on living." Tears streamed from her eyes, tiny drops plinking into the water. "We waited for over two hundred years. And you're still alive? You could have come to us? You could have stopped Mom's death? You ditched us, you fucking bastard! You ditched us!" The ripples emanating from Cassie turned into wavelets as she spoke. Abner bobbed in the waves of his daughter's fury.

She began sobbing and just stared at him, her face twisted with grief and questioning. She opened her mouth several times as if to say something but closed it and sobbed quietly.

Abner took a deep breath, causing ripples to span out across the surface of the wavelets right up to the edges of the pool. He spoke slowly. "I'm so very sorry, sweetheart." And now tears broke from his eyes as well. He took another deep breath. "I did something very stupid."

Cassie glared at him, the rage returning, eyes boring into his as if to say, "You're damn right you did something stupid." But she stayed silent.

"I worked out a program that I thought would allow me to turn myself into software." He stared at the surface of the water around him, as though looking for justification or reason on its swaying surface. "It didn't work."

"I'll say it didn't work," sobbed Cassie "It... " She breathed in sobs for a minute.

Abner waited for her to speak. When she remained silent, he said, "Bella Bjork was waiting for me."

Cassie looked confused.

"She set a trap for me."

"A trap?" asked Cassie sarcastically. "Bella Bjork?"

"She was still after my program, thinking it would help her to live forever."

"But why didn't she just try to kidnap me and Mom again?"

"Because it didn't work the first time. Without my program, you and your mother would die. She needed to get the program from me."

"But then... " Cassie looked thoughtful, doubtful. "Why would she let me live all this time? Even after your program for sentient VRs was re-created by her programmers? That was over a hundred years ago."

"She needed you to compete in the Reality Wars." He sent more ripples across the water with another deep breath. "Your performance in the Wars was one of her devices for keeping control of Quannet, of helping humans to accept the presence of VRs. She didn't want wars in Quannet between humans and VRs."

Cassie looked up, then down, then at the water around her, which was beginning to calm as she calmed. "So, she's been using me for the last thousand years?"

"I'm afraid so."

A dark fury started to fill Cassie's eyes. "All this time I was told that everything I had came from yours and Mom's Quanstates. But it was really coming from Bella?"

"She confiscated everything I had." He sighed ripples across the water. "I'm back and I'm going to make things right between us."

Before Cassie had a chance to respond and before either had a chance to resist, father and daughter were Quanned out of Cassie's pool and into a new space across the universe.

CHAPTER 74 - ALMOND FLAVORED

She almost got you this time. She gets better with each one she sees.

"She's not a problem," said the Assassin. He sipped almond-flavored coffee from a large cup with gold inlaid on a light-blue ceramic surface. The gold formed patterns of snakes twining around swords. If you looked closely, you would notice that the snakes were moving continuously from sword to sword. "I've gotten better myself since the last time she messed with me."

That stuff she gave to the last one to smoke allowed her to see you.

"That stuff is called marijuana, and what she saw was a man sitting outside a cafe drinking coffee. The drug she smoked caused her to hallucinate. She could have seen cows jumping over the moon. She'll never... "

This one saw you as well. The only difference was the flavor of the coffee. The drug she gave Shade was much more powerful than the marijuana. She may have seen your face.

"No one sees my face."

How can you be sure?

"I'm sure."

I'm not convinced.

"Nobody's asking you to be convinced."

You may have to go back to your old ways to finish this one. How do you feel about that?

"She'll get a beautiful death."

You're running out of time.

"She'll be ready to die when she arrives at the Wars."

Elli brings a wild card into your plans. Perhaps kill her the old way, then give the other a beautiful death.

The Assassin sipped from his cup. Steam curled around the brim. In this place the coffee was always hot. "First, I'd never get past the Celtenan defenses. Second, I'm not being paid to kill the old woman. Third, I beat her before, I'll beat her again. Fourth, do you ever shut up?"

You should know.

***

"How did you know that?" asked Shade. She was sitting on the couch beside Elli, who held her left hand, stroking it gently.

"The last one saw a man in a cafe drinking coffee," said Ellie. "He wore a beret... and it appeared that he was talking to himself."

"What did he look like?"

"She didn't see his face clearly. It was distorted. She could barely pick out his lips moving as he spoke."

"What happened to her?"

"Three days later, her body was found in her quarters on the Marl asteroid. She'd been stabbed in the heart. Strange, though."

"Strange?" asked Shade. "How?"

"She had a peaceful, almost happy look in her face." She paused. "Did you see his face?"

259

"Yes." She shuddered visibly, and felt a cold chill run up her back. "He had two faces."

"Two faces?

"One normal face, and another one, a smaller one in his left cheek. It looked like it was talking with the big one, but the smaller one's mouth didn't move. What can I do to defeat this thing?"

"Only one thing, dear." She smiled and squeezed Shade's hand. "You need to keep your will to live strong. You've seen his face. For some reason, I think this may lessen his power over you." She squeezed Shade's hand tighter. "I think he kills by stealing your will to live. I don't know how he does this, but I think, by the time he's finished, you almost want to die. I think you'll be safe while you're on Celtenan. The others were killed on their home asteroids, after they left Celtenan. I'm sure that he finishes the job physically with a weapon. I'm guessing that he'll make his move when you and Loac arrive at Canak for the Reality Wars."

"You really think that's when he'll come for me?"

"I think that will be his only opportunity."

Shade smiled widely. "Good. Then that's when I'll kill him."

"Be careful, though. He'll be trying to get into your head more and more frequently right up till the Wars."

Shade thought about this a moment. "Maybe I'll set up a little trap for him."

260

CHAPTER 75 - A HOLE IN THE HEAD

Outside the dome, light exploded in colorful bursts as a meteor storm obliterated itself against a nanshield powerful enough to stop a planet. Seated in his command chair, Nels Horne watched, fascinated, even though he'd seen this thousands of times. It had a calming effect, and he needed to be calmed.

Below him, standing off to the side on the nanmarble floor, Chaine glowered. The wires twisting around his lips were bright red. Nels had never seen them red before. *What the hell is red supposed to mean? God, I hate these people*.

"The surveillance of the Cappel Dark Matter Field has not been stopped," said Chaine coldly.

Nels regarded him calmly, saying nothing. In the pitch black of deep space behind him, meteors exploded noiselessly in flashes of blue and orange light. With his right index finger, he touched one of the manual controls on his chair and floated smoothly down until he was a few feet directly in front of Chaine. His Black Tree Mission Regulator stood unflinching, lips glowing, anger smouldering in his eyes. Slowly, Nels touched his feet to the floor and stood. He towered over the squat Clansman. He entertained the idea of thrusting his jaw down and burying his nansteel goatee in whatever brain inhabited the head of this vile little man.

Instead, he smiled coldly. "Something is going on there," he said. "Something that might have an impact on our mission, Mission Regulator."

Chaine frowned. "Whatever is going on there is no longer any business of ours. Bella's orders are to focus on reaching the Texture."

"First," said Nels sharply.

Puzzlement replaced the frown on Chaine's face, but he said nothing.

Nels leaned forward and downward. "First, Mission Regulator. Bella wants us to reach the Texture first. Why do you think she sent an armada?" He swept his right arm in an arc to include most of the dark view outside the dome, where both men knew vast numbers of Bella's warships slipped through the folds of deep space. "We need to get there first and set up a blockade to make sure that we're the only ones who get there. The clone ship... "

"The clone ship has a breached hull. The clones are no longer a concern of ours."

Nels' eyes narrowed angrily. He pushed his face to within inches of Chaine's face, causing Chaine to back up slightly. "The clone ship... can go to hell... Mission Regulator," He wanted desperately to thrust his chin down. "Someone or something from the Cappel Field contacted the clone ship using an impossible technology and saved them from my solar bomb. There's no way they could have escaped that fast-not that ship, not that crew. I don't know what's in the Cappel Field, but until I do... "

"You'll withdraw your surveillance immediately," said Chaine venomously. "That order comes directly from Bella."

Nels glared at Chaine, wanting to kill him on the spot, but he knew that he was beaten. The order had come from Bella. Herself. Although Nels was Commander, Chaine was in charge of the whole Cappel Field incident. Time to eat crow, gracefully. He Quanned into Commandspace and ordered the surveillance of the Cappel field terminated. Still glaring at the Clansman, he said, "It's been withdrawn, Mission Regulator." He nodded slightly. "You can go now."

Without changing expression, Chaine turned and walked toward the portal.

"One other thing, Mission Regulator," said Nels.

Chaine turned. His wires were back to gold. "Commander?" he asked, his voice tainted with animosity.

Nels passed his right hand slowly over his goatee. "If you ever interrupt me again when I'm speaking, I'll put a hole in your head."

***

As the portal closed after Chaine, Nels knew that the only thing keeping him alive was his experience and the closeness of his mission to completion. Within moments of securing the Texture, he knew that he would be dead.

How're you going to get yourself out of this one, Commander?

CHAPTER 76 - FEEDING BELLA

"It was pure chance," said Bavn. "No security compromises or treason was involved. A young captain acted impetuously."

"His impetuosity could have upset our plans," said Wrenne. A long strand of blonde hair shone with the glow of the golden eye it covered, creating a luminous backlight on her forehead. Overhead, the asteroids of Blood Citadel profiled sharply against the gaseous glow of Vala. "But I agree, this looks like it was mere chance. The captain involved has a history of carelessness."

"Five hundred years of planning and we almost lose it to carelessness from the other side," said Triste through a holographic image beamed to his spot in the circle. "And they picked the one ship with the one bomb that would compromise the whole operation. A detailed search would have revealed it. I would have been forced to give the attack command before their security party boarded, and we would have been forced to play our hand sooner. This was a close one."

Bavn nodded agreement along with others in the circle, most of them over seven feet high-a circle of giants in furs and armor. "God was on our side in this one," said Bavn. "And our plans continue. For now, though, we have another problem." He looked at the blue kilted man to his left and said, "Carlse... ?"

Carlse nodded, his face dark, eyes grave. "Brann of the Eyes of Blood Clan Quanned me a few days ago. He said that he had something of great importance to tell me. We were to meet. He has since disappeared. No one in the Eyes-not even his family-knows where he is." He looked around at the circle of giants. "Brann was a good friend of mine and has always been a supporter of peace and cooperation among the Clans. His disappearance at this time is suspicious." He looked at Wrenne. "As high priestess of security, Wrenne, what do you say?"

Wrenne nodded. "I agree with you. The timing is close to large events and too close to other things that have been happening as well."

"Such as?" asked Bavn.

"I'll let Triste answer that." She nodded toward his holo projection.

"An hour ago I reported what seemed to be a security concern to Wrenne," he said. "Certain of our naval assets have been cloaking their Quansends. These are not spread randomly through the navies... they recur within the same ships-all of them belonging to the same groups of Clans."

"I've seen strange things in my dreams," said the Owene, seeming larger than normal in her flowing red robe. "Red snakes eating blue snakes. Stars colliding. Babies eating babies. These things mean something. I intuit their nature as the sameness of things turning on itself. Rebellion. Treason. War within."

"The preponderance of cloaking tracks to the Womb of the Universe ships," said Triste. "Traditionally, they've been lightly armed ambassadorial ships. Recently, they've been arming heavily."

A long slow sigh flowed from Bavn's lips as his chest heaved slowly. "Maebh." It was almost a whisper. "She never forgave us for the Wars." He looked at Triste. "How many have they won over?"

"About a fifth, counting all of our fleets."

Bavn winced. "That many?"

"It's not enough to defeat us," said Triste.

"But enough to weaken us, especially at a time when we can least afford it."

"Only a small number of the ships we suspect are in the armada going to the Texture. They can be eliminated, if need be."

"And the rest?" asked Bavn.

"Perhaps we find a way to feed them to Bella."

CHAPTER 77 - COMPANY'S COMING

"Where is this place?" asked Cassie, looking around the cavern with Abner and Benji standing in front of her and what looked like a six-inch-high Buddha sitting very Buddha-like in the air behind them.

"It's a place called the Cappel Dark Matter Field," said Abner. "It's pretty far away from home."

Cassie looked at her father and giggled. Abner gave her a questioning look. "I know all about the Cappel Field, Dad," said Cassie. "They didn't have Quannet where you've been for the last two thousand years, did they?" Cassie caught the look of regret that flashed into her father's eyes and flickered out. It suddenly occurred to her that, even living her own personal hell all these years with her parents gone, it was possible that Abner's hell may have been much worse.

She walked up to him and put her hand on his face. "I'm sorry, Dad. That was kind of thoughtless, wasn't it? I mean... " She lifted her hand off Abner's face, and her eyes filled with intense curiosity that quickly changed to astonishment. "I can feel you!" She looked around excitedly. "This isn't Quanspace! This is Realspace! I know it is. I can feel the tightness. I'm in SolidHolo! Dad, how did you do this?"

Abner pointed a thumb behind him. "You can thank Buddha."

Cassie looked at the seated figure floating in air and smiled at him. "I'll get to you in a minute." She threw her arms around her father and hugged him tightly. "I can feel you, Dad. I can feel you in Realspace. I missed you so much all those years. It was so lonely with you and Mom gone. I kept trying to find you, even after Mom died. I hated you for what you did to us... or what I thought you did to us, but I kept hoping to find you, to find out why you left us. I hated you, Dad, but I still loved you."

Abner held tightly, patting her back, eyes teary. "I'm sorry, sweetheart. I should never have tried to do something so stupid. I just wanted to be with you and your mother all the time. I thought that if I could become software, then I could live online with the both of you without ever having to leave you for the... "

"It's OK, Dad. I understand. And I remember how much you loved me and Mom. You risked your life for us when Bella had us kidnapped. That's why it didn't make any sense to either of us that you would just leave us without any warning, or any kind of message or reason."

Abner kissed her on the forehead. "I'm back now. And I won't ever leave you again."

Hearing this, Buddha lifted an eyebrow.

Cassie noticed. "What?" She pulled away from her father and faced Buddha.

Buddha remained silent.

"I saw that," said Cassie accusingly.

"Saw what?" asked Abner.

"The look in his face when you said you wouldn't leave again. I didn't like it."

Buddha sighed deeply as only Buddha could sigh... from a deep inner peace that had just been rippled. "Your father and I have things to do."

"Then I'll join you in your *things*," said Cassie defiantly.

"You have other things to do," said Buddha.

"Hold it a minute," said Abner. "You didn't mention any *things* that we have to do."

"You didn't ask," said Buddha, shrugging.

"And what exactly are these thing?" asked Abner.

"Changing the universe," said Buddha with a wink.

"And me?" asked Cassie.

"The same, only in another place."

"And me?" asked Benji.

Buddha smiled. "Back to Soul Ship."

"I don't get to change the universe?"

"Of course you do. But you'll be doing your thing from Soul Ship."

Benji smiled and offered his hand to Cassie. "I'm Benji."

Cassie smiled as she took his hand. "Please to meet you, Benji. I'm Cassie."

Benji's smile stretched the width of this face. "I know. The whole universe knows you." He began to blush. Cassie giggled.

"Hate to break up a party," said Buddha. "But we have company on the way."

"Company?" asked Abner and Cassie.

"Black Tree," said Buddha. "Lots of them. Be here in minutes. Plus, Bella has Quansors on the way trying to track down this location. I'm guessing she's been monitoring you to find out if your father contacts you."

Anger flashed in Abner's eyes. "I haven't seen my daughter in two thousand years and you're saying we have to go now?"

"We'll all meet again," said Buddha. He snapped his fingers and the cavern was empty. Not far away, a fleet of warships released hundreds of solar bombs into the area of the Cappel Dark Matter Field where the cavern was about to disappear.

***

Cassie opened her eyes. She was back in her pool, floating quietly. It had all happened with the quickness of a dream, but she knew that she'd been with her father, that he was alive and had been all these years. In a deep place, she'd always known.

***

The emerald-green snake winding around the gold sword was happy to hear that a large section of the Cappel Dark Matter Field had been turned into dust.

The wires on Chaine's lips glowed blue. He would live to serve Bella another day.

***

Lovesong sighed. *Missed you this time, Abner Hayes, but you'll try to see her again. I know you will.*

270

CHAPTER 78 - A SHORT CUT

Jeli's heart dropped into his stomach at the view through his Quantrols. The port side of Soul Ship had an eighty-foot-long hole in it. Lifeless crew members floated into space, ones that had held on for dear life when their cabins decompressed and everything not nailed down rushed into the void. They looked stiff and glassy as they floated, surrounded by blood and body parts like frozen entrails dangling from their lifeless bodies.

"I've locked down all portals and connecting compartments, Chief Magistrate," said Starr. "The rest of the ship is airtight."

"How many people were in the breached cabins, Sheriff Starr?" asked Jeli.

He took a few seconds to check his Quantrols. He took a deep breath, let it out slowly and said, "One hundred and seventy-three."

The other crew members looked at each other ominously, except Lation, who seemed completely unphased, floating in a command chair by the console. He looked around at the others and lifted his arms, palms out as though to ward off their glares. "What?" he said. "Maybe some of them were still flies."

Skype dipped a forefinger into drool on her lip and flicked it at him. "And maybe you should be making the rounds, looking for injured people, practicing medicine."

"Not the way it works," said Lation, propping his feet up on the console. "They report to the infirmary. I tend to them." My Quantrols are showing an empty infirmary."

"The infirmary has been breached," said Field.

"I'm not the one who changed course," said Lation.

"What the hell is that supposed to mean?" asked Jeli as a deep flush spread over his face. "We were about to be solar bombed."

"Just saying," said Lation, shrugging.

"Shut up, asshole," said Skype. "If the Chief Magistrate hadn't changed course, we'd all be space dust by now. Not that it wouldn't have been an improvement in your case."

Lation raised his eyebrows in mock insult. "Chief Magistrate, I'd like to lodge a harassment complaint against Colonel Skype. As this ship's medical officer, I-"

"Shut up," said Jeli, disgusted. "Save it for when we get home." He scanned the damage again. "If we get home."

Starr, who was also checking the damage, said, "I think we have the breach contained enough to continue, Chief Magistrate. Supplies and life support are all intact." He looked around at the walls and false control equipment of the command deck and smiled. "Maybe this ship wasn't called Soul Ship for nothing. It looks like we can continue our journey... " He clenched his lips together and opened them with a popping sound. "Away from the Texture."

At that moment, the phone rang beside Lation. He gave it a puzzled look and turned to Jeli. "This is the thing you were talking about with Parx's voice in it?"

"Pick it up," said Jeli. "Hold the top part to your ear. Speak into the lower part."

Slowly, Lation did as he was told, noticing Skype moving toward him in what he assumed was a threatening manner. He listened for a moment and turned to Jeli, holding the phone out to him. "It's for you."

Jeli walked over, took the phone from Lation and put it to his ear. A moment later, he handed the phone back to Lation and turned toward Starr. "It was Benji Parx again... with new coordinates. We're going to an anomaly, and Benji is going to join us there."

"An anomaly?" asked Field. "You mean the Texture?"

"No," said Jeli. "Apparently, a short cut to the Texture." He looked around at his executive crew, and smiled. "In the meantime, maybe we should all go to our quarters and put on some clothing."

Maybe it was some psychic remnant of being flies that caused his executive crew to overlook the otherwise obvious fact that they were all naked.

CHAPTER 79 - POUTING (A.K.A. STEWING)

"You're pouting."

"I'm not pouting."

"You're doing something like pouting."

"What I'm doing is called stewing."

"Stewing?"

"It means being withdrawn and unhappy because I only got to see my daughter for a few minutes before you whisked me off to this place."

"The other place no longer exists."

"So we had to leave. But couldn't Cassie have come with us?"

"She's being traced by Bella. She knows you'll try to contact your daughter, and she'll destroy galaxies to get you back."

"So, I can only see my daughter for a few minutes at a time because she's being traced?"

"For now, Abner, yes. But I'm working on it... we're working on it."

"Working on what?"

"Erasing the registry."

"What registry?"

"The one containing the names and numbers for every birth human and clone in the universe."

"And what will that do?"

"It'll make everyone equal."

"So I only get to see my daughter a few minutes at a time till then?"

"You get to see her once more before then. For a few minutes."

"A few minutes."
Silence.
"Pouting again?"
"I'm not pouting."

CHAPTER 80 - THE DEADLIEST KILLERS IN THE UNIVERSE

"A man with a face in his cheek?" Loac seemed almost angry. "In a Quanspace cafe? Drinking coffee? Talking to himself? Wearing a beret?" Each burst of speech was like an accusation, an attack. "That witch, Elli, tricked you into doing drugs. You hallucinated all this."

"It wasn't a hallucination. It was real. I saw the man who's been digging into my head, into my life force." Shade had her nancouch set so that it kept her upright. This was no time for relaxation. "I know the face in the cheek part sounds absurd, but it *was* in Quanspace. It might have been symbolic or something. But I know... I know that he's the one who's been doing this to me."

Images of misty fiords panned across Bavn's walls, casting a quiet, reflective light over the room. Loac, sitting in her ivory chair, looked skeptical.

Bavn reclined in a lounge chair, wearing his white robe, hood down, hands clasped under his chin. He looked thoughtful.

Noticing this, Loac said, "Father, you really don't think this crazy figment from some ancient drug really means anything, do you?"

Bavn took his time answering, his deep-blue eyes wistful. "I've known Elli for centuries. She may seem a little crazy sometimes. Unlike most of us, she's never lost her sense of humor, even after the Clan Wars. She's not of this age. Her spirit dwells on old Earth, in the traditions and stories of cultures we've long since forgotten, many of them not even recorded in the Archives. She's not stupid. She's not a witch. And she's not crazy. Her awareness goes in different directions than what the rest of us deem to be normal."

He paused for a moment. "No one else here was able to look into you, Shade, and see what was causing the nightmares and the drops in energy. I was the one who sent the three others to her. She told me what happened to them. I knew of this strange apparition you saw before I sent you to her. All we knew about was the beret and the cafe... and the fact that he talked to himself. Their life energy was drained from them, and then they were killed, physically."

Loac spread her arms apart. "So then, you think that this... apparition is real?" She looked concerned now. "You think that someone will try to kill Shade after destroying her will to live?"

"Like Elli says, he's been doing this for hundreds of years." He rubbed his hands together and re-clasped them, resting his chin on them. "There have been stories of assassins used by Bella for thousands of years. They have access to her technologies, to her wealth, to all the resources they need to become the deadliest killers in the universe. My guess is that this may be one of them."

Shade stood up. "Then it's Bella who wants me dead!"

"Why?" Loac was standing as well. "*I'm* the one who's supposed to beat the girl and prove once and for all that Bella's so-called sentient VRs are no match for humans. Why would she attack Shade?"

Bavn spread his hands apart. "I don't know. Possibly to distract you, take the edge off your skills just before the Wars. Attacking you outright would be too blatant, something the Gamblers might see as manipulation. It might hurt their profits, and I suspect that the Gamblers hold considerable power over Bella. This is a way of coming at you from the side."

Loac smiled evilly. "I can hardly wait to slit the bitch's throat."

Calmly, Bavn turned his eyes toward her. "Never mind Bella. She'll be taken care of. You need to do just one thing... focus on the Reality Wars. You and Shade leave for Canak tomorrow. That's where this assassin is most likely waiting. Canak is a free planet, open to everyone without question. There's no security other than what we bring ourselves. He'll have certain advantages, and if he can get to you psychically here, then he'll be even stronger on Canak."

Loac shook her head slowly. "I'll be glad when our plan comes to fruition and our enemies choke on their own hatred... "

"Think only of winning the Reality Wars, of defeating the girl. That's your mission, what you've been groomed for." He looked at Shade. "And your role is to aid her in defeating the girl, no matter what the cost."

Shade nodded, her mouth set firmly. "And I think I may have an idea about how to unbalance this assassin."

Bavn raised an eyebrow as he leaned forward.

CHAPTER 81 - CHANGING HANDS

It was a mixture of Old West saloon and Riviera casino, the biggest and busiest Quansino in the universe, and it was owned by a man they called the Cormorant. Hundreds of thousands of Gamblers lost everything they had nonstop, twenty-four hours a day. They were from all points in the universe, and most of them, after losing their savings, their homes and everything else they owned, would quietly kill themselves in Realspace. Losing everything at the Las Quan would be their last hurrah, their last big splurge before jumping into the void.

At the moment, attendance was down. It had been dipping for over a decade as the Reality Wars neared, with people saving their money for the Big Event, the one that came once a century. The Cormorant couldn't have cared less; after all, he controlled most of the betting on the Wars and this would be his most profitable year ever.

Through an oval window in his office, he overlooked the gambling with a sense of deep satisfaction. He'd started small, betting on air cars on his home planet, Attia, over fifteen hundred years ago. He was good at it. And smart. He understood that business acumen would take him further than luck, so when he'd saved enough, he built his own casino on Quannet, Las Quan. Maybe it was the name. Maybe it was the fact that he sponsored the first technology that allowed people in Realspace to taste and smell the things they ate and drank in Quanspace. Las Quan had a four-star restaurant and the most well-stocked bar in Quanspace. And there were the "intensifiers," special Quantunes that intensified the excitement, the thrill of winning, the lights, the noise, the sex. There had been ways to intensify emotions and experiences for hundreds of years but nothing like the Las Quan experience.

Then he hit on his masterpiece. He contacted all the biggest Gamblers in the universe, the ones who controlled at least 90 percent of the gambling, and they formed a cartel. He gave money to Bella Bjork to finance some of her ventures. In return, she eliminated Gamblers who didn't join the cartel. She made him the most powerful Gambler in the universe and now he was almost as powerful as Bella.

The time to use that power was near.

For a man more than fifteen hundred years old, he was remarkably youthful, like someone in his late teens or early twenties. He sat in a high-backed red leather chair with shiny brass trim. His bright-blue eyes sparkled under the crystal chandeliers. Spread before him at table after table were the most powerful of all the Gamblers. Over a hundred of them, dressed in Stetson Royal Flush fur hats, wide-brimmed Panamas, black vests with gold-and-red trim, thick moustaches, long dress overcoats-the women in fish net nylons with garters prominently displayed, corseted and tied, long red and blonde hair curling and flowing over their blushed cheeks and bare shoulders.

They all glittered and sparkled as they drank, bourbon and scotch and beer in heavy glass mugs for the men and champagne for the women.

The Cormorant was king of it all.

"His" people were laughing and joking, smoking cigars so big and wide they barely fit into the mouths of the smokers. The women flirted madly, the men stuck hundred dollar bills into their garters and bras. It was a party and the Cormorant loved parties, especially the ones where he was the focus of attention, and tonight, that's exactly what he was. The excitement in his office was almost palpable, even in Quanspace. The Cormorant had good news and everyone knew it.

He reached under the polished oak table in front of him and pulled out a silver Derringer with ivory inlay. He pointed it at the ceiling and pulled the trigger. The "bang" from the gun would have been barely enough to get their attention. What did the trick were the diamonds that fell out of the ceiling when the gun went off. Thousands of them, sparkling and flashing as they fell onto the tables and heads of the whooping and hollering crowd.

The Cormorant was wise in the ways of feeding loyalty with attention to greed.

"They're yours to keep!" he yelled. Each of the diamonds was registered and tracked to its counter in Realspace. The mob went nuts.

After they'd quieted to a dull roar, the Cormorant made his announcement. As he began to speak, the crowd quieted further; everyone focused on the Cormorant. "My advisors... " He winked and smiled. "Who some would call... my spies... " Quiet

281

laughter rippled through the crowd. "Are certain. Bella and the Clans will be going to war soon. It's unavoidable." Dead silence. "In response to this tragedy, I've made some special arrangements." He let them think about that for a moment. "A special Quanspace where we can control betting on who wins, who takes the greatest number of casualties, who wipes out the greatest number of planets, and who shows the greatest ingenuity in surprise weapons development. And if anyone has ideas for new categories, I'm all ears."

The room was quiet for a minute, everyone staring at the Cormorant, digesting his words, making sense of them. And then the cheering started. For them, a war that would send the universe reeling with death and destruction, that would strip life out of entire planetary systems... would be profitable.

"Oh, and I've been talking to Bella." Eyes rolled as dozens in the crowd made nasty comments. Several of the men let out long loud belches. "She wants us to keep our eyes open for none other than Abner Hayes."

"He's dead!" yelled a tall man with a handlebar moustache.

"He's just a myth," hollered another.

Murmurs and chatter spread through the room.

The Cormorant raised his hands for silence. "He's alive. Bella's been keeping him prisoner for two thousand years."

A wave of whispers and exclamations washed over the sparkling assembly.

282

The Cormorant pointed his Derringer at the ceiling again. Silence. He smiled. "He escaped."

There was a brief hush of disbelief, followed by an explosion of laughter and sneering remarks, some still unbelieving.

"Escaped from Bella? No one escapes from... "

"Then it must be true that... "

"The Queen is dead... "

"She must be up to... "

He fired another bullet. Nothing dropped out of the ceiling this time, though heads turned upwards expectantly. "I don't know how he escaped." He let that sink into the silence that followed. "But I've suspected for some time now that the Queen of the Universe is slipping. She's losing it. Her power wanes as our power increases."

Cheers erupted throughout the room.

"If any of you hears anything at all about Hayes. Pass it on to me and I'll give you my home planet."

Wild cheering swept through the room.

"A war between Bella and the Clans is anyone's guess as to the outcome. Both are in disarray across the universe as she focuses her attention on the Texture."

"Hundred million says it's just another anomaly!" yelled a weasel-faced man in a too-big black Stetson with a red brim.

"Done!" returned the tall man with the handlebar moustache.

The crowd roared.

My kind of people. The Cormorant fired another shot into the ceiling. No one looked up this time.

"I'm sure we all have our shares of booking on the Texture, but now I'd like to talk about the biggest gambling event since the invention of the Royal Flush... " The crowd quieted as glasses touched lips and mouths sucked deeply on gold-ringed cigars, all eyes intent on the Cormorant. "In the past, entire worlds and planetary systems changed hands after the Reality Wars. After the 10th Centennial Reality Wars, the *universe* will change hands!"

In Realspace, the thundering cheers that broke from the Gamblers would have shaken the foundations of the Cormorant's buildings for miles around.

CHAPTER 82 - GALAXIES

"Is everyone else seeing what I'm seeing?" Chief Magistrate Jeli Role stared unbelievingly into his Quantrols.

Manns Field, dressed in black panties and bra so sheer that her nipples and pubic hair were fully visible, sat in a floating command chair, legs crossed and eyes closed, trying to focus just that extra nanpixel on what she was seeing. "I still can't believe that we got to this place so fast. Who gave you those coordinates again?"

"Supposedly a dead member of our crew," said Jeli.

Inside her antique astronaut helmet, Jannn Tolne nodded her approval.

Jeli wondered where she'd managed to dig up the relic. It still had a life support hose attached that she dragged with her when she clogged around the command deck in the oversized magnetic boots.

"Where is this place, Chief Magistrate?" Starr had traded his black Stetson in for a white one. He actually looked good in it. "I've never heard of anything like this."

Jeli didn't know what to say. The coordinates Benji Parx had given them had taken them to somewhere in the universe that didn't appear anywhere in their Quantrol navigation. The Quanreadings were completely nonsensical. Nothing made sense. Everything was as scrambled and confused as their mission.

At least there was calm throughout Soul Ship. His executive crew-with the exception of Lation-had checked on things when they went to their quarters for fresh clothing. Everyone seemed calm. Most of the crew seemed to be unaware of having just been flies, even though the smell of feces was almost overpowering. Even more strange, nobody seemed to be aware of, or missing, the crew members who had hurtled into space when the hull breached.

"I'm not getting any readings, Chief Magistrate." Skype, dressed in fresh kakis, sweated adrenaline. She wanted to hit something after being forced to be a fly. "This place doesn't exist."

"It exists, Skype." Jeli's voice was calm. "It just doesn't exist anywhere that's been charted."

"Beg pardon, Chief," said Skype. "But the entire universe has been charted to some extent or another, and something this big would be hard to miss."

She has a point. It was big, too big to be missed by the millions of craft that had traversed the universe for thousands of years looking for proof of intelligent life and ending up with a well-charted universe, but one in which human intelligence seemed to be the only intellect in existence. And it was just too damned bursting with energy to be missed.

It was breathtaking. There were thousands of them, spread over millions of miles of space. Galaxies. Some spread for over a thousand miles. Some were just a few feet wide but they were all galaxies, with stars and dark matter and vast micro-expanses of space dust forming ellipses, spirals and rings."

"It's like a mini-universe inside our own," said Field, eyes wide with wonder.

"But I've never seen anything like that in our universe," said Starr. A tiny red dot appeared on everyone's Quantrols in the area where he was looking.

"Oh my God," gasped Field. "Is that real?"

She was looking at a square galaxy. It was about a hundred miles by a hundred miles, a perfect cube.

"Oh look! There's another one!" A red dot appeared where Field had found another cube galaxy, this one less than a mile in length but bursting with stars. As they continued to Quanscan, they found more of the cube-shaped galaxies, hundreds of them. And then round globes, like huge beach balls filled with stars and boot-shaped galaxies.

"Where the hell is this place?" asked Lation, showing emotion for the first time Jeli could remember.

"I think I can answer that."

Everyone's eyes turned on the man who had suddenly appeared out of nowhere on the command deck.

"Benji?" asked Jeli. "Benji Parx?"

CHAPTER 83 - TURNING A NEW LEAF

Buddha swerved to the left, barely avoiding a comet the size of a pea. "Maybe you should slow down." Pea size or not, Abner was aware that if the comet had punctured their deep space pod, it could have put a hole the size of a baseball in Abner's chest.

"Nervous, Abner?" Buddha smiled mischievously.

"I still don't see why this thing can't be shielded."

"I'm sentient software in Solidholo operating in several Quanspaces simultaneously. The field created by the shielding interferes with my processes. But my reflexes are fast." He smiled wider. "And I'm Buddha."

"You're sentient?"

Abner was still shaken by having suddenly appeared in the cockpit of a deep space pod in what Buddha said was the outskirts of Control. Apparently, this was their holding pattern until it was time to go in. In the meantime, they would just fly around dodging comets and other space debris.

"It was your computer." Buddha looked over at Abner admiringly. "The longer I stayed on it, the more my program evolved in strange ways, and when you switched it over to Quan-"

"I noticed that you didn't seem to be around shortly after that."

Buddha shrugged. Through the cockpit windows, the stars and planets of Control produced a seemingly warm glow. "It was time to leave. The universe was calling. I was software, and the strings were my operating system. I rolled out of Earth into the cosmos and just traveled around the universe for a few hundred years. Then I found a quiet little place where I could spend a couple of thousand years seeking enlightenment. Atoning."

"Atoning?"

The smile slowly drifted away from Buddha's lips. He took his hands off the control stick. Abner's eyebrows raised, eyes on the abandoned stick. "Don't worry," said Buddha. "I've been using Quantrols to fly this thing all along. The control stick is just for appearances." He chuckled.

Abner stared at him.

Buddha made a sound like clearing his throat. "When I brought down the city states, I killed billions of humans and VRs, not sentient VRs, but they would have been by now, if I hadn't destroyed them."

"But you didn't destroy them. The city states went to war with each other. They're the ones who brought the whole thing down."

"But I'm the one who instigated the war, the one who gave them the viral weapons and manipulated them into going to war. I designed the war, they just carried out my design."

"But you were just doing what you were programmed to do. It's what you were created to do, and it's not like you had any choice."

"Evil, no matter where or how it originates, is still evil."

"But you weren't evil. You were a software program."

Buddha looked at Abner questioningly. "I killed billions of human beings."

"And you saved my wife and daughter."

Another shrug. "Details."

"And you just saved me from Bella."

"Well, let's not go getting sentimental. Hang on." Before Abner had a chance to do anything, the pod streaked to the right, plastering Abner to the side of his seat. "Comet."

"Thanks for the warning," said Abner reluctantly.

"Anyway, I found a place in just about the most remote region of space I could find, a place that I was sure wasn't going to be overrun with settlers and explorers anywhere near the end of time."

Abner thought a moment. "The Cappel Dark Matter Field."

Buddha nodded. "My home for nearly two thousand years. I holed up in that little cavern, tuned into the frequencies of Creation and just meditated on the meaning of it all. I had time to deal with my guilt over killing those people, and I had time to work out a plan to atone."

"So what does it all mean?"

"I'll need another few thousand years to figure that one out. The atonement, I've got though."

"And that is?"

"Instead of the destroyer of things, I'm going to be the savior of things. You're going to become software again, and we're going right into the heart of Quannet and erase every existing file recording information about birth humans and clones."

"And maybe even save the universe?"

Buddha smiled. "Maybe. Just Maybe."

CHAPTER 84 - NEVER BET ON A SURE THING

The Cormorant chuckled to himself. *What a bunch of gullible losers*. He'd fooled them all with that slop he'd fed them about Cassie Hayes being at her lowest in a thousand years, fed up with the Wars and ready to throw it all away.

"I mean, what does she get out of it?" he'd asked them. Nobody knew. They sat, looking around at each other, looking to see if anyone knew what he was talking about.

"Nothing!" The Cormorant's voice had echoed with conviction in the silence. "She gets nothing! She's software. She can have any Quanspace she wants. She's immortal. She doesn't need the money, and she doesn't want the fame."

He'd let them chew on that for a minute-and then the clincher. "Loac has been bred for half a millennium to beat her. She'll have Shade backing her up, clearing the field, cutting down the competition." Sitting back in his red leather chair, he'd crossed his legs, the Derringer resting in his lap. "Ladies and gentlemen-and I use the term gentlemen loosely." Laughter had erupted. "And ladies, even looser!" Screams and laughter. Someone had thrown a glass that zinged by his head, bringing a frown to his lips. Even in Quanspace, he hadn't been amused. That was a sign of disrespect.

He'd raised a hand for silence and the room had gone quiet. "I think we're going to see a whole new era in the Reality Wars, an era of birth-human domination of the greatest sport in the universe." He'd counted three breaths. "And we, the Gamblers, stand to win whole galaxies when Cassie Mae Hayes loses the Reality Wars for the first time in a thousand years."

The roar had been deafening, even in Quanspace.

Idiots.

He'd planted it masterfully. He'd all but told them that Cassie Mae Hayes was going to lose the Wars. They would all be thinking the same thing, *He's got something up his sleeve. The Cormorant has found a way to fix the Reality Wars. Cassie Hayes is going to lose.* This translated as *Take all bets on the VR girl and throw everything on the Clanswoman.*

They would own the universe.

Idiots.

All of the Cormorant's money would be going on Cassie Mae Hayes. The other Gamblers were right. He *was* fixing the Reality Wars. And after that, he would have Abner Hayes's head brought to him to present to Bella in repayment for killing whoever had thrown the glass at him.

CHAPTER 85 - KARMATIC WAVE

"Your employer has no idea what repercussions will spread throughout the universe if your mission is successful."

"You again?" The assassin sipped from his cup and savored the sweet Hazelnut Cream flooding his palate. It was nighttime, and the street was lit with the flickering of candles burning on tables the length of the street. The dark-blue sky, tinted heavily with lapis green looked like something pulled out of a Van Gogh and rolled over the top of the Assassin's Quanspace. "This is supposed to be a private Quanspace. Not only are you not supposed to be here, you're not supposed to find this place. You're not even supposed to know about this place."

"I'm Buddha."

"Right. And I'm Kali." The Assassin sipped again. In spite of the intrusion, the coffee was just as sweet. "I'm not abandoning my contract." He leaned back in his wrought-iron chair, holding his left hand over his cup as though the steam rising from it were massaging his palm.

"You might want to reconsider that." Suddenly, Buddha had a chocolate milkshake before him. He sipped through the straw.

"Fattening," said the Assassin, pointing at the milkshake with his right hand.

"I'll eat lentils and rice for a month."

"I always thought you'd be a little more serious."

"I'm a little of everything. Depends on who wrote about me."

"Pity."

"How's that?"

"Being at the mercy of the people who write about you."

"Not a problem you would have, I suppose."

"They've written about the results of my work, but not about me. I have a strong veto on that."

"A veto?"

"I've had to kill two journalists. Too bad, though. To get onto me, they had to be good."

"String veto."

The Assassin nodded and sipped his coffee as Buddha sipped his milkshake through the straw. "They make a great milkshake here."

"I wouldn't know. Not something I built into the place."

"Your employer is insane."

"All my employers have been insane. I'm not sure if I'm playing with a full deck myself."

"If you kill the Clanswoman before the Reality Wars, you'll set in motion a Karmatic wave that could affect the entire universe. This could have dire consequences for all life, everywhere."

"There's no such word as Karmatic."

"I'm Buddha. Don't tell me about Karma."

"I'm an assassin. Don't tell me about who needs to die."

Buddha took another sip of his chocolate milkshake, smiled at the Assassin and disappeared.

***

You're messing with forces beyond yourself this time.

"There are no forces beyond myself. I am the force of my own force."

And just what does that mean?

The Assassin sipped his coffee, enjoying the rich flavor of hazelnut, and smiled without answering.

CHAPTER 86 - REALIZATION

The pulsing red walls of the Womb of the Universe ship were getting on Uillium's nerves. Everything about his alignment with the Womb and with Maebh was getting on his nerves. He was certain that something was going on that he hadn't bought into, and he was beginning to realize that trusting her had probably been a foolish thing.

But he'd been proud, too proud. Like Maebh, he'd seen the relationship between the Tears and the other Clans as one of subservience to the Tears. Not because they'd ever treated the other Clans as less than equal, but because they were the most powerful, the ones who'd won the Clan Wars, the ones who'd been merciful and spared the lives of his own people even after they'd joined the Clans warring on the Tears and their allies.

And now he was joining forces against them again.

A dread tangible enough to push bile into his throat grew in his stomach. He felt cut off from his Clan and all the Clans, alone with the enemy—and there was little doubt that Maebh was exactly that, the enemy. Enemy to all the Clans.

And where did that put him?

In danger of being eliminated. He knew too much. Things were moving faster than he'd dared imagine. Pacts had been made, sides had lined up. His role in bringing other Clans on board was over. He was expendable, if not a liability. He'd witnessed what Maebh had done to Brann.

He'd been a fool to trust her. All the signs had been there right from the start. The hatred, the secrecy, the nanmagic... all leading to Brann's horrifying murder. But even before that, he knew of the Womb, their seclusion from the other Clans, their strange magic dating back to ancient Earth. Some said they dated back to a time of advanced civilizations that had disappeared before recorded Earth history. The more Uilliam dealt with them, the more he'd begun to realize that these were not ones who would integrate with the other Clans. These were a closed order, a rule and word unto themselves.

The dread in Uilliam's stomach turned into ice. It was all so obvious. The armaments on the Womb ships. The campaign to spread hatred of the Tears of Blood centuries after the Clan Wars.

Maebh wants to take over the universe.

Uilliam had just barely enough time to complete the thought when he noticed a movement to his right. He wasn't alone. An icy chill raced through his chest. His scream was cut short by a red claw slicing through his skull.

CHAPTER 87 - THE CONSEQUENCE OF CONTEXT

Magic and mystery permeated the air at the pinnacle of Mount Keri. It was a place of worship and devotion to things beyond the strings and stuff of the known universe. Standing on the domed surface of the mountain with the asteroids of Blood Citadel forming a panorama of power and majesty around Vala, a feeling of confirmation warmed Bavn's chest, an excitement in the knowing of things beyond sight and reason that would soon reveal themselves to believers and unbelievers throughout the universe.

This was the Temple of the Oracle, a holy place where the energies of the Tears of Blood Clan focused. Its place in the asteroid belt and its peculiar rotation kept it eternally in light. It was rumored that the end of time would begin the day darkness crept over the expanse of white marble under the dome topping Mount Keri.

Bavn and Owene stood dead center in the marble plateau. War and other large movements were imminent, and it was time to consult the oracle. Owene, usually dwarfed by the towering Bavn, seemed larger with her red robes fluttering in the artificial breeze pumped into the dome through tunnels beneath the asteroid's surface that formed a complex series of burial channels for Clansfolk killed in battle. Though scrubbed and filtered, the breeze carried a faint scent of old death.

Bavn, dressed in the traditional purple robes of war, stared down into the blue eyes of his oracle. The Clan leader looked almost sad, though the occasion was supposed to be one of jubilance. He spoke slowly and heavily. "Owene, great times approach."

Owene nodded. Blue hair flowed over her shoulders, strands waving in the breeze. Her irises were wide with the sacred drugs she'd been taking for the last few days, drugs that would open her spirit to the otherworldly, the domain of chance and future. They would allow God to touch her soul and show her the paths. "And times of great confusion. I've counseled you many times in the past, before battles and at the beginnings of great plans, but never have the paths been so obscured with question marks. Every path holds danger of equal weight, and there are no paths of choice. The time of war is near but this is not a choice. This is a consequence of context."

Bavn scowled, not at Owene, but at the truths he'd already felt, the outcomes he'd already known were inevitable. They were so close to the plan they'd begun a thousand years ago. Things would not be easy. These would be the days that would change the universe. "I'm not surprised at these words, but I'm not sure that I understand what you mean by a consequence of context."

"The movement of all things around the Tears of Blood Clan includes our own destiny, the destiny of others and the destiny of the universe that contains the ultimate destiny of everything. This is the context. The consequences are when those

300

movements interact. War may be thrust upon us, and my sense of this is that our enemies may in some form be our allies and our allies, our enemies."

"Of that I'm sure." Bavn sighed deeply. "The intrusion into Shade's life force, the daily conflicts between the Clans... these point to enemies within and without. I also sense a great confusion as we near the culmination of our plans, a splitting of ultimate goals within the Clans."

"You cannot allow yourself to trust anyone but the closest of allies."

"You're certain of this?"

Owene smiled. "Other than being certain that nothing else is certain, I'm certain of this."

They thought about this for a moment. Bavn was the first to smile. He waited for Owene to return the smile before he spoke. "So, you're saying that everything is unclear?"

"All war is unclear, especially when it seems certain."

Their smiles deepened. Bavn's huge mass visibly relaxed. "Thank you, my friend. These will be both splendid and terrible times, but I feel ready now." He breathed deeply again. "Ready for whatever gallops across our horizon."

"There is one other thing... "

Bavn's smile lapsed slightly. "Yes?"

"There is a being that has recently awakened. Its nature is withheld from me. It will play a key role in our destiny as the days ahead unfold. Its goals are not ours, but it will not be our enemy."

"A mystery player in the eleventh hour."

301

"That would be one way to put it."

"And you say 'it'?"

"I don't know what it is. Its nature is withheld."

"I'll be sure to keep an eye out for it."

With that, Bavn marched across the parapet, leaving his oracle to stare at the asteroids and stars.

CHAPTER 88 - THE TRAP

The trap was set.

They'd discussed it at length with a reluctant Elli, still very much aware of the others she'd lost to the monster in the cafe. It was, all things considered, an outrageous plan, a dangerous plan. They still had no idea whom they were up against, knowing only that he was deadly, that he'd killed successfully and had been doing so for centuries, possibly millennia.

But it was a plan that just might work. There was no way the stranger could know what he would be sinking his killing consciousness into, and by the time he was in, it would be too late.

Then it would be up to the two women to deal with an experienced and precise unknown, and maybe it was just that factor of unpredictability that had tipped the scales for them. This would be a game for warriors, a test of skills and battle readiness, a wonderfully timed preparation for the Reality Wars.

They'd asked if they could use Elli's quarters to do it, but that was where Shade had already encountered him and seen him. He wouldn't touch her there, so it had to be in their own quarters. They'd asked if Elli could be with them, but even that might upset the balance of the trap, create an extra psychic scent in the strings that might tip him off.

She'd given them the drug and instructions on how to prepare it, the exact dosage, the way to crush the cube into the right consistency of powder.

They shared a cup of the tea and then walked together naked to their bedroom and merged vapors.

The trap was set. Loac was inside Shade, their vapors flowing into each other but with a difference from their lovemaking fusion. Tonight, they ignored each other, did everything in their power to not acknowledge the other. They were one and they were separate. They lay in bed for almost an hour, joined mentally and emotionally only by their common goal.

And he came.

It was the slightest disturbance in the frequencies of Shade's mind, a submolecular sliver of intent, but it was unmistakably there, creeping through the essence of Shade's energies, slithering snake-like into her life force. They let it enter. They let it spread through the frequencies that defined the cells and atoms of Shade while Loac nudged everything that was herself away from its intrusion. They let it suffuse her. Shade felt its presence more than ever, powerful inside her, aggressive now after so many failures. *It's becoming desperate. Careless.*

She felt the beginnings of its sucking on her will to live, its attempt to taint her ability to savor life. No longer the needle of poison, it was becoming a maw, and Shade knew that this would be his last frantic attempt on her.

She could feel the confusion and desperation, sensing that this was someone experiencing failure for the first time and unable to deal with it. Suddenly, he froze, fearful, startled, sensing that he wasn't alone with his prey. But it was too late.

304

They attacked together, blistering straight into his Quanspace where he sat cross-legged, alarmed, taken by surprise. They rushed into his Quanmind, slashing and bashing the emotional content of his Quanpresence, driving him to the brink of insanity, battering the essence of his intellect and awareness. Sluggishly, reeling with pain, he crawled out of Quanspace, screaming in Realspace.

***

"You said he finishes his victims in Realspace?"

"That's what Elli suspects."

Loac shifted on her side and ran a finger down the side of Shade's face, down her neck and across her breasts. "He's going to be really pissed when he comes face-to-face with you."

"He's going to be even more pissed when he feels my sword slice into his gut."

***

I don't think she'll want to die. It won't be a beautiful death.

"I want her to love life with every cell in her being when I kill her. And it will be an ugly death."

305

CHAPTER 89 - SPACE SHIPS

Strange things were beginning to happen aboard the Clans' ships as they approached the Texture, as though they'd entered a place where all the rules that had guided them throughout their lives were suddenly turned upside down and replaced with something new and strange. But this didn't worry Zethar. His powerful Clans' navy was prepared for anything that the deep recesses of space could throw at them, even here at the edge of the universe. Their approach to the Texture was a spearhead pointed at the weakest formation in Bella's navy. He was surprised at the size of the fleet. Obviously, the madwoman wanted the Texture desperately. But the Clans would arrive first. Bavn's cloaking nanmagic kept them invisible for now, but Zethar wondered if they would withstand the strange shifts in realities the closer they came to the anomaly.

He was surprised by the report of the attack on the Cappel Dark Matter Field. Strange things were happening there as well. Someone or something in the Field had pissed off Bella, and the viciousness of the Tree Clan's attack left no doubt in Zethar's mind that they wouldn't be pissing her off again, ever. Zethar had never liked the Tree. They were like pus dripping out of a sore inflicted on the Clans.

And then there was the matter of communications. They were breaking down, and Zethar feared they would break down further the closer they came to the Texture. They might lose communications completely. He prayed the Clan navies would fare well under Bavn's leadership because Zethar Locklan was certain that he would have his hands full at the edge of the universe.

***

Captain Shona Ureil felt her stomach tighten as she gazed out the viewport at the masses of Bella's ships stretching beyond the limits of vision along every horizon. It was like space was solid with Bella's power.

The Clans were about to take a pounding, but the navies filling her viewport were going to taste the fury of the Clans, a taste that would sour their appetite for war for a long time. If any survived the pounding.

***

They were going to lose contact with Control before they reached the Texture, but Nels had expected that. Already, there were inconsistencies in the way things worked, as though they'd stepped into another dimension and it would get worse the closer they got to it. He'd gone through the last transmissions of the Finder hundreds of times. The crew had literally gone insane. The ship itself had gone insane. And now they were approaching it with an entire fleet of warships armed with enough firepower to bring galaxies to their knees.

And a big chunk of the Cappel Field had been destroyed. Obviously Chaine had something to do with that, acting directly under Bella's orders. There would be a showdown between the two of them soon. Nels expected it would come shortly after they reached the Texture.

And there was the matter of Bella's other navies. They were right off the Quan horizon, lost somewhere in the universe, millions upon millions of warships. And there were Clans' ships passing alarmingly close to Control, supposedly on some religious trek.

Not likely. They were up to something. Nels couldn't imagine they would be foolish enough to attack Control itself. The warships surrounding Control were the most heavily armed in existence and armed with weaponry that not even Nels was privy to. Not even the total number of ships was known, and some estimated that there was one warship for every single Clansman.

So what the hell are they up to?

**

So, what are they doing here? Supreme Commander Daman Haley adjusted the nanglass of his observation dome for close-ups, long range and depth coordinates. Ship after ship, some heavily armed, some conspicuously unarmed. Daman hadn't seen a Clans' navy as formidable as this since the Clan Wars. They'd bashed the shit out of each other across the known universe. Some had said they would simply annihilate each other, but then the Tears of Blood had begun a vicious campaign of

308

slaughter equal to the worst that he himself had unleashed in the name of Bella.

Bella's navies had stayed out of that one, letting the Clans slug it out as long as they kept their war away from her interests. When it was over, all the Clans had been weakened. That's when Bella should have attacked them. It would have been simpler, less costly and there would have been minimal loss of life in Daman's navies.

Now, after five hundred years of rebuilding, it was hard to guess just how powerful the Clans' navies were. And it was impossible to imagine what weaponry they possessed, especially of the nanmagic sort from that old tyrant, Bavn.

But they would soon find out. Daman's first wave of attack ships sailed quietly through space, passing through his defense formations from every possible attack coordinate. When the time came, they would descend upon the Clans' navies and rectify the mistake they'd made half a millennia ago.

**

Commander Colin "Crash" Duncan scratched his cheek as he watched the attack cruiser, *Farewell*, come to rest just behind the outermost lines of defense. It was one of the plainest of Bella's ships, a gray tube of destruction five hundred miles long and thirty miles wide. The firepower of this single ship was equal to entire fleets. And there were thousands of them.

At least they're propping things up at the front just in case the Clans try something. And if they would just attack anyway, how sweet that would be.

***

Commander Borne Caine gazed through the magnified view of his observation port at the vast expanse of asteroids, millions of them, each a fortress. Borne was tall, lean and dark-skinned with deep-black eyes and an aura of calm. He'd commanded hundreds of missions across the universe, but he'd never seen anything like this. The firepower of the asteroids was awesome and he was seeing just the ones on this side of the planet.

There would be heavy losses in this battle, even with the millions of Bella's ships cloaked and waiting for the word to attack and begin the destruction of the Clans.

Maebh felt no remorse in killing Uilliam. He'd just been another tool in her plans. She'd Quanned her messages to all the Womb navies to maneuver into positions that would allow quick retreat when the fighting began.

When the battles were over, the Womb would be the mightiest force in the universe, and she would have the Texture and whatever unknown powers it might bring to the table.

And every member of the Tears of Blood Clan would die.

***

"So," asked Jeli, "do you have any idea where and what this place is?"

Benji smiled at the Chief Magistrate. "It's more like... when."

"When?" Jeli raised his eyebrows, though he wasn't all that surprised by anything he heard on Soul Ship. After all, he was standing in the command deck talking to a dead man who'd suddenly appeared out of nowhere and made telephone calls in space.

"It's complicated," said Benji.

"I don't doubt that it is." Jeli smiled. "So, you seem to be our new navigator. Where do we go next? I'm hoping that you'll say *toward* the Texture. That is, after all, our destination."

Benji returned the smile. "For now, we wait."

"What?" asked Skype.

"Sounds good to me," said Lation.

"Wait for what?" asked Field.

Benji waited for the questions to stop before answering. "We wait for Buddha to tell us what to do."

Jeli and his executive crew stared speechless at Benji Parx. Levels of Absurdity Officer, Jannn Tolne, stared through the visor of her ancient astronaut's helmet, nodding approval.

CHAPTER 90 - AND THEN WE'LL KILL THEM

Lovesong tried not to stare at the white foamy spittle gathering at the corner of Bella's mouth. She'd been raving for over an hour, pacing the emerald floor, throwing herself onto the divan. Its hard crystal surface gave gently when it recognized her skin and clothing. She sat on it now, legs crossed Indian style, like a spoiled teen throwing a tantrum, weeping quietly, body shaking, alternately frowning and smiling frantically. Her eyes were wild, flashing a mad panorama of insane colors. Her hands shook like motorized gel. "They'll soon know," she whimpered. "They'll know and then it'll be too late. Then they'll fall. They'll all fall."

The liquid walls of Bella's control room swirled and churned shades of green. Windows linked into Bella's Quans appeared and disappeared. She was monitoring her universe, her navies and her empire. Images from her mind wavered onto the screen and disintegrated to be replaced by others, some of them breaking into alternate or subscreens displaying vast navies spanning immense stretches of space. As the story behind the screens unfolded, Lovesong felt his stomach tighten. At first, he thought he might have been mistaken, that the images on the screen were not what he suspected. Slowly, as Bella raved, it sunk in.

Bella was going to wage war with the Clans. Fleets in the outlying regions of the universe and in systems where there were no Clans had been pared to the bone, the main bodies consolidating with large fleets, all of them moving toward heavily populated Clans sectors.

And the most startling of all-millions of Bella's most advanced warships were within striking distance of Blood Citadel. Lovesong knew what kind of weaponry they carried. It would be the bloodiest battle of all time, and when it was over, Blood Citadel and every living being in its millions of asteroids would be vapor.

And on the perimeters of Control, a huge force of the Clans' ships passed, oblivious of the deadly warships moving into attack formations.

The woman he loved was about to start a war that would span the entire universe.

Lovesong sat in his own crystal divan, tuned to his frequencies, and watched in horror as the navies of both sides moved into positions of annihilation and wondered how she'd managed to keep all of this a secret from him. But then, she was Bella, a goddess, ruler of the universe, his creator, his love.

But she was dying. Her body was beginning to break down regardless of the most advanced life support sciences and technologies. Her mind was chaos, becoming less coherent with each passing hour.

Lovesong watched a massive warship move into position at the outer reaches of Control, its weaponry targeting the Clans' ships, ready to release death. This was madness, insanity.

It was pure Bella.

"My," he said, "this certainly is a surprise."

She threw him a scorching look and stared at him as though just realizing that he was there and who he was. Her face loosened. She wiped the spittle from her lips and stared at it on her finger with a look that asked: What is this? Her lips twisted into a strange smile. Her cheeks had lost their luster, and dark patches were spreading over the skin of her forehead as though something inside her that had been holding itself together for thousands of years suddenly decided that it was time to just let go.

"None of them are my friends." A deep sad darkness suffused her voice. She was going fast. It occurred to him that, possibly, she was aware of this at some deep level, and she'd decided that she was going to take the universe down with her.

"You're all I have." And now her face was open, beseeching, lost. "My love." Suddenly, her face hardened. "They'll pay for both of us. When I have the Texture, I will have it all back." The madness leaped back into her eyes. "We'll kill every living thing in the universe. Start it all over. Create it in my likeness."

Lovesong did the only thing he could-he smiled and nodded. "Yes, my love, we'll start it all over."

"And then we'll kill him and his daughter. We'll keep them alive long enough to see it, to see the beauty and grandeur of the new universe. And then we'll kill them."

"Yes, and then we'll kill them."

Oh, Bella.

CHAPTER 91 - ENTIRE EMPIRES

This is why the Assassin never brought his clients to his Quancafe , preferring to meet them in their own or a neutral space. Kingston Cormorant as a twenty-foot-high gold coin would have done serious damage to his cafe ambience.

The Assassin presented in Old West garb, a huge black Stetson with a long rim throwing his face in shadow. He titled his head forward, puffing on a cigar. They were in Kingston's office, overlooking flashing lights and spinning wheels, desperation and excitement igniting the eyes of thousands upon thousands of humans and VRs, their bodies swaying from table to table in a wave-like motion that turned the Quansino into an ocean of thrills. The Assassin liked this place-the lights, the subdued noise filtering through the muting program, and the color. But he had a hard time getting his mind around Kingston presenting as a gold coin in his own space.

"So everything is going as per the plan?"

The movement of the lips around the wide-toothed smile was a bit much, thought the Assassin.

"She'll be dead just before the Wars start."

Might want to qualify that, pardner. The two of them almost got you.

The coin's lips stretched from edge to edge, the lower lips bulging as a wide obscene smile of satisfaction spread across the coin. After thousands of years in his line of work, the Assassin had no doubts that all his clients were insane, or well on their way. Maybe there was just something in the ability to cause the death of others that was too much for the stable mind to handle.

Strange thought for you to hold.

"It has to be just before they start."

"Everything is going according to plan."

One microsecond close to being totally brain dead from the two lesbians-and you call that going to plan?

"Entire empires depend on your work moving forward flawlessly."

"I've never failed."

There's always a first time.

The coin smiled again. It was disturbing, that wide white smile spread across the surface of the coin. Time to close this. "Her death will be beautiful."

The Cormorant liked the sound of this. A beautiful death. Yes, it would be exactly that. It would be a beautiful death that would make him the richest man in the universe. Eventually, he might end up the most powerful man in the universe. Maybe he wouldn't kill the arse who had thrown the glass. Possibly keep him as a pet that he could kick around whenever he thought of that glass flying past his head. "Yes, a beautiful death. That's exactly what it will be." In an instant, the Cormorant was alone in his office, and the Assassin was sipping coffee in his Quancafe.

***

But it won't be beautiful, will it?

"No, it won't be beautiful.

***

Something strange about that man, thought the Cormorant as he stretched back in his red leather chair. Being a successful Gambler required a keen ability to read people, to see things that others missed, including the people themselves.

There was something about this assassin, something about the pauses in his speech, the shifts in his posture, almost as though he were talking to someone else in the room.

But he was well aware of the assassin's reputation. He was practically a myth. After this was all over, maybe he would put him on the payroll permanently.

CHAPTER 92 - A Different Kind of Quan

"I can only stay a few minutes before they trace even this.

It was dark, pitch black in this place.

"It's just not fair that I don't have you and Mom with me all this time, and then you're back and now you have to go... "

"This will all be over soon, and then we'll be back together."

The dark was so thick you could bite it. They couldn't see each other. It was a different kind of Quan. It felt strange.

"I don't want you to go."

"I don't have a choice."

Only their voices existed here, and the presence behind the voices, the pain and the fear.

"You can say no. It's dangerous. I mean, it's Control. It's the most well-guarded place in the universe. Even if you could get in, you'll never get out alive."

"We'll slip through and be gone before they even know we were there."

It was like they were talking to each other's souls. Every word had the solidity of a heartbeat.

"You don't have to go."

"He helped me save you and your mother. He saved me from being a cloud of fog floating around a pile of rot."

"Just to put you right back into danger."

"No more danger than what you'll be facing."
He paused. "Sweetheart, you have to know something."

"What?" Her voice was almost pouty. He wished there was a way he could hug her.

"Your backer all these years... "

"You mean backers. Thousands of them."

"No, sweetheart, just one."

Silence. The dark was suddenly suffocating.

"Bella."

An even deeper silence permeated the darkness before a pained whisper broke through it. "No."

"Yes. She's been using your victories to quell antipathy toward VRs."

Again, the heavy silence. "Then... that was a good thing. Wasn't it?"

Abner chuckled and the darkness, though still impenetrable, seemed a shade or two lighter. "In a way, I guess. But, soon, it won't matter."

"What do you mean by that?"

"You'll see... soon. I have to go now."

"I love you, Daddy."

"I love you too, Sweetheart."

***

"And you swear that you can keep her safe in the Reality Wars."

"She'll be safe." The finality in Buddha's voice, even with its suggestion of all-knowingness, was little consolation for Abner. He was going to the most dangerous place in the universe to change the universe, and the only thing that would keep him

alive through all of this was an ancient computer
virus that thought it was Buddha.

What the hell am I doing?

CHAPTER 93 - SWALLOWED

"He turned me into software a fraction of a second before I died," said Benji. "The poison was neutralized in the process. And then he brought me back to my physical self."

He was alone now with Jeli on Soul Ship's control deck. Jeli was still having a hard time accepting Benji's presence, the fact that he was still alive. But then it occurred to him-no one had gone to the viewing room to recover the body, and if they had, no one had reported it to Jeli. If things hadn't unfolded the way they had, Jeli assumed that Benji's lifeless body might still be slumped in the aft observation deck.

"And he did this all from a cavern in the Cappel Dark Matter Field?"

"What can I say... he's Buddha."

Jeli tightened his lips and nodded. "And he's on our side?"

"He gave me the coordinates for you to escape the solar bomb."

"And then had us turned into flies."

Benji looked gravely into Jeli's eyes. "Who are we to question the ways of Buddha, Chief Magistrate?"

Annoyed, Jeli narrowed his eyes and tightened his lips until they turned white. He breathed deeply, and an air of calm settled over his face as his lips loosened and their color returned. He sighed. "I suppose you're right. But I think the breached hull was a bit much. People died."

"Control over the course of large things is never exact." Benji's eyes rose in momentary surprise. He wasn't used to saying things that hinted of so much depth of thought. But then, he'd just been hanging with Buddha.

Jeli didn't know what to make of Benji. His Quanfile described an innocuous man with an unexceptional past who didn't seem to be crazy or suicidal. His profile described the same person that everyone else was, someone trying desperately to believe in something, and the Texture seemed to offer that last hope that there might be something out there bigger than themselves, bigger than the human empires and bigger than the vastness of space with all its disappointments.

"So... what next?"

"Check out your Quantrols."

Benji quanned into the viewscreen in his mind and felt his blood turn into ice water. There were no stars out there. No brilliant swatches of space dust swirling for millions of miles. He was looking at light-years of empty space without even the felt presence of dark matter. He was looking into a terrifying expanse of nothingness.

He tried to keep his voice calm. "And what's Buddha sending us into now?"

"It's a wormhole."

"And where's it taking us?"

"Apparently, right into the middle of a war zone."

"And Buddha will be there to protect us in the war zone?"

"No, uh, he'll be busy somewhere else."

Without warning, a tremor rocked Soul Ship, almost sending Jeli and Benji onto their knees. Everything disappeared as the wormhole swallowed them.

CHAPTER 94 - A PLAN

It was like being in space. The four walls and the ceiling of Bavn's quarters showed projections of the asteroids of Blood Citadel. It was almost dizzying.

"She tells me we're to be sparing with our trust, even within the Clans." The blue aura from Bavn's eyes and beard seemed brighter than normal. He feared the days ahead would test him more than any of the days of his life, even more so than the Clan Wars, and he prayed that they would be the last time he would be needed in his natural element: war. He was, above all, a warrior. And these were times for a warrior leader. "She also mentioned a being, recently awakened."

The two women stiffened. "The one we encountered?" asked Loac.

"I don't think so." Bavn shifted in his posture. "This one, apparently, is not an enemy, though its goals may run counter to our own. But it's an unknown. Be mindful of its presence but refrain from immediate action until you understand its intention."

"Got to love these cryptic warnings from Owene." Shade smiled as she spoke, as did Bavn. Loac remained straight-faced.

"What she gives us are guidelines for an attitude coming into great events," said Bavn. "The specifics of the future are always a mystery, but the large movements are implicit in all the events of the present and past. Attitude determines how these become the future."

324

"Then we'll deal with this... *being* when we encounter it," said Loac. "In the meantime, we expect Shade's assassin to be physically present at Canak. According to Elli, he finishes his kills in Realspace after destroying their psyche and will to live. We're guessing that he'll make his move before the Wars, or during them."

"You're probably right." Bavn nodded, the smile gone. "That would make sense. You'll be on your own."

"We've worked out a few scenarios," said Shade. "He'll be alone. That seems to be the way he operates. He's probably already on Canak, as a Wars official or with the Gamblers... or maybe even as one of the competitors. Probably not spectator. That wouldn't give him a chance to get close enough."

"It doesn't matter how he's there," said Loac, eyes steely and determined. "When he shows himself, we'll kill him."

"Just be careful." Bavn stood and walked over to the wall, gazing out over the spacescape of asteroids lit up with the light bouncing from Vala's daytime. "This man has been killing for hundreds of years, maybe thousands. He's good at what he does, and Elli says that he's never failed."

"We've already confronted him," said Loac. She almost smiled. "And kicked his ass."

Bavn turned to face the two women. "Yes, you did." He sighed. "I just wish that I could be there with you, but I need to be here while things unfold on so many borders." His eyes darkened. Shade and Loac glanced at each other.

Loac stood, vibrating with defiance. "Don't worry about us, Father. We're ready for this—the Wars aren't. And we'll be killing the assassin just as we almost got him through his own mind."

Bavn smiled. "Yes. Yes, you will. But still, never overestimate yourself or underestimate your enemies. The two of you still have to be tested in the arena for which you were bred, the Reality Wars. You leave tomorrow. You'll be on your own." He breathed deeply. "And while you're competing, our quest for the Texture will finally be realized." He faced Loac. "We need you to beat the girl. We need a win for humanity, to bring respect back to flesh and blood. Without it, we'll never rid the universe of these so-called sentient VRs. And with all eyes in the universe on the Reality Wars and your victories, our ships at Control stand an even better chance of completing their mission."

"I've always wondered what that part of the plan will be," said Shade, curiously.

Bavn breathed deeply as he smiled and said, "Something that will change the nature of the universe, probably even more so than whatever surprises await us with the Texture."

CHAPTER 95 - THE ONLY WAY TO BE A HAPPY HUMAN

In vapor they were a single being with two souls, every thought and feeling, the sum of their mutual experience and breeding, their fear, their love, two endless oceans merging their biosystems into a place of sharing. It wasn't reading each other's minds so much as feeling their mutual thoughts, walking two separate paths blended into a single experience spanning the distance of their lives on their way to a single purpose.

Shade's doubts became certainties as they brushed the perimeters of Loac's iron resolve, tempered now with something that had never been there before, and she felt that, for the first time, she was feeling her love. She knew this was a good thing, something to strengthen her drive and draw a sense of commitment beyond a half millennium of breeding and indoctrination. This, Shade knew, would prepare her more for the Reality Wars than anything. The purpose beyond politics, religion and blood.

***

It was a feeling beyond anything she'd allowed herself to experience in all the years of her training and growth as a weapon, like she'd only known half of her life, half of the purpose of being human. And now she was full. Now, she knew she was ready for the Wars. She let go of her hatred and let herself sink into the sweet embrace of Shade's vapor.

***

Cassie glided through the water, feeling every lick of the fluid as it flowed over her body. For the first time in hundreds of years, she was at peace. She would win the Wars again, for the last time. She no longer needed them to fill the pit that the absence of her parents had left in the center of her life. Her father was back. He hadn't left her. He still loved her. She worried that he was in a place of danger again. But he was with Buddha. She smiled as she plied through the cool water. *He's with Buddha.*

It was so much like her dad.

***

Sara wanted to be with Cassie tonight... especially tonight, the night before leaving for the Wars, but she knew that her friend needed this time alone, like she always did, especially now that she had so much else on her mind-the appearance of her father right out of nowhere, saved from Bella Bjork by, of all people, Buddha.

She looked around. The Beer was almost empty tonight with everyone plastered at the Reality Bars, Quanning in on the betting, the competitor bios, interviews, the endless flow of previous Wars footage and the stories of millions of spectators who'd chosen these Wars to die, who'd paid top dollar to be right where the action would most likely kill them.

Well, Sara had her own way to prepare for the Wars the night before-she lifted the glass to her mouth and savored the flavor and fluid texture of the beer as it spilled over her tongue and bubbled down her throat.

***

Maxilim Marx lay beside his wife, daydreaming about the glory that would be his when he became the first clone to win the Reality Wars. He wondered how many worlds would change hands when he beat the girl, not that he had anything against her, but she'd hogged the center stage long enough-it was time to share the limelight. And this time, she would be competing in his world.

Clones would be looked at in a new way after these Reality Wars. *They'll finally take us seriously, accept us as real humans*. But even as he pictured himself idolized on Quan by breathless billions across the universe, he knew that was probably unlikely.

***

Centos Kama slept dreamlessly and snored loudly. He didn't care what the birth humans thought. He was happy to be a clone. After all, most of the humans he knew wanted nothing more than to be dead, as though being dead was the only way to be a happy human.

***

One of the most well-guarded secrets in the universe was the location of a planet named Canak. Not a single navigation program in the universe registered its existence. There were those who thought it was no more than a Quanspace where the minds of humans, clones and VRs were transported to compete in the Reality Wars. But this year, the truth was out. Canak was real-not just an idea, but a place that existed in the universe of flesh and blood. The Reality Wars were going to be in both Quanspace and Realspace. Just outside the planet's capital city, also called Canak, a quantum landing strip awaited the arrival of thousands of competitors and vast hordes of spectators.

Across the surface of the planet, millions of tubes awaited the spectators who had paid to be in the most dangerous places as the Wars progressed, the deal being, that even if they didn't die in the Wars, their bodies would never leave those tubes.

***

The assassin's body lay in his bunk in the employee quarters on Canak. He planned on being the only employee who would leave after the Wars, the others having paid for the privilege of spending eternity-if they lived that long-on a planet that would be, in essence, a burial ground after the Wars.

As he waited for the competitors-and his prey-to arrive, he sipped a steamy cup of Columbian roast in his Quancafe, fantasizing the painful death of the Clanswoman. He had a very special surprise waiting for her, and if the chance presented itself, he would take the other as well.

The voice in his head was strangely quiet tonight.

CHAPTER 96 - A MATTER OF CHOICE

Maggie: This is Maggie Westork reporting live from Canak for the Tenth Centennial Reality Wars... and I can't believe the energy here. You could cut the air with a laser net. This is sizing up to be the greatest, wildest and bloodiest Reality Wars of all time.

Childen: That's right, Maggie. The fields outside Canak's only city-also called Canak-may be filled with endless rows of burial tubes but the energy suffusing this planet is unmistakable.

Maggie: Childen! (laughs overloud) I'm SO sorry. I was so caught up in... well... never mind! Today, my co-host is Childen Shan, third-place finisher in last century's Reality Wars. Good to have you here, Childen.

Childen: (chuckles) It's good to be here, Maggie. And it looks as though the audience can see us this time.

Maggie: That's right, Childen. Not that you'll be taking up a lot of Quanscreen. (laughs)

Childen: (begrudging chuckle) Got me there, Maggie. I'd give you the gotme point, but as everyone can see, I have no arms. (smiles widely) Lost them in the last Reality Wars. And, yes, I could have new ones grown. But, no, I won't. Why? Because I swore I'd stay the way I emerged from the Wars for the rest of my life. So! Maggie! Anything to add?

Maggie: (looking confused, lost for words, recovers vigorously) Childen, I've never seen you like this before. Feeding on the atmosphere here, Childen? All abuzz and gung-ho on a tidal wave of pure Reality Wars frenzy? All-

Childen: So, Maggie, these Wars are shaping up to be different than any other since the inaugural Wars a thousand years ago.

Maggie: That's right, Childen. Lots of fresh-and-new on the go here. First, this will be the first time ever that the Reality Wars will take place in both Realspace and Quanspace.

Childen: And so much for complaints from the Clans that the VRs are competing in the Wars with a huge advantage.

Maggie: (irritated) That's right, Childen. This year, the contestants will be zapped in and out of Real and Quanspace without warning. They could be in some Quan war arena, and then, ZAP! They're in one of the arena's under the surface of Canak along with any number of the other contestants and a few million spectators hoping to die.

Childen: It's my understanding that over a thousand arenas have been set up inside the planet, and most of them have never been run in Quanspace in previous Wars. Some may be used, some not. It's all completely random.

Maggie: That's right, Childen. Rumor has it that this was a demand from the Gamblers, to ensure that none of the contestants could possibly come into the Wars with an advantage. You're in one reality and... ZAP! You take what you get.

333

Childen: And then there's the rivalry between the Clans and the VRs.

Maggie: That's right, Childen. And this year, it's more obvious than ever, with both camps having their icon to represent everything that each side stands for. The VRs have, as usual-and since the Wars began-Cassie Mae Hayes. She's never lost, no matter how much they've weighted the Wars against her to compensate for her being software.

Childen: After the last Wars, they applied that same software to several hundred VRs and burned them out of existence. That's one tough little girl in the VR camp.

Maggie: One tough little two thousand year old girl, Childen. She's older than you or I.

Childen: If only my own kids would stay kids young so long.

Maggie: And how do you have kids, Childen? Grow them? (laughs)

Childen: Exactly.

Maggie: (startled, mouth open, recovers) But this year, the big talk-and the big betting-is centered on the Tears of Blood Clan's Loac. This woman could be the ultimate Reality Wars weapon, bred and genetically enhanced for this one event.

Childen: They say that she's had every past Reality Wars programmed into her cells, every winning strategy, every losing move, every possible outcome of every action taken by every competitor for the last thousand years, plus projections on the possibilities of the new arenas. She's like a chess game with every move by every player ever to play the game hard-wired into her brain and body.

334

Maggie: That's right, Childen. And she doesn't like Cassie Hayes or her friend, Sara, especially after the Clean Test. Almost had a pre-event blood bath there.

Childen: They're definitely going to be carrying some animosity in these Wars, but I think a lot of it may be centered more on Sara.

Maggie: That's right, Childen. Sara's been a thorn in the side of the Clans for centuries, and after the look she got from Loac at the end of the Clean Test, I wouldn't want to be in her shoes. The Clans will almost certainly be looking for a clean kill on her.

Childen: And, at last count, over eighty million spectators were entangled with Sara-

Maggie: And this year, the entanglement promises to be a big surprise. In past Wars, they just allowed spectators to tap into the Quanostics of the competitors, giving an approximation of their physical and emotional stress...

Childen: And killing or maiming the spectators who weren't up to what the competitors were experiencing.

Maggie: Only if they were foolish enough to not take the filtering pills, or choose the wrong competitor.

Childen: In a universe where half the population just wants to die, the pills aren't really a big seller.

Maggie: Ancient history this year though, Childen. The Wars have taken a quantum leap, using entanglement to tie the spectators to the competitors. Your competitor dies, you die. Your competitor stresses out, you stress out. And there are no pills to overcome the entanglement. And once the Wars start, you're in till the finish.

Childen: (looking out the observation windows at the rows of tubes) And then millions more perish just for the hell of it.

Maggie: It's that kind of universe, Childen. Get used to it. (laughs) It's a matter of choice. And we'll be talking to a group of spectators from Zinin-over a thousand of them, all gathered in one of Zinin's largest burial crypts, all of them soon to be entangled with Sara.

Childen: Making her one of their favorites to be killed.

Maggie: That's right, Childen. (laughs) Get used to it.

CHAPTER 97 - MAKING MEANING

The competitors' quarters on Canak were among the most luxurious living accommodations in the universe-specially designed by the most gifted and sought-after Quan and Realspace designers, they rivaled the opulence of the most imaginative virtual environments to be found in all of Quannet.

The Reality Wars would be cast throughout the universe and maybe even into those unknown regions where the familiar laws of existence began to break down. Trillions of birth humans, clones and VRs would be following every word and movement of the Wars. Planetary systems would go bankrupt while others would be flooded with new wealth. For the duration that it took the last entrant to finish, the Reality Wars would be the central focus of almost every man, woman and child in Creation. With billions of lives happily expiring or flickering out in astonishment at having made the wrong pick, no one would be unaffected. The people who transcended realities to make this possible were regarded as gods.

"Nothing I couldn't get myself in Quanspace," said Cassie, shrugging.

"Speak for yourself, my VR compatriot." Sara sprawled leisurely in a nanchair, relaxing in the waves of movement created by the bots moving across its surface. Both women wore one-piece black suits that clung like second skins. "That steak I had for supper tonight was the most delicious piece of meat I've ever tasted. Like, it was the real thing. No cloning. No nanhancements. Just pure beef off the hoof from some planet where they still raise real cows that eat real grass. Makes me wonder if all these technological enhancements really enhance or just make bigger numbers."

Cassie, in SolidHolo, feeling the Realspace massage, made a face. "Real meat. Software or not, the idea of eating flesh turns me off. I mean, that cow was something that lived and breathed at one time. Same as you."

"No, my mistaken friend, not the same as me. This was an animal that didn't know how to add one and one. It had no opposable thumbs, no bicameral brain and no connection to Quannet. It was alone in a field munching grass, getting big and fat, waiting for me to eat it with a baked potato smothered in sour cream."

"And it was born naturally from another cow."

"Of course, that's what made it a natural-born cow."

"Then it had a family, other cows that would miss poor little Belle." Cassie leaned forward and spoke in a deep male voice. "Betty, have you seen Belle?" She shook her head no; then, in a high-pitched female voice, "No, Jonathan, I haven't. I hope they haven't cut our baby up into pieces for Sara to eat."

Sara threw a star shower at her. It exploded noiselessly, its glittering stars taking the shape of a cow. "Sorry, Mr. And Mrs. Cow, but I ate a big chunk of your daughter." She belched loudly and laughed. "Hope you don't get too mooooooody about it."

Cassie laughed and threw a shower at Sara. It formed a cow skull. "And now she's gnawing Belle's bones to sharpen her meat-eating incisors."

"Admit it, though, this place is... " She looked around at the crystalline walls and fixtures, rumored to have come from the same piece of emerline that had been used to build Bella Bjork's space mansion. It was also rumored to enhance perceptions on Canak, even the perception of dying. "Lavish."

"It's OK."

Sara sighed deeply. "This is the place to be, Cass. And we're the people to be. What's wrong with enjoying the spotlight a little?"

"I'm not here for the spotlight," said Cassie. She was tense in spite of the frantic action of the bots to relax her muscles. "In fact, I don't even want to be here. And I don't want to go into the Wars tomorrow."

"Don't want to go into the Wars?" Sara almost slammed her feet on the crystal floor sitting erect. "What's that supposed to mean? You *are* the Wars. Trillions of people Quan into the Wars just to watch you win. You're the measure of the whole thing."

"The whole thing is stupid. I'm sick of it." She stood up and began pacing around her nanchair. She wanted to tell Sara about Bella's role in the Wars, how she was the one backing her all these years, and possibly even the one behind the Reality Wars in the first place. But she wasn't about to lay something that big and disturbing on her friend just before the Wars began. "In the last Wars, millions of people died from attacks that barely missed me. They died, Sara."

339

"Of course they did, Cass. That's what they signed up for, to go down in a blaze of glory in the Reality Wars. If they hadn't been killed that way, they would probably have killed themselves at one of the death parties after the Wars. You had nothing to do with their ultimate fate, Cass. Blame that on the universe, on that wonderful sense of pointlessness it inspires-we're born, we live, we die. End of story."

"Is this supposed to cheer me up?"

"It's supposed to enlighten you. We have to find meaning in life itself, in the everyday act of living it, in things like the Wars, eating real steak, enjoying the most lavish quarters in the universe, being the idols of trillions of people throughout the-"

"We're not the idols of the people whose loved ones-sometimes their whole families-die in the Wars because we make a mistake, avoid an attack, or kill an opponent... or just experience something so powerfully that the intensity of it kills a few thousand people, wipes out half a family, or turns another few million people into mind dead zombies."

"Oo... I'm getting chills from your conviction, Cass. But here's the truth... those people are going to become whatever they will be after the Wars-dead or alive-whether they do it in the Wars or not. We give them their last meaningful moments in this life, and the better we are at it, the more meaningful those moments will be."

Cassie thought about this for a moment and faked a pout. "It still sucks."

340

"So why *are* you here?"

"Two reasons."

"Yes?"

"Buddha and my Dad want me here."

"And?"

"To keep you out of trouble."

Sara faked a look of disgust and then laughed. "To keep *me* out of trouble, huh? And just what trouble do you think I'm going to get into?"

"I think Loac and Shade are going to do everything in their power to kill you, just to make an example of you."

"My take on that scenario is... I take them out first."

"This isn't just a competition with them. This goes far beyond that. This is, like, some kind of religious statement for them. They believe I'm soulless, and if they have souls, then they should be able to beat me in events that go beyond the physical. My winning the Wars flies in the face of everything they believe. And your supporting me and being my friend makes you just as evil to them as I am. But at least I don't goad them and try to make fools of them in a Quancast that goes out to the entire universe."

Sara sat up quickly, eyebrows furrowing in anger. "I don't give a snake's ass what their religious beliefs are. And I don't need you riding shotgun for me. I can take care of myself. All you have to do is worry about *me* not beating *you*, because you're just not with it this year. I'm beginning to think that you want to be beaten."

"Well, I don't plan on winning."

341

"You don't plan on winning! What the hell do you plan on doing?"

"Riding shotgun and letting you win."

Sara jumped up, blustering with fury. "Don't you dare! I mean it! I don't need you to let me win. If I win, it'll be because I did it against your doing everything you can to win, the same as me. And listen, Cass... " She leaned her head forward and pointed a finger at Cassie, fist curled underneath like a gun. "If the Gamblers detect even one micro-instant of deliberate hesitation, or any move, no matter how miniscule, they'll file to have your program deleted. They'll kill you. And they might just kill me as well if they think we're both in on it."

Cassie stuck her tongue out at her. "I have friends who won't let that happen."

"Yeah, Buddha," she said with mock awe. "He may have helped your father escape from Bella, but if you have both Bella *and* the Gamblers after you, then eventually you're going to die."

"Well, like you said, I'm not up to par. You just might win."

"Just keep a look out for your own ass. You'll be in Realspace as well this time. And they would much rather kill you than me. That would be the ultimate victory for them. For them, it would prove humans are better than VRs. It would... "

"Oh shut up," said Cassie, smiling. "Let's go to the dining room and have one of those stupid streaks."

"You'll try a steak?"

"I'll try a bite and take it from there."

"Now, this is what I was saying... putting meaning into every moment. You're going to love-"

"Yeah, yeah, yeah. Let's go."

Interesting. Lovesong watched the spycast from Cassie and Sara's quarters. *Abner Hayes... saved by Buddha?*

CHAPTER 98 - REALITIES WITHIN REALITIES

"He'll strike soon," said Loac. "Probably tomorrow." The emerline bed shaped to her body as she shifted onto her side. "It'll be crazy at the Gates."

They'd just merged vapors and Shade was still reeling from Loac's hunger. There'd been urgency in the way her vapor had swarmed through Shade's body, grasping and caressing every muscle and bone, mingling lovingly with every cell. They'd never been so close to becoming a single entity, throbbing with an indefinable need to confirm and accept, and Shade had no doubts now that Loac was in love with her, deeply and powerfully. What they'd just experienced had no roots in duty or ultimate mission. It was love, uncompromising, unquestioning-close to the brink of that pit of ecstasy into which you fling yourself and know that you'll land sated and happy.

It was the kind of thing that could get them both killed.

She ran a finger down Loac's cheek and neck, tracing a slow line over her shoulders and breasts down to her thigh. "Let me worry about him. You need to focus on the other competitors."

"And what if he's one of them?"

"Could be, but I don't think so. Getting into the Wars takes hundreds of years, backing from organizations, media coverage. The process would have started too long ago for a contract assassination. He's here, but I'm guessing he'll be working here, or maybe he'll just flash in from nowhere with a knife in his hand." She made a motion to laugh, and stopped herself. "We have so many realities within realities. It's hard to know what to expect anymore."

"Which is exactly what the Reality Wars are all about." She put a palm tenderly against Shade's cheek. "And we've been preparing for this for five hundred years. He may have been in his element in his past contracts, but he's in our element now." She leaned forward and kissed her on the cheek. "And, together, we've already won the first round. He kills after he's weakened his victims. You're not weakened. If anything, you're stronger than ever, and he's the one whose strength has been lessened. We've seen him, sensed him, we know him."

"Well, I'd like to know him a little better, like face-to-face where I can slice that thing growing out of his cheek. And I think we'd better take turns sleeping tonight."

Shade thought about this and nodded. "You take the first sleep."

"And what about the girl's friend? Is it really necessary to kill her?"

"Our victory has to be complete." Cold again, eyes hard, void of feeling. "The entire universe will be watching this. The message we send will be a sign that flesh and blood are still the essence of sentient life in the universe." Once again the icon with an ultimate mission.

CHAPTER 99 - THE MEANING LURKING BEHIND THE WORDS

You're nervous.

"I'm not nervous."

You've never met anyone like her. And there are two of her now.

"She's just another mark."

They almost tore your mind out.

"They got lucky."

Or you got unlucky.

"I don't depend on luck."

You're acting out of anger. You've never done this before.

"I'm acting out of a need to finish this contract and get back to beautiful deaths. This is personal."

You're angry.

"I'm not angry, I'm disappointed."

Disappointed?

"She wouldn't let me give her a beautiful death."

Maybe she doesn't want to die.

"I was trying to take care of that."

Maybe her will to live is stronger than your need for her to die.

"The people I work for control the movement of history. She's just one woman."

And you're a force of history?

"I'm the Roman legion tearing the forest apart from around the last Germanic horde. I'm the Panzer division Blitzkrieging into Poland, the Airborne storming across the desert, the Tears of

Blood terraforming Annan Q before the Dragon Fire Clan had a chance to evacuate. I'm the action behind the words, the iron around the fist, the meaning lurking behind the policy..."

You're working for a guy to presents himself as a coin and calls himself the Cormorant. He's a sleazy little asshole-

"Who controls a large part of the universe and will soon control a lot more. Ultimate power rarely sits with decent people."

You could at least make it quick.

"If that will make you happy."

I think it will make you happy at some level.

"Quick, then. But not beautiful."

CHAPTER 100 - WE'RE ALL GONNA DIE!

Maggie: We're talking to a group of spectators from Zinin. Now, these folks are right into the mood of the Reality Wars with ten thousand of them gathered in one of the largest burial crypts in the universe.

(Cut to Quancast of thousands of revelers, drinking, hugging, having sex, smoking, dancing. Quancast focuses in on one group standing in a circle. Seven women and three men)

Maggie: (laughing) Hello from Canak! Looks like you folks have a party going on there.

(Laughter and shouts from the crowd. Quancast focuses on a young woman with long blond hair)

Childen: This is Childen Shan from Canak. Who's your favorite to win?

Young woman: (laughs hysterically, obviously on drugs) No favorites to win, Childen. We're all here for Sara Beth to lose. (laughs madly)

Childen: You mean, your group?

Young woman: (laughs, points around) No! All of us! All ten thousand of us. We're the Sara Beth Ten Thousand. When she dies, we all die.

Maggie: That's the most amazing thing I've ever heard! You mean everybody in the crypt is entangled with the same competitor?

(Young man with sandy brown hair steps into focus)

Young man: That's right, Maggie! (laughing nervously) When Sara goes down, we all go down.

Childen: But what if she doesn't go down?

Young man: (laughs) Sure, Childen, sure. The Tears are gonna take her down just on principle. I think they want her dead more than they want to win the Wars. Did you lose brain matter along with your arms!

Young woman: Don't listen to Dann! He's on drugs! (pokes him in the ribs and laughs) We're hoping that she at least gets through the first Reality. Maybe even the second. But there's no way the Tears are going to let her finish the Wars. No way!

Maggie: And then you're all going to die?

Young woman: That's right! All ten thousand of us. All together. Just... (snaps her fingers)... boink into the... (throws her arms up) whatever!

Childen: You seem to want to die.

Young woman: Now, you're getting it, Chilly.

Childen: But why?

Young woman: Why? (points upwards) Because there's nothing out there. (points to her chest) There's nothing in here. There's nothing. (looks momentarily distraught, recovers, laughs) Yahoo! We're all gonna die!

Group: Yahoo!

Maggie: Now, that's getting into the Wars! You folks have a great time! And we'll check back with you tomorrow!

Group: Yahoo!

Childen: Folks... just one last question. (group looks into Quanscreen of Childen, smiling, laughing) Given the off chance that Sara Beth does finish the Wars alive... what then?"

349

Young man: We stay here.

Childen: You stay there?

Young man: The crypt's been sealed.

Childen: You mean, you can't get out?

Young man: (laughs nervously) Hey, we paid top dollar for this. It's sealed.

CHAPTER 101 - SOMETHING TO TIE IT ALL TOGETHER

Lorsies Sharmain floated in her tube. It was comfortable, warm and lit up with a pleasant green glow, probably the micro bit of emerline crystal used to sooth her mind and enhance the effects of the nandrugs. This was the most peace she'd experience for most of her adult life, nearly seven hundred years.

She'd sold everything she owned-in Realspace and Quanspace-to be here. Unfortunately, everything she owned wasn't enough for entanglement with one of the competitors, plus be on Canak for the Wars. That would have been the way to go if she could have afforded it, but this was OK. She was going to be one of the millions who would receive a Quansurge from the start of the Reality Wars. It would be a rush of energy from the competitors, the spectators and everyone else connected, no matter how remotely, to the Wars. Their energy, their excitement, their stress, fears, happiness, expectations, disappointments-everything they felt-was going to come rushing into Lorsies. The sheer intensity of it would be lethal-and it would grow as it surged over the planet for those who could at least have afforded to die on Canak, and then out across the universe to those who couldn't.

As death followed death, the intensity of the surge would feed on those deaths and grow even more lethal until every life subscribed to it blinked out.

Lorsies wasn't the least concerned about the end of the Reality Wars; she was concerned just with her own end, an end to that huge gnawing emptiness that grew inside her like a spiritual cancer after exhausting all the possibilities she'd tried over the hundreds of years of her life. She'd forgotten most of the things she'd experienced in both Quanspace and Realspace, all the jobs, the families, the romances, the careers, the leisure activities, the discovery mission across the universe, the introspection, the shamans, the religions, the lifetime after lifetime of searching for something to tie it all together, the disappointments following each new experience, the emptiness following each new find in the universe that might suggest the existence of something beyond the trap of her life. It was bottomless. What the hell, they were making life now. Clones. Sentient VRs. What was the value of being human when the copies were better than the originals? What was the value of endeavor when it had no ultimate goal? What was the value of life when software was happier than you?

There was nothing out there. Nothing beyond. No mystery. No ultimate meaning. Nothing to unite it all into some higher meaning. As far as Lorsies was concerned, death was the only thing that would tie it all together.

CHAPTER 102 - IMAGINATION

Maxilim Marx's friends respected his athleticism in every plane, physical, mental and spiritual. He'd been a top contender in the last four Wars and was the favorite to win for the clones this year, just as he had in the last Wars, finishing fourth overall behind the girl, Sara Beth and Childen. But this year, he wasn't finishing third overall, he was finishing first. He knew it. It was his destiny. This would be the year that clones were finally taken seriously, as seriously as any blood and flesh human.

And it didn't matter that they might still claim he was soulless. Could the birth humans killing themselves by the millions-and the hundreds of millions, maybe even billions in the Wars alone-really lay claim to having souls themselves? Would souls give them the strength to stay alive? Possession of something existing beyond the life-draining mundane-wouldn't that be enough to sustain their will to live? But it didn't.

If soul existed at all, it certainly didn't exist in any of the birth humans he knew.

Except maybe in the Clans. Their suicide rates appeared to be nil. But then, many would say the Clans had manipulated themselves genetically to the extent that they might not even be human anymore. They might be something else. And Loac appeared to be the ultimate the Clans had to offer. Maxilim would be hard-pressed to beat her. He wasn't even sure if the girl or her friend could beat her, though they had bested both Loac and her bodyguard at the Clean Test.

But might that not be Maxilim's key to winning? Somehow... play the four of them against each other? Let them fight their little VR-hating battles amongst themselves, while he surged to the forefront and became the first clone to win the Reality Wars and the first life form other than software ever to win.

Maxilim Marx lay in his emerline crystal bed imagining the universe that he was about to inspire and the changes in perception that his win and example would provoke across billions of galaxies.

He imagined the new galactic order that he would create for his wife and children, his friends and the billions of other clones who just wanted to live without some registry at Control branding them with the greatest insult Maxilim could imagine: less.

CHAPTER 103 - THE PLAINS OF PEACE

The North Tower of Canak City's only hotel, The Plains, overlooked the Plains of Peace. Once, the Plains had been thousands of square miles of lush yellow and green grass peppered with towering mushroom-like yellow trees. Now, thousands upon thousands of rows of tall entanglement tubes stretched to every horizon, casting an eerie green glow in the Canak night.

Millions of people floated in those tubes, waiting to die.

Close to the top of the sparkling North Tower, a strange sound emitted from an open window. It had a powerful steady beat, and it came in loud waves, its silences all the more powerful for the battering wave of sound.

Centos Kama rolled over in his emerline bed and scrunched a pillow under his head, awakened by the sound of his own snoring.

355

CHAPTER 104 - A BALANCE OF POWER

Maggie: As you all know, the Reality Wars are the single biggest gambling event in the universe, and this year promises to be the biggest money maker-or loser, depending on your luck-ever.

Childen: Entire star systems are expected to change hands. Galactic empires will be made and others broken. Coming into the Wars, the betting was triple any previous year. Now, It's ten times the highest it's ever been... and counting.

Maggie: That's right, Childen. And the odds seem to be pretty much splits between Cassie Hayes and the Tears of Blood Clan's Loac. These Reality Wars could begin a change in the balance of power throughout the universe.

Childen: That's right, Maggie. (Maggie throws him a blistering glare) Nobody knows exactly how powerful the Gamblers are, but there are rumors that Bella may be into them to the point where they may be in a position to exercise control over her. (Maggie looks suddenly worried, remains quiet) And with the breakdown of Quannet after the VR Outpouring, there's even talk that any kind of alliance between the Gamblers and any of the other power nodes in the universe-the Clans, for instance-might lead to a force powerful enough to-

Maggie: (still worried, cuts in) That's very interesting, Childen. And now, on Plaaten V, the entire planet has been converted into one huge party, with every city and nation on the planet giving nonstop fireworks, live entertainment and group Quans, the biggest one coming from a five-mile-high screen carved right into the side of Mount Cambers...

CHAPTER 105 - SWEATING

Far from Canak, on a planet hidden just as well as Canak, appearing on no charts or navigation systems, it was nighttime. Sleep time. But the planet's most powerful denizen was sleepless. He'd been sleepless for several days. So much was riding on the next day or two. Everything that he'd built over centuries was riding on someone who was just short of being a ghost doing something that any sane person would deem to be impossible.

The Cormorant sipped from his brandy glass, replaying the Quans of Shade arriving on Canak, looking healthy and fit, as ready for the Wars as she'd ever been. She wasn't the tired, lifeless wreck waiting to die that his assassin had predicted.

Not only could he not sleep, he was sweating.

CHAPTER 106 - SOON

Lovesong's soft snore soothed Bella as she lay against him, her head snuggled into is chest, her right leg draped over his right leg. Their lovemaking had gone deep into the night, enhanced by their genetics, the drugs they'd been doing more often these days and the fire of victory fevering her mind and body. Everything had been set in motion; there was no turning back. But then, Bella Bjork had never in her life been one to turn back. She'd gone against the Powers and defeated them, all of them, tracked them down across the universe and killed them one-by-one... and their families, and their friends-she'd given orders to the Tree to eat the babies alive while their parents watched. She'd slaughtered entire star systems and brought galaxies to their knees just by going forward ruthlessly.

The only person in the universe to ever thwart her was Abner Hayes. And she knew that he'd had an ally. He had to have had help. The Old Earth Archives left over from the first Internet showed traces of another being, something not human, but not quite software. Something in between. And whatever it was, it was back. That being had helped Abner Hayes escape.

But that was all right. Soon, the Clans would be smashed. The greatest military threat to her power would be decimated and all their ships and crews turned to vapor. All life on their planets would be exterminated, humans, animals and plants-the planets turned into lifeless deserts with lethal atmospheres. Soon, the asteroids of Blood Citadel would be space dust. Soon, the Gamblers-and that insect Kingston-would be obliterated, their wealth in Bella's coffers. Soon, she would have the Texture.

The Texture.

It was the key, her hope, her destiny. It would unlock the powers of other dimensions, give her understanding of eternity, grant her everlasting life. She would have access to new powers, born of new properties that she would unite with the properties of this dimension. Her hold over this universe would be complete. She would rule over every atom and string. There would be nowhere for her enemies to hide that she didn't have control over right down to the frequencies that defined the air they breathed.

Soon, she would have Abner back and his ally. And his daughter.

And they would all die.

CHAPTER 107 - SECOND THOUGHTS

You're going to die.

"I'm not going to die."

This is just plain crazy.

"This is the only way."

Your getaway plan is flimsy at best.

"It'll work."

She's not just a competitor, she's a warrior.

"She's another human. She can die."

You're human. You can die.

"I won't."

You'll have a fraction of a second.

"Plenty of time."

She still wants to live. She won't be like the others.

"I've killed thousands who wanted to live."

But not in hundreds of years.

"I still have it."

They'll be together.

"It won't help her."

Together, they almost got you once.

"Once."

Buddha doesn't want her to die.

"Buddha wasn't contracted to kill her."

He says that you'll destroy the potato.

"I never liked potatoes."

You ate French fries on Halion once.

"I needed something to dip into the mayonnaise."

But you still enjoyed the fries.

"Fries are not potatoes. They're processed potatoes."

You might say they're one of the paths.

"One of the possibilities."

Potato potential.

"A spud pattern."

You don't have to kill her.

"I accepted the contract."

But now you're having second thoughts.

"I never have second thoughts."

And what exactly do you think I am?

CHAPTER 108 - RULES AND RANDOM PLATFORMS

Maggie: Here we are at the beginning of the Tenth Centennial Reality Wars, and the whole universe is watching! These are the biggest Wars since they were started a thousand years ago! More competitors, more arenas, more betting, more at stake.

Childen: Not to mention all new rules. And one at the very last minute-

Maggie: (irritated) That's right, Childen. Competitors are no longer permitted to work in teams. They go in alone and they fight for their lives alone. This year, it's everyone for themselves.

Childen: That's going to make a serious dent just about everyone's training, Maggie, especially for those who depend almost entirely on team work.

Maggie: That's right, Childen. But what's going to make this the most interesting of the Wars ever certainly has to be the hatred steaming around four of the women in this year's event... Loac and Shade from the Tears of Blood Clan and Cassie Hayes and Sara Beth in their own camp.

Childen: I wouldn't exactly say that Cassie Hayes has hatred steaming out of her, Maggie. In fact, her ability to control her feelings is probably the main reason she's been winning for-

Maggie: She's software, Childen! She-

Childen: Sentient software, Maggie. She feels.

Maggie: (shakes here head while rolling her eyes) And we have some new arenas this year, and

with Solidholo, this will be the first Wars ever to be run in both Realspace and Quannspace for both humans and VRs.

Childen: And the randomly rotating arenas will push them in and out of realities without warning, sometimes in the middle of an event.

Maggie: While at the same time switching between Quanspace and Realspace. Now, I've been informed that this is a new technology that really hasn't been tested for anywhere near infinite possibilities. Things could go wrong. Some of the competitors might just find themselves streaking off into... wherever.

Childen: With millions of spectators entangled in their fate.

Maggie: (shrugs) Be interesting to see what happens to them.

Childen: (looks at her skeptically) Hopefully, nothing.

Maggie: Not what they signed up for, Childen. (laughs) But who knows? With hundreds of possible arenas, all of them rotating randomly, plus switching between Real and Quanspace, this promises to be the best Wars ever.

CHAPTER 109 - THE LEAST LIKELY PLACE

"I still don't see the point in this." Shade's irritation was mixed heavily with a sense of embarrassment that Loac seemed somehow to be taking the lead in security, insisting they use the stairs rather than the tubeway. "This seems more likely a place to make his move than the tubes."

Both were wearing Reality Wars black skintight body suits-called Wars suits-with the red tears insignia of their Clan. "He won't expect us to take the stairs," said Loac. There was a hint of excitement under her words, as though they were playing some potentially dangerous children's game. Shade sensed that she was enjoying this. "Everybody takes the tubes. That's where he'll be waiting. It's the perfect ambush. For that fraction of a second, just as you step out, you're disoriented."

"And he knows that we know that."

"So?"

"So, he'll be waiting where we're not likely to be."

"You mean the stairs." A shadow of doubt flickered in her eyes but only momentarily. "On the other hand, he may think that we'll expect him in the least likely place."

Shade let out a sigh. "Do what you want, lover, but as soon as that port opens, I'm killing anything that's within two feet of it."

The thought of Shade springing viciously out of the port and mercilessly killing whatever was on the other side sent a thrill through Loac's body and an intense tingling sensation in her loins.

"And remember to stick to our deal," said Shade. "I'll be first out."

"That still sounds odd to me. You're the one he's after."

"I have a surprise for him."

"I wish you would tell me what's going on with that."

"You'll see soon enough." *When I kill that bastard.*

***

How can you be so sure they won't take the tube?

"It's what everyone does."

So why wouldn't they?

"They're not everyone."

CHAPTER 110 - PEACE TUBES

Maggie: (Quancast pans a convex metallic gold wall several miles long and at least a mile high) What you're seeing now is the War Wall. This is where the contestants will arrive. The ports will open first on the ground level and then begin opening in lines across the wall until they open right to the top, an entire mile up! Childen, you exited the tubes close to the top in Quanspace once, didn't you?

Childen: Yes, Maggie, about fifty feet from the top. It was a great way to enter. There were thousands of contestants floating down, even VRs. That was the last time that VRs other than Cassie Hayes competed in the Wars.

Maggie: (suddenly excited) We've just received word that the contestants have entered their tubes and are on the way down to the center of Canak. Yes, that's what I said... the center of Canak!

Childen: A move to increase security given the millions of Realspace spectators. And... it just happens to make plenty of room for suicide tubes on the planet's surface. Makes me wonder what will happen when they run out of room on the surface to install tubes for future Wars.

Maggie: (laughs) Childen, Childen, Childen. I believe the proper terminology is Peace Tube. Those people will be at peace for the rest of time in those tubes, released from-

Childen: They go into the tubes knowing they'll die in them, either during the Wars or after. Maggie, they're committing-

Maggie: (excited) The first contestants will be coming out in just a few seconds!

CHAPTER 111 - WORRIES

"Stop worrying. He'll be OK." Sara lay her head on Cassie's shoulder, still fascinated with being able to actually feel her best friend in SolidHolo. "So... how does it feel?" she said, lifting her head and turning toward Cassie as the two plummeted to the center of Canak in the tubeway.

"It feels like crap." She looked worried. "I don't know where he is."

"I mean SolidHolo. How does it feel?"

"The strangeness has mostly passed and it's starting to feel normal... not as tight as at first." She sighed deeply. "But that's the least of my problems. I mean, I finally get to see my Dad after all these years... "

Sara put her hands on Cassie's shoulders and looked into her eyes with a mixture of sympathy and irony. "He's with Buddha. He'll be OK."

"I wish you wouldn't say his name in that tone. I know he's not the real Buddha, but-

"I know, he saved your father." She gripped Cassie's shoulders tightly. "And I'm thankful to him for that as well. But just think of it... if he can help your father escape from Bella, then your father is probably in good hands."

Cassie thought about this for a moment. Sara hugged her lightly and turned toward the port. "And I'm just as worried about you," said Cassie. "Especially now that we're not allowed to do any teamwork and might not even meet in the same arenas."

"Don't worry about me. I'll be OK."

369

"They'll try to kill you. I mean, you've got them backed into some kind of corner of honor. The only way they'll be happy is with you dead."

"I really don't like those people."

"They really don't like you." She put her hand on Sara's shoulder. "Don't take any unnecessary chances, Sara. I mean it. You're the only real friend I have. I need you."

Sara smiled. "And you're the closest friend I have. Don't worry about me. I know they'll try to kill me. I expect it. But I've killed in the Wars before. If I have to, I'll do it again."

A slight frown creased Cassie's face.

The tube came to a halt and the port began to slide open. "Well," said Sara, "the show begins."

CHAPTER 112 - FAMILIES

Maxilim Marx ran his hand over the hairless landscape of his head. It wasn't a nervous movement, just something he did because it felt good.

"Yes," said Centos Kama, smiling. "Your head's still on your shoulders."

Maxilim winked. "Just checking."

Centos chuckled. "How's the family?"

"Proud. Nervous. Happy for me. Nervous."

"Must be hard on the families. Never had one myself-but times like this, it don't bother me." He shrugged. "Maybe a few hundred years or so."

"You would make a great husband and father, Centos. For all your bulk and brash, you're one of the gentlest souls I've met."

"Don't ever say that in public," said Centos, mocking sternness. "Especially right before a Wars."

Both men were laughing as the tube slowed and stopped and the port began to open.

CHAPTER 113 - THE RUSH

Maggie: Look! Look! The walls are reddening! (Quancast zooms in on a section of the wall where the gold surface begins to turn red) The first tubes are arriving on the ground level!

Childen: And this should be interesting Maggie. Only the top contenders, those who have finished well in past Wars, and those who have the highest odds with the Gamblers are allowed to enter at ground level so we'll be seeing the cream of this year's Reality Wars crop, all entering at the same time.

Maggie: So why did you have to enter from the top two Wars ago, Childen? Haven't you always been a contend-

Childen: I asked to be released from the top, Maggie.

Maggie: (looks dumbfounded) Why?

Childen: For the rush, Maggie, the rush.

CHAPTER 114 - DEADLY ENTRANCE

"Oh that," said Loac, seeing the silver metallic device in Shade's hand. She smiled.

"You have a beautiful smile," said Shade.

The smile promptly dropped from Loac's mouth but was back within seconds.

"When it opens," said Shade, "hold back a moment."

Loac nodded as the port slid open.

A dozen feet to the left, Cassie and Sara stepped out of their tube and into the Wars Chamber, while at the same time, a dozen feet to their left, Maxilim and Centos left their tube, still laughing.

Sara glanced to her right and saw Loac and Shade exiting from the utility stairs, looking straight ahead with Clan arrogance. *Why did they use the utility stairs? And what was that on the other side of them?* An instant before she could scream a warning, a man dressed in a black Wars suit thrust his hand forward to propel a dart-like object at Shade. He was in mid throw when suddenly, both Sara and Cassie saw a life-size Buddha appear directly in the line of fire. In a fraction of a second, the dart flew through Buddha and through Shade's head as she continued to walk, oblivious of the attempt on her life. The dart streaked past Cassie's head, missing her by a microinch and shot directly into Maxilim's head. The clone was in mid-laugh when his head exploded, tossing bits of brain, bone and skin tissue into Centos's face.

Before the Assassin could lift his other arm with another dart, Shade and Loac disappeared.

They used a holo.

"No time to... "

Shade and Loac tumbled out of the tube, firing lasers in the Assassin's direction. A chunk of his right shoulder disappeared at the same time that a swatch of his stomach sizzled into nonbeing.

He disappeared.

Shade and Loac looked into each other's eyes, then into the shocked eyes of Cassie and Sara, and all four turned their eyes on Centos, eyes ballooned, head shaking, holding the headless body of Maxilim Marx.

Sara turned to Cassie. "They used a holograph to draw fire away from them. Cassie, if Buddha hadn't appeared to deflect the dart, it would have gone into your head. In SolidHolo, it would have killed you.

Cassie nodded, not taking her eyes off Centos, still propping up Maxilim's body, crying now as his eyes narrowed in murderous anger.

***

On Illim Cent, over a hundred light-years away, Quenith Kamp, like millions of others across the universe entangled with Maxilim Marx, lay slumped in death. All the walls of his room were littered with memory panels playing out all the experiences of his life from birth to the moment he watched

Maxilim Marx die a hundred light-years away. He'd spent his last moments watching them, looking for something to make sense of it all, and right up to the moment of his death, he'd found nothing that would have made him want to disentangle from Maxilim Marx.

CHAPTER 115 - MAGGIE AND CHILDEN

Maggie: Did you see that! Did you see that! Maxilim Marx has just been killed by a puff dart by one of the other competitors! Maxilim Marx has just been killed!

Childen: Did you see who that competitor was? I didn't see who that competitor was. He just disappear-"

Maggie: Maxilim Marx has just been murdered! An illegal kill! Before the Wars even started! Maxilim Marx has just-

Childen: And Maggie, who was that fat guy with the big smile? Did you see the fat guy with the big smile! I've seen him before! I've seen that face, that shape... and then he just-

Maggie: Centos Kama is holding Maxilim Marx's dead body! His head has completely disappeared! Blown off with a puff dart! Maxilim Marx is dead! The first competitor killed in these Wars! Killed illegally...

CHAPTER 116 - MY JOB

Yep, that went well.

"I don't need this."

The dart would have torn the upper part of her body off. She would have had a horrible death.

"And what of it?"

Don't you think that would have been a bit much?

"She came into my Quanspace with her bitch friend. Into my personal space."

You were trying to kill her.

"That's my job."

And maybe it's her job to live.

"Maybe it's your job to shut up."

What will you do now?

"Sleep."

Good place for that.

Suspended inside a luminescent green tube, the Assassin gazed at thousands of rows of Peace Tubes stretching into the Canak horizon.

You're sure you know how to get out of here.

"When it's time."

How long do you think it'll take them to trace the SolidHolo track to the tubeway.

"Doesn't matter. It tracks back to another tube."

But they know you're here now.

"I set up a false trail."

Silence.

"But you know all this."

Yes, I know all this.

"Then why do you ask me these questions?"

It's my job.

The Assassin closed his eyes and slept.

378

CHAPTER 117 - A CHANGE IN ODDS

The Cormorant's eyes bulged with fury. Blood vessels swelled obscenely on his neck. He opened his mouth and closed it, opened and closed, words mired in the glue of his disbelief. If he'd been watching the Wars on a screen, he would have thrown something heavy and destructive to smash the Quanned images. Maybe that's why he dug his fingers into his head and pulled down hard enough to draw blood.

Something gurgled up from his throat. It was a sound of sorts. But nothing intelligible. It barely sounded human. It had the resonance of rage, the pitch of desperation, the tone of hatred-pure unbridled hatred.

His assassin had failed him. The Clanswoman was still alive. She would still enter the Wars and her Clans girlfriend wouldn't be the slightest put off by the death the assassin was supposed to have given her. In fact, they would both be pumped up by what had just happened, primed to raise havoc in the Wars. Primed to win.

He checked the odds. Betting on Shade and Loac was climbing. Strangely, Shade was favored to win just under the VR.

CHAPTER 118 - A SURPRISE

"It wasn't your fault."

The Buddha Abner faced was anything but a happy Buddha, more like despairing. "I knew that your daughter was in danger if he made the attempt on Shade. I didn't know that the clone would pay his life for my intervention. I should have thought this-"

"You're not God. You can't control the future. You saved my daughter's life. You did good."

"The clone had a family. They won't feel so good about what I've done."

Abner regarded Buddha with a look of deep compassion. "If Cassie had died, hundreds of millions of lives across the universe would have disappeared with her."

"That would have been their choice."

"But not the choice of their loved ones."

Buddha thought about this.

Abner was taken aback by the sigh coming from a piece of software-remnants of human genetic coding-that had once caused the deaths of hundreds of millions of people, a program written for the purpose of causing war and destruction, now remorseful over the death of one clone. "You've changed in the last couple thousand years."

"I had a lot of time to think things out, change my purpose and meaning." Buddha smiled. "I'm enlightened now, you know."

"And now you're going to bring equality to billions of people across the universe. And maybe even save the universe." Abner smiled wryly. "Any hints on how that might happen?"

"I'm still a little uncertain about that part."

"That doesn't make me feel much good about all this. C'mon, any hints?"

"It's the Texture. I'm not exactly sure what it is. It's not from this universe."

"You're sure of that?"

"I've probed it."

"Everybody rushing across the universe to find out what the damn thing is, and you've already been there?"

"It helped to enlighten me."

"How so?"

"It taught me a different song."

Silence.

"And?"

"It just taught me a different song."

"Is that supposed to make me feel better?"

"It shouldn't make you feel any worse."

Abner shrugged. "Will we be going to see this Texture?"

Buddha smiled. "We may not have to."

Abner rolled his eyes.

CHAPTER 119 - VERY UNCLANSMANLIKE

After their plans had been carried out, it didn't matter if it took the rest of his life-he would find the man who tried to assassinate Shade. His heart was still beating madly after seeing how close she'd come to dying. Very unclansmanlike. But that was beside the point now. Shade was like a second daughter to him, much more human than Loac, but maybe their combination of humanity and cold sense of purpose would give them an advantage in the Wars. Yes, it was even possible that Shade's particular character-considered an aberration by many-was something given by God to give them that extra dimension in the Wars.

For now, he could relax in the knowledge that the assassin had failed. It was unlikely that he would try a second attempt. The Wars would begin in minutes. The competitors were already dispersing across the launching field in the War Chamber, taking their places to begin an event that was watched by trillions of spectators across the universe.

In the meantime, Bavn had other things to deal with. Communications were all but nonexistent with the ships he'd sent to the Texture. They, like his daughter and Shade, were on their own now. What happened there would happen there. It was in God's and Zethar's hands, and Bavn knew that the outcome would be known to him the very moment

Zethar's ships succeeded. And they would succeed. One way or another.

What worried him most now were the reports from Triste. Strange new ships like none the Clans had ever seen in Bella's navies were moving to the front lines at Control. It might mean nothing, possibly their commander Daman Haley taking extra precautions after the incident with the young captain. On the other hand, he'd told Triste to be ready for anything, even though he knew he would be.

And then there was the disappearance of millions of Bella's ships. This bothered Triste more than the movement of ships at Control. It bothered Bavn as well. It wasn't unusual for entire fleets of Bella's navies to disappear, so thoroughly cloaked that none of the Clans' intelligence experts could locate them until they just reappeared, back from missions somewhere in the universe, doing Bella's will.

But millions of ships. At this particular time. Right at the doorstop of extraordinary events. He looked around at the Vorgell asteroids surrounding Vala, darkened and formidable, and more heavily armed than any navy in the universe. A fortress traveling thousands of miles an hour around a planet that was, itself, a formidable weapon. If war with Bella came, the Clans would be ready. They would always be ready.

He just wished that Lethar would reach the Texture soon.

CHAPTER 120 - ADRENALINE

They walked slowly but purposefully, emanating pure energy as thousands of them made their way across a field of perfectly sheered crystal-green grass. The variety of human and clone was breathtaking-enlarged heads, shrunken heads, extra arms or legs, strange faces with even stranger eyes and noses and mouths. Some had antenna; others, monitors for heads-monitors that displayed every experience they had in Real or Quanspace. Among them, they displayed every imaginable color in the universe at every conceivable frequency.

They were the product of genetic choice.

Precisely every ten feet, gray metal disks rose out of the ground to the exact height of the grass. As competitors reached them, they stopped and stepped onto the disks. There they stood quiety, waiting.

***

Maggie: This is it, folks, the beginning of the Tenth Centennial Reality Wars. We've been told that the man who killed Maxilim Marx has disappeared. Security devices have been released, but there seems to be no trail and no sign. Childen, what happened there?

Childen: Who knows, Maggie? It could have been anything. It's hard to even say who he was trying to kill. If it hadn't been for Shade's holo, she would be dead. But maybe it was just a wild shot. Maybe Maxilim really was the target."

Maggie: Any thoughts on why, Childen?

Childen: Again, who knows? A grudge? Somebody trying to change the odds in the gambling? An irate fan? Somebody looking for a moment of fame? We won't know until they catch him, and that's unlikely to happen until the end of the Wars. Until then, the focus of everyone and everything on Canak will be on the Wars.

Maggie: Possibly then, a fitting start to a Reality Wars that promises carnage beyond any we've seen yet. (Smiles widely)

Childen: Maggie, have you ever thought about getting help?

Maggie: (Confused) I beg your pardon?

Childen: Nothing. (Shifts his head) It seems to have little effect on the competitors-

Maggie: Yes, they're walking across the launch field, thousands of them, as more descend from the wall and stride toward the field. Childen, can you tell our viewers why they have to take the first disk in their path instead of just choosing one on their own?

Childen: It's the new ruling against teams entering the Wars. This is how they're separated, Maggie. Most of them enter the field in pairs or in groups. When they enter the launch field, they have to walk a straight line until they come to the first unoccupied launch disk. If they're walking with someone and come to a disk, the person next to them might have to walk a hundred feet or more before coming to the first unoccupied disk in their path. The first person to find a disk will be surrounded by strangers. This is why many of the competitors have separated from their groups before entering the field. They have a better chance of being together if they go in randomly.

Maggie: And this prevents them from working out group strategies.

Childen: Not exactly, Maggie. You see, they can still end up together in one or more arenas. It's completely random. This should make for some interesting adaptations and maybe even some new alliances.

Maggie: (looking bored) Very interesting, Childen. Oh look! Sara and Shade are walking into the field together. And it looks like they're talking to each other. And they appear to be smiling? Do you think they might actually be getting along?

Childen: Somehow, Maggie, I doubt that.

***

"So, your little girlfriend's messing around on you?" asked Sara, sarcastically. "Trying to get it on with my best friend?"

"I think my little girlfriend would love to eat your little best friend's heart," said Shade, smiling. "If she had one."

Sara laughed, forced, loud. "She does. Bigger than any machine that beats in the chest of any Clanswoman."

"You underestimate us, Sara." She put added emphasis on the "ah"-something Sara took to be an insult of some sort. "Our hearts are likely the only true hearts left in the universe. Look around you. Billions of lives will perish in these Wars, willingly, happily. They signed up for it. Not one of those death-wishers will be from the Clans."

"That's not heart, Shade. That's stubbornness. You all just want to stick around to be a pain up everybody else's ass." Sara stopped before a launch disk. "Looks like this is where I begin."

Shade stopped walking and turned to face Sara. "The Clan Wars may have watered down our humor, but soon, very soon, our hearts will be as light as any in the universe."

"Believe it when I see it," said Sara, stepping onto the ramp. "And by the way, your girlfriend had a message for me." Shade cocked her head to the side, curious. "I'm not the one who needs to be watching my back. My advice to you and her... watch your front. That's where I'll be."

Shade nodded, smiled and walked on, finding her disk about fifty feet beyond Sara's.

***

Maggie: I don't know, Childen. It looks like they might actually be getting along-a little pregame bantering. A lot of smiling going on there.

Childen: And then there's the old saying that the only time Clansfolk smile is just before killing somebody. That's...

Maggie: And just look at that! Loac and Cassie Hayes walking together. Now, this time I believe they won't have anything good to say to each other. And I'm not seeing any smiles on their faces.

***

Both women walked with long confident—almost threatening—strides.

"Harm Sara, and I'll kill both of you." Cassie looked straight ahead as she spoke, expressionless.

"Your threats don't worry me, VR." Also looking straight ahead. "If your friend crosses my path, there will be no mercy. If you cross my path, there will be no mercy. A new universe is nearing, and there will be no room in it for your kind. There will be no room for anyone who supports your kind. It will be a universe of flesh and bone and soul."

"These Wars may give you a new insight into soul, Clanswoman." Cassie stopped at her disk and stepped onto it. "If you're still alive when they end."

"Don't worry about me being alive, VR. Just pray that we don't come face-to-face." She walked on without a glance in Cassie's direction.

***

Maggie: Yes, no love lost between those two.

Childen: They're disks are far apart, but as I said, the Wars are completely randomized. They could end up in a Quanspace spread across galaxies, or in any of the hundreds of Realspace arenas under Canak's surface.

Maggie: Centos Kama looks calm after the death of such a close friend.

Childen: They were friends, Maggie, but not really all that close. In the past, Maxilim has pulled some dirty tricks on Centos to pull ahead of him. One of those stunts almost got Centos killed. I'm guessing that all that's on his mind right now is doing his best in the Wars.

***

If there was one thing that Centos Kama was sure of, it was this-when these Wars were over, he would hunt down the man who'd killed his friend and kill him slowly. He stepped onto a disk and closed his eyes, calmly waiting for the Wars to begin.

***

Maggie: Everyone's almost in place now. Strange, isn't it, Childen, how calm they all look, almost relaxed.

Childen: That's the way to go into the Wars, Maggie. Competitors are well-trained in these first moments. In a few moments, they'll be wrenched from this reality into something that goes beyond any of their past experience. They've all trained for this moment, to stay calm, control their breathing, relax their muscles, empty their minds of thought. To be ready for anything.

Maggie: And yet, dozens of them will die at the launch from Quan glitches, the sheer excitement... and my favorite, the launch pad kills. I don't know how they do that, but watching the victims falling into the arenas with pikes sticking out of their heads... I wonder if that will happen...

Childen: (rolling his eyes) And millions more will die, the spectators who signed up for the launch rush, the exact second the Wars start. It's said to be the biggest adrenaline rush in the universe. It takes the feelings of the competitors at the exact moment they launch-the moment the composure lets loose-and mixes it with the Quanned emotions of trillions of viewers. It's called the Reality Launch, and it kills.

Maggie: And the Reality Launch is about to begin! All the competitors are in place, Childen. The Tenth Annual Reality Wars are about to begin!

***

On the launch field, half the competitors began to glow red. These were the ones going to arenas in Quanspace. The disks under the remaining competitors began to spin and suddenly lowered, taking the people standing on them to arenas somewhere in the bowels of Canak.

***

Lorsies Sharmain smiled and breathed, let out a long contented breath as the surge of energy from the Reality Wars launch closed down her mind and body forever.

The surge spread through the universe, killing over thirty million people, some of whom had waited a century for this.

390

CHAPTER 121 - CREATION UPON CREATION

"You fixed the Wars?"

"I'm curious." Something giant with green wings flapped slowly by the ocean viewing port. Bella's eyes glowed green. The divan she lay upon breathed and undulated with every breath she took. "I want to see how these four women meet in the Wars. Every arena will pit one of the Clanswomen against either Cassie or Sara, maybe both."

Lovesong lifted two long-stemmed glasses filled with orange liquid from the top of a crystal pillar and crossed the floor, handing Bella one of the glasses before seating himself beside her. He smiled. "The audience will love it. The Gamblers will go crazy taking bets. It's genius." He lifted his glass to hers for a toast.

Bella smiled wildly. The corners of her mouth shook. Faint wrinkles spread from the corners of her eyes. "To hell with them, all of them. I did this for myself. And for you, my darling. For our entertainment."

"And the fleets?"

"They stand ready for my word." She sipped from her glass, let the fluid run over her tongue and swallowed. "Has the girl been in touch with her father?"

"Yes. Not long enough to get a precise fix, though."

A bright streak of red flashed through the blue of Bella's eyes and disappeared almost as soon as it appeared.

"But they'll be in touch again. They can only meet so many times before we have them. And they won't stop seeing each other. They can't."

"Then don't do anything yet." She shifted her position and curled up beside him, resting her head against his shoulder. "Wait until after the Wars, when the universe is mine once again. There will be nowhere for them to hide. We'll let them think they're safe before we capture them and torture them side by side for a thousand years so they can feed on each other's pain. And then we'll destroy them."

"As you wish." Lovesong sipped from his drink as he thought. "Did you know about the assassin?"

More red flashed from her eyes and subsided. "That was as much a surprise for me as it was for you. I have a feeling that our little Cormorant may have been trying to manipulate the gambling. I'll have to make his death all the more horrifying."

"And the assassin?"

"He dies." The right side of her lip twisted into a snarl. "They all die."

"It'll be a clean sweep."

"A great purging."

"A new universe."

They toasted again.

She turned her head up and kissed him under his chin. "A universe created in my likeness. A universe joining all other universes for all time with

392

every life and every frequency vibrating to my rhythm."

"Creation upon Creation existing within your perfection."

"They all die."

CHAPTER 122 - WHITE

And suddenly everything was blindingly bright. Color blanched out of the control console of Soul Ship. Color blanched out of Benji Parx. Color blanched out of Jeli Role. Everything was white, shades of white outlining the whiteness of objects. Shades of white filling the outlines. Everything impossibly white. Jeli watched the shades of white in Benji's eyes widen as his own must have widened.

Was that a scream? It was the sound of the color white. It made no sense as just a single shade of audible white with no tones of blue or red or green. Just screaming white. All the colors of creation blending into one whiteness, erasing themselves in their perfect blended balance of white.

Was that his scream or Benji's scream? It was impossible to distinguish across the sameness of the white, blanching out still further, losing the shades of white and blending into a whiteness of unbelievable intensity.

Was that even a scream? Or was it the sound of Soul Ship shattering as the colors that defined its existence merged into the sameness of one color, the sum of all colors, balanced so that they defined one thing, one object, even the sound of the scream blending its physical identity into the screaming of Soul Ship's battered structure bending and twisting beyond any stress that it was ever intended to withstand.

And the last thought that distinguished Jeli's mind from the air around him and the scream that shrieked into one sound with the scream of the ship was white.

CHAPTER 123 - LOTS OF TIME

"We're getting close." The wires in Chaine's lips glowed orange.

Nels wanted nothing more than to tear them out of his mouth and stuff them into one of his eyes.

"It's strange, Commander. We've lost all Quan with Control and the rest of the universe, but it's working onboard and within the radius of our ships. Outside that-nothing."

"We expected something like this." Nothing in Nels appearance suggested that he was anything but in control and unphased by the loss of Quan, but he was actually troubled by this latest development. No Quan meant they were cut off from news from Control. From what he knew of ship movements, he suspected that Bella was up to something big, possibly a move on the Clans. He wasn't worried about the outcome of anything that went on anywhere else in the universe, just so long as it didn't affect his mission, just as long as there would be no surprises from the Clans' ships when they arrived at the Texture, and he knew there would be the Clans' ships there.

"This breaks off our ability to monitor," said Chaine. "It makes us vulnerable to attack by those who would interfere with our mission."

"We have enough firepower to destroy several star systems, Mission Regulator. I think we'll be relatively safe."

"We've entered a zone of unknowables. I suggest we put our ships at ready... "

"*My* ships, Mission Regulator."

Chaine glared. His wires went from orange to red. Nels stared straight down into the squat man's eyes.

"These are *my* ships, *my* command. We may have entered an area of unknowns, but so far there has been no threat. I'm not going to put thousands of ships' crews on alert over nothing. I want them calm and-"

A message Quanned in from his Chief Intelligence Officer. Nels Quanned into the coordinates.

There it was, less than a day away, nothing more than a faint aberration in the darkness of space. It wasn't within view through his observation ports yet, but there it was in Quan. *Strange, it should be far out of range of our Quan according to Chaine. But there it is. Almost like it's making itself visible to us. Like a beacon, an invitation. A trap.*

"Perhaps we should put *your* ships on alert now, Commander?" He'd obviously been informed as well.

Nels thought wistfully about ending his Mission Regulator's smugness with a tap of his goatee through the top of his head and out one of his evil little eyes. "Time for that, Mission Regulator. You can go now."

As Chaine stepped hard heeled across the command deck floor to the portal, lip wires glowing bright red, Nels wondered if the little asshole had already been given the order to kill him once the Texture was secured.

With communications completely broken off from Control and the rest of the universe, there might very well be a different ending. The only sphere of influence that Bella exerted in this quadrant of the universe, was the sphere that Commander Nels Horne exerted, and his options had suddenly expanded to infinite possibilities now that they were alone.

As he gazed out the observation port toward where the Texture lay waiting for them, he felt a strange sensation in his forehead. It wasn't an ache or pain, not a flush or a tightening of muscle, not a shake or a twitch. It was something he couldn't quite put his finger on, something he'd never felt before. Maybe he *should* have put his crews on alert. No, there was time for that. Somehow, he knew there was lots of time.

CHAPTER 124 - A SHIVER DOWN THE SPINE

Every crew member on every ship in Zethar's fleet was prepared to die. Unlike the rest of humanity Clansmen did not seek death, but they accepted that when it was time to die, it was time to die. Sacrificing their lives for the glory of their Clans was an honorable death. And Zethar would gladly lay down his life for his Clan. But this was madness.

He accepted the loss of contact with Blood Citadel and the rest of the Clans' navies. He'd expected it and he welcomed the other side of the coin-Bella's ships would also be cut off, able only to Quan between other ships in their fleet.

He accepted the strangeness of this place, this strangeness that he couldn't name. It had been reported throughout his fleet-odd feelings, tingles across flesh, unusual thoughts, nothing anyone could point a finger at and say, "This is what it is."

He accepted that, as they approached the Texture, other things besides communications might break down. They might loose their targeting systems, their shields, their cloaking. Anything was possible at the end of the universe, where the rules of Creation itself began to break down.

He accepted that they were alone, that the outcome of their journey would be entirely in his hands as commander of the fleet. And if he failed, then he and every crew member of every ship in his fleet was prepared to die.

He also accepted that, if it were his choice, he would destroy this thing called the Texture and end the madness that sent navies streaking across the universe for something that would just prove to be another disappointment.

For no reason he could imagine, a shiver rushed down his spine.

CHAPTER 125 - THE TRADE

Damn.

It was Cassie's first time in this arena. She'd been lucky for nine hundred years, hoping for a thousand, especially since this would be her last Wars. She'd heard much about this place, enough to know that she'd rather be just about any place else. They called it the Trade and it was said to be the weirdest-and most dangerous-of all the arenas. It felt strange here. A solid-blue sky hung over an ocher desert with a scattering of sagebrush and cacti. The parched earth glittered with a crystalline substance. There was no one in sight, but she knew she wasn't alone. They were out there. Dozens of them, maybe even hundreds, all feeling the same strangeness she felt. It wasn't just the place; it was she herself. Cassie looked down. The body she saw under the tight black Wars suits wasn't hers.

Damn.

Her Quan body had been traded for another competitor's body. And that competitor had her body. She hoped the other was good. Not just good-good and careful. If she died, Cassie died. If Cassie died, the other died, their fates entangled in Quanspace until one of them touched the other-not an easy thing to do while an unknown number of others were trying to kill both of them. Cassie would have to defend herself and the one with her body. The other would have to do the same.

She could feel them out there, spread across the landscape, adapting to the sparse cover, getting closer, crawling through furrows in the desert, frozen behind sagebrush, lying behind cacti, buried just under the surface of the sand, ready to spring out and attack. She looked down at her body again.

Damn.

Something about the suit, something very disturbing.

What? She spun to her left. She'd sensed movement. But nothing moved that she could see. No birds, no lizards, no spiders or snakes in this place. Just invisible people with other people's bodies, waiting to kill her. And the killing would start soon, just as soon as one competitor saw another without his or her body. That was the strategy-kill as many people as possible without your body, praying that you would recognize your own body because the uniforms were all alike, leaving you to rely on what you knew about you musculature, your bone structure, birth marks, old injuries, a certain posture... your general presence. As the numbers dwindled, it became easier to defend both you and the other. She hoped either she or someone on another team would touch hands early in the contest; otherwise, the only way out of there without killing somebody was to be killed. As the number of contestants dwindled, the remaining ones tended to get a little bloodthirsty and finished off the others just to get their kill count up. So it had always been kill or be killed... and Cassie had never killed.

She swung to her left, crouching, ready to pounce. Nothing. But she knew someone was there. She could feel the presence. She could almost hear their thoughts. But was it a target? Someone trying

402

to kill her? Or was it the other, trying to touch her? She was dead aware that a second's hesitation here could end her life. At the same time, a careless act could also end her life.

Something caught her attention, something right under her chin. Her stomach began to bundle up with just the knowing of what she was about to see. She looked down.

Damn.

Red tears, the insignia of the Tears of Blood Clan. There were only two of them in the Wars - Loac and Shade. One of them had her body.

Damn!

Behind the cactus thirty feet to her right. Someone was behind it. She reached into the Quanpack around her waist, the movement so fast it wasn't even a blur. In less than a second, a spike shot through the cactus and into whoever was behind it. She heard a muffled scream as she dove toward the cactus and rolled to the left, hoping that the wound hadn't been lethal. She saw him, a short man with tiny curls clinging tightly to his head, bearded face twisted in pain. Dense muscle rippled under his Wars suit. The spike protruded from his left shoulder.

His arm blurred as he threw his own spike at her, apparently aiming for her forehead.

She dodged it easily and rolled across the ground toward a shallow gully that ran about fifty feet before veering to the right. She scrambled through it, stopping just before it turned. She listened, felt the space around her, tuned herself into... not the movement, but the intent to move.

They were all around her, changing location, crawling nose to the ground, closing in on her and each other. She moved ahead slowly, peering around the corner.

A woman in a dark brown uniform hugged the side of the rut, frozen to it.

First-timer panicking. *Thinking twice about dying*. Cassie scurried on all fours and was beside the woman before she had a chance to move.

Tears streamed from the woman's eyes. Long black hair flowed over her shoulders. She was beautiful, but she was a mess. Again, the muscle rippling under the uniform. She'd probably trained for hundreds of years, full of dreams of winning, or just surviving, never expecting the intensity of being in the middle of a killing field and not knowing where your killers were, how many there were, if they were better than you. Death is so much more real when you can feel its breath on your neck.

She tapped the woman on the shoulder, putting a finger to her lips, a warning that the slightest sound here could be deadly. The woman smiled weakly. Cassie brushed her finger on the woman's cheek and smiled. This seemed to calm her. She wished the woman could go home, just leave the Wars and go home, but once in the Wars there was no way out but death or finishing. Cassie winked at her and moved on.

Ten feet away, a spike shot past her head from the direction of the woman. It had been a sloppy throw, one that had missed, and one that had made too much movement and too much noise. She heard the woman gag as another competitor killed her.

404

Something to the throat, Cassie guessed, not looking back and not moving any faster or any slower, not disturbing her surroundings enough to attract attention, though there would be those who would know, those who would feel her presence, the ones who'd survived the Wars for hundreds of years.

She sensed something familiar to her left, not far away-a hundred feet at most. She knew exactly what it was. It was her body. Either Loac or Shade was out there moving closer to her, sensing their own body within range. She dove over the top of the rut and rolled over the surface of the ground with lightning speed, eyes darting everywhere looking for attackers, seeing the tiny flash and ducking just in time as a red beam shot within microinches over her head. She twisted her body just enough to avoid another beam coming from the opposite direction. The beam flashed on something behind a thick ball of sagebrush to her left and someone screamed.

To her right, a man stood up, eyes wide, a hole the circumference of a medium-sized tree trunk in the center of his chest. He had just enough time to shake his head no, realizing that he'd just killed his counterpart-and himself -before he crumpled to the ground. Both of their Realspace bodies standing on the launch portals would be similarly crumpled.

She jumped into the air, arching her body over a blistering cloud of pellets. She was less than a second from throwing a spike at the bald man who'd unleashed the lethal pellets when his head exploded from a concussion dart. She looked to her left and saw Shade's head attached to her body. The other woman winked and smiled.

Don't expect me to buy you a beer for that. I could have taken him out without killing him.

Both women threw themselves down as an explosion rocked the ground and sent waves of heat through the air. Death shrieks and screams of pain followed the heat wave.

Sloppy way to kill somebody in a place like this. She glanced in Shade's direction and saw it instantly. Before Shade was even aware of her danger, Cassie's spike cracked against a spike headed straight for Shade, catching it less than an inch from her head.

In less than a second Shade sent a spike of her own through the top of a mound of sand. Someone screamed sharply as Shade rolled and scurried spider-like toward Cassie.

Just as Cassie was about to head toward her, the ground opened up in front of her and an arm, knife in hand, thrust out toward her. She drew back and the knife missed by less than an inch. Cassie's right leg shot out and buried itself into the ground just above the arm. The arm went limp.

Someone was suddenly beside her. She spun and stopped just short of delivering the blade of her right hand to Shade's skull.

Shade smiled. "I think this may be a new record for this arena."

Both women dove to the ground as dozens of spikes flew over their heads. "I guess we're even," said Shade.

406

"I could have handled that guy myself." Cassie's voice fell short of convincing anger.

"I knew that... just letting you know I was around."

There was something so unclanslike about this woman. Cassie couldn't help but feel that, under other circumstances, they might be friends. But then she remembered that this woman would try to kill her best friend. "Well, I can't say that I want you around me any longer. "Hurt Sara, and the next time we meet, I'll kill you." With that, she touched Shade on the arm and both of them disappeared from the Trade, as did all the other competitors there, dead and alive.

***

Across the universe, millions of spectators entangled with the killed competitors in the Trade drifted happily into death, over half of them from the explosion.

407

CHAPTER 126 - CHANGING THE UNIVERSE

"*All* communications?" Fire leaped out of Bella's eyes, flames licking the air around her head. "That's impossible! We didn't lose communications with the Finder! We had communications right up until they disappeared!"

"It's possible that whatever force is generating from the Texture is more powerful than it was fifty years ago." Lovesong's brows crunched together. He'd never seen her this agitated, not to the point of spitting fire out of her eyes. "That force may be blocking communications. We know that strange things happened to-"

"Something's wrong! Nels is up to something! He knows that I've ordered Chaine to kill him. He withheld information from me about the clone ship. He's up to something!"

"Commander Horne has been one of your most loyal servants. He's-"

"He's going to keep the Texture for himself! He's going to use it to take over the universe! He's going to usurp my control, destroy me with my own weapon!"

"I'm sure... "

"Or he's made a deal with the clones." The fire was beginning to subside, the flames growing shorter, less intense. But the desperation in her face was disturbing. "He covered for them. Chaine reported it. Why would he cover for them? He's made a deal with them. He's going to turn the Texture over to the clones. He's-"

He reached out and grabbed her, pulled her into him, wrapped his arms around her and pressed her head to his chest. It was all he could do. It took her by surprise, calmed her momentarily with confusion. He whispered into her ear, "We expected communications to break down. Everything's going as planned. Commander Horne is close to the Texture. He'll have it secured soon, and then it will be yours."

Bella whimpered. She reached her arms up and held him tightly around the neck, almost choking him. "So close, my love, so close. I can't lose it now. I can't lose my only hope."

Her eyes were suddenly sunken, her skin beginning to wrinkle, eyes frantic, filling with madness. She held him for several minutes, tightening her powerful grip until he was almost certain that she would break his neck. And then she suddenly let go. Her face was sallow, sunken, wrinkled around the eyes and mouth. Her voice shook as she spoke. "Or maybe he's dealing with the Clans. They would make him a king. Oh, what they'd give to have him on their side." She released her grip, backed away from him and began pacing the crystal floor. "That's it! He's throwing in with the Clans. They're going to take over the universe together. Think about it. He hasn't been able to track the Clans' ships heading for the Texture. Does that make any sense? Not a single trace and we know they're out there. We logged their departure. But Nels claims they can't see them... "

"The Clans' cloaking devices have eluded us in the past."

"And we've broken through them, every time, without fail. Why not this time, and why not with the most sophisticated technologies in any of my navies at his disposal? He should have had them ages ago. He should have destroyed them!"

"But we're not at war with the Clans. Destroying their ships... "

"Is exactly what I'm going to do."

"What do you mean?"

"We attack now, on every front, throughout the universe! That's it! He sold out to the Clans. He's going to give them the Texture, and they're going the make him a king. That fool! They'll just kill him! They'll use him to get the Texture from me, and then they'll kill him! And then they'll take over the universe!"

She dropped to one knee, saliva dripping from her lower lip, foam gathering at the corners of her mouth, tears streaming from her eyes, glowing now with a deep red.

Oh Bella.

She turned on him, like a feral cat about to spring. "Well, let's see what they have to come back to. Give the order!"

"But we don't know-"

"We know enough! Nels has sold us out! We attack now! With or without the Texture! We attack now! Give the order!"

Lovesong felt his blood turn to ice, his entire body numbing as he sent out the order that would

410

claim billions of lives and change the nature of the entire universe.

CHAPTER 127 - THE DUST OF BELLA'S ENEMIES

And so it starts.

Supreme Commander Daman Haley switched his Quan to war mode, blocking all communications that weren't directly related to one thing: annihilating the Clans from one end of Creation to the other. Billions were about to die, and he would be the one orchestrating the slaughter. The plans were in place. The ships were in place. Blood Citadel would soon be space rubble, its asteroids transformed into meteors pouring into Vala's atmosphere, coating the planet's surface with the dust of Bella's enemies.

And the Clans had been so cooperative in sending an entire fleet right to his doorstep, where he could watch their destruction up close and personal. It would be a magnificent display. He loved the sight of an enemy warship, miles in length, flipping through space uncontrollably with its crew incinerating. Sometimes they crashed into their own ships. The light show was breathtaking.

His new heavy cruisers were in place. They were virtually indestructible, the largest ships ever built, each of them armed with enough firepower to take on entire fleets. Unless the Clan ships had some serious surprises, this would be a short battle.

He gave the order to attack. Simultaneously, the order went to the foremost of the large ships positioned and the forefront of his Control navies and to every one of the billions of ships in Bella's navy, and to the millions of cloaked ships waiting to attack the asteroids of Blood Citadel.

You've just unleashed hell, and the universe is about to become a different place. Supreme Commander Daman Haley seemed happy with this thought.

***

Commander Borne Caine took a deep breath. This day would go down in history as one of the most infamous of all acts in history. Billions of lives-men, women and children-were about to perish. An entire civilization was about to be exterminated. On the other hand, what did history matter? History from this day forward would be whatever Bella Bjork wrote it to be. If there were ever any doubt that she was the supreme being in the universe-after this day, those doubts would be forgotten, and the doubters would be dust.

Almost the instant he gave the command to attack, millions of ships in his fleet shed their cloaking and streaked toward Blood Citadel.

CHAPTER 128 - GOD WILLING

"You might want to Quan into the long range systems." Wrenne's voice was at once calm and agitated. Something was up. "We're under attack."

For the first few seconds, Bavn's mind rejected the words. What fools would attack Blood Citadel? Who would be crazy enough? But he was a warrior-all too familiar with these words. His mind instantly cleared of skepticism and accepted the reality. Blood Citadel was under attack. "From where?"

"Everywhere."

He Quanned into the long-range observations four quadrants at a time. Another four. And another four. That magnificent feeling returned to his chest, that feeling he'd missed for five hundred years that he would get just before battle—excitement and dread twining around each other so powerfully they almost took his breath away.

There were millions upon millions of them-warships from Bella's navy converging on Blood Citadel like a storm of angry wasps, some of them firing solar bombs in advance. In Quadrant 16, he saw a ship overtake its own solar bombs, destroying itself and a dozen other ships. They'd been sitting, cloaked, just outside Blood Citadel's security watch, waiting for the order to attack.

Just like that witch. Attack when the entire universe is absorbed in the Reality Wars. Attack just before they had the Texture.

"Just waiting for your orders, Bavn." He sensed the humor in Wrenne's voice. Something about war seemed to bring it out in the Blood Clan.

"Well, Wrenne, perhaps we should throw something at them."

She smiled widely as Bavn traced her actions through his own Quantrols. Within seconds, all of Blood Citadel became a deadly weapon as billions of ordinance emplacements sprung to life and spun madly, marking targets and firing patterns. The asteroids of Blood Citadel lit up as the weaponry fired in unison, pouring out a mass of laser beams and bombs that mushroomed into space like an exhalation of deadly breath in every direction. This was the initial volley that would take out most of the incoming solar bombs. The second volley would take out most of the first wave of ships just before the first solar bombs struck the asteroids.

He switched from quadrant to quadrant. They were everywhere. He'd never seen or heard of this much firepower brought to bear by Bella's navy. But then, nothing like Blood Citadel had ever existed before. He changed the holo in his room into a real-time view of Vala. *God willing, we won't have to use it.*

He tried to Quan Triste's fleet at the edge of Control. Nothing happened. The attackers had cut off their Quan. All the Clans throughout the universe were on their own now. But that was all right with Bavn-they'd always been on their own, and Bella's navies were about to experience their first defeat.

The first volley began to strike targets, exploding solar bombs and the war ships following close behind them. The noiseless flashes and bursts of fire obscured the stars all around Vala like a

415

sphere of flame surrounding the planet from deep space. And the guns of Blood Citadel fired their second volley just before the solar bombs struck.

He looked again at the holo of Vala. *There will be no defeat for the Clans*.

CHAPTER 129 - BACK OF THE PACK

Captain Colin "Crash" Duncan was strung tautly between ecstasy and disappointment. He'd been waiting his entire career for a crack at the Clans, and that time had finally arrived. They were going to destroy the Clan fleet. His body vibrated with the thought of slaughtering thousands of Clansmen. He was the deadliest killer in all of Bella's navies. His crew was the most well trained and ready to kill the Clans with relish. He wanted to kill. His crew wanted to kill. Kill in the name of Bella. And first on the list was Captain Ureal. He'd known there was something funny about the Clan fleet, something not right about their arrogance. He wanted to kill them all.

But he was at the back of the pack, thousands of miles away from the action, the last wave of backup in case things went wrong. But nothing was going to go wrong. The weaponry of the new ships was enough to control the universe. They were going to wipe out the Clans' fleet in minutes. Crash Duncan was going to miss the most important battle of his life. He wanted to strangle Supreme Commander Daman Haley to death, watch the life drift out of his old dinosaur eyes. He wanted to kill. His crew wanted to kill. But they were at the back of the pack.

His body vibrated with rage as he Quanned the front lines and saw the big ships moving into firing position and then let hell loose on the Clans. He broke into a cold sweat as he watched the solar bombs loosed from the Clans' ships, aimed futilely at the mass of warships at the front of Control. Nothing was going to get through the barrage of firepower heading toward them. He watched as the missiles, bombs and beams from both sides streaked through space—two deadly walls of death about to collide. He watched as the distance closed to within impact range.

And then the universe outside Control turned in a fireball so huge its light might be mistaken for a star thousands of years from now in some distant star system.

CHAPTER 130 - GOOD THOUGHTS

Shit. A white Quanspace. Sara was almost at home with most Quanspaces as any VR, probably because of her close friendship with Cassie, something that had led her into places where most humans hadn't been and likely wouldn't want to be. But she'd never been much for the white spaces, the ones with nothing but your own Quanpresence and maybe the presence of someone you were with. They were mostly intense places, places of tremendous focus either internally or externally. There were no distractions in a white place, nothing to alleviate the intensity. In fact, the absence of everything magnified every doubt, fear and worry a hundred times. People had gone crazy in these places-even VR programs had been known to break down in white spaces.

She sensed the presence of another— just one. It looked like this would be a one-on-one arena. Time to move. That would be problematic here. Up and down were whatever you wanted them to be. You could walk straight ahead in whatever position to which you were oriented, or you could walk straight up, turning your front into your bottom. The presence of the other didn't seem to be making any moves on her yet. Time for some practice. She spun around, turning her left side into up, landing on the ground of what had been her right side. She jumped up, spun and landed on what had previously been up. She tried something different-she planted one foot firmly on her right side and the other on her left and pushed up, spinning as she pushed and turned a diagonal into her new up, spiraling through it like a gyroscope. She stopped suddenly and froze.

The other presence was close. Too close. Somewhere to her right. She looked.

Standing just a few yards away in empty space, upside down, was Loac-not moving, not smiling or frowning, not threatening in any way except maybe the absence of threat.

Sara felt a deep sense of dislike for the Clanswoman "So," she said. "I heard that you've been hitting on my best friend."

The other woman stared, ice blue eyes showing no anger or resentment, just staring at Sara as though she were an afterthought or something of no real significance, as though she were waiting patiently for a movie or other entertainment to begin.

And then it came, strong, hard, like a physical thing striking through her stomach and chest. It hurt like hell. She nearly fell into the white beneath her.

She quickly sprung into ready position, facing Loac, who was now several feet closer, but still not attacking, still not making any threatening motions, just staring expressionlessly.

"I don't know how you did that," said Sara. "But you're going to pay for it in spades." As soon as she finished speaking, she had a strange feeling of regret, of having said the wrong thing, of having set something in motion that she wasn't going to like.

Loac smiled.

What was it they said about when a member of the Clans smiled?

That's when she realized where she was. The Karma Corridor. Of all places to be with Loac. She was in a place with the one person in the universe she hated most, a place where your own hatred would turn on you, where every action, every word and possibly every thought in the Corridor came back on the person who sent it out. Hating someone here could get you killed. Killing someone here could get you killed.

In fact, the only person who had ever gotten out of here alive was Cassie.

How did she do it? She'd been in here with a clone. Both of them had come out alive, but the clone had gone insane. She'd asked Cassie many times how she did it, but she'd never been sure, her only answer being, "Guess I just had good thoughts."

Good thoughts. That was the key. No bad thoughts. They hurt. No attempts on the other's life. They killed. Loac was just a few feet from her now, standing eye to eye with her. Still smiling. She hated that smile. Another bolt of pain, this time through her thighs. Time to think of something else. She focused on Loac's long dark hair.

"You have beautiful hair."

No answer. Just the smile. No movement. Just the smile, the look of indifference, the complete lack of commitment, like a blank slate. It was obvious the Clanswoman had trained well for this. She was feeling nothing.

That was it. Feel nothing. That's what Loac was doing, setting herself free of emotion, not giving into her hatred for Sara, and Sara knew well that the

421

Clanswoman hated her almost as much as she hated Cassie, maybe even more. Sara suddenly felt a sense of peace suffusing her chest, the karma from the compliment. She and Loac were almost nose to nose now.

How did she do that? She hadn't seen her move. It was like she was frozen in the white space, no flexing of muscles, not a ripple of motion. Their bodies were almost touching. She was looking directly into the other woman's dark-blue eyes, like liquid sky. Beautiful, but cold and unfeeling. Sara's body filled with a mixture of feelings, none of them bad, apparently. There was no pain but no pleasure either. She wondered if there were such a thing as neutral karma. Would that even be karma? Karma was a disruption in the fabric of intent, a pebble of good or evil dropped into the pool of a still life, a force that spread across the landscape of a life, bounced off the horizons and sent back a tsunami of like feelings.

They stood face-to-face in nothing, not daring to make a move against each other, not daring to think a negative thought, not daring to think anything. Stalemate. Stuck. Impasse. They could stay here forever, not thinking anything. But then, wasn't that what it was all about? A waiting game until one of them gave into their feelings, and the longer they waited, the stronger those feelings were likely to be, a sudden deluge of bad thought followed by a wave of karma powerful enough to kill.

And suddenly Loac was against her, touching her, the Clanswoman's body starting to envelope

422

Sara's body. *What the hell?* Loac's body was folding around hers. She watched, fascinated, as the other woman's face spread out from the sides and began to wrap around her own face.

Vapor!

The stories of vapor were true! The Tears of Blood could actually turn into vapor, and Loac had carried that power over to Quanspace with the same power is in Realspace. And that, somehow, gave her the ability to move through this place without seeming to move. Somehow, she nudged the vapor of herself through Quanspace. That would explain the absence of muscle movement, the seeming lack of effort. Like mist, she flowed through space without movement. Sara was beginning to feel an overwhelming sense of nothingness, a pit into which she was falling where there was no meaning for her. The Clanswoman was telegraphing her feelings directly into her as she encased her with her VR body. There was no hatred or love, good or bad, in what Loac was projecting. There was only the absence of anything and, in this place of heightened emotion, Sara was like a sponge, absorbing the pure indifference into herself. It was becoming what she was.

But how to fight it? She tried to throw out her own indifference, but it was too late-she'd been taken by surprise. Loac had her at a disadvantage. Her move was completely unattached to anything that could be translated into karma. There were no feelings that would ripple the stillness of this place. Sara pushed against the other woman. Too late, she realized the emotional attachment of the push, a

423

mixture of revulsion and hatred, and a good measure of fear. The vapor of Loac dispersed around her, effortlessly, completely giving. Not so for Sara. All the feelings of revulsion, fear and hatred pounded through her like being battered with clubs from the inside. She doubled up with the pain. It hurt every part of her body and mind, draining her energy, sapping her life.

And Loac was upon her again, spreading herself over Sara and flowing over her body. Sara started gagging. She wanted to throw up, run, strike out, kill the Clans bitch who was doing this to her. The pain intensified a hundred fold. Darkness began to settle over her life. She knew that she was dying, killing herself with her own uncontrollable feelings.

Just as her life was about to flicker out, she sensed a scream that seemed to stretch across the universe, a scream of unrelenting anguish. The vapor that was Loac began to throb violently, erupting and tearing apart, shredding into shards and blobs, and the voice of the scream, she knew, was Loac. Within seconds, there were only floating threads of the Clanswoman. Sara watched in wonder as they dissolved into the whiteness. Loac was dead. She was alive.

***

What have you done?
"I've killed the bitch's lover."
Why?
"To hurt her."
You don't take losing too well do you?

"No, I don't."
How did you do that?
"You don't know?"

CHAPTER 131 - THOSE WHO REALLY DO NEED TO DIE

"It was him. I know it was him. He's the only one in the universe who could have pulled that off."

Lovesong was surprised by Bella's reaction to Loac's death. He'd braced himself for a cataclysmic meltdown the moment Loac's body disintegrated, but instead of outrage spitting from her eyes, she'd been disturbingly calm and said, "One less of the Clans to wipe out." And her lips had twisted into a chilling smile. "But I know who did it." She was quiet a moment as she replayed the murder in Quan. "It was my own assassin. He's working for someone else." She spread her legs apart, placed her hands on her hips. "Now, I wonder who that could be?"

"Given the sheer impossibility of contacting the Assassin," said Lovesong, "the list of suspects should be small. "And only a handful of people in the universe even know of his existence-the only ones rich enough to afford him."

Bella turned quickly toward Lovesong, pinching her chin with a thumb and forefinger. "And it has to be someone with an interest in swaying the outcome of the Reality Wars, someone who could not just afford the Assassin, but could afford the bribes and technology to get the Assassin not just into Canak but into one the Reality Wars arenas. That must have been close to a miracle." Her tone was almost admiring. Her lips twisted into a nervous smile. "And something that could only have been achieved with more money than just about anyone else in the universe."

"Kingston," said Lovesong.

Bella nodded. "Our little cormorant is definitely trying to fix the Reality Wars." She tapped her index finger against her cheek. "But I think we'll let that go for now. He's just added something to the Wars."

"And what would that be?"

"Vengeance, my love, vengeance." She walked slowly toward him, pressed her body into his and put her arms around his neck. "I'm sure the Clanswoman's lover already knows of her mate's death. Everyone in the universe will think that somehow Sara Beth killed Loac, including Shade. She'll be after both of them-Sara and Cassie. There won't be any spear-tipped bantering, no snide remarks or taunting. Shade will be going directly for the kill." She placed her lips against Lovesong's cheek and kissed lightly, moving her lips across his cheek to his mouth, where she slid the tip of her tongue against his. Her breath was hot against his mouth.

Lovesong's heart began to beat faster, his pulse quickened. She was his universe, even as the cracks and wrinkles around her eyes and at the edges of her mouth increased by the hour. Even as he felt her deteriorating in his arms, sensed her brain beginning to shut down, her organs on the verge of failing.

"The Clanswoman will give us the greatest Reality Wars spectacle of all time. And if she lives through it, we'll keep her around for a while. After we've exterminated all the Clans, we'll make a spectacle of her, execute her publicly, Quan it all around the universe. The execution of the last member of the Clans." She pressed her lips hard into his and her tongue flowed into his mouth. She pulled her head back, her eyes were glowing green. "And we'll have to add the Assassin to the list of those who really do need to die."

CHAPTER 132 - FURY AGAINST FURY

Across the universe hundreds of millions of men, women and children slumped lifeless in chairs, beds, tubes, on floors and sidewalks, in their vehicles, in the homes of friends, in special dying rooms where groups ranging into the hundreds to the thousands gathered to die when Loac died, all of them entangled in the Clanswoman's fate. Strangely, their faces spoke of either relaxation or indifference.

But not so at Blood Citadel where Bavn, though blocked from Quannet by Bella's attacking navies, knew that his daughter was dead. The reality of her death washed over and through him like tangible pain. He felt that his heart would drop out of his body. He swooned in his recliner and began to howl. The walls shook with the force of his voice. The skin around his eyes twisted and crimped, lids clamped shut. His body shook. And then he stiffened as the shock waves from the first volley of the attacking ships pounded across the surfaces of Blood Citadel's asteroids, impacts from concussion bombs killing hundreds of thousands of the Tears of Blood deep under the surface. He Quanned into the battle.

What had been empty space around the asteroid belt just minutes ago was now a gargantuan wall of fire, smoke and dust shot through with laser beams and exploding spacecraft. He watched as ship after ship of Bella's fleets were blasted into oblivion, but they kept coming, they kept firing as the second powerful volley from the asteroids fired up the rocks' surfaces with blinding light. Thousands of missiles were struck by the incoming projectiles even as they lifted from the surface, creating towering balls of curdling flame. Laser canons spewed lines of light into the oncoming force, thousands of them bursting into flames as they were struck haphazardly by the mass of incoming death.

Bavn choked down his grief and watched. There were no orders to be given. *Except maybe one*. The Tears of Blood warriors of Blood Citadel were prepared for this. Every one of them had been trained from childhood for the fight that had been brought to them, and they would gladly die to defend their home. They would return the fury of the attacking forces tenfold.

Bavn set his walls to outside monitor to watch in both Realspace and Quan as the battle for Blood Citadel raged just above his head.

CHAPTER 133 - THE WAY HUMANS RESOLVE THINGS

"My God." Abner could find no frame of reference for what he was seeing. He'd seen war movies, read about famous battles, even played some of the bloodiest war games imaginable when he was a teenager-but everything he'd ever seen paled in comparison with the horror that unfolded before his eyes. It spread across vast distances of space like a wave of fire shot through with blinding streaks of red and blue laser beams, millions of them. He watched as giant orb-like ships the size of moons fired thousands of beams and projectiles into the fleet of Clans' ships, their firepower hurtling through space with unbelievable speed, traversing the distance to their targets in just seconds, only to be met by an equally deadly wall of death. Some of the beams and missiles actually made it through the wall, slamming into the ships from both sides, lighting them up with explosions that disrupted the fabric of space for miles. Abner watched as a barrage of explosions crept across the surface of one of the moon-sized ships threatening to slice it in half, but they kept spewing death at the other ships.

"What the hell is going on?"

"War," said Buddha.

"You have anything to do with this?"

"Not this time. This is human killing human, trying to take over the universe. Those are Bella's ships at Control firing on the Clans' ships."

"But their fleet is so small. They don't stand a chance. Why would they attack Bella's fleets right in her stronghold?"

"They didn't. Bella launched the attack. The Clans' fleet itself is just a diversion."

"A diversion?"

"They think they only need one ship."

"Just one ship? And they brought an armada."

"They think they can bring down Quannet with a single ship attacking in the right place."

"And?"

"Bad intel."

"So, what will happen to them?"

"Remember that Old Earth phrase 'shit kicking'?"

Abner turned his attention back to the battle. "Yeah, I remember you and I delivering one to forces far bigger than us."

Buddha smiled, then looked doubtful. "But this wasn't supposed to be the plan. I'm guessing that something's happened that Bella doesn't like, and she's starting her war sooner than expected."

"Sooner than expected? You mean, you knew this was going to happen?"

"The very moment she reached the Texture. But something's happened. Something's set her off, and she's started ahead of schedule. This is going on all over the universe-Bella's navies attacking Clans' worlds and any ship with a Clans' signature"

"Could you have stopped this?"

"Nothing could have stopped this. Too many powerful people have too much to gain for too

432

many reasons. And this is the way humans resolve these things."

"And software too, I might add."

"I was programmed by a human, as you so eruditely pointed out. *I might add*."

Abner smiled and nodded. "Good point. So, what do we do now?"

"We go in early."

"You mean now? While all *that's* going on?"

"Best time. They have their hands full here and all over the universe. They won't be looking for us inside their defenses."

"I'm not sure if I-"

An instant later, they were in another world.

CHAPTER 134 - THE MEEK SHALL INHERIT THE EARTH

Her word went out across the universe, to every Womb of the Universe world, ship, and member of the Womb Clan. Flee. Fall back. Hide. It was the beginning. Maebh, Queen of the Womb, licked her lips as a red glow illuminated the interior folds of her hood.

"Fall back. Wait," she commanded. When it was over, they would spring out of hiding and attack whatever was left of Bella's and the other Clans' navies. Everything would fall in their path, and the Womb of the Universe would give birth to a new order.

"Hide." An ignoble way to recreate Creation, but wasn't it written by the ancients, "the meek shall inherit the earth?" Meek at first, perhaps, but not so meek when the time arrived, when the Womb would thunder across the universe, spreading death and submission.

If they think Bella ruled with a fist of steel, wait till they meet their new queen. Under the hood, she licked her lips again.

CHAPTER 135 - NORMAL COLOR

Color returned. But it wasn't the color of normality-if anything about Soul Ship could be termed normal. The color wavered like slow breathing. Reds and blues and yellows seeped into each other like liquids spilled into the spaces defining the Soul Ship command deck, blending into each other and redefining the nature of things.

Benji looked around the room, taking in the bleeding of colors re-forming the useless antiques comprising the control panels. Jeli's eyes were still wide in wonder, mouth still in the shape of a scream. His eyes darted from one point in the room to another and slowly his mouth closed and his eyes returned to normal. The colors of his face were still a mishmash of tints in motion. Benji lifted his right hand and gazed at it curiously. Colors snaked across the surface of his skin, twining around each other, melding into tones and disintegrating into solid primaries, then merging into each other. He looked again at Jeli's astonished face as he stared at his hands. Jeli tore his eyes away from his hands and gazed at Benji with wonder. Benji smiled. "Hear that?"

Jeli listened, cocked his head to the side as though trying to scoop up sounds with his eyes. Puzzlement drifted across his face. "Hear what?"

"Nothing."

"What?"

"The ship. It's stopped making all those falling apart sounds. We're still alive."

435

Jeli thought for a moment and began to smile. Slowly, the color of the room mixed into its natural hues and tones. The movement stopped. Color was back to normal. Jeli began to laugh. Benji joined him. They laughed hard, and then harder, and soon they were laughing hysterically. Until, at the same time, their laughter stopped abruptly and their eyes widened again as they looked out the observation port.

"Holy shit," whispered Jeli.

"Yep, we must be getting close," said Benji with a shrug.

On one side, space was practically solid with Bella's massive fleet. On the other side, space throbbed with the density of millions of Clans' ships. Both fleets appeared to be on a collision course at some point ahead of them.

And there it was. Ahead of them. Spreading across their field of vision, astonishing and terrifying. It defied description. It obliterated all boundaries of comprehension.

The Texture. They'd reached it.

In an instant, Jeli's Quantrols sprang to life with reports from all over what remained of Soul Ship. At the same time, he felt a strangeness washing over and through his body and for some reason, this seemed to be OK with him. It didn't worry him in the least. In fact, it seemed almost like this strangeness was something he *should* be feeling, like it was the only thing that could be felt. The reports mushroomed as though a madness bacteria were infecting everyone aboard Soul Ship. But that was all right with Jeli.

Benji felt the right side of his body turn into water and was fascinated by its amazing ability to stick to the left side of his body without flowing across the control room floor. It tickled. He giggled. He tried to move his right arm but it wouldn't respond. *Of course it won't; it's water*. A sudden surge of what seemed like pure energy shot through his left side, and Chief Magistrate Jeli Role burst into laughter as Benji Parx collapsed onto the floor with a loud splash.

CHAPTER 136 - THE HUB OF THE UNIVERSE

Captain Shona Ureal watched as the giant fireball exploded throughout space where the firepower of two walls of death crashed into each other. *And theirs is just from the big ships.*

After the flames were extinguished by the vacuum of space, there would likely be another barrage from them, followed immediately by the smaller ships streaking in to attack individual ships. This didn't bother her. In all the 'unofficial' encounters between Bella's ships and the Clans, the Clans had always won. They were the better fighters. They had the better ships. They had the most experience in large scale war from the Clan Wars. And they didn't even have to win this battle. All they had to do was get one Clans ship into Control. Hers.

Of course, they were destined to die, but their deaths would be rewarded in honorable death for having done their part in the creation of a universe connected by faith, not by Bella Bjork's Quannet. Quannet would be a thing of the past, its power broken.

It had taken hundreds of years to pinpoint it, lost in the scattered star systems of Control. It had taken the deaths of hundreds of Clan spies and millions in currencies from around the universe, but its location had been found, and that location had been built into her ship's targeting systems. It was just beyond this wall of death-the Hub of the

Universe, the heart of Quannet. Its destruction would bring quiet to the universe, leaving only the flesh and blood to fill the universe with meaning.

She Quanned her crew to be ready, aware that this would be one of the last Quans in a universe where soon, distance would once again be meaningful, and mystery would return.

All they had to do was get within a light-year.

Triste filled her Quanscreen. "Captain, this will be a glorious day for you."

"Yes, Commander. I've been waiting a long time for this."

"And your crews are ready?"

"Biting at the bit."

"They're lining up for their next volley. Their tactical ships are in place to follow right in behind it. When we punch the hole, you'll have just a few seconds before we split space open at your entry point."

"I understand, Commander." She thought a moment. "How will the rest of the fleet fare?"

"Once you're in, we'll retreat. That should draw a good portion of their navy away from you. And the new cloaking device should keep you virtually invisible until you reach the rear of their navy. That will be mostly communications and support ships. You should be able to outrun them easily."

"Piece of cake, as the Archives say."

Trite's eyes turned away for a moment. "And here comes the second volley. God speed, Commander Ureal."

The Quan ended, and Captian Ureal turned her attention to the navies guarding Control. The missiles had already been unleashed, millions of them, followed by hundreds of thousands of attack ships, their lasers blasting even though they were still far out of range. She wondered how many of those ships would outrun their own firepower and die in their lust to kill for Bella.

Let them. Soon, they would be like pebbles scattered mindlessly throughout the vast distances of space.

CHAPTER 137 - WHEN PLANETS DIE

Maggie: Did you see that! Did you see that! Loac is dead! Loac is dead! The Clans' Reality Wars weapon is dead! She's dead!

Childen: (staring at Maggie calmly) Maggie-

Maggie: (grabs Childen's arm) She's dead!

Childen: (pulling his arm away from her grasp) Get a hold of yourself, Maggie.

Maggie: (looking at Childen wide-eyed, looks around, calms): And there we have it! Somehow Sara Beth has managed to kill Loac in the Karma Corridor just as the Clanswoman was invading her psyche and turning Sara's own will to live against her. Just a few seconds more, and she would have been toast.

Childen: (raises his eyebrows) Toast?

Maggie: Expression from the Archives, Childen. Sara Beth would have been dead within seconds, but somehow she managed to turn it around and shred Loac to pieces. Definitely one of the most amazing turnarounds ever in the Reality Wars! Childen, any thoughts on how she did it?

Childen: No, Maggie. That came completely out of the blue. One second, she was almost dead and suddenly, Loac was in shreds. It's almost like it came from somewhere else.

Maggie: (looks at Childen, astonished) What are you saying, Childen? That Sara Beth had help? We all saw it. It was just the two of them. There was no one else in that arena, Childen.

441

Childen: None that we could see, Maggie.

Maggie: (skeptical) Childen, these are the most highly guarded events in the universe. The Quansors would have picked up anything that had tried to interfere with the Wars.

Childen: It was done in Quanspace, Maggie. Just about anything is possible in Quanspace.

Maggie: (shaking her head, disgusted) Right, Childen. But for all intents and purposes and nothing else having been detected, it looks like a legal kill for Sara Beth. Which leads us to...

Childen: (waiting for Maggie to finish) Leads us to... ?

Maggie: (points to the launch area where Shade is standing on her portal, tears streaming from her closed eyes, chest heaving) It looks as though Shade is aware of her mate's death, and she's going to be coming after Sara Beth with a vengeance if the two of them end up in any of the same arenas. I wouldn't want to be in that arena when those two come face-to-face. This is shaping up to be the bloodiest Reality Wars ever!

Childen: I'm afraid I have to agree with you on that one, Maggie. (she gives him a puzzled look) If Shade goes after Sara, then Cassie Hayes will be after Shade. This could very well be the first time Cassie kills anyone in a thousand years of Reality Wars.

Maggie: (excited) And this just in from Carba Galant in the Sorba system. The entire planet has just committed suicide.

Childen: What? The entire planet? That's just not poss-

442

Maggie: Getting the Quans in now, Childen. They bet the entire planet's GNP on Loac to win the Wars.

Childen: But why would they commit-

Maggie: And... they entangled every human and clone and VR on the planet with Loac. Guess they didn't want to be sold off by the Gamblers.

Childen: (looking sad) That's billions of lives, Maggie. And by the way, it's not humans and clones, its just... people.

Maggie: (fakes a pout) Nothing personal meant, Childen. You know I respect all life.

Childen: (rolls his eyes) Too bad the people on Carba Galant didn't feel the same way.

Maggie: (shrugs) Looks like the Gamblers just came into possession of a planet full of dead people.

Childen: And how many others across the universe?

Maggie: (checks her Quan) Looks like over four billion and counting. A lot of people wanted to go down with the Clanswoman. Yep, shaping up to be the greatest Reality Wars ever.

Childen: Or maybe the saddest Reality Wars ever.

Maggie: (rolls her eyes) Whatever, Childen, whatever.

***

There was an unsubtle change in the nature of the planet Carba Gallant after the death of Loac. Planes on automatic systems soared through the heavens, landed and departed from majestic airborne skyports, fueled and ran maintenance checks, informed their passengers of delays and arrival times. None of the passengers were aware of how well the automatic systems were taking care of them. They were slumped in their seats, dead. Collapsed on portable toilets, dead. Sprawled in the aisles, dead. No one disembarked or boarded at the skyports. Massive lines of men, women and children littered the floors, silent and lifeless.

Intercity transit pods stopped for corpses and left still carrying the macabre fares that would miss their stops in an endless round of transits. Elevators in buildings that speared through the clouds zoomed up and down with cargos of the dead, stopping at floors cluttered with the dead.

Automated home care systems sensing a change in the nature of their resident owners applied first aid and other emergency treatments uselessly. Emergency response centers were beginning to overload with the calls for ambulances, fire trucks and other emergency vehicles. They were becoming confused. Nothing in their programming had ever prepared them for this. No one had ever considered running a scenario as insane as every resident on an entire planet dying simultaneously.

CHAPTER 138 - TEARS

Get a hold of yourself. The whole universe is watching you. Shade Quanned into Loac's death once more as tears glistened on her cheeks. *But how?* It still didn't register as real. How could it be? Loac was the most perfect weapon in the universe. She was more than equipped to kill the VR's friend. It wasn't supposed to be like this. Loac was essential to the beginning of a new universe. The seed had been planted over half a millennium ago, waiting all these hundreds of years for the day.

She can't be dead.

But she was. There it was, all over Quannet, being replayed and replayed through all parts of the universe. And the reports of billions dying, all of them entangled with Loac's life. An entire planet, dead, gone with the woman she loved more than anything in Creation.

She stood on her launch portal, forcing her body to remain still, breathing deeply to squelch the sobs she felt rising in her chest. She didn't dare let her chest heave, her face quake, her legs fall from under her. She was Tears of Blood, the strongest of the strong in the Clans, the fiercest warriors in the universe, and she was one of the most formidable weapons ever to walk on two legs. She practiced her breathing, drawing strength and calm from the air around her, from the surface of the ground she stood upon, from the stillness of space beyond Canak's atmosphere.

She had a new mission now. The Reality Wars could go to hell. She had one goal only-destroy Sara

Beth. And then she would destroy her VR friend. And then she would destroy other VRs. Bavn and Loac had been right all along. They were the evil of the universe, and from this day forward, Shade would be their nemesis. She would kill every VR she encountered. She almost hoped the mission to Control would not succeed so that there would be lots of VRs for her to kill.

She waited for the next arena, praying that it would bring her face-to-face with the VR's bitch friend.

CHAPTER 139 - THE LAST BLOOD STANDING

After the first wave of attack, Bavn ordered the Clans' ships to move into areas where the asteroids had been all but decimated by Bella's ships. He monitored the damage to the attackers. It was substantial. Almost the entire first wave had been destroyed. But they kept coming. The Quanblock from Bella's forces limited Bavn's range but he was able to Quan far enough into the attackers to see that their numbers were formidable. There were millions more of them. And there would be millions beyond them-the giant attack ships, small tactical ships, and beyond them, he knew there would be the moon-size command ships, the ones blocking Quannet, cutting Blood Citadel off from the rest of the universe, cutting Bavn off from sending warnings. He knew that Bella wouldn't just attack Blood Citadel, she would be attacking every Clans population across the universe.

But Blood Citadel was far from defeated. There were millions of asteroids. Millions of Blood ships. Billions of the greatest warriors in the universe, men and women who weren't afraid to die, who would fight to the last breath. By the time the space dust had dispersed, Bella's attack fleet would be all but destroyed, and there would still be armed asteroids to meet them.

He tried desperately to push aside thoughts of Loac. He knew that Shade would be after her killer. There would be no mercy, no doubts about what she must do. Her mind would be clear, focused. And she would kill.

And if all else failed at Blood Citadel, that one defiant Clansman standing against the enemy would turn whatever was left of Bella's fleet into nothingness.

CHAPTER 140 - QUESTIONS

Light from the fireballs between Blood Citadel and Bella's fleet ignited orange pinpoints of light in the eyes of Commander Borne Caine. It spread a deep orange glow throughout the observation deck. He'd expected the first wave to do substantially more damage, but the firepower from the asteroids had been a surprise-he hadn't counted on the long-range weapons. He'd always thought their armaments were primarily short range. The asteroids appeared to be designed just as much for offense as defense. The first wave had been all but decimated. He'd expected they would take a pounding but nothing like what he'd witnessed. And now the second wave was meeting the same resistance.

He didn't doubt that he would win this battle. Blood Citadel would be nothing more than a memory before he moved his fleet on to other Clans' targets but it was clear that the cost would be astronomical.

He Quanned to Control. The Clans' fleet there was holding their ground even in the face of overwhelming numbers. But their presence at Control didn't make any sense. There was absolutely no way they could meet with anything but defeat against the largest and deadliest of Bella's navies. So why were they there? And why would they send such a small fleet? With weapons systems hot, it was obvious this was no peaceful religious pilgrimage. It was a strike force. They'd been sent to attack the navy that guarded the only entrance to

Control, the rest of space around it being protected by a force field that drew its power from a gargantuan black hole at the center of Control.

Was it their intent to take over Quannet? That would be impossible. A fleet that size wasn't nearly big enough to take Control even in the improbable event they got past Daman Haley's monstrous fleet. Or was their presence at Control a ruse, something to draw attention away from... what? The Texture. All contact had been lost with Nels Horne's fleet. God knows what was happening there. There would be Clans' ships at the Texture. They wanted it just as much as Bella. Borne hoped that the Clans' ships were just as incommunicable as Nels' ships. But would that stop a battle from taking place to take control of the anomaly?

Probably not.

So why were the Clans waging war at the gateway to Control? Borne had a bad feeling about that. The Clans were up to something, and the sooner his fleets took out Blood Citadel, the sooner he could prepare for whatever it was.

CHAPTER 141 - THE USUAL EXPLOSIVE CARNAGE

It was like being on the inside of a furnace. Millions of missiles and solar bombs from Bella's attacking force exploding all around the Clans' feet spread for immense distances in every direction, covering the Clans' ships with fire and an impact that shook her craft like a child's rattle. But their ships were built for this. Nothing short of a direct hit with a solar bomb was going to put more than a dent in them, and the attackers were firing wildly, just spraying space with explosions and making the occasional lucky hit. Shona watched through her observation deck as the Jaggeer exploded, throwing burning shrapnel and flaming body parts for miles.

She received a Quan from Triste. It was time. "Captain Ureal. Any losses?"

"No Commander. A bit shaken but ready to go."

"Did I mention that you'll be navigating through hell?"

Shona smiled. "I thought that's what we were taking to Bella."

Triste returned the smile. "I don't want you to fire. Save everything you have until you get inside Control. You know where the target is but you don't know what's guarding it."

"Right, Commander."

"And good luck."

"Good luck to you too, Commander."

451

She Quanned out and waited. It was a short wait. It started as an almost imperceptible vibration whose intensity grew quickly. And then it was thunder. It was the entire Clan fleet, with the exception of Shona's ship, turning loose a wall of missiles and bombs that made space dense with death. It cut right through the fireballs and headed straight for Bella's fleet, where she knew they were preparing for the usual explosive carnage. But this time, they were in for a surprise.

And right behind it, Shona Ureal streaked toward Control.

CHAPTER 142 - A BUDDHA THING

It was crystal. But not like any crystal Abner had ever seen. It was crystal in motion, waves of sparkling crystal flowing into waves of sparkling crystal, glistening but not wet and not dry, spreading endlessly around the two of them, Abner in his form, Buddha in his, but both in the substance of crystal.

"So this is the heart of Quannet?"

"An entire galaxy of servers controlling the whole universe," said Buddha.

Mesmerized by the waves of crystal flowing through his hands and arms, Abner wondered why he didn't feel anything but normal. "And this won't turn us into something weird?"

"You've been mist for two thousand years, Abner. I don't think it gets any weirder than that."

"I'll keep that thought in mind." A swarm of shimmering blue crystals passed through his chest, and that's when he began to hear it. It wasn't anything he could define, a sound of sorts, but more like the presence of sound, the impression of sound, or maybe the potential for sound. "Do you hear anything?"

Buddha smiled widely. "You can hear it?"

"I think so. I'm not sure. What is it."

"It's the frequencies of Creation, Abner."

In the crystalline distance, a ball of orange crystal the size of a city bounced slowly through great tidal waves of crystals of every shape, size and color without disturbing a thing in its path. Rather than moving through anything in its way, it blended into everything without losing its form and without any apparent affect on the form of anything it touched. The sound grew more intense, and then drifted off, like a current washing against Abner's awareness.

"So all this is vibration?"

"You got it. This is beyond the strings that make the universe. This is their substance, the frequencies that make the strings."

"So, it doesn't get any smaller than this?"

"Everything can get smaller, Abner. But this is very small."

Abner watched, fascinated, as the ball of crystal expanded and then seemed to fall apart on itself in a brilliant sprinkle of glittering rain, all of them disappearing into the waves surrounding them. "And we're supposed to find one little gateway into... " His eyes squinted. He cocked his head to the side. "Um, Buddha... " He cocked his head in the other direction. "Call me crazy, but I think I just heard something that sounded very human, like a voice, or voices, but... "

Buddha chuckled. "That would be the servers."

"The servers have human voices?"

"The servers *are* human."

Abner stared at Buddha as a mist-like wave of crystal passed through both of them. "Human computers?"

"Genetically bred over hundreds of years to use their full brains, including all that brain power that's not normally used, as a galaxy-wide peer network. Billions of them, all with hundreds of backups. They form a giant data warehouse and a single executable program that controls all the programs. And that program is controlled by the Master Program."

"And that's what we're going after?"

"That's right, Abner."

"And it's somewhere in this galaxy? Somewhere in the millions of light-years in an entire galaxy?"

"No. Actually, it's not anywhere near Control."

"So, where is it?"

"In Bella's fortress."

"And where's that?"

"Only Bella knows that. Everyone who had anything to do with building it was slaughtered when it was finished."

"And I'm guessing that we somehow have to find Bella's fortress and go there to get the Master Program?"

"Exactly. It's the only way to erase the registry and ensure that it's been destroyed everywhere."

"And it's not here."

"But the gateway to Bella's fortress is."

"I see. And that's definitely where we're going?"

Buddha half frowned and half smiled. "Just as soon as I locate it."

"You don't know where it is?"

"It wouldn't be much of a secret gateway if I did."

"So how do you plan on finding it... in an entire galaxy. It better be a big gateway."

"Actually, it's one of the smallest things in the universe."

"Great. Ever hear the old expression 'finding a needle in a haystack?'"

"I've come across it. But then, if you turn the needle into the haystack and the haystack into the needle, it becomes easier to find."

"I have no idea what you're talking about."

"I let my awareness float down to something smaller than the vibrations."

"You can do that?"

"I'm Buddha."

"Right. So how does that help you find the smallest thing in the universe?"

"Because then, Abner, it becomes the biggest thing in the universe."

"And just how does that work?"

"It's a Buddha thing."

CHAPTER 143 - SOME WARS DON'T HAVE WINNERS

The Cormorant was ecstatic. It no longer mattered that the Assassin hadn't killed Shade, though he wondered why in hell he would kill Loac, even after the games started. But that worked out perfectly for the Cormorant. Shade didn't stand a chance against Cassie Hayes, and there simply were no other contenders. He'd bet the equivalent of galaxies on the VR girl, and now his money was safe.

And the reports he was getting from his spies, the ones paying off gambling debts in Bella's navies and in the Clans all confirmed what he knew was going to happen. Bella was at war with the Clans. There were major battles at the gateway to Control and on Blood Citadel. Bella's fleets were attacking Clan worlds and settlements throughout the universe. One by one Quans from those worlds were disappearing as were Quans from entire fleets in Bella's navies. This would be the bloodiest war of all time, Creation-wide, with each side determined to exterminate the other. There would be no survivors among the losers of this war.

There might not even be a winner. Bella's navies were larger, but the Clans were born warriors. They knew how to do much with little, and they were always pulling surprises out of their robes. If, in fact, there were such things as magic, the Clans would have it.

And there was something about Bella. She wasn't the Bella he'd been dealing with for hundreds of years, the one he'd lusted for in countless fantasies. Though still the most beautiful woman in the universe, she didn't have that same old sparkle. Something was wrong. Could death finally be catching up to her after more than two thousand years? Or was she just going crazy? Whatever it was, she was losing it, her power over Quannet and her power over the universe.

The Cormorant was certain that Bella Bjork was about to lose her first war, but she would decimate the Clans in the process of losing. This was why the Cormorant, though all the other Gamblers were betting heavily on the wars, hadn't bet a thing on them. No one was going to win this war, and when it was over there would be a new order in the universe.

The Cormorant would be an essential player in that order. He watched as Shade and Sara Beth entered an arena together, wondering what the odds were of that happening?It looked like Bella might be tampering with the Reality Wars. Now he knew his money was safe.

CHAPTER 144 - AND NOW SHE WAS DEAD

She replayed the Quancast over and over, not understanding what she was seeing. Standing on her launch port, Sara Beth looked calm and in control to the trillions of viewers Quanning in on the Reality Wars, but calm was nowhere close to what she felt. She replayed it once more. She couldn't understand what had happened. Whatever or whoever killed Loac, she knew that she had nothing to do with it. The Clanswoman had almost killed her, somehow using her vapor powers in Quanspace to invade her mind and body and turn her fear and hatred on her like a lethal weapon. Another few seconds, and she would have been dead.

And then suddenly the Clanswoman was screaming and her vapor was struggling and thrashing inside her and she could feel the life force draining out of her. And then the woman who was supposedly the deadliest human weapon in the universe was nothing more than threads of mist dissolving into Quanspace.

Sara looked toward the launch portal where Loac's body lay slumped on the ground. They left the bodies there until after the Wars. By then it was a grim spectacle of hundreds, sometimes thousands, of dead competitors. If anyone thought the Reality Wars were anything but the bloodiest game in town, those rows of corpses would be quick to change that misconception.

Though Loac's death had been horrific, she'd fallen gracefully. She lay on the grass with her long legs crossed one over the other, her dark hair draped around her neck and face elegantly, eyes closed serenely, her face tranquil, all the hatred of her breeding death-drained out of her features.

Sara felt a pang of regret-such a beautiful woman but so steeped in hatred and so-called duty. What were the Clans thinking? What kind of hatred would lead them to spend half a millennium building a human being for no other purpose than to guide all of humanity into hating a life form born out of humanity? And now she was dead. Five hundred years of planning and scheming and manipulating the human genome for an evil purpose, all down the toilet.

But how?

On that thought, her launch port fell from under her, and she was whisked off at lightning speed to her next arena. This one, she knew, would be in Realspace, somewhere deep inside Canak.

CHAPTER 145 - PURE WEAPON

This is new. Sara was in a pit about thirty feet deep with a dirt floor. She was aware of noise coming from the top of the pit. There were dozens of them along the walls-something strange about them. They weren't human. They were twisted stone-like creatures with hideous faces and lizard-like bodies. Some had leathery wings, and their legs and arms were like something out of horror stories from the Archives-bent, warped, like something between reptile and bird with enormous claws. Huge fangs protruded from their monstrous jowls. Their eyes glowed red. Some were huge-over ten feet high-others, the size of dogs. They jumped and growled and scurried along the tops of the walls with their terrible red eyes fixed on her, waving their clawed arms and screeching obvious obscenities as repugnant dark liquids dripped from their mouths. The stench from their breath and ugly bodies flowed down into the pit.

Gargoyles. She remembered the stories. They'd been bred by one of the early outer colonies as an abominable army in one of the early colonial wars. Millions of them had been set loose on whole systems of planets, where they'd slaughtered entire populations, sterilizing them of human life before their creators had sterilized the gargoyles and then moved into the decimated planets. But when they had come to the attention of Bella, she'd sent her navies to destroy both the gargoyles and their creators. These creatures had been exterminated over a thousand years ago, or so everyone had thought.

Obviously, some had been spared. And the only person who could have spared them was Bella. And now they were here. That could mean only one thing-Bella was running the Reality Wars. But that didn't really surprise Sara.

Something felt strange. She moved her hands quickly to her hips. Her weapons were gone. She was unarmed. She sensed movement behind her and spun sharply to face it.

It was Shade, standing at the other end of the pit, blond hair flowing over muscular shoulders, arms by her side, standing still and composed, emanating deadliness. There was something different about her, something changed at a basic level-something removed? This was not the same Shade that Sara had confronted at the Clean Test. The woman standing before her had been emptied of anything that might smile. Sara was facing a weapon. Hatred burned brightly in her eyes as she stood glaring at Sara.

Sara remained silent, letting her surroundings sink into her awareness, making subconscious notes on the consistency of the dirt floor, the texture of the walls, the distance between her and her opponent.

Slowly, Shade opened her mouth and spoke. "Looks like we fight this one out hand to hand." Her lips twisted into a cruel smile. "I get to strangle you to death with my bare hands." She looked up at the gargoyles. "And then I think I'll feed your dead body to our audience."

462

"I think those things would be more into Grade B meat, Clans bitch. And that would be you."

Shade narrowed her eyes and practically growled. "How did you do it?"

Simultaneously, both women began moving to the side slowly, forming a circle between them. "Do what?"

"Kill her. How did you kill her? She had you. You were gone, dead. And suddenly she was dead. How did you do it?"

"I didn't."

Shade's eyes narrowed further as a hint of confusion flickered in them. "I watched it on Quan. Somehow, you shredded. How did you do it?"

"It was just as much a surprise to me as it was to you. I don't know what happened. One moment, I was losing consciousness; the next, she was in pieces and I was back on my launch port."

"That's impossible! I watched it. There was no one else there but you and Loac, and you were just seconds away from dead."

"Maybe she slipped."

The crouched now as they circled, ready to spring or defend.

"What's that mean?"

"It was the Karma Corridor, Shade. Maybe just before I was about to die, she slipped and let the hatred take her over. It would have come back on her in spades. And she had a lot of hatred in her... five hundred years worth of-"

Shade covered the distance between them in less than a blink of the eye, her right leg flying spearing at Sara's face and missing by a fraction of an inch as Sara moved to the left and spun around, sending her right leg up and catching Shade's right arm as she twisted in the air to land on her feet.

"You'll have to be faster than that," said Sara between clenched teeth.

The two women backed away from each other as the gargoyles howled at the top of the pit, falling over each other in their madness, the larger ones crushing the smaller under giant clawed legs.

"She was a good woman!" screamed Shade. "She wanted what was right. She wanted a return to respect for humankind."

"By destroying trillions of VR lives. That's not what's right, that's insanity."

"Spoken like a true VR lover. They're filling up Creation, despoiling it with their numbers, taking over Quannet, taking it away from its flesh and blood owners."

"Most of them are off somewhere on Quannet where they don't even come into contact with humans. Hell, some people say they're not even on Quannet anymore. Almost all the ones you see work at jobs where they serve humans and VRs alike."

Shade attacked, springing so fast she was barely visible.

Sara reacted instantly.

Both women collided, knocking each other to the ground, where they scrambled dizzily to fighting stances and attacked again. Sara scored a hard jab into Shade's mouth, cutting her lower lip on her teeth in almost the same instant that Shade came down painfully in the top of Sara's right foot with a stomping kick.

Both women backed away from each other again, in low fighting stances. They attacked again, but this time, something strange happened in the pit. It was just a fraction of a microsecond, but it changed things infinitely. They were in Quanspace.

***

Maggie: And there it is! For the first time ever, a Realspace Wars arena has switched in mid-engagement to Quanspace! And there's definitely no love lost between these two. This is a fight to the death!

Childen: (obviously not happy) Too bad. From all accounts, Shade was one of the more reasonable and open-minded of the Clans, but it appears that the death of her mate has changed that.

Maggie: Exactly the stuff of a great fight, Childen. Sara has just killed

Shade's mate, and now she's face-to-face with what she's done. This day will go down in the books as the greatest Reality Wars battle of all time.

Childen: (doubtful) And just what are the odds that these two would come face-to-face?

Maggie: (frowning) Childen, the odds are what they are, and these are some of the best Reality Wars moments ever. Get with the program.

***

She was in Quannspace, oriented and ready, and she wasn't about to fall for the vapor trick

465

again. Shade stood before her, arms by her side in a wide stance, eyes measuring the battleground.

They were still in the pit, but now it was hundreds of feet in diameter with walls soaring up over a hundred feet. Thousands of gargoyles shrieked and wailed from the tops of the walls, their dark profiles gruesome against a blood-red virtual sky with roiling dark clouds.

A movement from Shade's direction and Sara sprung to the right just in time to avoid a foot that might have ripped her head off her shoulders. She drove her right hand into the ground and pivoted her body around it, throwing her left leg directly at Shade's head.

Shade ducked back and the foot shot by her face by less than an inch.

In barely a second Sara pushed herself at Shade, grazing her throat with her left foot.

As though her foot had missed her completely, Shade spun around blindingly and landed the back of her right foot firmly in Sara's midsection. It bounced off.

Facing each other, they backed away in low fighting stances.

Suddenly, they were back in Realspace. Sara ducked just in time to avoid a strike to her head from Shade's flying thrust kick. She dropped to the ground and kicked upward in the direction where the other woman would land but Shade managed to twist her body to avoid the blow and landed on two feet and an arm, her right arm up and ready to block an attack.

Chests expanding and contracting slowly as they replenished their oxygen-deprived bodies, both women faced each other, eyes glaring.

"Just want you to know one thing before I kill you," said Sara without a trace of fatigue. "I wasn't the one who had the pleasure of killing your little girlfriend. But I wish I had."

Shade attacked instantly, arms swinging like a threshing machine. Sara jumped and spun, flailing her left leg out and smashing it into Shade's right hand. Shade yelped and came at her harder.

Without warning, they were in another Quanspace, in the center of a pit that had grown to the proportions of a lifeless plains, dirt floor spreading for miles in every direction until it came upon walls that stretched hundreds of feet in the sky. Thousands upon thousands of gargoyles jabbered and howled, some of them over a hundred feet high. They squirmed and slid between each other like a grotesque wall of vile life above the walls of the pit. Towering clouds in the sky over them boiled over with bloody rain, and the gargoyles thrived in it, opening their mouths to swallow ball-sized drops that splashed over their faces.

There was movement all around her. She spun her head and body, startled. She was all around herself, thousands of replica Saras. And in front of them, thousands of Shades. All of them astonished. But the surprise was short lived. Both sides attacked, two screaming walls of fists and feet, colliding in the center of the pit. Thousands of Shades and Saras kicking and punching, gouging eyes, pulling hair, ripping the flesh from each others' faces with their fingernails.

And both Shade and Sara could feel every blow that landed on their replica bodies. They could feel every gouged eye, every kick to the face, every crushing kick to their arms and legs. It was impossible for either to tell which was the real other, and which were the copies.

Sara fended off attack after attack, all of them solid in Quanspace. She could feel her own blows penetrating deeply, causing damage. *Take that you Clans bitch, whichever one you are*.

And that's when she saw her, beating her way toward her through dozens of virtual Saras, and Sara could feel every one of the blows.

The gargoyles were going insane, their screams and howls filling the air in the pit with a foul solid sound. The stench was strangling. The creatures' red eyes grew increasingly intense, turning into a crimson glow that lit up the upper walls of the pit.

From the center of the glow, directly in front of Sara, an opening appeared like a curtain rising into another place. Something moved on the other side of the curtain, a burst of white. It shot like a tiny bolt of pure energy without a trail, without warning, straight into Sara's forehead.

Before she even started to fall to the ground, she was dead.

***

Standing almost breathless on her launch port, Shade knew. She'd seen the white flash penetrate

468

Sara's forehead, and she'd looked back just in time to see the white curtain fold on itself and disappear. And she knew-someone had fixed the Reality Wars.

***

On Zinin, the bodies of the Sara Beth Ten Thousand lay lifeless in their party tomb amid thousands of empty and half-empty liquor containers. Some lay slumped in groups, some were crumpled together still joined to each other's bodies in acts of sex, some lay with their arms to their sides with others forming perfect geometrical shapes-a death game they played before their lives disappeared into the void.

The young man and young woman who'd been interviewed just hours before lay beside each other, holding hands, smiles frozen into their pale faces.

CHAPTER 146 - SOMETHING THE AUDIENCE WILL NEVER FORGET

It was chilling, watching the woman he loved laughing so hysterically. Her eyes spilled streams of red and orange light. Her hair was in flames, her face contorted with cruel amusement. Her laugh was a choked cackle and then snorts and hyperbreathing and snatches of giggles and guffaws. Her body racked spasmodically.

Lovesong watched from the other side of the nancouch, eyes sad, horror filling his heart. The lines around Bella's eyes and mouth were deepening at a startling rate.

"That makes us even! That... that makes us even," she yelled between gulps of air. "That bastard assassin killed Shade's mate, so I... " She pointed a long finger, beginning to bend with age, at her chest. "I killed Cassie's best friend." She turned on Lovesong with crazed eyes, looking for what? Confirmation? "I killed her, my darling Lovesong. Killed her!" Another fit of laughter. "We're even! Even!"

Lovesong smiled weakly and remained silent. He reached out to her and wrapped his fingers around her hand. Slowly, she began to calm with ever decreasing spurts of giggles and grunts. Her face was a mess, covered with tears. Tiny muscle spasms bubbled across her cheeks and jaw.

"He wants to interfere with my Reality Wars, then I'll interfere with his. And when it's all over, I'll interfere big time with his very life." She slid over the couch and curled up against his side, putting her arms around his neck. She kissed him passionately on the cheek, leaving a splotch of spittle and lay her head on his shoulder. Her chest still heaved, but not so violently.

After a few moments, she whispered, "And what did you think of the gargoyles, love?"

Lovesong chuckled. "I thought you had both them and their creators exterminated."

"Kept a few as souvenirs. You never know when a gargoyle or two might come in handy." She giggled maliciously. "They're beautiful creatures in their own right, wouldn't you say?"

"They were definitely a spectacle. Something the audience will never forget."

"Yes. Yes, they'll never forget. And with those two women fighting for their lives... and fighting well, I might add... didn't you think they fought well?"

"It was one of the most spectacular fights ever in the Wars."

"And they did it for *my* glory, to make *my* Wars the grandest show in the universe."

"They served you well."

"They did. They served me well. And what did you think of the death bolt? It certainly did kill that Sara Beth."

"It certainly did."

She raised her head and looked into Lovesong's eyes, questioning. "You... you have troubles, my Lovesong?"

He shrugged lightly and smiled. "It was a wonderful show and the ending is sure to make these Wars the most interesting and talked about ever."

She looked deep into his eyes, searched his face and came back to his eyes. She brought her face closer to his. "You have doubts?" She stuck a long finger into his chest, the nail almost painful. "Tell me."

"I was just wondering if anyone might have seen the death bolt. They were in full view of trillions of viewers."

"The bolt was cloaked to that one Quanspace. No one outside the arena could see it."

"And the Clanswoman?"

"She might have," she said coyly. "But it doesn't matter. As far as the audience is concerned, she could have been killed by one of the thousands of Shades attacking her. It will go down as her kill. And if she knows, who will listen to her, even if she could get out of the Wars. After all, darling Lovesong, once in the Reality Wars, there's no way out until the finish... " She ran a fingernail down the side of his face, then kissed him again on the cheek. "If... I let her finish."

Oh, Bella.

For an instant, her body froze, eyes wide, mouth opened as though surprised by a sudden thought. It was just for an instant but Lovesong noticed.

What now?

CHAPTER 147 - A THOUSAND THOUGHTS

She knew even before she saw Sara's body slumped over her launch disk. She'd just returned from the Smallness arena after being compressed to the smallest particle in the universe, or as small as virtual reality could shrink an object into half its size and then half again until it reached something so infinitesimally small that it became the opposite of size, and continued to grow smaller. This in itself would have been difficult, but to make it even more interesting, she engaged in hand-to-hand combat with another competitor who was shrinking along with her.

There had been hundreds of them in the arena. Over half of them had gone insane whether they won their individual battles or not. Many had died from shock or had just stopped living as the only escape from the claustrophobic horror of falling between atoms in a universe of smallness.

She knew it even before the Quan replays reached her. Sara was dead. Dead. Her friend of nearly a thousand years-killed by Shade. Her upper body began to heave. The muscles around her mouth shook. A thousand thoughts converged on her mind, scrambling through her awareness like phantoms screaming for attention. Sara was dead-killed by Shade.

She replayed the Quan a thousand times each second as the reality of Sara's death took root in her universe. She couldn't be dead. But there it was, second after second, thousands upon thousands of replays. But Sara hadn't even met her father yet. But now, she never would. She was gone. They would never go to the Beer again. Sara would never try to get her hooked up again. They would never again lounge around talking about everything in the universe. Never train together again. Sara was dead-killed by Shade.

She replayed the Quan again and again and again. She watched Sara fall, watched in horror as the thousands of virtual Saras fell. It wasn't right. It was impossible to tell which of them had taken the fatal blow from Shade, which of them had taken that final impact that had erased her best friend's life. It couldn't be right. She knew the Clanswoman was no match for Sara. And Loac-dead so early into the Wars, in her first arena. Something was wrong.

But she had no time to think about it, no time to mourn her friend. Something was happening, and she knew that she wasn't going to like it.

474

CHAPTER 148 - ON THE CREST OF DESTRUCTION

It was like riding on the crest of a supernova. Strapped into her command chair, Shona Ureal ordered all observation ports closed and armored as they followed the wake of the missiles from the Clans' fleet. It was breathtaking, watching the sheer numbers and collective mass of the deadly ordinance that filled all of space in front of them. Detecting her ship in all that explosive bulk would be impossible. She Quanned into the scene outside, saw the fury released by Bella's fleet to meet the missiles and beams from the Clans. Just a few more seconds and they would see if Bavn's nanmagic armor would withstand the impact and heat they would have to race through to break into Control.

And then it hit. Her ship lurched ten feet in one direction and was thrown back another twenty in the other. But the guidance system was locked in strongly and brought her back on course. There was no Quanning the outside at this point. They were inside a giant fireball that would turn any other ship into space soup. Bavn had worked on this nanmagic shielding for years. Though the storm of destruction outside the ship wouldn't penetrate the shielding, the force of it rocked her ship from side to side, up and down, sometimes sending them in wild spirals and neck-wrenching jolts. The ship spun like a top but the sheilding held. The ship groaned and bucketed, and the booming from explosions outside pounded Shona's ears.

And suddenly the booming stopped.

They'd made it through the first set of explosions, the ones that were planned to ignite at the forefront of the Control fleet. And now Bella's forces were getting a little surprise. Nearly a third of the Clans' missiles, including her ship, were equipped with nanboosters that would propel them at almost the speed of light for a microsecond, taking them right into the center of Bella's fleet where the missiles would explode simultaneously.

Which is exactly what they did. Suddenly, Shona Ureal was aware that she was inside what amounted to the destructive detonation of an exploding star. Hundreds of Bella's ships burst into flames and disintegrated within seconds. The temperature in her ship rose unbearably, but the shielding held. Shards of exploding vessels hammered her ship from one end to the other, and still the shielding held. And then, her facial muscles stretched painfully as the second nanbooster shot her ship forward to the rear ranks of the Control fleet.

They were in. And there were no attackers. The shielding had brought them through.

Now to bring down Quannet.

***

There was a lot to be said for observation ports. They let you see things the way they were. If something tried to be invisible, it had to actually be invisible, and nothing was invisible. It was only for a brief instant and it was just a blur, but Captain

Crash Duncan knew exactly what it was. He could feel it. He could taste it. It was a Clans' ship. It couldn't be anything else. He was picking nothing up on his Quantrols. *Got themselves a new cloak*. It couldn't be anything else.

He Quanned into the ships in his vicinity, most of them older ships, a few light cruisers and a few reserve heavy attack ships.

"We've got intruders, folks. Get your cloak breakers scanning for a Clans' ship on this side of the line. Spread out and start searching."

Almost immediately, a response from one of the cloak breakers. "Captain Duncan, you're right. We have a Clans' ship in Control."

Even before the cloak breaker had finished his sentence, Crash Duncan knew who was piloting the Clans' ship. It was Shona Ureal. He knew it.

CHAPTER 149 - SABOTAGE

All around her the other competitors began dropping to the ground. A woman in an orange Wars suit beside her let out a small sigh as her eyes went dead blank and her feet crumpled under her. She fell straight down. Cassie heard a bone crack as the weight of the woman's upper body snapped it. She was dead before her head touched the grass surrounding her launch disk. Thousands of them fell almost simultaneously. All of them dead.

Somebody's killing us. Killing everybody.

Bella. She's killing off all the competitors. In less than a minute, she was surrounded by lifeless bodies. She saw the massive body of Centos Kama sprawled on the ground just a few yards to her left. His face relaxed, loose. Death had come quickly enough that he'd had no chance to know what was happening.

Why? Why would she do this?

The Wars had been hers for a thousand years, according to Buddha. *Why would she just throw it away by killing off all the competitors?* And then she knew why.

About a hundred feet to her right, Shade turned slowly, eyes glowing blue. It was down to just her and the Clanswoman. Their eyes met and held. Neither said a word as they stood quietly, staring into each other's eyes.

This is the woman who killed Sara. This is the woman who killed my best friend. Anger welled up in her Realspace body. It felt strange to feel such a strong emotion and to feel it physically. She'd felt anger off and on for over two centuries, but this was different. This anger was sickening in its intensity. She suddenly had new insights into why physical humans acted the way they did. It wasn't that she'd never felt emotions strongly as virtual software-it was just that it had always been more contained. What she was feeling now raged beyond her body. It hurt. It was everywhere. She felt it creeping through the follicles in her head, slashing into her Realspace kidneys, raging through the muscles of her arms and legs, thrashing sickeningly in her stomach.

For the first time in her life, she wanted to kill something.

* * *

Maggie: (stunned, eyes wide) Did... did you see... ?

Childen: (puzzled, ignoring Maggie, staring with wide eyes)

* * *

It all started to make sense. The light in the pit had killed Sara Beth, but she wasn't murdered by somebody trying to fix the Reality Wars. She looked around at the bodies slouched in death all around her. She looked back at Cassie Hayes, the VR woman's eyes filling with hatred and rage, thinking that she was facing her best friend's killer.

It struck her like a sheet of ice passing over and through her body-they killed Loac. Sara Beth had

479

been telling the truth. She'd had nothing to do with Loac's death. Whoever was doing this had killed her mate, and then they'd killed Sara Beth. They weren't just fixing the Wars...

Somebody's sabotaging the Wars.

Somebody had just ended the Reality Wars for all time. And the battle between d Cassie Hayes and her would be the last Reality Wars combat in the universe. Even though the VR existing at the moment in Realspace in some sort of simulated physical presence, the last Reality Wars was down to flesh and blood against software.

CHAPTER 150 - THE GREATEST SLAUGHTER OF ALL TIME

It was the greatest slaughter of all time-spanning every galaxy, every star system and habitable planet in the universe. Hundreds of billions lives, tied into the fate of the Reality Wars competitors, winked out as though someone had flicked the switch of the universe to OFF. But it wasn't just the immensity of the horror, it was the timing-it was so perfect, so precise. At exactly the same second that death swept over the launch area on Canak, death's brood swept through the universe erasing life. Conversations ended suddenly when the person on the other side of the table suddenly crumpled silently and fell to the floor.

Throughout the universe mighty space freighters drifted aimlessly, their holds and quarters littered with bodies. Planet-sized space stations faced massive cleanups before the gases of soon-to-be-rotting bodies threatened to overpower their life support systems.

Like a single massive wave of confused and expired life, it crashed upon itself in every direction, and it was felt everywhere. Plants across Creation felt an instant of wilting as life forms too small to see with the eye suddenly froze in their microscopic worlds, feeling the slaughter at levels too small to understand.

It was felt as a cry. It was felt as a scream and a sigh of release. It was felt as something like abandonment, of giving up on an entire universe made small by too much knowing and not enough mystery.

It was a single wave of sadness permeating the basic structure of the universe, and it soured all reality at some essential level of being.

Such was the power of hopelessness.

CHAPTER 151 - THE END OF ALL THAT WAS

Lovesong stared unbelieving at the mass of dead competitors. This was beyond anything he'd ever dreamed Bella would do, an act of pure madness, of immeasurable ruthlessness.

But looking into her alarmingly creased eyes, sinking faster and faster with the breakdown of her life force, he knew that he still loved her and would accept all of her last acts without question.

"Now we know who's master of the universe!" she screamed. "Let them wonder on this! Let them see the power I exert! Let them... " She choked on spittle draining into her throat, coughed hoarsely, her eyes two dying embers of a fire that had burned brightly for two millennia and still glistening with an insane inner light.

He wrapped his arms around her and pulled her to him, burying her head into his chest. He massaged her back slowly, feeling the heaving of her breath. The coughing subsided and her breathing returned to normal. She lifted her face to his. The smoothness of her skin was giving way to mild pruning, losing its sheen to undercurrents of yellow and gray. She lifted a misshapen finger to his lips. "I've decided to make this the last of the Reality Wars, my love. They were beginning to bore me anyway. A thousand years of them is enough, and if I'm done with them, then the universe is done with them." She looked deep into his eyes, cocked her head to the side, questioningly.

"You look so sad, my love. You should be happy. This is the beginning, the start of a new universe. A time to rejoice!"

He smiled. "I'm a little surprised, I suppose. I'd always thought that the Wars were something dear to you."

"In their time." A wistful look spread over the increasingly gaunt features of her face. "But these are new times, times that call for new entertainment for the cosmic masses. When I have the Texture, and my powers over all life are restored, I'll give them something new, something bigger and better and spectacular beyond anything that has ever been. Something befitting an eternal queen of the universe."

She laughed loudly, madly, and there was just the slightest taint of panic in her voice from that part of her, buried deep inside that must have knowledge of what was happening to her, something that sensed the irreversible breakdown of the nanhancements, the genetic modifications, the failing implants that had kept her alive beyond any human science or technology no matter how close they came to godly powers.

"And this should put a dent in the Gamblers. I wonder what this will do to their odds, their betting, their payouts and... " She stepped away from him, laughing wildly. "They'll just have to cancel! Ha! Cancel!"

She was sinking fast, but he knew that the universe needed for her to die soon, before she could wreak any more havoc on it. He wondered how many billions of entangled lives had perished with the killing of those thousands of competitors, whether it was their wish to die or not. How many billions would die in her war against the Clans? How many planets would be stripped of life to extinguish an entire people?

He Quanned into the battlefronts. As if she were in his head, she asked, "And how goes the extermination of those pesky little Clans? Tell me they're perishing by the billions, my love."

They were. And so were her own navies. The Clans were putting up fierce resistance, much more stubborn than anyone had dreamed. This would not be a war with a clear winner. This would be a war to devastate the most powerful forces in the universe, leaving all of Creation in chaos. That would be Bella Bjork's legacy-the end of all that was.

"They're falling like ash from the fire clouds of Ponea."

"And my navies are leaving no survivors?"

"No survivors."

"That's important, you know. I want this to be final. It must be the end of them. There can be no survivors... even the babies must die."

"Our navies will be thorough. This war will be the end of the Clans."

"Wonderful!" She stepped up to him, putting her arms around his neck, pressing her body hard against his but not with the same firmness and strength of just an hour earlier. She kissed him hard on the lips and her lips seemed less full, less heated, less moist than just an hour ago. She ended the kiss with a flick of her tongue. "And now to make the last of my Reality Wars the best of them ever with the best of human against the best of software." She narrowed her eyes. "And if Cassie Hayes wins, I'll put her in Realspace forever and turn her into mist as I did her father. And I'll do the same to him when I have him back."

"And if the Clanswoman wins."

"We kill her immediately."

CHAPTER 152 - ALONE

The ship was going mad. The entire fleet was going mad. Chaine, had turned into a snake and had slithered off to god knows where. But it didn't matter. The snake was an improvement, easier to look at, and more in keeping with the reptilian evil of the little bastard. It still had those damn wires around its snake jowls though. There was no point now in bringing the crews of his ships to alert. Everyone was caught up in the same madness playing out on his command deck. His own reality was wavering no matter how much he tried to hold onto it. Things changed, things moved. The walls appeared to have a strange sheen, emitting waves of diffused light like rainbows in oily water.

All their weapons had been disabled along with their navigation systems. Nels was no longer in charge of his ship, no longer in command of his fleet. It appeared that the strange object in space was in control. The Texture. It was visible now through his observation windows. There was no way it could be that big. It spanned galaxies, yet it was right there in front of them in its entirety, possibly the size of a planet, or maybe a moon. Or a basketball. Its shape was impossible to describe. It was like a tear in space, with vast expanses of energy pouring out of it, spilling its cosmic contents into the space around it, but containing it all within boundaries that seemed possible to understand in one instant beyond anything the mind could handle in the next instant.

It defied anything that human logic could get its cold head around. Nels had given up even trying to understand it. All he knew was that they'd arrived, and somehow he had to figure out what this thing was all about and then get his ships out of there and back home to whatever was left of home. He stared into it. It just wasn't possible. Nothing like this could exist in the rules and laws of this universe. Perhaps Bella was right. Perhaps this was from another universe. Perhaps this is where our time/space touched another time/space and leaked something from one to the other, creating a pocket of rules and laws that were somehow trapped in this place unable to move beyond these borders and into the rules and laws that contradicted everything they were trying to be.

It was something that was never meant to exist here but there it was, trying to exist. It looked confused, yet confident; alone, yet teeming with life. *What am I thinking?* He suddenly realized that he was endowing it with feelings, sentience, a knowing of its state. But how could that be? Was this a living thing? Could something like this be said to be living? Everything he knew told him no. Everything he knew told him... why not?

One thing he knew for certain. They were no longer flying through space to the Texture. The Texture was drawing them to it.

CHAPTER 153 - A PURPOSE

"They're leaving?" Supreme Commander Daman Haley Quanned the Clans' fleet. Sure enough, they were pulling back from the battle leaving a deadly wake of missiles in their departure. *Why would they suddenly run?* This wasn't like the Clans. Their defense against his superior forces and firepower had been unexpectedly effective, especially the last salvo that had somehow boosted from the forward lines right into the middle of his fleets. They'd taken out hundreds of ships with that little trick. *And now they're running?*

Something was wrong. They were up to something. He knew it. The Clans never did anything without some purpose to it, and there had to be some purpose in bringing their fleet this close to Control. Daman was certain they'd expected a confrontation. Given the size of their fleet, he hadn't been in the least worried by their presence. Meeting their first attack and striking back was just like the Clans. But they hadn't even stayed long enough to engage in close range fighting. That was their specialty, the only warfare that would have won the day for them... if they hadn't been outnumbered thousands to one. But it was unlike them to not even have tried. It would have been something for them to talk about, something to recount over the centuries to add to the legend of their warrior image.

They're passing the opportunity to make new myths.

Somewhere in the back of Daman Haley's mind, an alarm sounded quietly. There was a purpose in their leaving. Either it was their intention to lead his navies into a trap, or they had achieved whatever purpose had brought them here. He weighed the possibilities. Their cloaking technologies were the best in the universe. It was possible they had a larger force far beyond the battlefront and the retreating force would lead his navies to them. He Quanned his intelligence crew and ordered them to scan for light-years in the direction the Clans' fleet was traveling and search for cloaking devices. He ordered three fleets to give chase to the Clans and destroy them. If he'd been confident there would be no ambush, he would have sent ten fleets. But given the uncertainty, three was all he was prepared to sacrifice for the chase. He would send others as events unfolded.

Almost as soon as he gave the order, he received the Quan. It was Captain Juna Rillie stationed in the rear guard. Captain Colin "Crash" Duncan had just broken formation and taken several attack ships streaking into Control.

"And his reason?" he asked the obviously nervous Captain Rillie.

"It looks like they're in pursuit of a Clans' ship, Sir."

"Clans' ship? Inside Control?"

"It looks that way, Sir."

That was their purpose. And it looked like they'd achieved it.

He ordered five fleets into Control to hunt down the Clans' ship and destroy it. He was puzzled though-that they would send just one ship into an entire galaxy-but wary.

There would be a purpose for sending just one ship.

CHAPTER 154 - AN ICICLE OF DREAD

They never stopped coming, swarm after swarm. Bavn couldn't begin to imagine how many of the attacking ships had been destroyed, but they kept coming. Such was the fear and power of Bella-these fools believed her to be a goddess to die for, to sacrifice their lives for her will. And her will was to destroy Blood Citadel. The toll on the asteroids had been heavy-the toll on the attackers astronomical, but they kept coming, and there were still millions stretching into unseen reaches of space.

He was beginning to wonder how long they could withstand the onslaught. And he knew they were on their own. Blood Citadel was the most powerful of all the Clans' strongholds. Their navies battled ferociously but they were outnumbered hundreds to one. Every Clans' ship cost the attackers ten of their own. Every attack on an asteroid cost them dearly. But they kept coming.

Bavn still had faith they could withstand the assault. There would be little left of the Clans' navies but there would still be battle-ready asteroids left at the end. Of this he was certain.

At the very moment this thought traveled through his mind, he received a Quan from the far side of Vala.

"Bavn," said Ulmach Diorn, chief of the Machlan asteroid. "There's an unusual array of

492

Bella's ships clustering just beyond our short-range weapons. They have the emblem of the Tree Clan."

Damn. Bavn thought they were merely assassins these days, not an attack force. "What are they doing?"

"They seem to be aligning themselves into a formation, but it doesn't look like any attack formation I've ever seen."

"Can you reach them with your missiles?"

"We've tried. They have thousands of ships running shotgun for them. Most of them suicidal, some of them taking full hits from the missiles just to stop them. And our lasers seem to have no effect on them."

Somewhere in the back of Bavn's mind an unease began to take root. The Trees were up to something, and whatever it was, it would be bad for Blood Citadel.

"Strange," said Ulmach. "It looks like the defending ships are clearing away."

Bavn Quanned into the quandrant and saw the masses of Bella's ships clearing the area, leaving a strange formation of several hundred Tree ships still out of tactical weapons range. He felt the unease growing in his chest now. Whatever was about to happen, it wasn't good.

And it wasn't.

Suddenly, the Tree Clan ships boosted full speed straight at Machlan. Long-range missiles took out a few dozen, but the lasers bounced off them. When they came into short weapons range, several dozen more were blown into space dust, but they kept coming at the asteroid in full booster. It looked like they were going to crash into the surface, a foolhardy suicide strategy that would do no more than surface damage. The war machines under the surface would still be intact and ready to be moved to the surface.

Then the unimaginable happened. As one, the entire attacking force exploded just above the surface of the asteroid. The force of the explosion lit up the surrounding asteroids and the surface of Vala with the brilliance of a nova. But something else was happening. A strange aura emanated from the explosion, something iridescent and filled with dancing spectrums like immense rainbows twisting and undulating. Bavn gazed in horror as the aura seemed to solidify and fall onto the asteroid, spreading over its surface like a shimmering blanket. The asteroid began to glow dull red, then bright red and yellow and then the Machlan asteroid broke from its orbit, picking up speed as it veered toward Vala. Bavn watched incredulously as Machlan traveled with alarming speed and crashed Nathin, an asteroid smaller than Machlan—and now the two were hurtling wildly through space taking out two more asteroids before streaking toward Vala's upper atmosphere. Cold dread gathered in Bavn's chest.

The Tree had found a way to destroy Blood Citadel.

CHAPTER 155 - A GAMUT OF ASTONISHED EMOTIONS

Jeli laughed uncontrollably as he watched Benji splash over the control deck. His water was every color in existence and colors that Jeli had never seen, colors that didn't exist, colors for which he had no words, no ability to comprehend or respond to-except to laugh like a madman. After all, this *was* madness. The very idea of pilgrimage to this impossible phenomenon was madness. The journey to this place had been madness. The ship and the crew were madness.

Foam gathered at the edges of his mouth and he laughed harder.

The portal opened and Bingo rushed in eyes wide with panic. "The ship is out of control," he yelled.

Jeli laughed still harder, falling to his knees, his stomach feeling ready to explode with the sheer physical exertion of his laughter. His body heaved as he gulped air and tried to bring the laughter under control enough to speak. It took several minutes, with Bingo staring ball-eyed at him. Through spasmodic breaths, Jeli finally managed to mutter, "The ship... the ship has always been out of control." Another fit of laughter. "It's... it's... we've never been in control."

Bingo gawked, jaw hanging.

"Don't you see it? Can't you see it? It's why they sent *us*. It's why they picked the most absurd crew they could imagine and put us on the most

495

absurd ship they could create. They knew it would be impossible for us to get here. They knew we didn't stand a chance in hell. That's why they sent us." Another fit of laughter. "It was impossible for us to get here. That's exactly why it *was possible* for us to get here." He pointed out the observation port at the Texture. "That... that is impossible."

Bingo's gaze followed the direction of Jeli's finger. His mouth opened slowly. He tried to speak. Nothing happened. He stood as though glued to the surface of the deck, speechless, as his mouth moved, trying to put into words what his mind was unable to comprehend. Impossible shades of light reflected off his face and spread over his features. He raised his hand and pointed in a direction off to the side. Jeli followed with his eyes and saw them.

They were lined up row after row, thousands and thousands of them. Bella's ships. And to the other side of Soul Ship, the Clans' ships. Jeli and Bingo reached a simultaneous realization—they were sitting directly in the line of fire between two of the largest battle fleets they'd ever seen.

"And was it impossible for them to get here?" asked Bingo, pointing at the waves of ships. As the last word lifted away from his lips, both he and Jeli turned into water and splashed onto the deck.

CHAPTER 156 - A THOUSAND THOUGHTS

"I didn't kill her," said Shade slowly. They were twenty feet from each other, closing the distance slowly, working around the corpses—some calm-faced, others unbelieving—not attacking, but measuring. "There was a beam of light. Sara fell when it hit her. I think someone is trying to sabotage the Wars."

A barrage of thoughts pummeled Cassie's mind, a thousand possibilities, and infinite ways to end this, so many of them variations on strangling the life out of the Clanswoman. She wanted to stare into Shade's eyes as her life flickered and evaporated into nothingness.

But the Clanswoman's words rang true. She had no reason to deny killing Sara. If anything, she would more likely have flaunted her kill, using it as an emotional weapon.

"And I don't think Sara killed Loac." Something in Shade's eyes, an undertone in her voice, sliced through Cassie's anger and deflated it. There was nothing threatening in Shade's stance. She was relaxed, trusting, open.

"And what were the chances that Sara and Loac would be matched in the first round, and then Sara and I? And now, you and I—and everybody else is dead."

"Bella."

"Bella?"

"She runs the Wars. She started them."

A look of recognition crossed Shade's eyes, like suddenly remembering something that was in front of her but unseen for a long time. She nodded. "That makes sense. No one has ever been able to figure out how a backwater planet like Canak could afford the money and resources needed to keep something this big going for a thousand years."

"Shade?"

"Yes."

"She can kill both of us anytime she wants."

The truth of Cassie's words, and their implications, sank instantly into Shade's mind. Bella was watching them. Bella wanted the Reality Wars battle of all time. She wanted Cassie and her to provide that, the final showdown between human and software, an epic that would shine gloriously through the ages. And there was no doubt who had to win. Bella's empire had been built not just on her vast navies and ruthlessness but on her command of Quannet and the VRs. A VR would have to win the last of the Reality Wars. That was the way Bella would want it. She would let this last battle play out for however long it would last, but the winner would not be Shade. She'd be doomed the moment the battle began. She already was.

"You see it, don't you?" asked Cassie.

"Unfortunately, I do."

"We have to play this out with neither of us winning."

"That could go on for a long time."

"Got something else to do?"

Shade smiled. "Sooner or later, she's going to get bored... and just end it."

498

"Maybe we can figure something out. In the meantime... " Cassie lunged at Shade, screaming, and raked the side of her face with her nails.

Shade spun with lightning speed, sending a blistering kick into the back of Cassie's right leg. Blood dripped from the side of her face. The two stood facing each other in fighting stances.

"Well," said Shade, "that certainly convinced *me*."

Cassie stifled a smile, hoping that Bella hadn't heard their conversation. As she thought about this, Shade attacked.

CHAPTER 157 - THE SMALLEST SPACE AND THE SMALLEST TIME

"We're going to a place that's only a theory?" Normally, Abner would be surprised, but Buddha had long since stopped surprising him. "So it might not even exist?"

"It exists." He seemed so implacably smug, sure of truth in absurdity.

"Then it's not just a theory."

"Let's just say that the theory has had a practical application-one that worked."

"And just what was that practical application?"

"Quannet."

"Quannet?"

"It's when and where Quannet exits."

"When and where?"

Buddha breathed out a long noisy sigh.

Abner couldn't help but smile. It seemed that his questions had finally ruffled Buddha's implacableness.

"We're going to compress ourselves into the smallest particles imaginable but not like the smallness they compress themselves into in the Reality Wars, something your daughter excels at, by the way. We're going to compress both space *and* time. We're going to shrink to the smallest space and the smallest time-or at least, as close to it as we can get. There's no end to smallness, just as there's no end to largeness."

"So, just how small is this smallness?"

"Smaller than the strings, smaller than their vibrations. That's where the gateway to Quannet exists. That's where Quannet was conceived."

"And Bella did that?"

"Don't underestimate Bella, or the billions of human computers she created."

"I still don't get it. We're going to find something so small within an entire galaxy... wouldn't we just be making the galaxy larger?"

"Exactly."

Abner frowned.

"We'll be so small," said Buddha, smiling patiently, "that the universe will swallow itself in its largeness, time will cease to exist in the infinity of its future and past. The only things that will exist for us will be the things as small as us to which we are entangled by our own will and belief."

"So how long will we be there?"

"Not long."

"How not long?"

"Less than an instant. However, it may seem longer to us."

"A long time?"

"Does infinity bring anything to mind?"

"I don't think I want to know any more."

"That's probably a good attitude. Some things are best not known before you experience them."

"And why's that?"

Buddha winked. "You might not want to experience them."

Abner frowned. Something occurred to him. "By the way, I can see how you might go there, but how the hell am I going to get there?"

501

"The same way we got here together-we're entangled. Ready?"

"Um... "

In an instant they were gone from where and when they were, and were nose to nose with infinity.

CHAPTER 158 - COSMIC PANDEMONIUM

"It's her," growled the Cormorant. "I know it's her." He presented himself as the Joker, the spades Joker-his symbol of vengeful power. It was time for vengeance, time for payback.

The other Gamblers presented themselves in every ornate form of card imaginable, from the simplest wallpaper fleur-de-lis to flowery concepts so intricate they defied description. They all had two things in common-they were face cards and the eyes were alive, alive and shocked.

"Not even Bella is capable of rigging the Reality Wars," said a Botticellian King of Hearts, with the assumed arrogance of a king. "The Wars are the sole property of Canak. Always have been. That was the basis of the Truce of All Entities. It's what's kept the Wars the most viable and, I might add, the most profitable gambling event in the universe."

The Cormorant turned both his top eye and mirrored bottom eye on the King of Hearts. The malevolence in their glare caused the other card's presence to waver. The Cormorant's voice cut through Quanspace with acidic menace. "In case you haven't been Quanning the Wars in the last hour... *I might add*... we've all been fucked!"

Hundreds of eyes embedded in every conceivable form of decoration blinked. Most knew that something terrible had just happened. None understood the full ramifications. Nothing like this had ever happened before.

All bets were off in the Reality Wars. The competitors had been murdered. Strange things had happened in the arenas-improbable things, impossible things. Something not right had happened to Sara Beth. And now Hayes was facing Shade-the odds were incalculable. And thousands of competitors had just dropped dead. Bella was interfering with the Wars, rigging them. Bella was interfering with the profits of the Gamblers. The biggest money event of all time had just been scuttled, and there would be cosmic pandemonium. It might even be the end of the Gamblers.

A Kandinsky Queen of Clubs asked, "How do you know it's her."

The Cormorant cast his eyes on her, mellowed immediately, knowing who she was and remembering the great sex they'd had both in Real and Quanspace. "She's the only one with the power to do this," he said, his voice beginning to calm. "Think about it... nobody has ever really known how Canak, a backwater planet with a completely unknown population, became hosts of the biggest sporting event in the universe. They had to have had lots of backing, backing on a scale that only Bella could have provided."

"But they started out small, Cormorant," said the Queen of Clubs. "They built up slowly."

"Exactly, my dear. But how did they make their money?"

"Well, from... " She went silent.

The Cormorant continued. "There's no way they could have raised the money from the Wars. There's no entrance fee. Having to be financially neutral, they have no gambling operations. It's outlawed planet wide. They made the Wars an intergalactic spectacle in its first century, and now they're running it in both Realspace and Quanspace. Where did they get the money to pay for that kind of technology?" He paused. "Bella has been running the Wars all along." He paused again. "And now we have to kill her."

If eyes could nod, they would have.

CHAPTER 159 - NOT ON MY WATCH

"We're on our way," said Brys, Shona's chief onboard intel officer. "I've located the cluster that forms the heart of Quannet. It's just like they described it. Now, that's damn fine intel."

"Nice work, Brys," said Shona, certain now that the rest would be a piece of cake. And a tasty piece of cake it would be—plant Bavn's nanmagic virus in just one of the human servers that made up the heart of Quannet, and within minutes, Quannet would cease to exist... along with every VR ever created. Humanity would reign over the universe once more."

She received an urgent Quan from her navigator, Waylande. "We have company."

Shona Quanned the area and saw the other ship immediately. It was the same one that had boarded them earlier. She almost flew into the air as her ship rocked from a direct missile hit. *These bastards mean business.*

"Evade! Evade!" she screamed.

***

On you now, bitch, thought Crash Duncan. *I don't know what you think you're going to do here, but you won't be doing it on my watch.*

"Time to turn that Clans bitch's ship into solar dust," he ordered. Every piece of ordinance on his ship locked onto the Clans' ship.

CHAPTER 160 - CERTAINTY

Blood Citadel was quickly becoming the biggest blood bath in the universe. The relentless suicide squadrons of Tree ships had taken out over a dozen asteroids, throwing them out of orbit and sending them tumbling into space or into Vala's atmosphere. Vast explosions dotted the surface of the planet, throwing up immense clouds of debris.

The Clans' short-range fighters fought desperately to stop the Tree ships' suicidal attacks, but they were far too outnumbered. Bella's navies were coming in faster and more furiously. Their losses were staggering but they kept coming.

Bavn had never felt more alone. Communications with all his fleets beyond Blood Citadel were gone. Communications with Clans across the universe were gone. He wondered how Shade was faring in the Reality Wars and was troubled by the growing awareness that he might never know. He'd lost his daughter. And now he was on the brink of losing Blood Citadel and the billions of lives under the surfaces of its asteroids.

He Quanned into another massive Tree explosion smashing into one of the bigger asteroids, lifting it out of its orbit like a marble, sending it reeling into half a dozen others. Within minutes they were burning through Vala's atmosphere. Bavn had never seen nor heard of weaponry like this that could take entire asteroids out of their orbit with what appeared to be just the normal explosions of solar bombs and whatever other known weaponry.

Whatever they were using was new... and deadly. If they kept it up, Blood Citadel was lost.

But they would take the attacking fleets with them. Of that Bavn was certain.

CHAPTER 161 - HOPING FOR BUDDHA

The dead stretched for miles on the surface of Canak, slumped lazily or sprawled gracefully or awkwardly with their arms under their heads or reaching over their heads as though trying to grasp onto the lives that had fled their bodies. Their faces were frozen with last thoughts, last feelings and realizations, from astonishment to puzzlement to peace. Centos Kama, his huge bulk sagging over his knees, looked silly with massive arms dangling lifelessly to the ground, his face a study in contentment. Beside him, a young woman lay with one leg straight, the other bent at the knee, as though she were running parallel to the ground. Her eyes were wide with terror. It was impossible to know if she'd died in an arena or when Bella had thrown the switch on the Wars.

Shade streaked past Cassie, slashing with her nails but Cassie turned with the attack at the last second and Shade's nails cut through the air harmlessly. Still turning at blinding speed, Cassie shot her right leg out in a long arc toward the back of Shade's head but the Clanswoman, expecting the counter, ducked just in time. The attack and counter were over in less than a second.

Cassie, right leg stretched over Shade's body, dropped her foot straight down, catching Shade's left shoulder with a sickening thud and a small crack that sounded like breaking bone.

Shade rolled away with lightning speed and sprung to her feet in a defensive stance, one arm by her waist ready to attack, the other forward and ready to block.

"Are you alright?" whispered Cassie, trying not to move her lips as she spoke.

"I'm fine. Nice move."

"Thought I heard something break."

"My shoulder. Does that all the time. No problem." Shade faked an attack.

Cassie slid back, crouching low.

"We can't do this forever. Any ideas?"

"Working on it. Been trying to Quan an old friend. But he seems to be out of range or something."

"Who's the old friend?"

"Buddha."

Shade almost laughed, then remembered. "The fat guy at the exits?"

"Yep. None other."

"I think he may have saved your life."

"Not the first time."

"You think he can help us?"

"Hoping for it."

"Just who is he?"

"Supposed to be some kind of god, I think."

"Good man to have on our side. If he gets here in time."

"He will. I hope." With that, Cassie lunged at Shade.

CHAPTER 162 - SCREAMING IN THE PAIN OF THEIR MUTUAL DESTRUCTION

Gaunt—the texture of Bella's face.

Sunken-the look and feel of her cheeks and eyes. Her skin was beginning to shrink and ripple, its immortal smoothness and glow succumbing to wrinkles and discoloration.

"Something's wrong! Something's not right!" Her voice was beginning to crack and grow shrill, anger giving way to panic. "They should be tearing each other to pieces! They should be locked in death holds, screaming in the pain of their mutual destruction!"

In spite of the centuries of genetic manipulation and nanhancements, Lovesong's eyes began to well with tears. He wasn't just born to serve this woman; he was created to love her. And he did. But everything that was Bella Bjork was shutting down, closing its essence forever. Dying.

"They're faking it! I know they are-faking and stalling for time!"

"But what could they possibly be stalling for?" Sitting on a crystal divan, legs crossed, hands folded in his lap, Lovesong tried desperately to maintain his composure, even though his white knuckles betrayed the effort to control their shaking. "There's nowhere for them to go or hide. Nothing and no one to save them. They each believe the other killed the closest people in their lives. They hate each other."

"Then one of them should be dead by now!" It was a shriek. "This is the last of the Wars! The last! And those two bitches are just pussyfooting! I know they are! I can feel it!"

"They're two of the greatest Reality Wars contestants of all time. They're sizing each other up, looking for strengths and weaknesses before they go for the kill."

Bella stopped in midstride and turned suddenly toward Lovesong. "You think so? Sizing each other up? They haven't really begun the fight?"

Lovesong smiled. "I'm sure of it. They'll do this for a while until they've each worked out their strategies." He leaned forward, spreading his arms in a gesture of grandeur. "And then they'll give us the greatest Wars ever, something befitting the last of the Wars, something befitting the entertainment of the queen of the universe."

Bella smiled weakly, the skin at the corners of her mouth beginning to droop. "Do you really think so? It's truly their attempt to honor me as I've honored them by giving them the last of the Reality Wars?" She thought about his a moment, facing Lovesong. He noticed something strange about her posture, something he'd never seen before. She seemed bent, crooked. She'd always stood so straight, firm, strong and commanding. And now she was beginning to bend into the stoop of an old woman. "But what about Nels?" Her dulling eyes were full of doubt and pleading. "What of the Texture? We haven't heard from them. They've broken contact. Something is wrong."

"Nothing's wrong," said Lovesong, calmly reassuring. "We expected to have communications problems as they approached the Texture. We just didn't expect the interference to begin so soon and to be so extreme. I'm sure Commander Horne remains faithful to you. He's always been... "

"Always means nothing in these times!" Panic was creeping back into her voice. Her eyes widened fearfully. "Many will see these as times of opportunity. There will be those who will take advantage of this, even those in the highest echelons on my empire... " She stopped, crooked her head to the side in a gesture of sudden realization. "Chaine is with him."

Lovesong relaxed back into the divan, feeling its nanproperties beginning to massage the tightness in his back. "Exactly. We have Chaine there to keep Commander Horne in order. The very instant the Commander acts in any manner that's not in your interests, Chaine will simply kill him."

"Unless he's sold out to Horne."

Lovesong blinked and took a moment to compose his reply. "Chaine is a member of the Black Tree Clan. No group of warriors have ever been more faithful to you. To them, you are a goddess. They would gladly lay down their lives for you, if for no other reason than you requested a demonstration of their faith. Even at this moment, squadrons of Trees are sacrificing their lives in suicide attacks on the asteroids, giving up their lives without question and happy to die for you."

"But there's so much power to be had from the Texture, so much temptation."

"You are the only power in Chaine's life."

"But what if he *has* been tempted? What if the Texture proves to be too much for him? What if the Texture changes him?" She was beginning to whine. *Bella, queen of the universe... whining.* Lovesong wondered guiltily how long her death would be drawn out, how long he would have to suffer her dying before he could join her in eternal peace. *It must be only a matter of hours now.*

CHAPTER 163 - LOOKING THROUGH THE EYES OF GOD

It was only an instant, a matter of time so small, a space so small that it stretched into the inner boundaries of the smallness of infinity. There were things that Abner would never be able to understand, things that were a part of everything he knew and at the same time the stuff of an impossible universe.

He remembered layers of matter and energy shuttering down to their essence, and then the layers of matter and energy of their matter and energy shuttering down still further until there were only a few objects that changed as he looked at them, becoming something else before he could define them.

Everything was up close, and he was floating alongside several objects that were at once orbs and planes and diamond-shaped objects, just a few of them, all of them somehow familiar, and then there was a tune, like a song without words that could be grasped in a foreign language that he half understood as it played itself beyond his comprehension.

It was the most beautiful sound he'd ever heard. It filled him with peace and an understanding of things that he would never be able to put into words, things that changed into something else as he tried to know them.

He stopped trying. He would go mad in the attempt, and most certainly he would be driven insane by any definition he could straitjacket that sound into. After the passage of all time and the passage of no time, he was aware of something entirely different-a flowing sensation, a sense of the way that he and Buddha were going. They were in motion in a place that defied motion. And the song was leading them.

The entire universe burst all around them, the power of its energy and light exploding for an instant. In that instant, he saw Cassie and Shade facing off inside Canak, and he understood that they were not a threat to each other, that some form of peace had been made, but that they were still in grave danger. He saw the wars raging outside Control, the carnage at Blood Citadel and the arrival of the ships at the Texture. He saw these things while at the same time seeing all the people on all the planets in all the galaxies across the universe. It was like looking through the eyes of God.

And then it flicked out almost the instant it started.

They were at the gates of Quannet.

CHAPTER 164 - FROM THE FRONT

The thrust of her evasive maneuver was nearly a right angle that threw Shona to the other side of the control deck. Her head banged heavily into the wall but the nanmaterials recognized her instantly and softened the blow enough to stop her skull from splitting open. Pain shot down her right side from the sudden twisting impact on her neck and spine.

She Quanned in. "Shit!" The other ship was still on them and closing in fast. They'd used up almost all their shielding getting past the ships outside Control. They couldn't withstand another direct hit now. She grabbed onto the back of her command chair just in time to prevent being thrown back across the floor as the ship lurched in evasion maneuvers. Her feet lifted from the floor, but she hung on.

Abruptly, the ship literally bounced straight up from the concussion of a tactical solar bomb that barely missed them. Immediately, Shona Quanscanned for damage, expecting the worst, but the ship was holding up.

"Fold!" she screamed into Quan, and suddenly they were at the center of Control. Shona's heart pounded madly. *Close, too close*. She stood up, hands and legs shaking. *Nothing can stop us now*. Slowly, the pounding in her chest began to subside, and her breathing began to return to normal. *Nothing*.

At that exact moment she saw the other ship coming straight at them. From the front. Too fast. Too reckless.

***

"Shit," said Crash just before he did.

CHAPTER 165 - UNDER ATTACK

"I count just over a hundred thousand of them, Commander."

Triste thought about Kayly's words. Her Chief Nav Officer had a point. A hundred thousand of Bella's ships to about ten thousand of hers. Ten to one. She arrived at a quick conclusion—these were acceptable odds.

"Do we engage, Commander?"

"Not sure if the odds are fair, Chief Nav."

"You think we might need reinforcements?"

"I'm thinking they might need them."

Kayly laughed.

"I'll put it to a vote."

"Aye aye, Commander."

Triste never failed to be amused by her Chief Nav's use of archaic expressions. Smiling, she Quanned a poll to the captains of her fleet. Immediately, the results were back and the vote was unanimous-engage.

She Quanned Kayly. "Attack formations. Close quarters tactical."

"Yahoo!" screamed Kayly, and yahoos resounded from the captains of the other ships. Seconds later, Triste's fleet broke into dozens of attack formations spanning the breadth of Bella's pursuing ships and streaked toward them.

***

Commander Robb Carls's jaw went slack at about the same time that he received Quans from all over his fleet. They were under attack.

CHAPTER 166 - TAPERING INTO THE TEXTURE

Commander Nels Horne was ready for anything, even the hissing and spitting coming from the long green snake that was once Mission Regular Chaine. Most of his seven or eight foot long body was inside an air duct high in the wall. Only the obscene scaled head with the abnormally large red eyes showed, jaw wide open, tongue darting in and out, face flashing reptilian fury.

Outside the viewport the impossible was happening. A corridor of ships from his fleet mixed with the Clans' fleets tapered into the distance toward the Texture. He couldn't help wondering what kind if madness overtook the ships up close to the anomaly. His own ship was pure insanity, his crew scurrying around the decks as lizards and snakes, some of them changing from one to the other in mid-scurry. And then all but Chaine began changing into other creatures, some hideous, some hilarious, creatures like no human would dream of in their most vulnerable sleep.

At first, they looked confused, sounded terrified, but then they began to laugh-or at least, that was what Nels took the sounds emitting from the orifices he assumed were mouths to be. They appeared to be less frantic, less disoriented, less fearful of each other, mingling in small groups, even seeming to communicate with each other.

He wondered what bizarre creatures roamed the decks and corridors of the ships closest to the Texture.

His ship was still too far for close observation through the viewport and Quan was down completely. All ships' controls were gone. Weapons systems were neutralized. It appeared the Texture was in control, and Nels and his crews were just along for the ride, just as were the ships in the Clans' fleet.

Nels watched in amazement as the clone ship floated eerily by itself down the center of the corridor of warships straight for the center of the Texture.

He wondered what would happen next, what insane impossibility would drop from the depths of space to try and drive him crazy.

He noticed a rustling to his left. He turned his head to see a beautiful woman with long dark hair and magnificent blue eyes walking toward him. She wore the uniform of a captain in Bella's navy. Nels recognized her immediately. It was Jana Reede, captain of the Finder. Supposedly dead for the last fifty years.

CHAPTER 167 - FINDING IT

"How big is this?" asked Abner.

"More like... how small," said Buddha. "Not as small as the route here, but almost as small."

"It's beautiful," said Abner, unable to hide the awe in his voice.

Around them, crystalline structures spread for as far as they could see. Two pale blue octahedron-like crystals floated past Abner's head, sending out tiny translucent tubes—hundreds of them—joining the two structures. They began to pulse as sparkles of red flashed in each of them.

"They seem to be alive," he said.

"They are. Sentient crystals. The tubes join them together as they process information. And both are entangled with all the other crystals in here."

"In here?"

"We're inside Bella's fortress, at the heart of the database that stores all the information on Quannet ever since it was conceived, along with all the information left over from the digital age-pretty much all the recorded knowledge from all of history."

"And this is where we'll find the registry?"

"This is it. This is where we wipe the slate clean."

"And make everybody in the universe equal."

"That's the plan."

Abner chuckled. "You know, you just might be Buddha after all."

"One of them, anyway."

"So, how do we find the registry?"

"I'm working on it."

"Any idea what it looks like?"

"More like... how it feels."

"Any idea how it feels?"

"That's the part I'm working on."

"I'm worried about Cassie."

"She's OK."

"Are she and Shade still fighting?"

"Yes, and putting on a pretty good show. Shade knows about Bella's control of the Reality Wars. Bella just killed all the other competitors."

"Killed them? I thought there were thousands of them."

"There were."

"And what's to stop her from killing my daughter."

"Me."

"You can do that?"

"I've just cut off all outgoing Quans from Bella. All she can do now is watch her empire crumble while she dies."

"She's dying?"

"You care?"

"She killed my wife, imprisoned me for nearly two thousand years, told me repeatedly that she was going to kill my daughter-if I could, I'd strangle her to death with my hands."

Buddha smiled ironically. "Doesn't sound like the Abner I used to know."

"Try being mist for a couple thousand years."

Buddha thought about this for a moment. "Interesting thought. I just might try that."

It was Abner's turn to smile. "It gets really boring after the first few hundred years."

"Just a matter of how you focus your mind."

The smile dropped from Abner's lips. "All I had to focus on was the loss of my wife and the fear that Bella might kill my daughter at any time."

"This is why I'm a loner."

"So Cassie's going to be OK?"

"I think she's making a new friend."

"From the Clans? The people who want to stamp out all sentient software in the universe."

"Shade's different. Not your typical Clanswoman."

"One thing... if Bella can't do anything to them now, why let them keep fighting?"

"Sending a Quan outside may tip off our location. Bella still has power here. And her mate, Lovesong, is almost as formidable as she was at her peak."

"So, how much longer?"

"I think I almost have it." Suddenly, he frowned. "Shit."

"Now, that was very un-Buddha-like. I'm assuming you found it."

Buddha nodded.

"So, where is it?"

"She's wearing it."

CHAPTER 168 - NOTHING'S PERFECT

"Something's different." Cassie crouched in a low stance, ready to defend high with her hands or attack low with her feet. Ten feet away, Shade was in a similar stance. They stood, weighing each other, expecting the next move, second guessing shifts in posture, tracking eye movements without committing, controlling their breathing, relaxing their muscles-all the time wondering how to respond convincingly without harming the other.

"What's different?" asked Shade, shifting her weight slightly to the rear, ready to spring forward.

"I don't know." Cassie crouched further, ready to meet Shade's attack.

"Then... " Realizing that she'd just telegraphed her attack, Shade moved her weight forward, ready for a spinning attack. "What makes you think something's different."

"Just a feeling." She raised her stance an inch, ready to dodge the spinning kick. "I don't know how to explain it, but something just changed a moment ago."

"Realspace or Quan?"

"Quan... I think."

"Is she going to kill us both?" Shade sprung backward, standing erect, and began to circle Cassie, who straightened as well and began to circle. Their movements flowed like water as they moved, eyes boring into each other, faces expressionless.

"I don't think so. It's hard to say. It was... yes, it was definitely Quan. Something changed. For just a micro instant."

"I don't want to die like them." Shade's eyes scanned briefly over the corpses surrounding them. She scowled. "Maybe we should make this for real. I need a warrior's death. I need to die in battle."

"No. We need to stall a little longer. I know my father... and he has Buddha helping him. They'll do something. They're doing it now. They'll get us out of this."

"Buddha. I still have a hard time with that."

"I trust him. Plus... " She sprang forward, missing Shade's head by a microinch with a blistering side thrust kick.

Shade spun as she lowered herself and delivered a foot sweep, catching Cassie's grounded foot and toppling her. She continued her spin and sent a low crescent kick to Cassie's head.

Cassie ducked under it and caught Shade's leg.

Shade jumped back with her grounded leg and jerked her foot out of Cassie's grasp.

"Plus, he made it possible for me to swim centuries before Quannet. By the way, nice move."

Shade smiled. "I thought so. You're the first person to ever live through one of those."

Cassie smiled inquisitively, staring into Shade's eyes. "Person?"

Shade smiled almost shyly. "There are a few Clans' beliefs that I've never completely accepted."

"So, you don't think that VRs are going to saturate the universe and bring about Armageddon?"

"I think we humans are perfectly capable of doing that without anybody's help."

"You're not like anyone else I've met from the Clans."

"I'm not supposed to be. They spent five hundred years making me different, making me into something to destroy you, in fact."

"Looks like they made a mistake somewhere along the line."

"Guess nothing's perfect."

"Well, maybe Buddha."

"Will you get off the Buddha thing and attack?"

Like a panther on steroids, Cassie jumped into the air over Shade and sent a side thrust kick straight at the back of her head.

528

CHAPTER 169 - LIKE BEING WATER

The control deck of Soul Ship glistened with the liquid that Jeli, Benji and Bingo had become. They sloshed across the floor, washed up onto the walls, formed rivulets and eddies, soaking the deck with their waterness. Laughter bubbled from the water-giggles and hoots and chortles.

This is fun, thought the water that was Benji.

Exhilarating! thought Jeli.

It's... it's... it's like being water, thought Bingo.

The water of Benji and Bingo screeched with merriment.

Jeli giggled. *You are water, Sheriff. We're all water! We're rivers, oceans, galactic seas!*

Suddenly, a sizable body of the water that was Benji splashed against the wall and cascaded down bubbling and foaming. *I'm a fucking waterfall crashing down from the summit of Mount Booning! Don't get caught in my boil!*

Jeli laughed madly. Bingo churned and huffed and turned into a whirlpool, squealing with laughter. Suddenly, he went quiet. Jeli and Benji fell silent as well.

Did you feel that? thought Jeli.

What was it? thought Bingo.

I don't know, something different, just a feeling... like...

The water of the three clones began to flow into the center of the deck, forming three large blobs of crackling effervescence. The blobs contracted slowly to the size of baseballs and then began to expand into shapes.

What the hell is happening to us? thought Bingo.

Damned if I know, thought Jeli. *We seem to be changing into something else.*

No shit, thought Benji. *I think I'm growing some kind of arms*.

Sure enough, the water blob that was Benji began to sprout spindly appendages as it bobbed up and other appendages emerged from its liquid interior.

Hey, I think I'm growing some kind've... I don't know... something, thought Bingo.

Jeli's blob began to expand up and out, its top flattening as reptilian tentacles shot out from under the blob.

An array of large surprised eyes formed at the end of the spindly appendages of Benji's blob, which continued to grow straight up without much growth to the sides. He was forming into a tall slender shape with a leathery surface mottled with dull stripes and splotches of red and yellow.

Bingo's blob expanded outward a few inches and then inward as though it were breathing, picking up speed faster and faster like a hyperventilating horror. It stopped abruptly... and disintegrated into dust-like particles on the surface of the deck. *I think I just died or something*, he thought.

You wouldn't be thinking about dying if you were dead, thought Jeli as a pair of massive gray eyes began growing under the flat surface at the top of his blob.

Sure feels like dead. I think I'm just... dust.

But, dust that can still think. Benji snickered as he continued to sprout up and stop just short of the deck's ceiling.

Suddenly, the dust that was Bingo exploded into brilliant flashes of blue and green light and floated into the air, glittering with the furious movement of thousands of tiny pinnacles of light all contained seemingly within an invisible membrane. *We all look like a bunch of aliens from a Quan*, he thought.

I think you just hit the nail on the head, thought Jeli ominously.

CHAPTER 170 - BUILDING A FORTRESS

Commander Rob Carls had never seen anything like it. He'd heard about the ferocity of the Clans, but he'd chalked most of it up to mythmaking. The Clans' forces were known for their almost mindless frenzy, attacking with suicidal viciousness, but there was nothing suicidal in the thousands of ships converging on his fleet from every direction. *How did they get into position so fast? How could we have missed their cloaking?*

Rob Carls didn't like having the table turned on him. He was supposed to be the hunter. The attackers were supposed to be the hunted. But there they were, the prey on the attack, literally blowing his ships away. They came in from the sides, the back, the front, from over them and under them. They were everywhere. His ships barely had time to fire desperately before they were destroyed. He'd never seen such accuracy, such precise tactics. It seemed like they flew right through barrages of defensive fire, spiraled around long lines of missiles and laser beams, almost like they were playing with them; and when they were all but brushing against their targets, they opened fire and were gone almost invisibly, leaving death and space debris behind.

"Close in!" he commanded. "Close in and form a defensive core!" It was their only hope, to condense their presence so tightly the attacking ships couldn't get inside their ranks. They still outnumbered the Clans almost ten to one. If he could just get enough of his ships into a solid mass without the Clans' ships inside, they could form something like a fortress, so much easier to defend.

He watched as his ships began the maneuver, flying toward a common core. They'd done this hundreds of times in training, but Carls wondered if it had ever actually been done in live battle. No one had ever attacked any of Bella's fleets like this before. He watched as one after another of his ships exploded into space dust as they tried to retreat into the core. It looked as though the Clans' ships were maneuvering in with them, still attacking, still on the inside. Still deadly.

He broke from Quan and stared out his observation port straight into an array of missiles heading directly toward him.

CHAPTER 171 - THE STRANGE PART

Childen: Something's wrong here, Maggie.

Maggie: Wrong! Childen, this is the fight of the millennium! Look at those two! They're tearing into each other. I've never seen such a vicious fight. And the scene, the scene! All those thousands of dead bodies, and these two women... software and human... fighting to establish the predominance of one over the other. This is...

Childen: This is all wrong, Maggie. They should both be ribbons by now. Only one should still be alive.

Maggie: (disgusted) Oh, Childen... jealous about not being on the field with those two for the greatest Reality Wars of all time?

Childen: (raises brow as he looks over the scene) Somehow I think I would have joined the bodies lying on the ground. This battle was pegged for these two.

Maggie: And just what are you saying, Childen? That the Reality Wars have been fixed?

Childen: Maggie, look around out there. They're all... dead.

Maggie: A glitch in the software. Maybe a virus of some sort. It could be anything, Childen. But it's led to this... species Armageddon.

Childen: They're not trying to kill each other, Maggie.

Maggie: Childen! Did you lose your eyes along with your arms? They're out there trying to kill each other!

Childen: No, it would have been over by now if they were.

Maggie: If they weren't trying to kill each other, Childen, they'd both be dead by now. You know the rules.

Childen: That's the strange part, Maggie. They're *not* dead by now.

CHAPTER 172 - PARTING WORDS

The asteroids of Blood Citadel fell one by one, crashing into each other, smashing through the atmosphere of Vala and pockmarking the surface of the massive planet. Large expanses of the planet's surface were shrouded in clouds of ash and dust. The skies over Vala blazed with death. Even as the asteroids were thrown out of orbit, the batteries of missiles and lasers continued to reign death on their attackers.

Bavn watched as the Tears of Blood Clan's orbiting fortress succumbed to the fury of Bella's suicidal navies. Millions of her ships had fallen, taking with them hundreds of millions lives. And they kept attacking, even as the Tree Clan destroyed asteroid after asteroid, the rest of her navies pulverized their surfaces and were incinerated as they attacked. Bella might take down the Tears of Blood, but it would be her costliest victory ever.

It will soon be time. Bavn's thoughts turned to his daughter, dead now. Five hundred years of the most sophisticated genetic engineering and nanhancements in the universe-all toward making her and Shade heralds of a new order with humans as the supreme beings. And now she was dead. And the fate of Shade, unknown.

The floor and walls rocked as Bavn's dwelling took a near hit. Bavn watched as the attacking ship burst into blazing fragments as a dozen laser beams sliced into it. He steadied himself and Quanned for a damage report. Nothing came back. It was over. They were cut off from the rest of the universe, and there would be no last minute salvation from navies sent by the other Clans. They were likely all under attack as well in a war that spread across the universe. This would be the end of the Clans.

Or would it?

He Quanned the attacking fleet and was channeled to its Commander, Borne Caine. Bavn presented as himself, as did Caine.

"Commander," he said. "It appears that Blood Citadel is fallen."

The commander appeared calm, an almost compassionate look in his eyes. "Your people have fought well today, Bavn. I've never encountered such remarkable fighters."

"It's what we live by, Commander. I have only one thing to ask."

"Go ahead."

"Will any be spared?" *Is that sadness in his eyes?*

The commander breathed in deeply and let it out slowly before he spoke.

"No."

"Not anywhere?"

"Bella has ordered the extermination of the Clans... throughout the universe."

"And the lesser Clans?"

"All the Clans."

It was Bavn's turn to breath deeply.

Caine continued. "I don't like this, but those were her orders. If it hadn't been for the Tree Clan, we might not have won this day."

Bavn smiled weakly. "It took a Clan to defeat the Clans."

Caine returned the smile. "You might say that."

"And then, what of the Tree Clan?"

Caine half shrugged but remained silent.

"I see," said Bavn. "Commander, thank you for granting me this interview."

"It was an honor, Bavn. You fought well today."

"And so did you, Commander. It's too bad neither of us will hear the myths and legends to which this day will give birth." Bavn Quanned out as Borne Caine's eyes began to squint in confusion.

So it's come to this. Bavn held his hand out, palm down. A section of the floor began to rise toward his hand, forming a narrow pillar. Its top melted away to reveal a brilliant orange jewel glowing with an inner light. When it reached Bavn's hand it stopped, and a low rumble crept ominously through all the mass and space around Vala.

CHAPTER 173 - A GUARANTEE

"You have a lot of nerve contacting me after fucking me this way." The Cormorant presented as the Ace of Spades—his power presence. "You were supposed to have killed the Clanswoman. She's still alive. She's in combat with the girl."

"There was a slight glitch in the program." The Assassin presented as a black silhouette, just the top half of his body, wearing a fedora.

"And just what would that glitch have been?"

"Someone from a long time ago."

"Well, let's just forget about your old enemies for now. You fucked me."

"You're right. But it wasn't intentional. On the other hand, Bella seems to be fucking all of you, every Gambler in the universe."

The Cormorant thought about this a moment. "We'll take a hit on much of the betting. But everything is switching over to the Clanswoman and the girl. Something might be salvageable out of this."

"I don't think so."

"You don't think so? And just what information do you have that I don't?"

"Shade and Cassie Hayes aren't fighting, they're faking it."

"I thought it was going on a bit too long."

"Bella's been cut off from the Wars."

"How do you know that?"

"I have my ways."

"And who would have the power to do a thing like that?"

539

"I'm guessing... Buddha."

"Buddha? That's just an ancient superstition. Are you trying to fuck with me again?"

"No, I'm trying to help you."

"And how can you do that?"

"I can kill Bella."

"You can guarantee that?"

"I can."

"It needs to be done right away. Where are you now?"

"In a safe place. But if I do this... we're square?"

"We are. Just make sure she's dead. Soon."

"She will be."

***

Now I know you're suicidal.

CHAPTER 174 - BELLA AND LOVESONG

"I'm cut off! Cut off!" She staggered around the room, staggered and tripped and staggered. Lovesong moved to help her. "Back! Back! I can hold myself!"

The beauty that once had been as perfect as her cruelty melted into gray skin, peeling and flaking—her sunken eyes shriveled like two dull gray balls suspended precariously in their sockets. She was shedding hair, exposing patches of gray flesh.

"How can I be cut off! Who would dare! I'm Bella Bjork! Bella! Bjork!"

"It might just be some form of cosmic interfer... "

"No!" She glared at him, the glare all the more disturbing from those eyes that seemed almost disconnected from the rest of her body. "Nels, Chaine, my Assassin, the Cormorant, Damon! They're all against me! They want to take my empire away from me! They want to destroy me, take the Texture away from me, take away my immortality. They hate me!"

"No, Bella. They're all loyal, loyal to you only. They exist to serve you. This is just some freak occurrence in Quannet. Possibly... "

"There are no freak occurrences in my Quannet! Not ever! I control it!" Suddenly, she stopped in midpace, almost falling over as she checked her forward momentum. "It's here."

"Here?"

"The thing that helped Abner Hayes escape. It's here. It's the only thing that could cut us off from Quannet. It's here to destroy me."

"Bella, that's impossible. Nobody even knows where this is. Everyone who might have known is dead. This is the safest place in the universe."

"It's here. I can feel it. I know it."

"But that's... "

Ten feet in front of Bella, Buddha appeared, legs crossed, palms on his knees, floating in the air—and right behind him, Abner Hayes, standing.

CHAPTER 175 - AN UNIMPOSING BEAM

It started with a beam of pure nanmagic. The beam, less than a nanometer in diameter, cut through the surface of Vala without disturbing a single pebble or scarring a single rock on the desolate surface of the planet. It shot through layer after layer of volcanic rock without leaving a trace of its passing, like a tiny pellet of phantom energy. Had it been sentient, it might have been mistaken for something almost apologetic, considerate in its passing, kind to a fault. So it was with this pellet of pure nanmagic.

Within seconds, it was in the planet's molten core. And it wasn't so nice anymore. Not that the planet would have a chance to sense this, it happened so fast. The beam's tiny mass seemed to breathe in for an instant and then breathe outward with the force of a universe birthing. In less than a second the giant dead rock that was Vala was a mass of fire and molten rock expanding into space, engulfing its asteroids, consuming Bella's navies and turning them into bone and metal spray.

All the billions of inhabitants of Blood Citadel evaporated in an instant, feeling nothing. Nor did the crews of Borne Caine's fleet, except maybe the crews of the ships ready to reinforce the attack thousands of miles away. They would have had a second or two of realization before they were washed away as so much space debris.

Within seconds, Blood Citadel and Vala and Caine's entire fleet were gone.

CHAPTER 176 - THE RIGHT DECISION

"Oh my God." Shade dropped her guard, shock spreading across her face. Cassie stopped just short of faking tearing her head off with a wicked roundhouse kick.

"What?"

"It's gone. Gone."

Cassie stared into her eyes, seeing the clash of horror and disbelief wresting deep in her irises, bubbling across her cheeks. "What's gone? What is it?"

"Blood Citadel. I can feel it. It's gone."

"Blood Citadel? How can it be gone? It's the biggest fortress in the universe."

"I can feel it, I tell you. I'm connected to it. I know it. It's gone."

Cassie looked bewildered. "That can't be good."

"It can mean only one thing. It's been destroyed. Completely. Bavn has set off Vala. That's the only thing that could have happened."

"Wait a minute... why would he do that?"

"Blood Citadel must have been under attack. It must have been close to falling. It's the only circumstance that would allow Bavn to ignite the planet. To allow the Citadel to be taken by an enemy would be the ultimate disgrace, not just for the Tears of Blood but for all Clans."

Disgusted, Cassie spat, "Bella."

"She's at war with the Clans." Shade grew paler by the moment.

"If you're right, then she'll be attacking the Clans everywhere, and... " She went quiet, startled eyes darting around.

"What?"

"We're not fighting. Nothing's happening. We should both be dead by now."

Shade looked around. Corpses spread for miles around the two. Her eyes settled on Loac's body, and just as her eyes began to dull with sadness, anger burned it away and her mouth tightened until her lips turned white. "I'll find that bitch if it takes the rest of my life. She's taken everything important in my life away from me. I'll kill her slowly." Her eyes squinted, boiling hatred through the narrow slits.

Cassie walked slowly to where Sara lay, eyes wide and unbelieving. She bent down as tears began to well up in the corners of her eyes. She reached out and gently closed her friend's eyelids. Still crouched, she turned to Shade. "You and me both."

The fury in Shade's eyes seemed to lessen slightly as she nodded. Then she looked around again. "But what's happening here? You said that Bella controlled the Wars. Why are we still alive?"

"Maybe Bella is having problems of her own."

Shade's eyes narrowed. "Well, whoever is giving them to her had better leave the killing for us."

"Spoken like a true Clanswoman."

***

546

Maggie: What's happening here? They've stopped fighting. They've just... stopped fighting. They can't do that. The Wars aren't over yet. They're both still alive. What are they doing?

Childen: It looks to me like they're ending the Reality Wars, Maggie, walking away from the bloodshed.

Maggie: But they can't do that! They have to decide which is the dominant species-humans or software. The entire universe is waiting for the answer.

Childen: No, Maggie, the entire universe is waiting for something, but it's not a decision on who's going to dominate whom. These Wars have ended exactly as they should have.

Maggie: And just how is that, Childen?

Childen: A tie.

CHAPTER 177 - CRYPTIC

Jana Reede looked exactly as she had in the records-half a universe away from nanhancents and any other technology to stop the aging process for half a century and she hadn't aged a bit. If anything, she was even more beautiful, but beautiful in a different way. An aura of deep composure glowed around her face and body, and her eyes were bright, shining with a sense of joy that touched even the war-hardened Nels. It was completely open, vulnerable, unafraid-not like the limp happiness that pervaded the soulless worlds of Bella's universe.

There was also a sense of knowing about her, like a great wonderful secret bubbling through her veins, pumping through her heart, permeating her brain.

"Hello, Commander." Her voice was deep and sonorous, like the voice of an angel. Her smile sent a shiver through his body. He savored it as he returned the smile.

"It's been fifty years. We thought you were lost."

"Quite the opposite. I was lost until I arrived here."

"And just where is here?"

She winked. "The beginning."

"I suppose that's one of those cryptic answers that I'll come to understand in time."

She laughed, so carefree and songlike.

He blushed.

"Yes, Commander, you'll come to understand it."

"My crew seems to be changing into things from a nightmare, except they all seem to be OK with the change." He nodded his head toward the duct where Chaine's reptile head still gazed out angrily. "Except him, of course."

Jana glanced at the monstrous head. "He'll find his way." She looked back at Nels. "You all will. Soon, the loneliness will be gone. The void will be filled.

"So, this is where you've been all these years? Out here hanging with the Texture?"

"The Texture is so much more than we thought it was. And no, not just here. Exploring."

"Exploring? Where?"

"Not so much as where, as when and how and what." She giggled. "And a little bit of where."

"More of the cryptic?"

"You seem like the kind of man who enjoys the cryptic."

She turned her head with a graceful sweep that seemed to move through time and space, like butter spreading across toast, and gazed out the observation port. The Texture was closer, the rows of ships closer, almost like they were touching, becoming one thing. Nels had a feeling at once of expansiveness and smallness. It was a feeling of elation.

They watched as the clone ship drifted gracefully into the Texture and disappeared.

Jana smiled and looked back at Nels. "They'll be fine."

"I'm sure they will be."

CHAPTER 178 - IT'S A SONG

We are aliens, thought Jeli, *aliens*.

Strange faces, sentient points of light, eye-tipped tentacles, and Jeli's massive gray eyes all turned at once to the observation port, where an impossible light containing every color of the universe and colors that had never been seen before poured into the control deck like a slow wave of cosmic liquid. It poured around the alien bodies of the three clones, and as it touched them, it glowed and the glow seeped into them and they glowed with the fluid light.

It feels like... thought Benji, his sparkles of light bouncing and dancing within the membrane that contained all that he was. *It feels...*

It's like something... thought Jeli through the gray-eyed blob of his body.

I can hear it, thought Bingo.

That's it, thought Benji. *It's a sound.*

Yes, thought Jeli, *a sound.*

No, thought Bingo, *it's a song.*

And whatever expression defined the alien equivalent of surprise and wonder mixing and mashing within their forms at the same time took shape and texture within the three clones as the light continued to engulf them until they all glowed brightly along with the entire control deck.

It's a beautiful song, thought Bingo ecstatically.

The most beautiful song, thought Jeli.

It's taking us, thought Bingo. *It's taking us.*

What we're here for, thought Benji. *Exactly what we're here for.*

551

Soul Ship glowed as it passed into the impossibility of the Texture and disappeared joyfully into something else.

CHAPTER 179 - THE OCCASION
MERITS A CIGAR

"You!" What remained of Bella Bjork-gaunt, bent and shedding life like acid rain-literally glowed with hatred. Fists clenched, turning yellow, skin white, she bellowed, "What have you done!"

Buddha gazed calmly into Bella's gray eyes, a wisp of smile crossing his lips. The tranquility he emanated could have soothed a herd of stampeding elephants. He sat in the air and stared.

Bella's fury turned on Abner. "And you! I turned you into mist. But you just wouldn't stay." Turning back to Buddha. "You helped him escape. It was you. You!"

Buddha tipped his head almost imperceptibly in agreement, enigmatic smile unchanged. This infuriated Bella. Around her neck the emerline crystal glowed vibrantly against the wilting landscape of Bella's body.

"And *you* can wipe that smirk off your face. I don't know what you are, but you are no god! I'm closer to godhead than you. I... Bella Bjork *am* a goddess! And soon my power will be replenished, my rule will be restored, my will be done." Her eyes darted hatefully between Abner and Buddha. "And you two will be my slaves for eternity. If you think it was bad being mist, just you wait till you see what kind of hell I can prepare for you!"

Lovesong watched the two carefully, ready to spring even though he knew instinctively that they meant Bella no harm, including the one who's wife she'd murdered. They were here for some other purpose, and Lovesong decided to bide his time until that purpose was revealed.

"And how did you get in here? How did you even know where this place is? Who betrayed me?" A sudden look of horror spread across her face, and she glanced desperately at Lovesong. He nodded no, and after a moment of mind seaching, her face relaxed and she turned back to Buddha and Abner. "Well, it doesn't matter now. You're both here. You can witness my ascent to godhood when my commander secures the Texture and my navies slaughter the Clans across the universe. Witness the beginning of a new universe with... "

"It's over."

He'd said it quietly and compassionately like the essence of a whisper... as only Buddha could have said it.

Bella glared at him, puzzled, head cocking spasmodically from left to right.

"I'm not here to harm you." His voice flowed across the room compassionately. "But something needs to be done." His eyes floated down to the pendant lying against her neck. "And it needs to be done now."

Bella grabbed at the pendant with both hands, covering it tightly as she pressed it to her chest. "No! You can't have it!" She looked at Lovesong, suddenly regal, and commanded in a haughty voice, "Darling. Kill them!"

The words were barely out of her mouth before Lovesong sprang like a bullet through the air directly at Buddha, but at almost the instant he moved, he froze as though time had suddenly stopped all around him. Only the confusion raging in his eyes suggested that he was still alive and not transformed into a lifeless statue.

Bella stared at him, unbelieving, dumbstruck and turned on Buddha, lashing out ferociously. "What have you done to him! What have you done to him! You monster! If you've hurt him... " For just a brief moment, Bella's hands loosened their grip on the pendant and it flew off her neck and out of her hands and into Buddha's extended palm. The moment it touched, he closed his fist around it. What danced across Buddha's palm when he opened his fist was not physical smoke. It was more like the etheric glow that surrounds every human being, purported by some to be the life force. All that was left of Bella's control over Quannet dissipated into the air and disappeared.

Bella's scream permeated the crystalline essence of her fortress. It cascaded in levels of horror and disbelief through the atoms of the walls and floors and filled the rooms and the ocean at the center of the fortress with a sound from the pits of despair. She screamed and screamed and screamed. Her face seemed to fold in on itself, her chest, almost drained of the beat of life suddenly expanded. Cracked ribs broke through the surface of her skin and clothing, spurting blood and the flatulent liquids of her deterioration.

This was the woman who had killed Abner's wife, kept him prisoner for two thousand years and threatened to murder his daughter, but he couldn't suppress a small feeling of sympathy. The most powerful human being in the universe—an object of unquestioning worship-reduced to a writhing mass of ugliness. This heap... once a dark angel setting in motion the destruction of worlds and civilizations, the slaughter of billions of men, women and children, was now powerless and dying ignominiously.

Lovesong suddenly broke from his spell, blinked his eyes and walked shakily to her side. He fell to his knees beside her. She looked into his eyes with her own sunken eyes and sobbed, opening and closing her mouth and twisting her flaccid lips as though trying to say something, but nothing came out. Lovesong brushed his hand over her forehead and through the colorless patches of her hair. Her mouth still moved, trying to break through the silence that cemented her tongue. He reached his arms around her and pulled her close, stared lovingly into her eyes and bent to kiss her twitching lips. Just as his lips were about to touch hers, both their heads exploded. It was a small explosion, more like an implosion. It erased both their heads, leaving their bodies erect, frozen together in a macabre statue like something from a sculpture's nightmare.

The Assassin looked at Abner and Buddha. "I think you two should get out of here fast."

"But... " said Abner.

Before he could finish, they were somewhere else.

***

So, this is it?

556

"This is it." The Assassin walked leisurely to the nandivan and sat down, crossed his legs, took out a large cigar and lit it with a tap at the end.

You haven't smoked in a long time.

"Only when the occasion merits."

Yes, I suppose this occasion merits. No more beautiful deaths?

"No more deaths, beautiful or ugly."

You did try, though.

"Yes, I did."

But it all comes down to the same thing, doesn't it?

"It does. It surely does."

It's just not fun anymore, is it?

"Lost a little of its glamour."

It surely has.

"Do you think death will be silent?

You mean, without voices?

"That's what I mean."

I suppose we'll find out soon.

The Assassin took a small nansteel device from his pocket and pressed a button at the top. The device sent a message to the bomb that he'd planted in the fortress's ocean centuries ago. It started off small, turning the water around it to steam and boiling the life out of a passing whale-like creature. Once started, it fed off the energy of the emerline crystal, growing more intense by orders of magnitude until it filled the entire structure and turned it into a molten cluster of plasma.

Where the Assassin had sat, there was silence.

CHAPTER 180 - WIN SOME, LOSE SOME

Supreme Commander Daman Haley wasn't happy. For the first time in his career, he didn't know what to do or what to think. For hundreds of years he'd been accustomed to victory and to fighting for a very specific purpose-the glory of Bella Bjork. Through the ranks, he'd killed for her, slaughtered entire populations, led thousands of her legions into suicidal oblivion to turn her enemies into space dust. And now, everything that had defined his existence was suddenly gone.

Rob Carls's fleet had just been obliterated by a much smaller force of Clans' ships. Blood Citadel had fallen and taken millions of his ships with it, not to mention one of his most able commanders. This was supposed to be the defining war of all time-destroy the Clans, the biggest threat in the universe to Bella's rule-but the campaigns had not gone nearly as planned. Some were successful, others not. They'd underestimated the ferocity and resolve of the Clans. Outnumbered hundreds and sometimes thousands to one, they'd won over half the battles, taking out hundreds of millions of his ships.

Strangest of all, the Reality Wars had just ended with only two of the contestants still alive-that had the ring of Bella's doing, but then, the two survivors had walked off the field without finishing their battle. That... Bella would not have allowed. Daman Haley had long suspected that Bella was behind the Reality Wars, and it seemed strange, if not unsettling, that she would allow the last two contestants to live after not fulfilling whatever purpose she had in mind for them.

There was no word from her. All his attempts to reach her had failed. Given the way the campaign had gone, that might have saved his life. At the moment, he wasn't sure. He didn't know what was going on with Bella. The Clans' attack on Control had been a complete failure, and he still wondered what in hell they could have been up to. Perhaps it had something to do with Bella's silence, but he thought not. Something else had happened, and knowing Bella's uncanny ability to guess instinctively when things were going wrong, his sense of unease deepened. There was a distinct possibility that Bella was dead. If that were true, all hell was about to break out from one end of the universe to the other.

And to top it all off, one faction of the Clans had been mysteriously absent from the battles. The Womb Clan seemed to have disappeared, their planets devoid of population, their ships lost somewhere in space. He'd never trusted them, especially that old witch Maebh, and he had a feeling their paths would cross at some point in the future.

CHAPTER 181 - A MUCH DIFFERENT PLACE

The red walls of the command deck of the Womb ship Alcyone pulsated, as though breathing. Hot red light glowed inside Maebh's hood as the Quans continued to flood in. The battles between Bella and the other Clans had gone just as she'd expected. Both sides had succeeded in decimating their navies with no clear winner on either side. And Blood Citadel was gone. Bavn was gone-the strongest of all the Clans' leaders had chosen death over defeat. No one had heard back from the Texture, but that was all right. She didn't need it. Eventually, the war between the Clans and Bella would be over. Both sides would be weakened, and the Womb Clan would begin its slow and unstoppable rise to power and the universe would be a much different place than it was.

CHAPTER 182 - A GOOD PLACE TO BE

It was a place without light or definition, without sound, feeling or presence. It was like the absence of place.

"So... " The sound of Abner's voice boomed against the backdrop of nothingness. It startled him. "Where are we now?"

"In a safe place." Buddha's words, of course, were soft, floating calmly over the absence of things.

"For how long?" Booming less.

"Until I get my bearings."

"You mean, we're lost?" A small panic curled inside Abner's intestines. The void around him tightened slightly.

"No, not lost. Just getting my bearings."

"What just happened back there?"

"An acquaintance making things right."

Abner thought for a moment and decided to leave it at that. "So now we just wait until you get your bearings?"

Buddha grunted.

"And then what?"

"We go see your daughter."

Abner's heart quickened. "She's OK?"

"She's fine. We'll be with her soon."

Abner let out a long sigh. "I still don't get the bearings thing, though."

After a moment's silence, Buddha said, "There's something happening somewhere else. This would be a good place to be when it happens. Afterwards, things will be much easier."

"I'm guessing that it's pointless to ask what that means."

"Best to just experience some things."

"And the registry? It's gone?"

"Forever."

Abner smiled. "You know, for a murderous, civilization-wrecking computer virus, you turned out all right."

Buddha smiled. "Of course I did. I'm Buddha."

CHAPTER 183 - THE SONG

Nels hadn't noticed anything actually changing, but there they were, not suddenly out of the blue and yet, surprisingly just there with Jana and himself-the rest of the Finder's crew: Balin, Martz, Kasna and... one was missing.

As though reading his mind, Jana said, "Tig decided to stay."

Nels nodded, then thought for a moment and asked. "Stay where?"

"In another place." The other crew members smiled knowingly.

"And you and the rest of your crew?"

"We're ready to go home."

"It's been half a century. Things will be different."

"Things have been different for half a century."

There was movement in her eyes like waves of light crashing against her irises. Something in those waves suggested strange and wonderful things. Nels spoke with a sense of wonder. "I imagine they have."

Something else crept into Nels mind. He wasn't sure what it was at first, but gradually, it worked its way into his awareness-the deck was fluctuating less now, solidifying into its natural state... but was it? Nels shook his head lightly, blinked his eyes. Yes, there was something else-an orange glow reflecting surreally off the surface of the walls and floor. It was pouring through the observation port. Nels and the Finder's crew turned their heads and stared out at the Texture. Nels' eyes glowed with awe. The Finder's crew looked on with an air of familiarity, almost as though acknowledging an old friend. The snake that was Chaine stuck its forked tongue out, its eyes fearful.

Up till now, it had been a state of gradual flux, like something breathing throughout thousands of miles of space. Or was it just a few feet? And now it began to transform slowly like optical liquid from orange to blue and then to some color that Nels had never seen before, something he'd never dreamed possible. It was simultaneously one color and all colors, white and not white. At the center of the Texture-or what he assumed was the center, if such a thing could have a center-a turbulence appeared, a swirling and washing of familiar and impossible colors. It was at once a roiling abyss and at the same time, an expanse of calm.

It was impossible.

The change began to accelerate, growing both larger and smaller by the moment. Normally, Nels would have called all personnel to arms but even if he could do that, he wouldn't. Nothing about what he saw suggested a threat. It was beautiful, indescribably beautiful. He stood in awe with the crew of the Finder and gazed quietly at the Texture. He whispered to Jana, "What's it doing?"

Not taking her eyes off it, she whispered back, "It's becoming."

"Where did it come from?"

"Another place. Many places. It's where they touched us."

"They?"

564

"Just watch, listen. You'll see. You'll hear."

It grew all around them, not swallowing, more like folding them into it protectively, lovingly. Wave after wave permeated the ships and their crews. It flowed through Nels's body and mind with a rhythm that soothed and completed. Behind them, Chaine-back to his wire-lipped self-floated down from his duct lair and bounced lightly onto the floor, giggling and moaning, rolling and twisting on the floor like a large slug in heat.

And then the sound began, starting as a low hum that seemed to come from within Nels and then from the Texture, and then from everything around him. It filled him with the rhythm of all the possible and impossible colors of the Texture. The crew of the Finder looked at each other, smiling, nodding, closing their eyes and savoring the sound.

Nels felt it growing stronger, vibrating within every cell of his body, caressing his skin, soothing his mind. "What is it?"

"It's a song."

"A song? Wasn't that the message you sent fifty years ago?"

They smiled.

***

Light-years away, Buddha turned to wherever Abner was in the absence of anything—which was now filled with something.

A song.

"Listen."

"What is it?" asked Abner.

565

"What we've been waiting for."

Abner felt more than heard it. "It's beautiful."

"Yes, it is."

"Is it everywhere?"

"Yes, everywhere."

"It seems to be saying something."

"It is."

"What?"

***

Shade and Cassie stood staring into each others' eyes, feeling the song flowing through them.

"It's beautiful," whispered Shade.

"It's telling us something," said Cassie.

"What is it?"

***

Daman Haley forgot about Bella, the losses in her war against the Clans, the ships under his command. Tears welled in his eyes as he listened to the song flooding his body and mind, its message seeping into his understanding.

***

Maggie: It's... it's...

Childen: It's what we've been looking for... ever since we were."

***

Their place without substance began to glow with the light of the song. Abner picked out the outlines of Buddha's form. His head was bowed. "I think I understand it," said Abner.

Buddha looked up at him. "Tell me," he said, smiling.

"It's the sound of other life forms, trillions of them, more than trillions. Where are they coming from?"

"From other universes, countless universes."

"But what are they saying?"

"It's an invitation."

"An invitation?"

"To join them." Buddha lifted his head higher, looked at their surroundings, no longer nothingness, now filled with light and form, all of it pulsing beautifully. "We're not alone."

"That's going to change the way a lot of people feel about things." He thought for a moment, remembering something. "By the way, I seem to remember your saying something about saving the universe. I don't remember that we did that."

Buddha cleared his throat. "Well, we would have... if it had been needed."

Abner was awed by what he saw—Buddha... blushing. He decided to let the saving the universe thing drop and said, "So, do you have your bearings now?"

"I do. Let's go get your daughter."

"Sounds good to me."

A second later, they were somewhere else.

CHAPTER 184 - WETNESS

The water in my pool is soothing, caressing, crystalline clear. And there's never going to be any more training for the Reality Wars. From now on... just enjoy every day as it comes, just float in my pool and think about nothing. Well, maybe I think about some of the past. I think about my Mom, and I miss her. I think about Sara, and I miss her as well. I think about the first home Mom and Dad and I had on the old Internet, and I miss it. But the pain is gone.

I mean, you can carry things for only so long.

I carried a lot of pain for a long time.

Now, I just immerse myself in my pool and think about... wetness.

It's a different universe now. With the exception of a few skirmishes between what's left of the Clans' and Bella's Fleets, the universe is pretty much a peaceful place. There're rumors of powerful forces stepping back and gathering themselves for the next big conflict. There's always a next big conflict. The Womb Clan mysteriously disappeared, but most people are pretty sure that they'll be back. When they're ready. The Gamblers who survived the sabotage of the Reality Wars joined up with the Cormorant, who played his cards right as usual and became the richest person in the universe. He owns galaxies now. Bella's supreme commander, Damon Haley, is his security chief. He inherited what was left of Bella's navies.

There's a rumor that trillions of VRs slipped into the Texture along with Soul Ship. How cool is that? Both the Clans' and Bella's fleets went in as well... after their weapons were turned into useful things like ornaments they could give out as gifts during their travels in other universes.

Knowing that we aren't alone after all, that there are infinite universes each with its own unique intelligent life forms, has really cut down on the suicide rates. We won't ever need anything like the Reality Wars again.

Shade and I are friends. I like her. She's not like the other Clansfolk. She accepts VRs as equals to humans, and there doesn't seem to be any hatred in her for anything. Of course, since that song permeated the universe, there's not been much hatred anywhere.

And Quannet seems to be running on its own. Some people are beginning to think that Quannet itself is sentient, that it might be some sort of conduit to godhood. I guess we'll have to wait and see about that.

Best of all, Dad and I are together again. In fact, he's floating in the water about ten feet away from me right now. Sometimes we're in Quanspace together, sometimes in Realspace. The possibilities are endless.

Oh yeah, and Buddha's mist now. He seems to like it. In fact, he says he might stay that way for a few thousand years. God knows what he'll come back as after that.

THE END

THE END